U0061853

Edgar Allan Poe 著

張瓊 張沖 譯

THE BLACK CAT

黑貓

商務印書館

本書譯文由上海譯文出版社有限公司授權使用

責任編輯　　陳朝暉
裝幀設計　　郭梓琪
排　　版　　周　榮
責任校對　　趙會明
印　　務　　龍寶祺

黑貓 *The Black Cat*

作　　者　　Edgar Allan Poe
譯　　者　　張　瓊　張　沖
出　　版　　商務印書館 (香港) 有限公司
　　　　　　香港筲箕灣耀興道 3 號東滙廣場 8 樓
　　　　　　http://www.commercialpress.com.hk
發　　行　　香港聯合書刊物流有限公司
　　　　　　香港新界荃灣德士古道 220−248 號荃灣工業中心 16 樓
印　　刷　　永經堂印刷有限公司
　　　　　　香港新界荃灣德士古道 188−202 號立泰工業中心第 1 座 3 樓
版　　次　　2024 年 7 月第 1 版第 1 次印刷
　　　　　　© 2024 商務印書館 (香港) 有限公司
　　　　　　ISBN 978 962 07 0443 7
　　　　　　Printed in China

Publisher's Note 出版説明

　　愛倫・坡素有"偵探小説之父"的美譽，其作品被認為是整個偵探文學的根源。本書精選了十篇愛倫・坡的經典之作，為讀者呈現一個黑暗神祕的文學世界。從《黑貓》中令人窒息的心理描寫，到《厄舍屋的倒塌》中令人毛骨悚然的恐怖氛圍，再到《紅死病假面》中撲朔迷離的懸疑情節 —— 每一篇作品都將帶領讀者進入一個充滿謎團和挑戰的世界，探索人類內心最深處的痛苦和恐懼，思考生命、死亡、瘋狂等永恆主題。

　　本書不僅是一部經典文學作品的集結，更是一次心靈的洗禮和啟迪。讓我們一起踏上這段奇幻之旅，領略愛倫・坡作品的獨特風格和深刻思想內涵，感受文學的力量與魅力。

　　初、中級英語程度讀者使用本書時，先閱讀英文原文，如遇到理解障礙，則參考中譯作為輔助。在英文原文後附加註解，標註古英語、非現代詞彙拼寫形式及語法；在譯文後附加註釋，以幫助讀者理解原文背景。讀者如有餘力，可在閱讀原文部分段落後，查閱相應中譯，揣摩同樣詞句在雙語中的不同表達。

商務印書館 (香港) 有限公司

編輯出版部

Contents 目錄

The Black Cat

1
The Black Cat

For the most wild, yet most homely narrative which I am about to pen, I neither expect nor solicit belief. Mad indeed would I be to expect it, in a case where my very senses reject their own evidence. Yet, mad am I not—and very surely do I not dream. But to-morrow I die, and to-day I would unburden my soul. My immediate purpose is to place before the world, plainly, succinctly, and without comment, a series of mere household events. In their consequences, these events have terrified—have tortured—have destroyed me. Yet I will not attempt to expound them. To me, they have presented little but horror—to many they will seem less terrible than baroques. Hereafter, perhaps, some intellect may be found which will reduce my phantasm to the commonplace— some intellect more calm, more logical, and far less excitable than my own, which will perceive, in the circumstances I detail with awe, nothing more than an ordinary succession of very natural causes and effects.

From my infancy I was noted for the docility and humanity of my disposition. My tenderness of heart was even so conspicuous as to make me the jest of my companions. I was especially fond of animals, and was indulged by my parents with a great variety of pets. With these I spent most of my time, and never was so happy as when feeding and caressing them. This peculiarity of character grew with my growth, and, in my manhood, I derived from it one of my principal sources of pleasure. To those who have cherished an affection for a faithful and sagacious dog, I need hardly be at the trouble of explaining the nature or the intensity of the gratification thus derivable. There is something in the unselfish and self-sacrificing love of a brute, which goes directly to the heart of him who has had frequent occasion to test the paltry friendship and gossamer fidelity of mere *Man*.

I married early, and was happy to find in my wife a disposition not uncongenial with my own. Observing my partiality for domestic pets, she lost no opportunity of procuring those of the most agreeable kind. We had birds, goldfish, a fine dog, rabbits, a small monkey, and a *cat*.

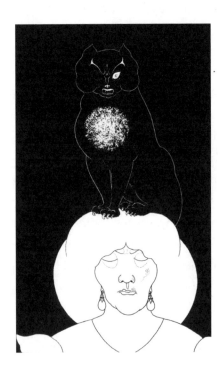

This latter was a remarkably large and beautiful animal, entirely black, and sagacious to an astonishing degree. In speaking of his intelligence, my wife, who at heart was not a little tinctured with superstition, made frequent allusion to the ancient popular notion, which regarded all black cats as witches in disguise. Not that she was ever *serious* upon this point—and I mention the matter at all for no better reason than that it happens, just now, to be remembered.

Pluto—this was the cat's name—was my favourite pet and playmate. I alone fed him, and he attended me wherever I went about the house. It was even with difficulty that I could prevent him from following me through the streets.

Our friendship lasted, in this manner, for several years, during which my general temperament and character—through the instrumentality of the Fiend Intemperance—had (I blush to confess it) experienced a radical alteration for the worse. I grew, day by day, more moody, more irritable, more regardless of the feelings of others. I suffered myself to use intemperate language to my wife. At length, I even offered her personal violence. My pets, of course, were made to feel the change in my disposition. I not only neglected, but ill-used them. For Pluto, however, I still retained sufficient regard to restrain me from maltreating him, as I made no scruple of maltreating the rabbits, the monkey, or even the dog, when by accident, or through affection, they came in my way. But my disease grew upon me—for what disease is like Alcohol!—and at length even Pluto, who was now becoming old, and consequently somewhat peevish—even Pluto began to experience the effects of my ill temper.

One night, returning home, much intoxicated, from one of my

haunts about town, I fancied that the cat avoided my presence. I seized him; when, in his fright at my violence, he inflicted a slight wound upon my hand with his teeth. The fury of a demon instantly possessed me. I knew myself no longer. My original soul seemed, at once, to take its flight from my body; and a more than fiendish malevolence, gin-nurtured, thrilled every fibre of my frame. I took from my waistcoat-pocket a pen-knife, opened it, grasped the poor beast by the throat, and deliberately cut one of its eyes from the socket! I blush, I burn, I shudder, while I pen the damnable atrocity.

When reason returned with the morning—when I had slept off the fumes of the night's debauch—I experienced a sentiment half of horror, half of remorse, for the crime of which I had been guilty; but it was, at best, a feeble and equivocal feeling, and the soul remained untouched. I again plunged into excess, and soon drowned in wine all memory of the deed.

In the meantime the cat slowly recovered. The socket of the lost eye presented, it is true, a frightful appearance, but he no longer appeared to suffer any pain. He went about the house as usual, but, as might be expected, fled in extreme terror at my approach. I had so much of my old heart left, as to be at first grieved by this evident dislike on the part of a creature which had once so loved me. But this feeling soon gave place to irritation. And then came, as if to my final and irrevocable overthrow, the spirit of PERVERSENESS. Of this spirit philosophy takes no account. Yet I am not more sure that my soul lives, than I am that perverseness is one of the primitive impulses of the human heart—one of the indivisible primary faculties, or sentiments, which give direction to the character of Man. Who has not, a hundred times, found himself committing a vile or a silly action, for no other reason than because he knows he should *not*? Have we not a perpetual inclination, in the teeth of our best judgment, to violate that which is *Law*, merely because we understand it to be such? This spirit of perverseness, I say, came to my final overthrow. It was this unfathomable longing of the soul *to vex itself*—to offer violence to its own nature—to do wrong for the wrong's sake only—that urged me to continue and finally to consummate the injury I had inflicted upon the unoffending brute. One morning, in cool blood, I slipped a noose about its neck and hung it to the limb of a tree;—hung it with the tears streaming from my eyes, and with the bitterest remorse at my heart;—hung it *because* I knew that it had loved me, and *because* I felt it had given me no reason of offence;—hung it *because* I knew that in so doing I was committing a sin—a deadly sin that would so jeopardise my immortal soul as to place it—if such a thing were possible—even beyond the reach of the infinite mercy of the Most Merciful and Most Terrible God.

On the night of the day on which this cruel deed was done, I was aroused from sleep by the cry of fire. The curtains of my bed were in flames. The whole house was blazing. It was with great difficulty that my wife, a servant, and myself, made our escape from the conflagration. The destruction was complete. My entire worldly wealth was swallowed up, and I resigned myself thenceforward to despair.

I am above the weakness of seeking to establish a sequence of cause and effect, between the disaster and the atrocity. But I am detailing a chain of facts—and wish not to leave even a possible link imperfect. On the day succeeding the fire, I visited the ruins. The walls, with one exception, had fallen in. This exception was found in a compartment wall, not very thick, which stood about the middle of the house, and against which had rested the head of my bed. The plastering had here, in great measure, resisted the action of the fire—a fact which I attributed to its having been recently spread. About this wall a dense crowd were collected, and many persons seemed to be examining a particular portion of it with very minute and eager attention. The words 'strange!' 'singular!' and other similar expressions, excited my curiosity. I approached and saw, as if graven in *bas-relief* upon the white surface, the figure of a gigantic *cat*. The impression was given with an accuracy truly marvellous. There was a rope about the animal's neck.

When I first beheld this apparition—for I could scarcely regard it as less—my wonder and my terror were extreme. But at length reflection came to my aid. The cat, I remembered, had been hung in a garden adjacent to the house. Upon the alarm of fire, this garden had been immediately filled by the crowd—by some one of whom the animal must have been cut from the tree and thrown, through an open window, into my chamber. This had probably been done with the view of arousing me from sleep. The falling of other walls had compressed the victim of my cruelty into the substance of the freshly-spread plaster; the lime of which, with the flames, and the *ammonia* from the carcass, had then accomplished the portraiture as I saw it.

Although I thus readily accounted to my reason, if not altogether to my conscience, for the startling fact just detailed, it did not the less fail to make a deep impression upon my fancy. For months I could not rid myself of the phantasm of the cat; and, during this period, there came back into my spirit a half-sentiment that seemed, but was not, remorse. I went so far as to regret the loss of the animal, and to look about me, among the vile haunts which I now habitually frequented, for another pet of the same species, and of somewhat similar appearance, with which to supply its place.

One night as I sat, half stupefied, in a den of more than infamy, my attention was suddenly drawn to some black object, reposing upon the head of one of the immense hogsheads of gin, or of rum, which constituted the chief furniture of the apartment. I had been looking steadily at the top of this hogshead for some minutes, and what now caused me surprise was the fact that I had not sooner perceived the object thereupon. I approached it, and touched it with my hand. It was a black cat—a very large one—fully as large as Pluto, and closely resembling him in every respect but one. Pluto had not a white hair upon any portion of his body; but this cat had a large, although indefinite splotch of white, covering nearly the whole region of the breast.

Upon my touching him, he immediately arose, purred loudly, rubbed against my hand, and appeared delighted with my notice. This, then, was the very creature of which I was in search. I at once offered to purchase it of the landlord; but this person made no claim to it—knew nothing of it—had never seen it before.

I continued my caresses, and, when I prepared to go home, the animal evinced a disposition to accompany me. I permitted it to do so; occasionally stooping and patting it as I proceeded. When it reached the house it domesticated itself at once, and became immediately a great favourite with my wife.

For my own part, I soon found a dislike to it arising within me. This was just the reverse of what I had anticipated; but— I know not how or why it was—its evident fondness for myself rather disgusted and annoyed. By slow degrees these feelings of disgust and annoyance rose into the bitterness of hatred. I avoided the creature; a certain sense of shame, and the remembrance of my former deed of cruelty, preventing me from physically abusing it. I did not, for some weeks, strike, or otherwise violently ill use it; but gradually—very gradually—I came to look upon it with unutterable loathing, and to flee silently from its odious presence, as from the breath of a pestilence.

What added, no doubt, to my hatred of the beast, was the discovery, on the morning after I brought it home, that, like Pluto, it also had been deprived of one of its eyes. This circumstance, however, only endeared it to my wife, who, as I have already said, possessed, in a high degree, that humanity of feeling which had once been my distinguishing trait, and the source of many of my simplest and purest pleasures.

With my aversion to this cat, however, its partiality for myself seemed to increase. It followed my footsteps with a pertinacity which it would be difficult to make the reader comprehend. Whenever I sat, it would crouch beneath my chair, or spring upon my knees, covering me with its loathsome caresses. If I arose to walk it would get between my feet and thus nearly throw me down, or, fastening its long and sharp claws in my dress, clamber, in this manner, to my breast. At such times, although I longed to destroy it with a blow, I was yet withheld from so doing, partly by a memory of my former crime, but chiefly—let me confess it at once—by absolute *dread* of the beast.

This dread was not exactly a dread of physical evil—and yet I should be at a loss how otherwise to define it. I am almost ashamed to own—yes, even in this felon's cell, I am almost ashamed to own—that the terror and horror with which the animal inspired me, had been heightened by one of the merest chimaeras it would be possible to conceive. My wife had called my attention, more than once, to the character of the mark of white hair, of which I have spoken, and which constituted the sole visible difference between the strange beast and the one I had destroyed. The reader will remember that this mark, although large, had been originally very indefinite; but, by slow degrees—degrees nearly imperceptible, and which for a long time my reason struggled to reject as fanciful—it had, at length, assumed a rigorous distinctness of outline. It was now the representation of an object that I shudder to name—and for this, above all, I loathed, and dreaded, and would have rid myself of the monster *had I dared*—it was now, I say, the image of a hideous—of a ghastly thing—of the GALLOWS!—oh, mournful and terrible engine of Horror and of Crime—of Agony and of Death!

And now was I indeed wretched beyond the wretchedness of mere Humanity. And *a brute beast*—whose fellow I had contemptuously destroyed—*a brute beast* to work out for *me*— for me, a man fashioned in the image of the High God—so much of insufferable woe! Alas! neither by day nor by night knew I the blessing of rest any more! During the former the creature left me no moment alone; and, in the latter, I started hourly from dreams of unutterable fear, to find the hot breath of *the thing* upon my face, and its vast weight—an incarnate Nightmare that I had no power to shake off—incumbent eternally upon my *heart*!

Beneath the pressure of torments such as these, the feeble remnant of the good within me succumbed. Evil thoughts became my sole intimates—the darkest and most evil of thoughts.

The moodiness of my usual temper increased to hatred of all things and of all mankind; while, from the sudden, frequent, and ungovernable outbursts of a fury to which I now blindly abandoned myself, my uncomplaining wife, alas! was the most usual and the most patient of sufferers.

One day she accompanied me, upon some household errand, into the cellar of the old building which our poverty compelled us to inhabit. The cat followed me down the steep stairs, and, nearly throwing me headlong, exasperated me to madness. Uplifting an axe, and forgetting, in my wrath, the childish dread which had hitherto stayed my hand, I aimed a blow at the animal, which, of course, would have proved instantly fatal had it descended as I wished. But this blow was arrested by the hand of my wife. Goaded, by the interference, into a rage more than demoniacal, I withdrew my arm from her grasp and buried the axe in her brain. She fell dead upon the spot, without a groan.

This hideous murder accomplished, I set myself forthwith, and with entire deliberation, to the task of concealing the body. I knew that I could not remove it from the house, either by day or by night, without the risk of being observed by the neighbours. Many projects entered my mind. At one period I thought of cutting the corpse into minute fragments, and destroying them by fire. At another, I resolved to dig a grave for it in the floor of the cellar. Again, I deliberated about casting it in the well in the yard—about packing it in a box, as if merchandise, with the usual arrangements, and so getting a porter to take it from the house. Finally I hit upon what I considered a far better expedient than either of these. I determined to wall it up in the cellar—as the monks of the Middle Ages are recorded to have walled up their victims.

For a purpose such as this the cellar was well adapted. Its walls were loosely constructed, and had lately been plastered throughout with a rough plaster, which the dampness of the atmosphere had prevented from hardening. Moreover, in one of the walls was a projection, caused by a false chimney, or fireplace, that had been filled up, and made to resemble the rest of the cellar. I made no doubt that I could readily displace the bricks at this point, insert the corpse, and wall the whole up as before, so that no eye could detect anything suspicious.

And in this calculation I was not deceived. By means of a crowbar I easily dislodged the bricks, and, having carefully deposited the body against the inner wall, I propped it in that position, while with little trouble I relaid the whole structure as it originally stood. Having procured mortar, sand, and hair, with every possible precaution, I prepared a plaster which could not be distinguished from the old, and with this I very carefully went over the new brickwork. When I had finished, I felt satisfied that all was right. The wall did not present the slightest appearance of having been disturbed. The rubbish on the floor was picked up with the minutest care. I looked around triumphantly, and said to myself, 'Here at least, then, my labour has not been in vain.'

My next step was to look for the beast which had been the cause of so much wretchedness; for I had, at length, firmly resolved to put it to death. Had I been able to meet with it at the moment, there could have been no doubt of its fate; but it appeared that the crafty animal had been alarmed at the violence of my previous anger, and forbore to present itself in my present mood. It is impossible to describe, or to imagine, the deep, the blissful sense of relief which the absence of the detested creature occasioned in my bosom. It did not make its appearance during the night; and thus for one night at least, since its introduction into the house, I soundly and tranquilly slept; aye, *slept* even with the burden of murder upon my soul!

The second and the third day passed, and still my tormentor came not. Once again I breathed as a free man. The monster, in terror, had fled the premises forever! I should behold it no more! My happiness was supreme! The guilt of my dark deed disturbed me but little. Some few inquiries had been made, but these had been readily answered. Even a search had been instituted—but of course nothing was to be discovered. I looked upon my future felicity as secured.

Upon the fourth day of the assassination, a party of the police came, very unexpectedly, into the house, and proceeded again to make rigorous investigation of the premises. Secure, however, in the inscrutability of my place of concealment, I felt no embarrassment whatever. The officers bade me accompany them in their search. They left no nook or corner unexplored. At length, for the third or fourth time, they descended into the cellar. I quivered not in a muscle. My heart beat calmly as that of one who slumbers in innocence. I walked the cellar from end to end. I folded my arms upon my bosom, and roamed easily to and fro. The police were thoroughly satisfied and prepared to depart. The glee at my heart was too strong to be restrained. I burned to say if but one word, by way of triumph, and to render doubly sure their assurance of my guiltlessness.

'Gentlemen,' I said at last, as the party ascended the steps, 'I delight to have allayed your suspicions. I wish you all health, and a little more courtesy. By the bye, gentlemen, this—this is a very well-constructed house.' (In the rabid desire to say something easily, I scarcely knew what I uttered at all.)—'I may say an *excellently* well-constructed house. These walls—are you going, gentlemen?—these walls are solidly put together;' and here, through the mere frenzy of bravado, I rapped heavily, with a cane which I held in my hand, upon that very portion of the brickwork behind which stood the corpse of the wife of my bosom.

But may God shield and deliver me from the fangs of the Arch-Fiend! No sooner had the reverberation of my blows sunk into silence, than I was answered by a voice from within the tomb!—by a cry, at first muffled and broken, like the sobbing of a child, and then quickly swelling into one long, loud, and continuous scream, utterly anomalous and inhuman—a howl—a wailing shriek, half of horror and half of triumph, such as might have arisen only out of hell, conjointly from the throats of the damned in their agony and of the demons that exult in the damnation.

Of my own thoughts it is folly to speak. Swooning, I staggered to the opposite wall. For one instant the party upon the stairs remained motionless, through extremity of terror and of awe. In the next, a dozen stout arms were toiling at the wall. It fell bodily. The corpse, already greatly decayed and clotted with gore, stood erect before the eyes of the spectators. Upon its head, with red extended mouth and solitary eye of fire, sat the hideous beast whose craft had seduced me into murder, and whose informing voice had consigned me to the hangman. I had walled the monster up within the tomb!

2

The Gold-Bug

What ho! what ho! this fellow is dancing mad!
He hath been bitten by the Tarantula.

—*All in the Wrong*

Many years ago, I contracted an intimacy with a Mr. William Legrand. He was of an ancient Huguenot family, and had once been wealthy; but a series of misfortunes had reduced him to want. To avoid the mortification consequent upon his disasters, he left New Orleans, the city of his forefathers, and took up his residence at Sullivan's Island, near Charleston, South Carolina.

This Island is a very singular one. It consists of little else than the sea sand, and is about three miles long. Its breadth at no point exceeds a quarter of a mile. It is separated from the mainland by a scarcely perceptible creek, oozing its way through a wilderness of reeds and slime, a favourite resort of the marsh-hen. The vegetation, as might be supposed, is scant, or at least dwarfish. No trees of any magnitude are to be seen. Near the western extremity, where Fort Moultrie stands, and where are some miserable frame buildings, tenanted, during summer, by the fugitives from Charleston dust and fever, may be found, indeed, the bristly palmetto; but the whole island, with the exception of this western point, and a line of hard, white beach on the sea-coast, is covered with a dense undergrowth of the sweet myrtle, so much prised by the horticulturists of England. The shrub here often attains the height of fifteen or twenty feet, and forms an almost impenetrable coppice, burthening the air with its fragrance.

In the inmost recesses of this coppice, not far from the eastern or more remote end of the island, Legrand had built himself a small hut, which he occupied when I first, by mere accident, made his acquaintance. This soon ripened into friendship—for there was much in the recluse to excite interest and esteem. I found him well educated, with unusual powers of mind, but infected with misanthropy, and subject to perverse moods of alternate enthusiasm and melancholy. He had with him many books, but rarely employed them. His chief amusements were gunning and fishing, or sauntering along the beach and through the myrtles, in quest of shells or entomological specimens—his collection of the latter might have been envied by a Swammerdamm. In these excursions he was usually accompanied by an old negro, called Jupiter, who had been manumitted before the reverses of the family, but who could be induced, neither by threats nor by promises, to abandon what he considered his right of attendance upon the footsteps of his young 'Massa Will.' It is not improbable that the relatives of Legrand, conceiving him to be somewhat unsettled in intellect, had contrived to instil this obstinacy into Jupiter, with a view to the supervision and guardianship of the wanderer.

The winters in the latitude of Sullivan's Island are seldom very severe, and in the fall of the year it is a rare event indeed when a fire is considered necessary. About the middle of October, 18—, there occurred, however, a day of remarkable chilliness.

Just before sunset I scrambled my way through the evergreens to the hut of my friend, whom I had not visited for several weeks—my residence being, at that time, in Charleston, a distance of nine miles from the Island, while the facilities of passage and re-passage were very far behind those of the present day. Upon reaching the hut I rapped, as was my custom, and getting no reply, sought for the key where I knew it was secreted, unlocked the door, and went in. A fine fire was blazing upon the hearth. It was a novelty, and by no means an ungrateful one. I threw off an overcoat, took an arm-chair by the crackling logs, and awaited patiently the arrival of my hosts.

Soon after dark they arrived, and gave me a most cordial welcome. Jupiter, grinning from ear to ear, bustled about to prepare some marsh-hens for supper. Legrand was in one of his fits—how else shall I term them?—of enthusiasm. He had found an unknown bivalve, forming a new genus, and, more than this, he had hunted down and secured, with Jupiter's assistance, a *scarabæus* which he believed to be totally new, but in respect to which he wished to have my opinion on the morrow.

'And why not to-night?' I asked, rubbing my hands over the blaze, and wishing the whole tribe of *scarabæi* at the devil.

'Ah, if I had only known you were here!' said Legrand, 'but it's so long since I saw you; and how could I foresee that you would pay me a visit this very night of all others? As I was coming home I met Lieutenant G——, from the fort, and, very foolishly, I lent him the bug; so it will be impossible for you to see it until the morning. Stay here to-night, and I will send Jup down for it at sunrise. It is the loveliest thing in creation!'

'What?—sunrise?'

'Nonsense! no!—the bug. It is of a brilliant gold colour—about the size of a large hickory-nut—with two jet black spots near one extremity of the back, and another, somewhat longer, at the other. The *antennæ* are—"

'Dey aint *no* tin in him, Massa Will, I keep a tellin' on you,' here interrupted Jupiter; 'de bug is a goole-bug, solid, ebery bit of him, inside and all, sep him wing—neber feel half so hebby a bug in my life.'

'Well, suppose it is, Jup,' replied Legrand, somewhat more earnestly, it seemed to me, than the case demanded, 'is that any reason for your letting the birds burn? The colour'—here he turned to me—'is really almost enough to warrant Jupiter's idea. You never saw a more brilliant metallic lustre than the scales emit— but of this you cannot judge till tomorrow. In the mean time I can give you some idea of the shape.' Saying this, he seated himself at a small table, on which were a pen and ink, but no paper. He looked for some in a drawer, but found none.

'Never mind,' said he at length, 'this will answer'; and he drew from his waistcoat pocket a scrap of what I took to be very dirty foolscap, and made upon it a rough drawing with the pen. While he did this, I retained my seat by the fire, for I was still chilly. When the design was complete, he handed it to me without rising. As I received it, a loud growl was heard, succeeded by a scratching at the door. Jupiter opened it, and a large Newfoundland, belonging to Legrand, rushed in, leaped upon my shoulders, and loaded me with caresses; for I had shown him much attention during previous visits. When his gambols were over, I looked at the paper, and, to speak the truth, found myself not a little puzzled at what my friend had depicted.

'Well!' I said, after contemplating it for some minutes, 'this is a strange *scarabæus*, I must confess; new to me; never saw anything like it before—unless it was a skull, or a death's-head, which it more nearly resembles than anything else that has come under *my* observation.'

'A death's-head!' echoed Legrand. 'Oh—yes—well, it has something of that appearance upon paper, no doubt. The two upper black spots look like eyes, eh? and the longer one at the bottom like a mouth—and then the shape of the whole is oval.'

'Perhaps so,' said I; 'but, Legrand, I fear you are no artist. I must wait until I see the beetle itself, if I am to form any idea of its personal appearance.'

'Well, I don't know,' said he, a little nettled, 'I draw tolerably—*should* do it at least—have had good masters, and flatter myself that I am not quite a blockhead.'

'But, my dear fellow, you are joking then,' said I, 'this is a very passable *skull*—indeed, I may say that it is a very *excellent* skull, according to the vulgar notions about such specimens of physiology—and your *scarabæus* must be the queerest *scarabæus* in the world if it resembles it. Why, we may get up a very thrilling bit of superstition upon this hint. I presume you will call the bug *scarabæus caput hominis*, or something of that kind—there are many similar titles in the Natural Histories. But where are the *antennæ* you spoke of?'

'The *antennæ*!' said Legrand, who seemed to be getting unaccountably warm upon the subject; 'I am sure you must see the *antennæ*. I made them as distinct as they are in the original insect, and I presume that is sufficient.'

'Well, well,' I said, 'perhaps you have—still I don't see them;' and I handed him the paper without additional remark, not wishing to ruffle his temper; but I was much surprised at the turn affairs had taken; his ill humour puzzled me—and, as for the drawing of the beetle, there were positively *no antennæ* visible, and the whole *did* bear a very close resemblance to the ordinary cuts of a death's-head.

He received the paper very peevishly, and was about to crumple it, apparently to throw it in the fire, when a casual glance at the design seemed suddenly to rivet his attention. In an instant his face grew violently red—in another as excessively pale. For some minutes he continued to scrutinise the drawing minutely where he sat. At length he arose, took a candle from the table, and proceeded to seat himself upon a sea-chest in the farthest corner of the room. Here again he made an anxious examination of the paper; turning it in all directions. He said nothing, however, and his conduct greatly astonished me; yet I thought it prudent not to exacerbate the growing moodiness of his temper by any comment. Presently he took from his coat-pocket a wallet, placed the paper carefully in it, and deposited both in a writing-desk, which he locked. He now grew more composed in his demeanour; but his original air of enthusiasm had quite disappeared. Yet he seemed not so much sulky as abstracted. As the evening wore away he became more and more absorbed in reverie, from which no sallies of mine could arouse him. It had been my intention to pass the night at the hut, as I had frequently done before, but, seeing my host in this mood, I deemed it proper to take leave. He did not press me to remain, but, as I departed, he shook my hand with even more than his usual cordiality.

It was about a month after this (and during the interval I had seen nothing of Legrand) when I received a visit, at Charleston, from his man, Jupiter. I had never seen the good old negro look so dispirited, and I feared that some serious disaster had befallen my friend.

'Well, Jup,' said I, 'what is the matter now?—how is your master?'

'Why, to speak de troof, massa, him not so berry well as mought be.'

'Not well! I am truly sorry to hear it. What does he complain of?'

'Dar! dat's it!—him neber 'plain of notin'—but him berry sick for all dat.'

'Very sick, Jupiter!—why didn't you say so at once? Is he confined to bed?'

'No, dat he aint!—he aint 'fin'd nowhar—dat's just whar de shoe pinch—my mind is got to be berry hebby 'bout poor Massa Will.'

'Jupiter, I should like to understand what it is you are talking about. You say your master is sick. Hasn't he told you what ails him?'

'Why, massa, 'taint worf while for to git mad about de matter—Massa Will say noffin at all aint de matter wid him—but den what make him go about looking dis here way, wid he head down and he soldiers up, and as white as a gose? And den he keep a syphon all de time—'

'Keeps a what, Jupiter?'

'Keeps a syphon wid de figgurs on de slate—de queerest figgurs I ebber did see. Ise gittin' to be skeered, I tell you. Hab for to keep mighty tight eye 'pon him 'noovers. Todder day he gib me slip 'fore de sun up and was gone de whole ob de blessed day. I had a big stick ready cut for to gib him deuced good beating when he did come—but Ise sich a fool dat I hadn't de heart arter all—he look so berry poorly.'

'Eh?—what?—ah yes!—upon the whole I think you had better not be too severe with the poor fellow—don't flog him, Jupiter—he can't very well stand it—but can you form no idea of what has occasioned this illness, or rather this change of conduct? Has anything unpleasant happened since I saw you?'

'No, massa, dey aint bin noffin onpleasant *since* den—'twas 'fore den I'm feared—'twas de berry day you was dare.'

'How? what do you mean?'

'Why, massa, I mean de bug—dare now.'

'The what?'

'De bug—I'm berry sartain dat Massa Will bin bit somewhere 'bout de head by dat goole-bug.'

'And what cause have you, Jupiter, for such a supposition?'

'Claws enuff, massa, and mouff too. I nebber did see sich a deuced bug—he kick and he bite ebery ting what cum near him. Massa Will cotch him fuss, but had for to let him go 'gin mighty quick, I tell you—den was de time he must ha' got de bite. I didn't like de look ob de bug mouff, myself, nohow, so I wouldn't take hold ob him wid my finger, but I cotch him wid a piece ob paper dat I found. I rap him up in de paper and stuff piece ob it in he mouff—dat was de way.'

'And you think, then, that your master was really bitten by the beetle, and that the bite made him sick?'

'I don't think noffin' about it—I nose it. What make him dream 'bout de goole so much, if 'taint cause he bit by de goole-bug? Ise heerd 'bout dem goole-bugs 'fore dis.'

'But how do you know he dreams about gold?'

'How I know? Why, 'cause he talk about it in he sleep—dat's how I nose.'

'Well, Jup, perhaps you are right; but to what fortunate circumstance am I to attribute the honour of a visit from you to-day?'

'What de matter, massa?'

'Did you bring any message from Mr. Legrand?'

'No, massa, I bring dis her pissel'; and here Jupiter handed me a note which ran thus:

MY DEAR—

Why have I not seen you for so long a time? I hope you have not been so foolish as to take offence at any little *brusquerie* of mine; but no, that is improbable.

Since I saw you I have had great cause for anxiety. I have something to tell you, yet scarcely know how to tell it, or whether I should tell it at all.

I have not been quite well for some days past, and poor old Jup annoys me, almost beyond endurance, by his well-meant attentions. Would you believe it?—he had prepared a huge stick, the other day, with which to chastise me for giving him the slip, and spending the day, *solus*, among the hills on the main land. I verily believe that my ill looks alone saved me a flogging.

I have made no addition to my cabinet since we met.

'If you can, in any way, make it convenient, come over with Jupiter. *Do* come. I wish to see you *to-night*, upon business of importance. I assure you that it is of the *highest* importance.

Ever yours,

WILLIAM LEGRAND

There was something in the tone of this note which gave me great uneasiness. Its whole style differed materially from that of Legrand. What could he be dreaming of? What new crotchet possessed his excitable brain? What 'business of the highest importance' could *he* possibly have to transact? Jupiter's account of him boded no good. I dreaded lest the continued pressure of misfortune had, at length, fairly unsettled the reason of my friend. Without a moment's hesitation, therefore, I prepared to accompany the negro.

Upon reaching the wharf, I noticed a scythe and three spades, all apparently new, lying in the bottom of the boat in which we were to embark.

'What is the meaning of all this, Jup?' I inquired.

'Him syfe, massa, and spade.'

'Very true; but what are they doing here?'

'Him de syfe and de spade what Massa Will sis 'pon my buying for him in de town, and de debbil's own lot of money I had to gib for 'em.'

'But what, in the name of all that is mysterious, is your "Massa Will" going to do with scythes and spades?'

'Dat's more dan I know, and debbil take me if I don't b'lieve 'tis more dan he know too. But it's all cum ob de bug.'

Finding that no satisfaction was to be obtained of Jupiter, whose whole intellect seemed to be absorbed by 'de bug,' I now stepped into the boat and made sail. With a fair and strong breeze we soon ran into the little cove to the northward of Fort Moultrie, and a walk of some two miles brought us to the hut. It was about three in the afternoon when we arrived. Legrand had been awaiting us in eager expectation. He grasped my hand with a nervous *empressement* which alarmed me and strengthened the suspicions already entertained. His countenance was pale even to ghastliness, and his deep-set eyes glared with unnatural lustre. After some inquiries respecting his health, I asked him, not knowing what better to say, if he had yet obtained the *scarabæus* from Lieutenant G—.

'Oh, yes,' he replied, colouring violently, 'I got it from him the next morning. Nothing should tempt me to part with that *scarabæus*. Do you know that Jupiter is quite right about it?'

'In what way?' I asked, with a sad foreboding at heart.

'In supposing it to be a bug of *real gold*.' He said this with an air of profound seriousness, and I felt inexpressibly shocked.

'This bug is to make my fortune,' he continued, with a triumphant smile, 'to reinstate me in my family possessions. Is it any wonder, then, that I prise it? Since Fortune has thought fit to bestow it upon me, I have only to use it properly, and I shall arrive at the gold of which it is the index. Jupiter, bring me that *scarabæus!*'

'What! de bug, massa? I'd rudder not go fer trubble dat bug; you mus' git him for your own self.' Hereupon Legrand arose, with a grave and stately air, and brought me the beetle from a glass case in which it was enclosed. It was a beautiful *scarabæus*, and, at that time, unknown to naturalists—of course a great prize in a scientific point of view. There were two round black spots near one extremity of the back, and a long one near the other. The scales were exceedingly hard and glossy, with all the appearance of burnished gold. The weight of the insect was very remarkable, and, taking all things into consideration, I could hardly blame Jupiter for his opinion respecting it; but what to make of Legrand's concordance with that opinion, I could not, for the life of me, tell.

'I sent for you,' said he, in a grandiloquent tone, when I had completed my examination of the beetle, 'I sent for you that I might have your counsel and assistance in furthering the views of Fate and of the bug—'

'My dear Legrand,' I cried, interrupting him, 'you are certainly unwell, and had better use some little precautions. You shall go to bed, and I will remain with you a few days, until you get over this. You are feverish and—'

'Feel my pulse,' said he.

I felt it, and, to say the truth, found not the slightest indication of fever.

'But you may be ill and yet have no fever. Allow me this once to prescribe for you. In the first place go to bed. In the next—'

'You are mistaken,' he interposed, 'I am as well as I can expect to be under the excitement which I suffer. If you really wish me well, you will relieve this excitement.'

'And how is this to be done?'

'Very easily. Jupiter and myself are going upon an expedition into the hills, upon the main land, and, in this expedition we shall need the aid of some person in whom we can confide. You are the only one we can trust. Whether we succeed or fail, the excitement which you now perceive in me will be equally allayed.'

'I am anxious to oblige you in any way,' I replied; 'but do you mean to say that this infernal beetle has any connection with your expedition into the hills?'

'It has.'

'Then, Legrand, I can become a party to no such absurd proceeding.'

'I am sorry—very sorry—for we shall have to try it by ourselves.'

'Try it by yourselves! The man is surely mad!—but stay!—how long do you propose to be absent?'

'Probably all night. We shall start immediately, and be back, at all events, by sunrise.'

'And will you promise me, upon your honour, that when this freak of yours is over, and the bug business (good God!) settled to your satisfaction, you will then return home and follow my advice implicitly, as that of your physician?'

'Yes; I promise; and now let us be off, for we have no time to lose.'

With a heavy heart I accompanied my friend. We started about four o'clock—Legrand, Jupiter, the dog, and myself. Jupiter had with him the scythe and spades—the whole of which he insisted upon carrying—more through fear, it seemed to me, of trusting either of the implements within reach of his master, than from any excess of industry or complaisance. His demeanour was dogged in the extreme, and 'dat deuced bug' were the sole words which escaped his lips during the journey. For my own part, I had charge of a couple of dark lanterns, while Legrand contented himself with the *scarabæus*, which he carried attached to the end of a bit of whip-cord; twirling it to and fro, with the air of a conjuror, as he went. When I observed this last, plain evidence of my friend's aberration of mind, I could scarcely refrain from tears. I thought it best, however, to humour his fancy, at least for the present, or until I could adopt some more energetic measures with a chance of success. In the mean time I endeavoured, but all in vain, to sound him in regard to the object of the expedition. Having succeeded in inducing me to accompany him, he seemed unwilling to hold conversation upon any topic of minor importance, and to all my questions vouchsafed no other reply than 'we shall see!'

We crossed the creek at the head of the island by means of a skiff; and, ascending the high grounds on the shore of the main land, proceeded in a northwesterly direction, through a tract of country excessively wild and desolate, where no trace of a human footstep was to be seen. Legrand led the way with decision; pausing only for an instant, here and there, to consult what appeared to be certain landmarks of his own contrivance upon a former occasion.

In this manner we journeyed for about two hours, and the sun was just setting when we entered a region infinitely more dreary than any yet seen. It was a species of table-land, near the summit of an almost inaccessible hill, densely wooded from base to pinnacle, and interspersed with huge crags that appeared to lie loosely upon the soil, and in many cases were prevented from precipitating themselves into the valleys below, merely by the support of the trees against which they reclined. Deep ravines, in various directions, gave an air of still sterner solemnity to the scene.

The natural platform to which we had clambered was thickly overgrown with brambles, through which we soon discovered that it would have been impossible to force our way but for the scythe; and Jupiter, by direction of his master, proceeded to clear for us a path to the foot of an enormously tall tulip-tree, which stood, with some eight or ten oaks, upon the level, and far surpassed them all, and all other trees which I had then ever seen, in the beauty of its foliage and form, in the wide spread of its branches, and in the general majesty of its appearance. When we reached this tree, Legrand turned to Jupiter, and asked him if he thought he could climb it. The old man seemed a little staggered by the question, and for some moments made no reply. At length he approached the huge trunk, walked slowly around it, and examined it with minute attention. When he had completed his scrutiny, he merely said,

'Yes, massa, Jup climb any tree he ebber see in he life.'

'Then up with you as soon as possible, for it will soon be too dark to see what we are about.'

'How far mus' go up, massa?' inquired Jupiter.

'Get up the main trunk first, and then I will tell you which way to go—and here—stop! take this beetle with you.'

'De bug, Massa Will!—de goole bug!' cried the negro, drawing back in dismay—'what for mus' tote de bug way up de tree?—d—n if I do!'

'If you are afraid, Jup, a great big negro like you, to take hold of a harmless little dead beetle, why you can carry it up by this string—but, if you do not take it up with you in some way, I shall be under the necessity of breaking your head with this shovel.'

'What de matter now, massa?' said Jup, evidently shamed into compliance; 'always want for to raise fuss wid old nigger. Was only funnin anyhow. *Me* feered de bug! what I keer for de bug?' Here he took cautiously hold of the extreme end of the string, and, maintaining the insect as far from his person as circumstances would permit, prepared to ascend the tree.

In youth, the tulip-tree, or *Liriodendron Tulipiferum*, the most magnificent of American foresters, has a trunk peculiarly smooth, and often rises to a great height without lateral branches; but, in its riper age, the bark becomes gnarled and uneven, while many short limbs make their appearance on the stem. Thus the difficulty of ascension, in the present case, lay more in semblance than in reality. Embracing the huge cylinder, as closely as possible, with his arms and knees, seizing with his hands some projections, and resting his naked toes upon others, Jupiter, after one or two narrow escapes from falling, at length wriggled himself into the first great fork, and seemed to consider the whole business as virtually accomplished. The *risk* of the achievement was, in fact, now over, although the climber was some sixty or seventy feet from the ground.

'Which way mus' go now, Massa Will?' he asked.

'Keep up the largest branch—the one on this side,' said Legrand. The negro obeyed him promptly, and apparently with but little trouble; ascending higher and higher, until no glimpse of his squat figure could be obtained through the dense foliage which enveloped it. Presently his voice was heard in a sort of halloo.

'How much fudder is got for go?'

'How high up are you?' asked Legrand.

'Ebber so fur,' replied the negro; 'can see de sky fru de top ob de tree.'

'Never mind the sky, but attend to what I say. Look down the trunk and count the limbs below you on this side. How many limbs have you passed?'

'One, two, tree, four, fibe—I done pass fibe big limb, massa 'pon dis side.'

'Then go one limb higher.'

In a few minutes the voice was heard again, announcing that the seventh limb was attained.

'Now, Jup,' cried Legrand, evidently much excited, 'I want you to work your way out upon that limb as far as you can. If you see anything strange, let me know.'

By this time what little doubt I might have entertained of my poor friend's insanity was put finally at rest. I had no alternative but to conclude him stricken with lunacy, and I became seriously anxious about getting him home. While I was pondering upon what was best to be done, Jupiter's voice was again heard.

'Mos' feerd for to venture 'pon dis limb berry far—'tis dead limb putty much all de way.'

'Did you say it was a *dead* limb, Jupiter?' cried Legrand in a quavering voice.

'Yes, massa, him dead as de door-nail—done up for sartain—done departed dis here life.'

'What in the name heaven shall I do?' asked Legrand, seemingly in the greatest distress.

'Do!' said I, glad of an opportunity to interpose a word, 'why come home and go to bed. Come now!—that's a fine fellow. It's getting late, and, besides, you remember your promise.'

'Jupiter,' cried he, without heeding me in the least, 'do you hear me?'

'Yes, Massa Will, hear you ebber so plain.'

'Try the wood well, then, with your knife, and see if you think it *very* rotten.'

'Him rotten, massa, sure nuff,' replied the negro in a few moments, 'but not so berry rotten as mought be. Mought venture out leetle way 'pon de limb by myself, dat's true.'

'By yourself!—what do you mean?'

'Why I mean de bug. 'Tis *berry* hebby bug. Spose I drop him down fuss, and den de limb won't break wid just de weight ob one nigger.'

'You infernal scoundrel!' cried Legrand, apparently much relieved, 'what do you mean by telling me such nonsense as that? As sure as you drop that beetle!—I'll break your neck. Look here, Jupiter, do you hear me?'

'Yes, massa, needn't hollo at poor nigger dat style.'

'Well! now listen!—if you will venture out on the limb as far as you think safe, and not let go the beetle, I'll make you a present of a silver dollar as soon as you get down.'

'I'm gwine, Massa Will—deed I is,' replied the negro very promptly—'mos' out to the eend now.'

'*Out to the end!*' here fairly screamed Legrand, 'do you say you are out to the end of that limb?'

'Soon be to de eend, massa,—o-o-o-o-oh! Lor-gol-a-marcy! what *is* dis here 'pon de tree?'

'Well!' cried Legrand, highly delighted, 'what is it?'

'Why taint noffin but a skull—somebody bin left him head up de tree, and de crows done gobble ebery bit ob de meat off.'

'A skull, you say!—very well!—how is it fastened to the limb?—what holds it on?'

'Sure nuff, massa; mus' look. Why dis berry curous sarcumstance, 'pon my word—dare's a great big nail in de skull, what fastens ob it on to de tree.'

'Well now, Jupiter, do exactly as I tell you—do you hear?'

'Yes, massa.'

'Pay attention, then!—find the left eye of the skull.'

'Hum! hoo! dat's good! why dey aint no eye lef' at all.'

'Curse your stupidity! do you know your right hand from your left?'

'Yes, I nose dat—nose all 'bout dat—'tis my lef' hand what I chops de wood wid.'

'To be sure! you are left-handed; and your left eye is on the same side as your left hand. Now, I suppose, you can find the left eye of the skull, or the place where the left eye has been. Have you found it?'

Here was a long pause. At length the negro asked,

'Is de lef' eye ob de skull 'pon de same side as de lef' hand ob de skull, too?—cause de skull aint got not a bit ob a hand at all—nebber mind! I got de lef' eye now—here de lef' eye! what mus' do wid it?'

'Let the beetle drop through it, as far as the string will reach—but be careful and not let go your hold of the string.'

'All dat done, Massa Will; mighty easy ting for to put de bug fru de hole—look out for him dare below!'

During this colloquy no portion of Jupiter's person could be seen; but the beetle, which he had suffered to descend, was now visible at the end of the string, and glistened, like a globe of burnished gold, in the last rays of the setting sun, some of which still faintly illumined the eminence upon which we stood. The *scarabæus* hung quite clear of any branches, and, if allowed to fall, would have fallen at our feet. Legrand immediately took the scythe, and cleared with it a circular space, three or four yards in diameter, just beneath the insect, and, having accomplished this, ordered Jupiter to let go the string and come down from the tree.

Driving a peg, with great nicety, into the ground, at the precise spot where the beetle fell, my friend now produced from his pocket a tape-measure. Fastening one end of this at that point of the trunk of the tree which was nearest the peg, he unrolled it till it reached the peg and thence further unrolled it, in the direction already established by the two points of the tree and the peg, for the distance of fifty feet—Jupiter clearing away the brambles with the scythe. At the spot thus attained a second peg was driven, and about this, as a centre, a rude circle, about four feet in diameter, described. Taking now a spade himself, and giving one to Jupiter and one to me, Legrand begged us to set about digging as quickly as possible.

To speak the truth, I had no special[1] relish for such amusement at any time, and, at that particular moment, would most willingly have declined it; for the night was coming on, and I felt much fatigued with the exercise already taken; but I saw no mode of escape, and was fearful of disturbing my poor friend's equanimity by a refusal. Could I have depended, indeed, upon Jupiter's aid, I would have had no hesitation in attempting to get the lunatic home by force; but I was too well assured of the old negro's disposition, to hope that he would assist me, under any circumstances, in a personal contest with his master. I made no doubt that the latter had been infected with some of the innumerable Southern superstitions about money buried, and that his phantasy had received confirmation by the finding of the *scarabæus*, or, perhaps, by Jupiter's obstinacy in maintaining it to be 'a bug of real gold.' A mind disposed to lunacy would readily be led away by such suggestions—especially if chiming in with favourite preconceived ideas—and then I called to mind the poor fellow's speech about the beetle's being 'the index of his fortune.' Upon the whole, I was sadly vexed and puzzled, but, at length, I concluded to make a virtue of necessity—to dig with a good will, and thus the sooner to convince the visionary, by ocular demonstration, of the fallacy of the opinions he entertained.

The lanterns having been lit, we all fell to work with a zeal worthy a more rational cause; and, as the glare fell upon our persons and implements, I could not help thinking how picturesque a group we composed, and how strange and suspicious our labours must have appeared to any interloper who, by chance, might have stumbled upon our whereabouts.

We dug very steadily for two hours. Little was said; and our chief embarrassment lay in the yelpings of the dog, who took exceeding interest in our proceedings. He, at length, became so obstreperous that we grew fearful of his giving the alarm to some stragglers in the vicinity,—or, rather, this was the apprehension of Legrand;—for myself, I should have rejoiced at any interruption which might have enabled me to get the wanderer home. The noise was, at length, very effectually silenced by Jupiter, who, getting out of the hole with a dogged air of deliberation, tied the brute's mouth up with one of his suspenders, and then returned, with a grave chuckle, to his task.

When the time mentioned had expired, we had reached a depth of five feet, and yet no signs of any treasure became manifest. A general pause ensued, and I began to hope that the farce was at an end. Legrand, however, although evidently much disconcerted, wiped his brow thoughtfully and recommenced. We had excavated the entire circle of four feet diameter, and now we slightly enlarged the limit, and went to the farther depth of two feet. Still nothing appeared. The gold-seeker, whom I sincerely pitied, at length clambered from the pit, with the bitterest disappointment imprinted upon every feature, and proceeded, slowly and reluctantly, to put on his coat, which he had thrown off at the beginning of his labour. In the meantime I made no remark. Jupiter, at a signal from his master, began to gather up his tools. This done, and the dog having been unmuzzled, we turned in profound silence towards home.

We had taken, perhaps, a dozen steps in this direction, when, with a loud oath, Legrand strode up to Jupiter, and seized him by the collar. The astonished negro opened his eyes and mouth to the fullest extent, let fall the spades, and fell upon his knees.

'You scoundrel,' said Legrand, hissing out the syllables from between his clenched teeth—'you infernal black villain!—speak, I tell you!—answer me this instant, without prevarication!—which—which is your left eye?'

'Oh, my golly, Massa Will! aint dis here my lef' eye for sartain?' roared the terrified Jupiter, placing his hand upon his *right* organ of vision, and holding it there with a desperate pertinacity, as if in immediate dread of his master's attempt at a gouge.

'I thought so!—I knew it! hurrah!' vociferated Legrand, letting the negro go, and executing a series of curvets and caracols, much to the astonishment of his valet, who, arising from his knees, looked, mutely, from his master to myself, and then from myself to his master.

'Come! we must go back,' said the latter, 'the game's not up yet;' and he again led the way to the tulip-tree.

'Jupiter,' said he, when we reached its foot, 'come here! was the skull nailed to the limb with the face outward, or with the face to the limb?'

'De face was out, massa, so dat de crows could get at de eyes good, widout any trouble.'

'Well, then, was it this eye or that through which you dropped the beetle?'—here Legrand touched each of Jupiter's eyes.

''Twas dis eye, massa—de lef' eye—jis as you tell me,' and here it was his right eye that the negro indicated.

'That will do—must try it again.'

Here my friend, about whose madness I now saw, or fancied that I saw, certain indications of method, removed the peg which marked the spot where the beetle fell, to a spot about three inches to the westward of its former position. Taking, now, the tape measure from the nearest point of the trunk to the peg, as before, and continuing the extension in a straight line to the distance of fifty feet, a spot was indicated, removed, by several yards, from the point at which we had been digging.

Around the new position a circle, somewhat larger than in the former instance, was now described, and we again set to work with the spades. I was dreadfully weary, but, scarcely understanding what had occasioned the change in my thoughts, I felt no longer any great aversion from the labour imposed. I had become most unaccountably interested—nay, even excited. Perhaps there was something, amid all the extravagant demeanour of Legrand—some air of forethought, or of deliberation, which impressed me. I dug eagerly, and now and then caught myself actually looking, with something that very much resembled expectation, for the fancied treasure, the vision of which had demented my unfortunate companion. At a period when such vagaries of thought most fully possessed me, and when we had been at work perhaps an hour and a half, we were again interrupted by the violent howlings of the dog. His uneasiness, in the first instance, had been, evidently, but the result of playfulness or caprice, but he now assumed a bitter and serious tone. Upon Jupiter's again attempting to muzzle him, he made furious resistance, and, leaping into the hole, tore up the mould frantically with his claws. In a few seconds he had uncovered a mass of human bones, forming two complete skeletons, intermingled with several buttons of metal, and what appeared to be the dust of decayed woollen. One or two strokes of a spade upturned the blade of a large Spanish knife, and, as we dug farther, three or four loose pieces of gold and silver coin came to light.

At sight of these the joy of Jupiter could scarcely be restrained, but the countenance of his master wore an air of extreme disappointment. He urged us, however, to continue our exertions, and the words were hardly uttered when I stumbled and fell forward, having caught the toe of my boot in a large ring of iron that lay half buried in the loose earth.

We now worked in earnest, and never did I pass ten minutes of more intense excitement. During this interval we had fairly unearthed an oblong chest of wood, which, from its perfect preservation and wonderful hardness, had plainly been subjected to some mineralizing process—perhaps that of the bi-chloride of mercury. This box was three feet and a half long, three feet broad, and two and a half feet deep. It was firmly secured by bands of wrought iron, riveted, and forming a kind of open trelliswork over the whole. On each side of the chest, near the top, were three rings of iron—six in all—by means of which a firm hold could be obtained by six persons. Our utmost united endeavours served only to disturb the coffer very slightly in its bed. We at once saw the impossibility of removing so great a weight. Luckily, the sole fastenings of the lid consisted of two sliding bolts. These we drew back—trembling and panting with anxiety. In an instant, a treasure of incalculable value lay gleaming before us. As the rays of the lanterns fell within the pit, there flashed upwards a glow and a glare, from a confused heap of gold and of jewels, that absolutely *dazzled* our eyes.

I shall not pretend to describe the feelings with which I gazed. Amazement was, of course, predominant. Legrand appeared exhausted with excitement, and spoke very few words. Jupiter's countenance wore, for some minutes, as deadly a pallor as it is possible, in the nature of things, for any negro's visage to assume. He seemed stupefied—thunderstricken. Presently he fell upon his knees in the pit, and, burying his naked arms up to the elbows in gold, let them there remain, as if enjoying the luxury of a bath. At length, with a deep sigh, he exclaimed, as if in a soliloquy:

'And dis all cum ob de goole-bug! de putty goole bug! de poor little goole-bug, what I boosed in dat sabage kind ob style! Aint you shamed ob yourself, nigger?—answer me dat!'

It became necessary, at last, that I should arouse both master and valet to the expediency of removing the treasure. It was growing late, and it behooved us to make exertion, that we might get every thing housed before daylight. It was difficult to say what should be done, and much time was spent in deliberation—so confused were the ideas of all. We, finally, lightened the box by removing two thirds of its contents, when we were enabled, with some trouble, to raise it from the hole. The articles taken out were deposited among the brambles, and the dog left to guard them, with strict orders from Jupiter neither, upon any pretence, to stir from the spot, nor to open his mouth until our return. We then hurriedly made for home with the chest; reaching the hut in safety, but after excessive toil, at one o'clock in the morning. Worn out as we were, it was not in human nature to do more immediately. We rested until two, and had supper; starting for the hills immediately afterwards, armed with three stout sacks, which, by good luck, were upon the premises. A little before four we arrived at the pit, divided the remainder of the booty, as equally as might be, among us, and, leaving the holes unfilled, again set out for the hut, at which, for the second time, we deposited our golden burthens, just as the first faint streaks of the dawn gleamed from over the tree-tops in the East.

We were now thoroughly broken down; but the intense excitement of the time denied us repose. After an unquiet slumber of some three or four hours' duration, we arose, as if by preconcert, to make examination of our treasure.

The chest had been full to the brim, and we spent the whole day, and the greater part of the next night, in a scrutiny of its contents. There had been nothing like order or arrangement. Every thing had been heaped in promiscuously. Having assorted all with care, we found ourselves possessed of even vaster wealth than we had at first supposed. In coin there was rather more than four hundred and fifty thousand dollars—estimating the value of the pieces, as accurately as we could, by the tables of the period. There was not a particle of silver. All was gold of antique date and of great variety—French, Spanish, and German money, with a few English guineas, and some counters, of which we had never seen specimens before. There were several very large and heavy coins, so worn that we could make nothing of their inscriptions. There was no American money. The value of the jewels we found more difficulty in estimating. There were diamonds—some of them exceedingly large and fine—a hundred and ten in all, and not one of them small; eighteen rubies of remarkable brilliancy;— three hundred and ten emeralds, all very beautiful; and twenty-one sapphires, with an opal. These stones had all been broken from their settings and thrown loose in the chest. The settings themselves, which we picked out from among the other gold, appeared to have been beaten up with hammers, as if to prevent identification. Besides all this, there was a vast quantity of solid gold ornaments; nearly two hundred massive finger-and ear-rings; rich chains—thirty of these, if I remember; eighty-three very large and heavy crucifixes;—five gold censers of great value;— a prodigious golden punch bowl, ornamented with richly chased vine-leaves and Bacchanalian figures; with two sword-handles exquisitely embossed, and many other smaller articles which I cannot recollect. The weight of these valuables exceeded three hundred and fifty pounds avoirdupois; and in this estimate I have not included one hundred and ninety-seven superb gold watches; three of the number being worth each five hundred dollars, if one. Many of them were very old, and as timekeepers valueless; the works having suffered, more or less, from corrosion—but all were richly jewelled and in cases of great worth. We estimated the entire contents of the chest, that night, at a million and a half of dollars; and upon the subsequent disposal of the trinkets and jewels (a few being retained for our own use), it was found that we had greatly undervalued the treasure.

When, at length, we had concluded our examination, and the intense excitement of the time had, in some measure, subsided, Legrand, who saw that I was dying with impatience for a solution of this most extraordinary riddle, entered into a full detail of all the circumstances connected with it.

'You remember,' said he, 'the night when I handed you the rough sketch I had made of the *scarabœus*. You recollect also, that I became quite vexed at you for insisting that my drawing resembled a death's-head. When you first made this assertion I thought you were jesting; but afterwards I called to mind the peculiar spots on the back of the insect, and admitted to myself that your remark had some little foundation in fact. Still, the sneer at my graphic powers irritated me—for I am considered a good artist—and, therefore, when you handed me the scrap of parchment, I was about to crumple it up and throw it angrily into the fire.'

'The scrap of paper, you mean,' said I.

'No; it had much of the appearance of paper, and at first I supposed it to be such, but when I came to draw upon it, I discovered it at once to be a piece of very thin parchment. It was quite dirty, you remember. Well, as I was in the very act of crumpling it up, my glance fell upon the sketch at which you had been looking, and you may imagine my astonishment when I perceived, in fact, the figure of a death's-head just where, it seemed to me, I had made the drawing of the beetle. For a moment I was too much amazed to think with accuracy. I knew that my design was very different in detail from this—although there was a certain similarity in general outline. Presently I took a candle, and seating myself at the other end of the room, proceeded to scrutinise the parchment more closely. Upon turning it over, I saw my own sketch upon the reverse, just as I had made it. My first idea, now, was mere surprise at the really remarkable similarity of outline— at the singular coincidence involved in the fact that, unknown to me, there should have been a skull upon the other side of the parchment, immediately beneath my figure of the *scarabæus*, and that this skull, not only in outline, but in size, should so closely resemble my drawing. I say the singularity of this coincidence absolutely stupefied me for a time. This is the usual effect of such coincidences. The mind struggles to establish a connection—a sequence of cause and effect—and, being unable to do so, suffers a species of temporary paralysis. But, when I recovered from this stupor, there dawned upon me gradually a conviction which startled me even far more than the coincidence. I began distinctly, positively, to remember that there had been *no* drawing upon the parchment when I made my sketch of the *scarabœus*. I became perfectly certain of this; for I recollected turning up first one side and then the other, in search of the cleanest spot. Had the skull been then there, of course I could not have failed to notice it. Here was indeed a mystery which I felt it impossible to explain; but, even at that early moment, there seemed to glimmer, faintly, within the most remote and secret chambers of my intellect, a glow-worm-like conception of that truth which last night's adventure brought to so magnificent a demonstration. I arose at once, and putting the parchment securely away, dismissed all further reflection until I should be alone.

'When you had gone, and when Jupiter was fast asleep, I betook myself to a more methodical investigation of the affair. In the first place I considered the manner in which the parchment had come into my possession. The spot where we discovered the *scarabœus* was on the coast of the main-land, about a mile eastward of the island, and but a short distance above high water mark. Upon my taking hold of it, it gave me a sharp bite, which caused me to let it drop. Jupiter, with his accustomed caution, before seizing the insect, which had flown towards him, looked about him for a leaf, or something of that nature, by which to take hold of it. It was at this moment that his eyes, and mine also, fell upon the scrap of parchment, which I then supposed to be paper. It was lying half buried in the sand, a corner sticking up. Near the spot where we found it, I observed the remnants of the hull of what appeared to have been a ship's long boat. The wreck seemed to have been there for a very great while; for the resemblance to boat timbers could scarcely be traced.

'Well, Jupiter picked up the parchment, wrapped the beetle in it, and gave it to me. Soon afterwards we turned to go home, and on the way met Lieutenant G—. I showed him the insect, and he begged me to let him take it to the fort. Upon my consenting, he thrust it forthwith into his waistcoat pocket, without the parchment in which it had been wrapped, and which I had continued to hold in my hand during his inspection. Perhaps he dreaded my changing my mind, and thought it best to make sure of the prize at once—you know how enthusiastic he is on all subjects connected with Natural History. At the same time, without being conscious of it, I must have deposited the parchment in my own pocket.

'You remember that when I went to the table, for the purpose of making a sketch of the beetle, I found no paper where it was usually kept. I looked in the drawer, and found none there. I searched my pockets, hoping to find an old letter—and then my hand fell upon the parchment. I thus detail the precise mode in which it came into my possession; for the circumstances impressed me with peculiar force.

'No doubt you will think me fanciful—but I had already established a kind of *connection*. I had put together two links of a great chain. There was a boat lying upon a sea-coast, and not far from the boat was a parchment—*not a paper*—with a skull depicted upon it. You will, of course, ask "where is the connection?" I reply that the skull, or death's-head, is the well-known emblem of the pirate. The flag of the death's-head is hoisted in all engagements.

'I have said that the scrap was parchment, and not paper. Parchment is durable—almost imperishable. Matters of little moment are rarely consigned to parchment; since, for the mere ordinary purposes of drawing or writing, it is not nearly so well adapted as paper. This reflection suggested some meaning—some relevancy—in the death's-head. I did not fail to observe, also, the *form* of the parchment. Although one of its corners had been, by some accident, destroyed, it could be seen that the original form was oblong. It was just such a slip, indeed, as might have been chosen for a memorandum—for a record of something to be long remembered and carefully preserved.'

'But,' I interposed, 'you say that the skull was *not* upon the parchment when you made the drawing of the beetle. How then do you trace any connection between the boat and the skull— since this latter, according to your own admission, must have been designed (God only knows how or by whom) at some period subsequent to your sketching the *scarabæus?*'

'Ah, hereupon turns the whole mystery; although the secret, at this point, I had comparatively little difficulty in solving. My steps were sure, and could afford but a single result. I reasoned, for example, thus: When I drew the *scarabæus*, there was no skull apparent upon the parchment. When I had completed the drawing I gave it to you, and observed you narrowly until you returned it. *You*, therefore, did not design the skull, and no one else was present to do it. Then it was not done by human agency. And nevertheless it was done.

'At this stage of my reflections I endeavoured to remember,

and *did* remember, with entire distinctness, every incident which occurred about the period in question. The weather was chilly (oh, rare and happy accident!), and a fire was blazing upon the hearth. I was heated with exercise and sat near the table. You, however, had drawn a chair close to the chimney. Just as I placed the parchment in your hand, and as you were in the act of inspecting it, Wolf, the Newfoundland, entered, and leaped upon your shoulders. With your left hand you caressed him and kept him off, while your right, holding the parchment, was permitted to fall listlessly between your knees, and in close proximity to the fire. At one moment I thought the blaze had caught it, and was about to caution you, but, before I could speak, you had withdrawn it, and were engaged in its examination. When I considered all these particulars, I doubted not for a moment that *heat* had been the agent in bringing to light, upon the parchment, the skull which I saw designed upon it. You are well aware that chemical preparations exist, and have existed time out of mind, by means of which it is possible to write upon either paper or vellum, so that the characters shall become visible only when subjected to the action of fire. Zaffre, digested in *aqua regia*, and diluted with four times its weight of water, is sometimes employed; a green tint results. The regulus of cobalt, dissolved in spirit of nitre, gives a red. These colours disappear at longer or shorter intervals after the material written upon cools, but again become apparent upon the re-application of heat.'

'I now scrutinised the death's-head with care. Its outer edges—the edges of the drawing nearest the edge of the vellum—were far more *distinct* than the others. It was clear that the action of the caloric had been imperfect or unequal. I immediately kindled a fire, and subjected every portion of the parchment to a glowing heat. At first, the only effect was the strengthening of the faint lines in the skull; but, upon persevering in the experiment, there became visible, at the corner of the slip, diagonally opposite to the spot in which the death's-head was delineated, the figure of what I at first supposed to be a goat. A closer scrutiny, however, satisfied me that it was intended for a kid.'

'Ha! ha!' said I, 'to be sure I have no right to laugh at you—a million and a half of money is too serious a matter for mirth—but you are not about to establish a third link in your chain—you will not find any special connection between your pirates and a goat— pirates, you know, have nothing to do with goats; they appertain to the farming interest.'

'But I have just said that the figure was *not* that of a goat.'

'Well, a kid then—pretty much the same thing.'

'Pretty much, but not altogether,' said Legrand. 'You may have heard of one *Captain* Kidd. I at once looked upon the figure of the animal as a kind of punning or hieroglyphical signature. I say signature; because its position upon the vellum suggested this idea. The death's-head at the corner diagonally opposite, had, in the same manner, the air of a stamp, or seal. But I was sorely put out by the absence of all else—of the body to my imagined instrument—of the text for my context.'

'I presume you expected to find a letter between the stamp and the signature.'

'Something of that kind. The fact is, I felt irresistibly impressed with a presentiment of some vast good fortune impending. I can scarcely say why. Perhaps, after all, it was rather a desire than an actual belief;—but do you know that Jupiter's silly words, about the bug being of solid gold, had a remarkable effect upon my fancy? And then the series of accidents and coincidences—these were so *very* extraordinary. Do you observe how mere an accident it was that these events should have occurred upon the *sole* day of all the year in which it has been, or may be sufficiently cool for fire, and that without the fire, or without the intervention of the dog at the precise moment in which he appeared, I should never have become aware of the death's-head, and so never the possessor of the treasure?'

'But proceed—I am all impatience.'

'Well; you have heard, of course, the many stories current—the thousand vague rumours afloat about money buried, somewhere upon the Atlantic coast, by Kidd and his associates. These rumours must have had some foundation in fact. And that the rumours have existed so long and so continuously, could have resulted, it appeared to me, only from the circumstance of the buried treasure still *remaining* entombed. Had Kidd concealed his plunder for a time, and afterwards reclaimed it, the rumours would scarcely have reached us in their present unvarying form. You will observe that the stories told are all about money-seekers, not about money-finders. Had the pirate recovered his money, there the affair would have dropped. It seemed to me that some accident—say the loss of a memorandum indicating its locality—had deprived him of the means of recovering it, and that this accident had become known to his followers, who otherwise might never have heard that treasure had been concealed at all, and who, busying themselves in vain, because unguided, attempts to regain it, had given first birth, and then universal currency, to the reports which are now so common. Have you ever heard of any important treasure being unearthed along the coast?'

'Never.'

'But that Kidd's accumulations were immense, is well known. I took it for granted, therefore, that the earth still held them; and you will scarcely be surprised when I tell you that I felt a hope, nearly amounting to certainty, that the parchment so strangely found involved a lost record of the place of deposit.'

'But how did you proceed?'

'I held the vellum again to the fire, after increasing the heat; but nothing appeared. I now thought it possible that the coating of dirt might have something to do with the failure: so I carefully rinsed the parchment by pouring warm water over it, and, having done this, I placed it in a tin pan, with the skull downwards, and put the pan upon a furnace of lighted charcoal. In a few minutes, the pan having become thoroughly heated, I removed the slip, and, to my inexpressible joy, found it spotted, in several places, with what appeared to be figures arranged in lines. Again I placed it in the pan, and suffered it to remain another minute. Upon taking it off, the whole was just as you see it now.'

Here Legrand, having re-heated the parchment, submitted it to my inspection. The following characters were rudely traced, in a red tint, between the death's-head and the goat:

'53‡‡†305))6*;4826)4‡.)4‡);806*;48†8¶60))85;1‡ (;:‡*8†83(88)5*†
;46(;88*96*?;8)*‡(;485);5*†2:*‡(;4956*2(5*—4)8¶8*;40692
85);)6†8)4‡‡; 1(‡9;48081;8:8‡1;48†85;4)485†528806*81(‡9;48;
(88;4(‡?34;48)4‡;161;:188;‡?;'

'But,' said I, returning him the slip, 'I am as much in the dark as ever. Were all the jewels of Golconda awaiting me upon my solution of this enigma, I am quite sure that I should be unable to earn them.'

'And yet,' said Legrand, 'the solution is by no means so difficult as you might be lead to imagine from the first hasty inspection of the characters. These characters, as any one might readily guess, form a cipher—that is to say, they convey a meaning; but then from what is known of Kidd, I could not suppose him capable of constructing any of the more abstruse cryptographs. I made up my mind, at once, that this was of a simple species—such, however, as would appear, to the crude intellect of the sailor, absolutely insoluble without the key.'

'And you really solved it?'

'Readily; I have solved others of an abstruseness ten thousand times greater. Circumstances, and a certain bias of mind, have led me to take interest in such riddles, and it may well be doubted whether human ingenuity can construct an enigma of the kind which human ingenuity may not, by proper application, resolve. In fact, having once established connected and legible characters, I scarcely gave a thought to the mere difficulty of developing their import.

'In the present case—indeed in all cases of secret writing— the first question regards the *language* of the cipher; for the principles of solution, so far, especially, as the more simple ciphers are concerned, depend upon, and are varied by, the genius of the particular idiom. In general, there is no alternative but experiment (directed by probabilities) of every tongue known to him who attempts the solution, until the true one be attained. But, with the cipher now before us, all difficulty is removed by the signature. The pun upon the word "Kidd" is appreciable in no other language than the English. But for this consideration I should have begun my attempts with the Spanish and French, as the tongues in which a secret of this kind would most naturally have been written by a pirate of the Spanish main. As it was, I assumed the cryptograph to be English.

'You observe there are no divisions between the words. Had there been divisions the task would have been comparatively easy. In such cases I should have commenced with a collation and analysis of the shorter words, and, had a word of a single letter occurred, as is most likely (*a* or *I*, for example), I should have considered the solution as assured. But, there being no division, my first step was to ascertain the predominant letters, as well as the least frequent. Counting all, I constructed a table, thus:

Of the character 8	there are	33.
;	"	26.
4	"	19.
‡)	"	16.
*	"	13.
5	"	12.
6	"	11.
†1	"	8.
0	"	6.
92	"	5.
:3	"	4.
?	"	3.
¶	"	2.
—.	"	1.

'Now, in English, the letter which most frequently occurs is *e*. Afterwards, the succession runs thus: *a o i d h n r s t u y c f g l m w b k p q x z. E* predominates so remarkably, that an individual sentence of any length is rarely seen, in which it is not the prevailing character.'

'Here, then, we have, in the very beginning, the groundwork for something more than a mere guess. The general use which may be made of the table is obvious—but, in this particular cipher, we shall only very partially require its aid. As our predominant character is 8, we will commence by assuming it as the *e* of the natural alphabet. To verify the supposition, let us observe if the 8 be seen often in couples—for *e* is doubled with great frequency in English—in such words, for example, as "meet," "fleet," "speed," "seen," "been," "agree," etc. In the present instance we see it doubled no less than five times, although the cryptograph is brief.'

'Let us assume 8, then, as *e*. Now, of all *words* in the language, "the" is most usual; let us see, therefore, whether there are not repetitions of any three characters, in the same order of collocation, the last of them being 8. If we discover repetitions of such letters, so arranged, they will most probably represent the word "the." Upon inspection, we find no less than seven such arrangements, the characters being ;48. We may, therefore, assume that ; represents *t*, 4 represents *h*, and 8 represents *e*—the last being now well confirmed. Thus a great step has been taken.'

'But, having established a single word, we are enabled to establish a vastly important point; that is to say, several commencements and terminations of other words. Let us refer, for example, to the last instance but one, in which the combination ;48 occurs—not far from the end of the cipher. We know that the

; immediately ensuing is the commencement of a word, and, of the six characters succeeding this "the," we are cognizant of no less than five. Let us set these characters down, thus, by the letters we know them to represent, leaving a space for the unknown—

t eeth.

'Here we are enabled, at once, to discard the "th," as forming no portion of the word commencing with the first *t*; since, by experiment of the entire alphabet for a letter adapted to the vacancy we perceive that no word can be formed of which this *th* can be a part. We are thus narrowed into

t ee,

and, going through the alphabet, if necessary, as before, we arrive at the word "tree," as the sole possible reading. We thus gain another letter, *r*, represented by (, with the words "the tree" in juxtaposition.

'Looking beyond these words, for a short distance, we again see the combination ;48, and employ it by way of *termination* to what immediately precedes. We have thus this arrangement:

the tree ;4(‡?34 the,

or, substituting the natural letters, where known, it reads thus:

the tree thr‡?3h the.

'Now, if, in place of the unknown characters, we leave blank spaces, or substitute dots, we read thus:

the tree thr...h the,

when the word *"through"* makes itself evident at once. But this discovery gives us three new letters, *o, u* and *g*, represented by ‡, ?, and 3.

'Looking now, narrowly, through the cipher for combinations of known characters, we find, not very far from the beginning, this arrangement,

83(88, or egree,

which, plainly, is the conclusion of the word "degree," and gives us another letter, *d*, represented by †.

'Four letters beyond the word "degree," we perceive the combination

;46(;88*.

'Translating the known characters, and representing the unknown by dots, as before, we read thus:

th.rtee,

an arrangement immediately suggestive of the word "thirteen," and again furnishing us with two new characters, *i* and *n*, represented by 6 and *.

'Referring, now, to the beginning of the cryptograph, we find the combination,

53‡‡†.

'Translating, as before, we obtain

.good,

which assures us that the first letter is *A*, and that the first two words are "A good."

'It is now time that we arrange our key, as far as discovered, in a tabular form, to avoid confusion. It will stand thus:

5	represents	a
†	"	d
8	"	e
3	"	g
4	"	h
6	"	i
*	"	n
‡	"	o
(	"	r
;	"	t
?	"	u

'We have, therefore, no less than ten of the most important letters represented, and it will be unnecessary to proceed with the details of the solution. I have said enough to convince you that ciphers of this nature are readily soluble, and to give you some insight into the *rationale* of their development. But be assured that the specimen before us appertains to the very simplest species of cryptograph. It now only remains to give you the full translation of the characters upon the parchment, as unriddled. Here it is:

' "A good glass in the bishop's hostel in the devil's seat forty-one degrees and thirteen minutes northeast and by north main branch seventh limb east side shoot from the left eye of the death's-head a bee line from the tree through the shot fifty feet out." '

'But,' said I, 'the enigma seems still in as bad a condition as ever. How is it possible to extort a meaning from all this jargon about "devil's seats," "death's-heads," and "bishop's hostels?" '

'I confess,' replied Legrand, 'that the matter still wears a serious aspect, when regarded with a casual glance. My first endeavour was to divide the sentence into the natural division intended by the cryptographist.'

'You mean, to punctuate it?'

'Something of that kind.'

'But how was it possible to effect this?'

'I reflected that it had been a *point* with the writer to run his words together without division, so as to increase the difficulty of solution. Now, a not over-acute man, in pursuing such an object, would be nearly certain to overdo the matter. When, in the course of his composition, he arrived at a break in his subject which would naturally require a pause, or a point, he would be exceedingly apt to run his characters, at this place, more than usually close together. If you will observe the MS., in the present instance, you will easily detect five such cases of unusual crowding. Acting upon this hint, I made the division thus:

> ' "*A good glass in the bishop's hostel in the devil's seat—forty-one degrees and thirteen minutes—northeast and by north—main branch seventh limb east side—shoot from the left eye of the death's-head—a bee-line from the tree through the shot fifty feet out.*" '

'Even this division,' said I, 'leaves me still in the dark.'

'It left me also in the dark,' replied Legrand, 'for a few days; during which I made diligent inquiry, in the neighbourhood of Sullivan's Island, for any building which went by the name of the "Bishop's Hotel"; for, of course, I dropped the obsolete word "hostel." Gaining no information on the subject, I was on the point of extending my sphere of search, and proceeding in a more systematic manner, when, one morning, it entered into my head, quite suddenly, that this "Bishop's Hostel" might have some reference to an old family, of the name of Bessop, which, time out of mind, had held possession of an ancient manor-house, about four miles to the northward of the Island. I accordingly went over to the plantation, and re-instituted my inquiries among the older negroes of the place. At length one of the most aged of the women said that she had heard of such a place as *Bessop's Castle*, and thought that she could guide me to it, but that it was not a castle, nor a tavern, but a high rock.

'I offered to pay her well for her trouble, and, after some demur, she consented to accompany me to the spot. We found it without much difficulty, when, dismissing her, I proceeded to examine the place. The "castle" consisted of an irregular assemblage of cliffs and rocks—one of the latter being quite remarkable for its height as well as for its insulated and artificial appearance. I clambered to its apex, and then felt much at a loss as to what should be next done.

'While I was busied in reflection, my eyes fell upon a narrow ledge in the eastern face of the rock, perhaps a yard below the summit upon which I stood. This ledge projected about eighteen inches, and was not more than a foot wide, while a niche in the cliff just above it, gave it a rude resemblance to one of the hollow-backed chairs used by our ancestors. I made no doubt that here was the "devil's seat" alluded to in the MS., and now I seemed to grasp the full secret of the riddle.

'The "good glass," I knew, could have reference to nothing but a telescope; for the word "glass" is rarely employed in any other sense by seamen. Now here, I at once saw, was a telescope to be used, and a definite point of view, *admitting no variation*, from which to use it. Nor did I hesitate to believe that the phrases, "forty-one degrees and thirteen minutes," and "northeast and by north," were intended as directions for the levelling of the glass. Greatly excited by these discoveries, I hurried home, procured a telescope, and returned to the rock.

'I let myself down to the ledge, and found that it was impossible to retain a seat upon it except in one particular position. This fact confirmed my preconceived idea. I proceeded to use the glass. Of course, the "forty-one degrees and thirteen minutes" could allude to nothing but elevation above the visible horizon, since the horizontal direction was clearly indicated by the words, "northeast and by north." This latter direction I at once established by means of a pocket-compass; then, pointing the glass as nearly at an angle of forty-one degrees of elevation as I could do it by guess, I moved it cautiously up or down, until my attention was arrested by a circular rift or opening in the foliage of a large tree that overtopped its fellows in the distance. In the centre of this rift I perceived a white spot, but could not, at first, distinguish what it was. Adjusting the focus of the telescope, I again looked, and now made it out to be a human skull.

'Upon this discovery I was so sanguine as to consider the enigma solved; for the phrase "main branch, seventh limb, east side," could refer only to the position of the skull upon the tree, while "shoot from the left eye of the death's head" admitted, also, of but one interpretation, in regard to a search for buried treasure. I perceived that the design was to drop a bullet from the left eye of the skull, and that a bee-line, or, in other words, a straight line, drawn from the nearest point of the trunk through "the shot" (or the spot where the bullet fell), and thence extended to a distance of fifty feet, would indicate a definite point—and beneath this point I thought it at least *possible* that a deposit of value lay concealed.'

'All this,' I said, 'is exceedingly clear, and, although ingenious, still simple and explicit. When you left the "Bishop's Hotel," what then?'

· 'Why, having carefully taken the bearings of the tree, I turned homewards. The instant that I left "the devil's seat," however, the circular rift vanished; nor could I get a glimpse of it afterwards, turn as I would. What seems to me the chief ingenuity in this whole business, is the fact (for repeated experiment has convinced me it *is* a fact) that the circular opening in question is visible from no other attainable point of view than that afforded by the narrow ledge upon the face of the rock.'

'In this expedition to the "Bishop's Hotel" I had been attended by Jupiter, who had, no doubt, observed, for some weeks past, the abstraction of my demeanour, and took special care not to leave me alone. But, on the next day, getting up very early, I contrived to give him the slip, and went into the hills in search of the tree. After much toil I found it. When I came home at night my valet proposed to give me a flogging. With the rest of the adventure I believe you are as well acquainted as myself.'

'I suppose,' said I, 'you missed the spot, in the first attempt at digging, through Jupiter's stupidity in letting the bug fall through the right instead of through the left eye of the skull.'

'Precisely. This mistake made a difference of about two inches and a half in the "shot"—that is to say, in the position of the peg nearest the tree; and had the treasure been *beneath* the "shot," the error would have been of little moment; but "the shot," together with the nearest point of the tree, were merely two points for the establishment of a line of direction; of course the error, however trivial in the beginning, increased as we proceeded with the line, and by the time we had gone fifty feet, threw us quite off the scent. But for my deep-seated impressions that treasure was here somewhere actually buried, we might have had all our labour in vain.'

'But your grandiloquence, and your conduct in swinging the beetle—how excessively odd! I was sure you were mad. And why did you insist upon letting fall the bug, instead of a bullet, from the skull?'

'Why, to be frank, I felt somewhat annoyed by your evident suspicions touching my sanity, and so resolved to punish you quietly, in my own way, by a little bit of sober mystification. For this reason I swung the beetle, and for this reason I let it fall it from the tree. An observation of yours about its great weight suggested the latter idea.'

'Yes, I perceive; and now there is only one point which puzzles . me. What are we to make of the skeletons found in the hole?'

'That is a question I am no more able to answer than yourself. There seems, however, only one plausible way of accounting for them—and yet it is dreadful to believe in such atrocity as my suggestion would imply. It is clear that Kidd—if Kidd indeed secreted this treasure, which I doubt not—it is clear that he must have had assistance in the labour. But this labour concluded, he may have thought it expedient to remove all participants in his secret. Perhaps a couple of blows with a mattock were sufficient, while his coadjutors were busy in the pit; perhaps it required a dozen—who shall tell?'

3
The Murders in the Rue Morgue

What song the Syrens sang, or what name Achilles assumed when he hid himself among women, although puzzling questions are not beyond all conjecture.

—*Sir Thomas Browne, Urn-Burial*

The mental features discoursed of as the analytical, are, in themselves, but little susceptible of analysis. We appreciate them only in their effects. We know of them, among other things, that they are always to their possessor, when inordinately possessed, a source of the liveliest enjoyment. As the strong man exults in his physical ability, delighting in such exercises as call his muscles into action, so glories the analyst in that moral activity which disentangles. He derives pleasure from even the most trivial occupations bringing his talent into play. He is fond of enigmas, of conundrums, of hieroglyphics; exhibiting in his solutions of each a degree of acumen which appears to the ordinary apprehension preternatural. His results, brought about by the very soul and essence of method, have, in truth, the whole air of intuition.

The faculty of re-solution is possibly much invigorated by mathematical study, and especially by that highest branch of it which, unjustly, and merely on account of its retrograde operations, has been called, as if par excellence, analysis. Yet to calculate is not in itself to analyse. A chess-player, for example, does the one without effort at the other. It follows that the game of chess, in its effects upon mental character, is greatly misunderstood. I am not now writing a treatise, but simply prefacing a somewhat peculiar narrative by observations very much at random; I will, therefore, take occasion to assert that the higher powers of the reflective intellect are more decidedly and more usefully tasked by the unostentatious game of draughts than by all the elaborate frivolity of chess. In this latter, where the pieces have different and *bizarre* motions, with various and variable values, what is only complex is mistaken (a not unusual error) for what is profound. The *attention* is here called powerfully into play. If it flag for an instant, an oversight is committed, resulting in injury or defeat. The possible moves being not only manifold but involute, the chances of such oversights are multiplied; and in nine cases out of ten it is the more concentrative rather than the more acute player who conquers. In draughts, on the contrary, where the moves are *unique* and have but little variation, the probabilities of inadvertence are diminished, and the mere attention being left comparatively unemployed, what advantages are obtained by either party are obtained by superior *acumen*. To be less abstract, let us suppose a game of draughts where the pieces are reduced to four kings, and where, of course, no oversight is to be expected. It is obvious that here the victory can be decided (the players being at all equal) only by some *recherché* movement, the result of some strong exertion of the intellect. Deprived of ordinary resources, the analyst throws himself into the spirit of his opponent, identifies himself therewith, and not unfrequently sees thus, at a glance, the sole methods (sometimes indeed absurdly simple ones) by which he may seduce into error or hurry into miscalculation.

Whist has long been known for its influence upon what is termed the calculating power; and men of the highest order of intellect have been known to take an apparently unaccountable delight in it, while eschewing chess as frivolous. Beyond doubt there is nothing of a similar nature so greatly tasking the faculty of analysis. The best chess-player in Christendom *may* be little more than the best player of chess; but proficiency in whist implies capacity for success in all those more important undertakings where mind struggles with mind. When I say proficiency, I mean that perfection in the game which includes a comprehension of *all* the sources whence legitimate advantage may be derived. These are not only manifold but multiform, and lie frequently among recesses of thought altogether inaccessible to the ordinary understanding. To observe attentively is to remember distinctly; and, so far, the concentrative chess-player will do very well at whist; while the rules of Hoyle (themselves based upon the mere mechanism of the game) are sufficiently and generally comprehensible. Thus to have a retentive memory, and to proceed by 'the book,' are points commonly regarded as the sum total of good playing. But it is in matters beyond the limits of mere rule that the skill of the analyst is evinced. He makes, in silence, a host of observations and inferences. So, perhaps, do his companions; and the difference in the extent of the information obtained, lies not so much in the validity of the inference as in the quality of the observation. The necessary knowledge is that of *what* to observe. Our player confines himself not at all; nor, because the game is the object, does he reject deductions from things external to the game. He examines the countenance of his partner, comparing it carefully with that of each of his opponents. He considers the mode of assorting the cards in each hand; often counting trump by trump, and honour by honour, through the glances bestowed by their holders upon each. He notes every variation of face as the play progresses, gathering a fund of thought from the differences in the expression of certainty, of surprise, of triumph, or chagrin. From the manner of gathering up a trick he judges whether the person taking it can make another in the suit. He recognises what is played through feint, by the manner with which it is thrown upon the table. A casual or inadvertent word; the accidental dropping or turning of a card, with the accompanying anxiety or carelessness in regard to its concealment; the counting of the tricks, with the order of their arrangement; embarrassment, hesitation, eagerness or trepidation—all afford, to his apparently intuitive perception, indications of the true state of affairs. The first two or three rounds having been played, he is in full possession of the contents of each hand, and thenceforward puts down his cards with as absolute a precision of purpose as if the rest of the party had turned outward the faces of their own.

The analytical power should not be confounded with simple ingenuity; for while the analyst is necessarily ingenious, the ingenious man is often remarkably incapable of analysis. The constructive or combining power, by which ingenuity is usually manifested, and to which the phrenologists (I believe erroneously) have assigned a separate organ, supposing it a primitive faculty, has been so frequently seen in those whose intellect bordered otherwise upon idiocy, as to have attracted general observation among writers on morals. Between ingenuity and the analytic ability there exists a difference far greater, indeed, than that between the fancy and the imagination, but of a character very strictly analogous. It will be found, in fact, that the ingenious are always fanciful, and the *truly* imaginative never otherwise than analytic.

The narrative which follows will appear to the reader somewhat in the light of a commentary upon the propositions just advanced.

Residing in Paris during the spring and part of the summer of 18—, I there became acquainted with a Monsieur C. Auguste Dupin. This young gentleman was of an excellent, indeed of an illustrious family, but, by a variety of untoward events, had been reduced to such poverty that the energy of his character succumbed beneath it, and he ceased to bestir himself in the world, or to care for the retrieval of his fortunes. By courtesy of his creditors, there still remained in his possession a small remnant of his patrimony; and, upon the income arising from this, he managed, by means of a rigorous economy, to procure the necessaries of life, without troubling himself about its superfluities. Books, indeed, were his sole luxuries, and in Paris these are easily obtained.

Our first meeting was at an obscure library in the Rue Montmartre, where the accident of our both being in search of the same very rare and very remarkable volume, brought us into closer communion. We saw each other again and again. I was deeply interested in the little family history which he detailed to me with all that candour which a Frenchman indulges whenever mere self is the theme. I was astonished, too, at the vast extent of his reading; and, above all, I felt my soul enkindled within me by the wild fervour, and the vivid freshness of his imagination. Seeking in Paris the objects I then sought, I felt that the society of such a man would be to me a treasure beyond price; and this feeling I frankly confided to him. It was at length arranged that we should live together during my stay in the city; and as my worldly circumstances were somewhat less embarrassed than his own, I was permitted to be at the expense of renting, and furnishing in a style which suited the rather fantastic gloom of our common temper, a time-eaten and grotesque mansion, long deserted through superstitions into which we did not inquire, and tottering to its fall in a retired and desolate portion of the Faubourg St. Germain.

Had the routine of our life at this place been known to the world, we should have been regarded as madmen—although, perhaps, as madmen of a harmless nature. Our seclusion was perfect. We admitted no visitors. Indeed the locality of our retirement had been carefully kept a secret from my own former associates; and it had been many years since Dupin had ceased to know or be known in Paris. We existed within ourselves alone.

It was a freak of fancy in my friend (for what else shall I call it?) to be enamoured of the Night for her own sake; and into this *bizarrerie*, as into all his others, I quietly fell; giving myself up to his wild whims with a perfect *abandon*. The sable divinity would not herself dwell with us always; but we could counterfeit her presence. At the first dawn of the morning we closed all the massy shutters of our old building; lighted a couple of tapers which, strongly perfumed, threw out only the ghastliest and feeblest of rays. By the aid of these we then busied our souls in dreams— reading, writing, or conversing, until warned by the clock of the advent of the true Darkness. Then we sallied forth into the streets, arm in arm, continuing the topics of the day, or roaming far and wide until a late hour, seeking, amid the wild lights and shadows of the populous city, that infinity of mental excitement which quiet observation can afford.

At such times I could not help remarking and admiring (although from his rich ideality I had been prepared to expect it) a peculiar analytic ability in Dupin. He seemed, too, to take an eager delight in its exercise—if not exactly in its display—and did not hesitate to confess the pleasure thus derived. He boasted to me, with a low chuckling laugh, that most men, in respect to himself, wore windows in their bosoms, and was wont to follow up such assertions by direct and very startling proofs of his intimate knowledge of my own. His manner at these moments was frigid and abstract; his eyes were vacant in expression; while his voice, usually a rich tenor, rose into a treble which would have sounded petulantly but for the deliberateness and entire distinctness of the enunciation. Observing him in these moods, I often dwelt meditatively upon the old philosophy of the Bi-Part Soul, and amused myself with the fancy of a double Dupin—the creative and the resolvent.

Let it not be supposed, from what I have just said, that I am detailing any mystery, or penning any romance. What I have described in the Frenchman, was merely the result of an excited, or perhaps of a diseased intelligence. But of the character of his remarks at the periods in question an example will best convey the idea.

We were strolling one night down a long dirty street, in the vicinity of the Palais Royal. Being both, apparently, occupied with thought, neither of us had spoken a syllable for fifteen minutes at least. All at once Dupin broke forth with these words:

'He is a very little fellow, that's true, and would do better for the *Théâtre des Variétés*.'

'There can be no doubt of that,' I replied unwittingly, and not at first observing (so much had I been absorbed in reflection) the extraordinary manner in which the speaker had chimed in with my meditations. In an instant afterward I recollected myself, and my astonishment was profound.

'Dupin,' said I, gravely, 'this is beyond my comprehension. I do not hesitate to say that I am amazed, and can scarcely credit my senses. How was it possible you should know I was thinking of—?' Here I paused, to ascertain beyond a doubt whether he really knew of whom I thought.

'—of Chantilly,' said he, 'why do you pause? You were remarking to yourself that his diminutive figure unfitted him for tragedy.'

This was precisely what had formed the subject of my reflections. Chantilly was a *quondam* cobbler of the Rue St. Denis, who, becoming stage-mad, had attempted the *rôle* of Xerxes, in Crébillon's tragedy so called, and been notoriously Pasquinaded for his pains.

'Tell me, for Heaven's sake,' I exclaimed, 'the method—if method there is—by which you have been enabled to fathom my soul in this matter.' In fact I was even more startled than I would have been willing to express.

'It was the fruiterer,' replied my friend, 'who brought you to the conclusion that the mender of soles was not of sufficient height for Xerxes *et id genus omne.*'

'The fruiterer!—you astonish me—I know no fruiterer whomsoever.'

'The man who ran up against you as we entered the street—it may have been fifteen minutes ago.'

I now remembered that, in fact, a fruiterer, carrying upon his head a large basket of apples, had nearly thrown me down, by accident, as we passed from the Rue C— into the thoroughfare where we stood; but what this had to do with Chantilly I could not possibly understand.

There was not a particle of *charlatânerie* about Dupin. 'I will explain,' he said, 'and that you may comprehend all clearly, we will first retrace the course of your meditations, from the moment in which I spoke to you until that of the *rencontre* with the fruiterer in question. The larger links of the chain run thus—Chantilly, Orion, Dr. Nichols, Epicurus, Stereotomy, the street stones, the fruiterer.'

There are few persons who have not, at some period of their lives, amused themselves in retracing the steps by which particular conclusions of their own minds have been attained. The occupation is often full of interest; and he who attempts it for the first time is astonished by the apparently illimitable distance and incoherence between the starting-point and the goal. What, then, must have been my amazement when I heard the Frenchman speak what he had just spoken, and when I could not help acknowledging that he had spoken the truth. He continued:

'We had been talking of horses, if I remember aright, just before leaving the Rue C—. This was the last subject we discussed. As we crossed into this street, a fruiterer, with a large basket upon his head, brushing quickly past us, thrust you upon a pile of paving stones collected at a spot where the causeway is undergoing repair. You stepped upon one of the loose fragments, slipped, slightly strained your ankle, appeared vexed or sulky, muttered a few words, turned to look at the pile, and then proceeded in silence. I was not particularly attentive to what you did; but observation has become with me, of late, a species of necessity.'

'You kept your eyes upon the ground—glancing, with a petulant expression, at the holes and ruts in the pavement (so that I saw you were still thinking of the stones), until we reached the little alley called Lamartine, which has been paved, by way of experiment, with the overlapping and riveted blocks. Here your countenance brightened up, and, perceiving your lips move, I could not doubt that you murmured the word "stereotomy," a term very affectedly applied to this species of pavement. I knew that you could not say to yourself "stereotomy" without being brought to think of atomies, and thus of the theories of Epicurus; and since, when we discussed this subject not very long ago, I mentioned to you how singularly, yet with how little notice, the vague guesses of that noble Greek had met with confirmation in the late nebular cosmogony, I felt that you could not avoid casting your eyes upward to the great *nebula* in Orion, and I certainly expected that you would do so. You did look up; and I was now assured that I had correctly followed your steps. But in that bitter *tirade* upon Chantilly, which appeared in yesterday's *Musée*, the satirist, making some disgraceful allusions to the cobbler's change of name upon assuming the buskin, quoted a Latin line about which we have often conversed. I mean the line:

Perdidit antiquum litera sonum.

I had told you that this was in reference to Orion, formerly written Urion; and, from certain pungencies connected with this explanation, I was aware that you could not have forgotten it. It was clear, therefore, that you would not fail to combine the two ideas of Orion and Chantilly. That you did combine them I saw by the character of the smile which passed over your lips. You thought of the poor cobbler's immolation. So far, you had been stooping in your gait; but now I saw you draw yourself up to your full height. I was then sure that you reflected upon the diminutive figure of Chantilly. At this point I interrupted your meditations to remark that as, in fact, he *was* a very little fellow—that Chantilly—he would do better at the *Théâtre des Variétés.*'

Not long after this, we were looking over an evening edition of the *Gazette des Tribunaux*, when the following paragraphs arrested our attention.

'EXTRAORDINARY MURDERS.—This morning, about three o'clock, the inhabitants of the Quartier St. Roch were roused from sleep by a succession of terrific shrieks, issuing, apparently, from the fourth story of a house in the Rue Morgue, known to be in the sole occupancy of one Madame L'Espanaye, and her daughter, Mademoiselle Camille L'Espanaye. After some delay, occasioned by a fruitless attempt to procure admission in the usual manner, the gateway was broken in with a crowbar, and eight or ten of the neighbours entered, accompanied by two *gendarmes*. By this time the cries had ceased; but, as the party rushed up the first flight of stairs, two or more rough voices, in angry contention, were distinguished, and seemed to proceed from the upper part of the house. As the second landing was reached, these sounds, also, had ceased, and everything remained perfectly quiet. The party spread themselves, and hurried from room to room. Upon arriving at a large back chamber in the fourth story (the door of which, being found locked, with the key inside, was forced open), a spectacle presented itself which struck every one present not less with horror than with astonishment.'

'The apartment was in the wildest disorder—the furniture broken and thrown about in all directions. There was only one bedstead; and from this the bed had been removed, and thrown into the middle of the floor. On a chair lay a razor, besmeared with blood. On the hearth were two or three long and thick tresses of gray human hair, also dabbled in blood, and seeming to have been pulled out by the roots. Upon the floor were found four Napoleons, an ear-ring of topaz, three large silver spoons, three smaller of *métal d'Alger*, and two bags, containing nearly four thousand francs in gold. The drawers of a *bureau*, which stood in one corner, were open, and had been, apparently, rifled, although many articles still remained in them. A small iron safe was discovered under the *bed* (not under the bedstead). It was open, with the key still in the door. It had no contents beyond a few old letters, and other papers of little consequence.'

'Of Madame L'Espanaye no traces were here seen; but an unusual quantity of soot being observed in the fireplace, a search was made in the chimney, and (horrible to relate!) the corpse of the daughter, head downward, was dragged therefrom; it having been thus forced up the narrow aperture for a considerable distance. The body was quite warm. Upon examining it, many excoriations were perceived, no doubt occasioned by the violence with which it had been thrust up and disengaged. Upon the face were many severe scratches, and, upon the throat, dark bruises, and deep indentations of finger nails, as if the deceased had been throttled to death.'

'After a thorough investigation of every portion of the house, without farther discovery, the party made its way into a small paved yard in the rear of the building, where lay the corpse of the old lady, with her throat so entirely cut that, upon an attempt to raise her, the head fell off. The body, as well as the head, was fearfully mutilated—the former so much so as scarcely to retain any semblance of humanity.'

'To this horrible mystery there is not as yet, we believe, the slightest clue.'

The next day's paper had these additional particulars.

'*The Tragedy in the Rue Morgue.* Many individuals have been examined in relation to this most extraordinary and frightful affair,' (the word "affaire" has not yet, in France, that levity of import which it conveys with us) 'but nothing whatever has transpired to throw light upon it. We give below all the material testimony elicited.'

'*Pauline Dubourg*, laundress, deposes that she has known both the deceased for three years, having washed for them during that period. The old lady and her daughter seemed on good terms—very affectionate towards each other. They were excellent pay. Could not speak in regard to their mode or means of living. Believed that Madame L. told fortunes for a living. Was reputed to have money put by. Never met any person in the house when she called for the clothes or took them home. Was sure that they had no servant in employ. There appeared to be no furniture in any part of the building except in the fourth story.'

'*Pierre Moreau*, tobacconist, deposes that he has been in the habit of selling small quantities of tobacco and snuff to Madame L'Espanaye for nearly four years. Was born in the neighbourhood, and has always resided there. The deceased and her daughter had occupied the house in which the corpses were found, for more than six years. It was formerly occupied by a jeweller, who under-let the upper rooms to various persons. The house was the property of Madame L. She became dissatisfied with the abuse of the premises by her tenant, and moved into them herself, refusing to let any portion. The old lady was childish. Witness had seen the daughter some five or six times during the six years. The two lived an exceedingly retired life—were reputed to have money. Had heard it said among the neighbours that Madame L. told fortunes—did not believe it. Had never seen any person enter the door except the old lady and her daughter, a porter once or twice, and a physician some eight or ten times.'

'Many other persons, neighbours, gave evidence to the same effect. No one was spoken of as frequenting the house. It was not known whether there were any living connections of Madame L.

and her daughter. The shutters of the front windows were seldom opened. Those in the rear were always closed, with the exception of the large back room, fourth story. The house was a good house—not very old.'

'*Isidore Musét, gendarme*, deposes that he was called to the house about three o'clock in the morning, and found some twenty or thirty persons at the gateway, endeavouring to gain admittance. Forced it open, at length, with a bayonet—not with a crowbar. Had but little difficulty in getting it open, on account of its being a double or folding gate, and bolted neither at bottom nor top. The shrieks were continued until the gate was forced—and then suddenly ceased. They seemed to be screams of some person (or persons) in great agony—were loud and drawn out, not short and quick. Witness led the way upstairs. Upon reaching the first landing, heard two voices in loud and angry contention—the one a gruff voice, the other much shriller—a very strange voice. Could distinguish some words of the former, which was that of a Frenchman. Was positive that it was not a woman's voice. Could distinguish the words "*sacré*" and "*diable*." The shrill voice was that of a foreigner. Could not be sure whether it was the voice of a man or of a woman. Could not make out what was said, but believed the language to be Spanish. The state of the room and of the bodies was described by this witness as we described them yesterday.'

'*Henri Duval*, a neighbour, and by trade a silversmith, deposes that he was one of the party who first entered the house. Corroborates the testimony of Musét in general. As soon as they forced an entrance, they reclosed the door, to keep out the crowd, which collected very fast, notwithstanding the lateness of the hour. The shrill voice, this witness thinks, was that of an Italian.

Was certain it was not French. Could not be sure that it was a man's voice. It might have been a woman's. Was not acquainted with the Italian language. Could not distinguish the words, but was convinced by the intonation that the speaker was an Italian. Knew Madame L. and her daughter. Had conversed with both frequently. Was sure that the shrill voice was not that of either of the deceased.'

'—*Odenheimer, restaurateur.*—This witness volunteered his testimony. Not speaking French, was examined through an interpreter. Is a native of Amsterdam. Was passing the house at the time of the shrieks. They lasted for several minutes—probably ten. They were long and loud—very awful and distressing. Was one of those who entered the building. Corroborated the previous evidence in every respect but one. Was sure that the shrill voice was that of a man—of a Frenchman. Could not distinguish the words uttered. They were loud and quick—unequal—spoken apparently in fear as well as in anger. The voice was harsh—not so much shrill as harsh. Could not call it a shrill voice. The gruff voice said repeatedly "*sacré*," "*diable*," and once "*mon Dieu.*" '

'*Jules Mignaud*, banker, of the firm of Mignaud et Fils, Rue Deloraine. Is the elder Mignaud. Madame L'Espanaye had some property. Had opened an account with his banking house in the spring of the year—(eight years previously). Made frequent deposits in small sums. Had checked for nothing until the third day before her death, when she took out in person the sum of 4000 francs. This sum was paid in gold, and a clerk went home with the money.'

'*Adolphe Le Bon*, clerk to Mignaud et Fils, deposes that on the day in question, about noon, he accompanied Madame L'Espanaye to her residence with the 4000 francs, put up in two bags. Upon the door being opened, Mademoiselle L. appeared and took from his hands one of the bags, while the old lady relieved him of the other. He then bowed and departed. Did not see any person in the street at the time. It is a by-street—very lonely.'

'William Bird, tailor, deposes that he was one of the party who entered the house. Is an Englishman. Has lived in Paris two years. Was one of the first to ascend the stairs. Heard the voices in contention. The gruff voice was that of a Frenchman. Could make out several words, but cannot now remember all. Heard distinctly "sacré" and "mon Dieu." There was a sound at the moment as if of several persons struggling—a scraping and scuffling sound. The shrill voice was very loud—louder than the gruff one. Is sure that it was not the voice of an Englishman. Appeared to be that of a German. Might have been a woman's voice. Does not understand German.'

'Four of the above-named witnesses, being recalled, deposed that the door of the chamber in which was found the body of Mademoiselle L. was locked on the inside when the party reached it. Everything was perfectly silent—no groans or noises of any kind. Upon forcing the door no person was seen. The windows, both of the back and front room, were down and firmly fastened from within. A door between the two rooms was closed, but not locked. The door leading from the front room into the passage was locked, with the key on the inside. A small room in the front of the house, on the fourth story, at the head of the passage, was open, the door being ajar. This room was crowded with old beds, boxes, and so forth. These were carefully removed and searched. There was not an inch of any portion of the house which was not carefully searched. Sweeps were sent up and down the chimneys. The house was a four-story one, with garrets (*mansardes*). A trap-door on the roof was nailed down very securely—did not appear to have been opened for years. The time elapsing between the hearing of the voices in contention and the breaking open of the room door, was variously stated by the witnesses. Some made it as short as three minutes—some as long as five. The door was opened with difficulty.'

'*Alfonzo Garcio*, undertaker, deposes that he resides in the Rue Morgue. Is a native of Spain. Was one of the party who entered the house. Did not proceed upstairs. Is nervous, and was apprehensive of the consequences of agitation. Heard the voices in contention. The gruff voice was that of a Frenchman. Could not distinguish what was said. The shrill voice was that of an Englishman—is sure of this. Does not understand the English language, but judges by the intonation.'

'*Alberto Montani*, confectioner, deposes that he was among the first to ascend the stairs. Heard the voices in question. The gruff voice was that of a Frenchman. Distinguished several words. The speaker appeared to be expostulating. Could not make out the words of the shrill voice. Spoke quick and unevenly. Thinks it the voice of a Russian. Corroborates the general testimony. Is an Italian. Never conversed with a native of Russia.'

'Several witnesses, recalled, here testified that the chimneys of all the rooms on the fourth story were too narrow to admit the passage of a human being. By "sweeps" were meant cylindrical sweeping-brushes, such as are employed by those who clean chimneys. These brushes were passed up and down every flue in the house. There is no back passage by which any one could have descended while the party proceeded upstairs. The body of Mademoiselle L'Espanaye was so firmly wedged in the chimney that it could not be got down until four or five of the party united their strength.'

'Paul Dumas, physician, deposes that he was called to view the bodies about daybreak. They were both then lying on the sacking of the bedstead in the chamber where Mademoiselle L. was found. The corpse of the young lady was much bruised and excoriated. The fact that it had been thrust up the chimney would sufficiently account for these appearances. The throat was greatly chafed. There were several deep scratches just below the chin, together with a series of livid spots which were evidently the impression of fingers. The face was fearfully discoloured, and the eyeballs protruded. The tongue had been partially bitten through. A large bruise was discovered upon the pit of the stomach, produced, apparently, by the pressure of a knee. In the opinion of M. Dumas, Mademoiselle L'Espanaye had been throttled to death by some person or persons unknown. The corpse of the mother was horribly mutilated. All the bones of the right leg and arm were more or less shattered. The left *tibia* much splintered, as well as all the ribs of the left side. Whole body dreadfully bruised and discoloured. It was not possible to say how the injuries had been inflicted. A heavy club of wood, or a broad bar of iron—a chair—any large, heavy, and obtuse weapon would have produced such results, if wielded by the hands of a very powerful man. No woman could have inflicted the blows with any weapon. The head of the deceased, when seen by witness, was entirely separated from the body, and was also greatly shattered. The throat had evidently been cut with some very sharp instrument—probably with a razor.'

'*Alexandre Etienne*, surgeon, was called with M. Dumas to view the bodies. Corroborated the testimony, and the opinions of M. Dumas.

'Nothing farther of importance was elicited, although several other persons were examined. A murder so mysterious, and so perplexing in all its particulars, was never before committed in Paris—if indeed a murder has been committed at all. The police are entirely at fault—an unusual occurrence in affairs of this nature. There is not, however, the shadow of a clue apparent.'

The evening edition of the paper stated that the greatest excitement still continued in the Quartier St. Roch—that the premises in question had been carefully re-searched, and fresh examinations of witnesses instituted, but all to no purpose. A postscript, however, mentioned that Adolphe Le Bon had been arrested and imprisoned—although nothing appeared to criminate him, beyond the facts already detailed.

Dupin seemed singularly interested in the progress of this affair—at least so I judged from his manner, for he made no comments. It was only after the announcement that Le Bon had been imprisoned, that he asked me my opinion respecting the murders.

I could merely agree with all Paris in considering them an insoluble mystery. I saw no means by which it would be possible to trace the murderer.

'We must not judge of the means,' said Dupin, 'by this shell of an examination. The Parisian police, so much extolled for *acumen*, are cunning, but no more. There is no method in their proceedings, beyond the method of the moment. They make a vast parade of measures; but, not unfrequently, these are so ill adapted to the objects proposed, as to put us in mind of Monsieur Jourdain's calling for his *robe-de-chambre—pour mieux entendre la musique.* The results attained by them are not unfrequently surprising, but, for the most part, are brought about by simple diligence and activity. When these qualities are unavailing, their schemes fail. Vidocq, for example, was a good guesser and a persevering man. But, without educated thought, he erred continually by the very intensity of his investigations. He impaired his vision by holding the object too close. He might see, perhaps, one or two points with unusual clearness, but in so doing he, necessarily, lost sight of the matter as a whole. Thus there is such a thing as being too profound. Truth is not always in a well. In fact, as regards the more important knowledge, I do believe that she is invariably superficial. The depth lies in the valleys where we seek her, and not upon the mountain-tops where she is found. The modes and sources of this kind of error are well typified in the contemplation of the heavenly bodies. To look at a star by glances—to view it in a side-long way, by turning toward it the exterior portions of the *retina* (more susceptible of feeble impressions of light than the interior), is to behold the star distinctly—is to have the best appreciation of its lustre—a lustre which grows dim just in proportion as we turn our vision *fully* upon it. A greater number of rays actually fall upon the eye in the latter case, but, in the former, there is the more refined capacity for comprehension. By undue profundity we perplex and enfeeble thought; and it is possible to make even Venus herself vanish from the firmament by a scrutiny too sustained, too concentrated, or too direct.

'As for these murders, let us enter into some examinations for ourselves, before we make up an opinion respecting them. An inquiry will afford us amusement' (I thought this an odd term, so applied, but said nothing), 'and, besides, Le Bon once rendered me a service for which I am not ungrateful. We will go and see the premises with our own eyes. I know G——, the Prefect of Police, and shall have no difficulty in obtaining the necessary permission.'

The permission was obtained, and we proceeded at once to the Rue Morgue. This is one of those miserable thoroughfares which intervene between the Rue Richelieu and the Rue St. Roch. It was late in the afternoon when we reached it, as this quarter is at a great distance from that in which we resided. The house was readily found; for there were still many persons gazing up at the closed shutters, with an objectless curiosity, from the opposite side of the way. It was an ordinary Parisian house, with a gateway, on one side of which was a glazed watch-box, with a sliding panel in the window, indicating a *loge de concierge*. Before going in we walked up the street, turned down an alley, and then, again turning, passed in the rear of the building—Dupin, meanwhile, examining the whole neighbourhood, as well as the house, with a minuteness of attention for which I could see no possible object.

Retracing our steps, we came again to the front of the dwelling, rang, and, having shown our credentials, were admitted by the agents in charge. We went upstairs—into the chamber where the body of Mademoiselle L'Espanaye had been found, and where both the deceased still lay. The disorders of the room had, as usual, been suffered to exist. I saw nothing beyond what had been stated in the *Gazette des Tribunaux*. Dupin scrutinised everything— not excepting the bodies of the victims. We then went into the other rooms, and into the yard; a *gendarme* accompanying us throughout. The examination occupied us until dark, when we took our departure. On our way home my companion stepped in for a moment at the office of one of the daily papers.

I have said that the whims of my friend were manifold, and that *Je les ménagais:*—for this phrase there is no English equivalent. It was his humour, now, to decline all conversation on the subject of the murder, until about noon the next day. He then asked me, suddenly, if I had observed anything *peculiar* at the scene of the atrocity.

There was something in his manner of emphasizing the word "peculiar," which caused me to shudder, without knowing why.

'No, nothing *peculiar*,' I said; 'nothing more, at least, than we both saw stated in the paper.'

'The *Gazette*,' he replied, 'has not entered, I fear, into the unusual horror of the thing. But dismiss the idle opinions of this print. It appears to me that this mystery is considered insoluble, for the very reason which should cause it to be regarded as easy of solution—I mean for the *outré* character of its features. The police are confounded by the seeming absence of motive—not for the murder itself—but for the atrocity of the murder. They are puzzled, too, by the seeming impossibility of reconciling the voices heard in contention, with the facts that no one was discovered upstairs but the assassinated Mademoiselle L'Espanaye, and that there were no means of egress without the notice of the party ascending. The wild disorder of the room; the corpse thrust, with the head downward, up the chimney; the frightful mutilation of the body of the old lady; these considerations, with those just mentioned, and others which I need not mention, have sufficed to paralyse the powers, by putting completely at fault the boasted *acumen*, of the government agents. They have fallen into the gross but common error of confounding the unusual with the abstruse. But it is by these deviations from the plane of the ordinary, that reason feels its way, if at all, in its search for the true. In investigations such as we are now pursuing, it should not be so much asked 'what has occurred,' as 'what has occurred that has never occurred before.' In fact, the facility with which I shall arrive, or have arrived, at the solution of this mystery, is in the direct ratio of its apparent insolubility in the eyes of the police.'

I stared at the speaker in mute astonishment.

'I am now awaiting,' continued he, looking toward the door of our apartment—'I am now awaiting a person who, although perhaps not the perpetrator of these butcheries, must have been in some measure implicated in their perpetration. Of the worst portion of the crimes committed, it is probable that he is innocent. I hope that I am right in this supposition; for upon it I build my expectation of reading the entire riddle. I look for the man here— in this room—every moment. It is true that he may not arrive; but the probability is that he will. Should he come, it will be necessary to detain him. Here are pistols; and we both know how to use them when occasion demands their use.'

I took the pistols, scarcely knowing what I did, or believing what I heard, while Dupin went on, very much as if in a soliloquy. I have already spoken of his abstract manner at such times. His discourse was addressed to myself; but his voice, although by no means loud, had that intonation which is commonly employed in speaking to some one at a great distance. His eyes, vacant in expression, regarded only the wall.

'That the voices heard in contention,' he said, 'by the party upon the stairs, were not the voices of the women themselves, was fully proved by the evidence. This relieves us of all doubt upon the question whether the old lady could have first destroyed the daughter, and afterward have committed suicide. I speak of this point chiefly for the sake of method; for the strength of Madame L'Espanaye would have been utterly unequal to the task of thrusting her daughter's corpse up the chimney as it was found; and the nature of the wounds upon her own person entirely preclude the idea of self-destruction. Murder, then, has been committed by some third party; and the voices of this third party were those heard in contention. Let me now advert—not to the whole testimony respecting these voices—but to what was *peculiar* in that testimony. Did you observe anything peculiar about it?'

I remarked that, while all the witnesses agreed in supposing the gruff voice to be that of a Frenchman, there was much disagreement in regard to the shrill, or, as one individual termed it, the harsh voice.

'That was the evidence itself,' said Dupin, 'but it was not the peculiarity of the evidence. You have observed nothing distinctive. Yet there *was* something to be observed. The witnesses, as you remark, agreed about the gruff voice; they were here unanimous. But in regard to the shrill voice, the peculiarity is—not that they disagreed—but that, while an Italian, an Englishman, a Spaniard, a Hollander, and a Frenchman attempted to describe it, each one spoke of it as that *of a foreigner*. Each is sure that it was not the voice of one of his own countrymen. Each likens it—not to the voice of an individual of any nation with whose language he is conversant—but the converse. The Frenchman supposes it the voice of a Spaniard, and "might have distinguished some words

had he been acquainted with the Spanish." The Dutchman maintains
it to have been that of a Frenchman; but we find it stated that
"not understanding French this witness was examined through an
interpreter." The Englishman thinks it the voice of a German, and
"does not understand German." The Spaniard "is sure" that it was that
of an Englishman, but "judges by the intonation" altogether, "as he
has no knowledge of the English." The Italian believes it the voice of a
Russian, but "has never conversed with a native of Russia." A second
Frenchman differs, moreover, with the first, and is positive that the
voice was that of an Italian; but, not being cognizant of that tongue,
is, like the Spaniard, "convinced by the intonation." Now, how
strangely unusual must that voice have really been, about which
such testimony as this could have been elicited!—in whose tones,
even, denizens of the five great divisions of Europe could recognise
nothing familiar! You will say that it might have been the voice of
an Asiatic—of an African. Neither Asiatics nor Africans abound in
Paris; but, without denying the inference, I will now merely call
your attention to three points. The voice is termed by one witness
"harsh rather than shrill." It is represented by two others to have
been "quick and unequal." No words—no sounds resembling
words—were by any witness mentioned as distinguishable.'

'I know not,' continued Dupin, 'what impression I may have
made, so far, upon your own understanding; but I do not hesitate
to say that legitimate deductions even from this portion of the
testimony—the portion respecting the gruff and shrill voices—are
in themselves sufficient to engender a suspicion which should give
direction to all farther progress in the investigation of the mystery.
I said "legitimate deductions"; but my meaning is not thus fully
expressed. I designed to imply that the deductions are the sole

proper ones, and that the suspicion arises *inevitably* from them as the single result. What the suspicion is, however, I will not say just yet. I merely wish you to bear in mind that, with myself, it was sufficiently forcible to give a definite form—a certain tendency—to my inquiries in the chamber.

'Let us now transport ourselves, in fancy, to this chamber. What shall we first seek here? The means of egress employed by the murderers. It is not too much to say that neither of us believe in præternatural[2] events. Madame and Mademoiselle L'Espanaye were not destroyed by spirits. The doers of the deed were material, and escaped materially. Then how? Fortunately, there is but one mode of reasoning upon the point, and that mode *must* lead us to a definite decision. Let us examine, each by each, the possible means of egress. It is clear that the assassins were in the room where Mademoiselle L'Espanaye was found, or at least in the room adjoining, when the party ascended the stairs. It is, then, only from these two apartments that we have to seek issues. The police have laid bare the floors, the ceilings, and the masonry of the walls, in every direction. No *secret* issues could have escaped their vigilance. But, not trusting to *their* eyes, I examined with my own. There were, then, *no* secret issues. Both doors leading from the rooms into the passage were securely locked, with the keys inside. Let us turn to the chimneys. These, although of ordinary width for some eight or ten feet above the hearths, will not admit, throughout their extent, the body of a large cat. The impossibility of egress, by means already stated, being thus absolute, we are reduced to the windows. Through those of the front room no one could have escaped without notice from the crowd in the street. The murderers *must* have passed, then, through those of the back room. Now, brought to this conclusion in so unequivocal a manner as we are, it is not our part, as reasoners, to reject it on account of apparent impossibilities. It is only left for us to prove that these apparent "impossibilities" are, in reality, not such.'

'There are two windows in the chamber. One of them is unobstructed by furniture, and is wholly visible. The lower portion of the other is hidden from view by the head of the unwieldy bedstead which is thrust close up against it. The former was found securely fastened from within. It resisted the utmost force of those who endeavoured to raise it. A large gimlet-hole had been pierced in its frame to the left, and a very stout nail was found fitted therein, nearly to the head. Upon examining the other window, a similar nail was seen similarly fitted in it; and a vigorous attempt to raise this sash failed also. The police were now entirely satisfied that egress had not been in these directions. And, *therefore*, it was thought a matter of supererogation to withdraw the nails and open the windows.'

'My own examination was somewhat more particular, and was so for the reason I have just given—because here it was, I knew, that all apparent impossibilities *must* be proved to be not such in reality.'

'I proceeded to think thus—*a posteriori*. The murderers *did* escape from one of these windows. This being so, they could not have re-fastened the sashes from the inside, as they were found fastened;—the consideration which put a stop, through its obviousness, to the scrutiny of the police in this quarter. Yet the sashes *were* fastened. They *must*, then, have the power of fastening themselves. There was no escape from this conclusion. I stepped to the unobstructed casement, withdrew the nail with some difficulty, and attempted to raise the sash. It resisted all my efforts, as I had anticipated. A concealed spring must, I now knew, exist; and this corroboration of my idea convinced me that my premises, at least, were correct, however mysterious still appeared the circumstances attending the nails. A careful search soon brought to light the hidden spring. I pressed it, and, satisfied with the discovery, forbore to upraise the sash.'

'I now replaced the nail and regarded it attentively. A person passing out through this window might have reclosed it, and the spring would have caught—but the nail could not have been replaced. The conclusion was plain, and again narrowed in the field of my investigations. The assassins *must* have escaped through the other window. Supposing, then, the springs upon each sash to be the same, as was probable, there *must* be found a difference between the nails, or at least between the modes of their fixture. Getting upon the sacking of the bedstead, I looked over the head-board minutely at the second casement. Passing my hand down behind the board, I readily discovered and pressed the spring, which was, as I had supposed, identical in character with its neighbour. I now looked at the nail. It was as stout as the other, and apparently fitted in the same manner—driven in nearly up to the head.'

'You will say that I was puzzled; but, if you think so, you must have misunderstood the nature of the inductions. To use a sporting phrase, I had not been once "at fault." The scent had never for an instant been lost. There was no flaw in any link of the chain. I had traced the secret to its ultimate result,—and that result was *the nail*. It had, I say, in every respect, the appearance of its fellow in the other window; but this fact was an absolute nullity (conclusive us it might seem to be) when compared with the consideration that here, at this point, terminated the clue. 'There *must* be something wrong,' I said, 'about the nail.' I touched it; and the head, with about a quarter of an inch of the shank, came off in my fingers. The rest of the shank was in the gimlet-hole, where it had been broken off. The fracture was an old one (for its edges were incrusted with rust), and had apparently been accomplished by the blow of a hammer, which had partially imbedded, in the top of the bottom sash, the head portion of the nail. I now carefully replaced this head portion in the indentation whence I had taken it, and the resemblance to a perfect nail was complete—the fissure was invisible. Pressing the spring, I gently raised the sash for a few inches; the head went up with it, remaining firm in its bed. I closed the window, and the semblance of the whole nail was again perfect.

'The riddle, so far, was now unriddled. The assassin had escaped through the window which looked upon the bed. Dropping of its own accord upon his exit (or perhaps purposely closed), it had become fastened by the spring; and it was the retention of this spring which had been mistaken by the police for that of the nail,—farther inquiry being thus considered unnecessary.

'The next question is that of the mode of descent. Upon this point I had been satisfied in my walk with you around the building. About five feet and a half from the casement in question there runs a lightning-rod. From this rod it would have been impossible for any one to reach the window itself, to say nothing of entering it. I observed, however, that the shutters of the fourth story were of the peculiar kind called by Parisian carpenters *ferrades*—a kind rarely employed at the present day, but frequently seen upon very old mansions at Lyons and Bordeaux. They are in the form of an ordinary door (a single, not a folding door), except that the upper half is latticed or worked in open trellis—thus affording an excellent hold for the hands. In the present instance these shutters are fully three feet and a half broad. When we saw them from the rear of the house, they were both about half open—that is to say, they stood off at right angles from the wall. It is probable that the police, as well as myself, examined the back of the tenement; but, if so, in looking at these *ferrades* in the line of their breadth (as they must have done), they did not perceive this great breadth itself, or, at all events, failed to take it into due consideration. In fact, having once satisfied themselves that no egress could have been made in this quarter, they would naturally bestow here a very cursory examination. It was clear to me, however, that the shutter belonging to the window at the head of the bed, would, if swung fully back to the wall, reach to within two feet of the lightning-rod. It was also evident that, by exertion of a very unusual degree of activity and courage, an entrance into the window, from the rod, might have been thus effected. By reaching to the distance of two feet and a half (we now suppose the shutter open to its whole extent) a robber might have taken a firm grasp upon the trellis-work. Letting go, then, his hold upon the rod, placing his feet securely against the wall, and springing boldly from it, he might have swung the shutter so as to close it, and, if we imagine the window open at the time, might even have swung himself into the room.

'I wish you to bear especially in mind that I have spoken of a *very* unusual degree of activity as requisite to success in so hazardous and so difficult a feat. It is my design to show you, first, that the thing might possibly have been accomplished:—but, secondly and *chiefly*, I wish to impress upon your understanding the *very extraordinary*—the almost præternatural character of that agility which could have accomplished it.

'You will say, no doubt, using the language of the law, that "to make out my case" I should rather undervalue, than insist upon a full estimation of the activity required in this matter. This may be the practice in law, but it is not the usage of reason. My ultimate object is only the truth. My immediate purpose is to lead you to place in juxtaposition that *very unusual* activity of which I have just spoken, with that *very peculiar* shrill (or harsh) and *unequal* voice, about whose nationality no two persons could be found to agree, and in whose utterance no syllabification could be detected.'

At these words a vague and half-formed conception of the meaning of Dupin flitted over my mind. I seemed to be upon the verge of comprehension, without power to comprehend—as men, at times, find themselves upon the brink of remembrance, without being able, in the end, to remember. My friend went on with his discourse.

'You will see,' he said, 'that I have shifted the question from the mode of egress to that of ingress. It was my design to convey the idea that both were effected in the same manner, at the same point. Let us now revert to the interior of the room. Let us survey the appearances here. The drawers of the bureau, it is said, had been rifled, although many articles of apparel still remained within them. The conclusion here is absurd. It is a mere guess— a very silly one—and no more. How are we to know that the articles found in the drawers were not all these drawers had originally contained? Madame L'Espanaye and her daughter lived an exceedingly retired life—saw no company—seldom went out—had little use for numerous changes of habiliment. Those found were at least of as good quality as any likely to be possessed by these ladies. If a thief had taken any, why did he not take the best—why did he not take all? In a word, why did he abandon four thousand francs in gold to encumber himself with a bundle of linen? The gold *was* abandoned. Nearly the whole sum mentioned by Monsieur Mignaud, the banker, was discovered, in bags, upon the floor. I wish you, therefore, to discard from your thoughts the blundering idea of *motive*, engendered in the brains of the police by that portion of the evidence which speaks of money delivered at the door of the house. Coincidences ten times as remarkable as this (the delivery of the money, and murder committed within three days upon the party receiving it), happen to all of us every hour of our lives, without attracting even momentary notice. Coincidences, in general, are great stumbling-blocks in the way of that class of thinkers who have been educated to know nothing of the theory of probabilities—that theory to which the most glorious objects of human research are indebted for the most glorious of illustration. In the present instance, had the gold been gone, the fact of its delivery three days before would have formed something more than a coincidence. It would have been corroborative of this idea of motive. But, under the real circumstances of the case, if we are to suppose gold the motive of this outrage, we must also imagine the perpetrator so vacillating an idiot as to have abandoned his gold and his motive together.'

'Keeping now steadily in mind the points to which I have drawn your attention—that peculiar voice, that unusual agility, and that startling absence of motive in a murder so singularly atrocious as this—let us glance at the butchery itself. Here is a woman strangled to death by manual strength, and thrust up a chimney, head downward. Ordinary assassins employ no such modes of murder as this. Least of all, do they thus dispose of the murdered. In the manner of thrusting the corpse up the chimney, you will admit that there was something *excessively outré*—something altogether irreconcilable with our common notions of human action, even when we suppose the actors the most depraved of men. Think, too, how great must have been that strength which could have thrust the body *up* such an aperture so forcibly that the united vigour of several persons was found barely sufficient to drag it *down!*'

'Turn, now, to other indications of the employment of a vigour most marvellous. On the hearth were thick tresses—very thick tresses—of gray human hair. These had been torn out by the roots. You are aware of the great force necessary in tearing thus from the head even twenty or thirty hairs together. You saw the locks in question as well as myself. Their roots (a hideous sight!) were clotted with fragments of the flesh of the scalp—sure token of the prodigious power which had been exerted in uprooting perhaps half a million of hairs at a time. The throat of the old lady was not merely cut, but the head absolutely severed from the body: the instrument was a mere razor. I wish you also to look at the *brutal* ferocity of these deeds. Of the bruises upon the body of Madame L'Espanaye I do not speak. Monsieur Dumas, and his worthy coadjutor Monsieur Etienne, have pronounced that they were inflicted by some obtuse instrument; and so far these gentlemen are very correct. The obtuse instrument was clearly the stone pavement in the yard, upon which the victim had fallen from the window which looked in upon the bed. This idea, however simple it may now seem, escaped the police for the same reason that the breadth of the shutters escaped them—because, by the affair of the nails, their perceptions had been hermetically sealed against the possibility of the windows having ever been opened at all.'

'If now, in addition to all these things, you have properly reflected upon the odd disorder of the chamber, we have gone so far as to combine the ideas of an agility astounding, a strength superhuman, a ferocity brutal, a butchery without motive, a *grotesquerie* in horror absolutely alien from humanity, and a voice foreign in tone to the ears of men of many nations, and devoid of all distinct or intelligible syllabification. What result, then, has ensued? What impression have I made upon your fancy?'

I felt a creeping of the flesh as Dupin asked me the question. 'A madman,' I said, 'has done this deed—some raving maniac, escaped from a neighbouring *Maison de Santé*.'

'In some respects,' he replied, 'your idea is not irrelevant. But the voices of madmen, even in their wildest paroxysms, are never found to tally with that peculiar voice heard upon the stairs. Madmen are of some nation, and their language, however incoherent in its words, has always the coherence of syllabification. Besides, the hair of a madman is not such as I now hold in my hand. I disentangled this little tuft from the rigidly clutched fingers of Madame L'Espanaye. Tell me what you can make of it.'

'Dupin!' I said, completely unnerved; 'this hair is most unusual—this is no *human* hair.'

'I have not asserted that it is,' said he; 'but, before we decide this point, I wish you to glance at the little sketch I have here traced upon this paper. It is a *facsimile* drawing of what has been described in one portion of the testimony as "dark bruises, and deep indentations of finger nails," upon the throat of Mademoiselle L'Espanaye, and in another (by Messrs. Dumas and Etienne), as a "series of livid spots, evidently the impression of fingers." '

'You will perceive,' continued my friend, spreading out the paper upon the table before us, 'that this drawing gives the idea of a firm and fixed hold. There is no *slipping* apparent. Each finger has retained—possibly until the death of the victim—the fearful grasp by which it originally imbedded itself. Attempt, now, to place all your fingers, at the same time, in the respective impressions as you see them.'

I made the attempt in vain.

'We are possibly not giving this matter a fair trial,' he said. 'The paper is spread out upon a plane surface; but the human throat is cylindrical. Here is a billet of wood, the circumference of which is about that of the throat. Wrap the drawing around it, and try the experiment again.'

I did so; but the difficulty was even more obvious than before. 'This,' I said, 'is the mark of no human hand.'

'Read now,' replied Dupin, 'this passage from Cuvier.'

It was a minute anatomical and generally descriptive account of the large fulvous Ourang-Outang of the East Indian Islands. The gigantic stature, the prodigious strength and activity, the wild ferocity, and the imitative propensities of these mammalia are sufficiently well known to all. I understood the full horrors of the murder at once.

'The description of the digits,' said I, as I made an end of reading, 'is in exact accordance with this drawing. I see that no animal but an Ourang-Outang, of the species here mentioned, could have impressed the indentations as you have traced them. This tuft of tawny hair, too, is identical in character with that of the beast of Cuvier. But I cannot possibly comprehend the particulars of this frightful mystery. Besides, there were *two* voices heard in contention, and one of them was unquestionably the voice of a Frenchman.'

'True; and you will remember an expression attributed almost unanimously, by the evidence, to this voice,—the expression, "*mon Dieu!*" This, under the circumstances, has been justly characterised by one of the witnesses (Montani, the confectioner), as an expression of remonstrance or expostulation. Upon these two words, therefore, I have mainly built my hopes of a full solution of the riddle. A Frenchman was cognizant of the murder. It is possible—indeed it is far more than probable—that he was innocent of all participation in the bloody transactions which took place. The Ourang-Outang may have escaped from him. He may have traced it to the chamber; but, under the agitating circumstances which ensued, he could never have recaptured it. It is still at large. I will not pursue these guesses—for I have no right to call them more—since the shades of reflection upon which they are based are scarcely of sufficient depth to be appreciable by my own intellect, and since I could not pretend to make them intelligible to the understanding of another. We will call them guesses, then, and speak of them as such. If the Frenchman in question is indeed, as I suppose, innocent of this atrocity, this advertisement, which I left last night, upon our return home, at the office of *Le Monde* (a paper devoted to the shipping interest, and much sought by sailors), will bring him to our residence.'

He handed me a paper, and I read thus:

CAUGHT—In the Bois de Boulogne, early in the morning of the—inst., (the morning of the murder), a very large, tawny Ourang-Outang of the Bornese species. The owner (who is ascertained to be a sailor, belonging to a Maltese vessel) may have the animal again, upon identifying it satisfactorily, and paying a few charges arising from its capture and keeping. Call at No.—, Rue—, Faubourg St. Germain—au troisiéme.

'How was it possible,' I asked, 'that you should know the man to be a sailor, and belonging to a Maltese vessel?'

'I do *not* know it,' said Dupin. 'I am not *sure* of it. Here, however, is a small piece of ribbon, which from its form, and from its greasy appearance, has evidently been used in tying the hair in one of those long *queues* of which sailors are so fond. Moreover, this knot is one which few besides sailors can tie, and is peculiar to the Maltese. I picked the ribbon up at the foot of the lightning-rod. It could not have belonged to either of the deceased. Now if, after all, I am wrong in my induction from this ribbon, that the Frenchman was a sailor belonging to a Maltese vessel, still I can have done no harm in saying what I did in the advertisement. If I am in error, he will merely suppose that I have been misled by some circumstance into which he will not take the trouble to inquire. But if I am right, a great point is gained. Cognizant although innocent of the murder, the Frenchman will naturally hesitate about replying to the advertisement—about demanding the Ourang-Outang. He will reason thus:—"I am innocent; I am poor; my Ourang-Outang is of great value—to one in my circumstances a fortune of itself—why should I lose it through idle apprehensions of danger? Here it is, within my grasp. It was found in the Bois de Boulogne—at a vast distance from the scene of that butchery. How can it ever be suspected that a brute beast should have done the deed? The police are at fault—they have failed to procure the slightest clue. Should they even trace the animal, it would be impossible to prove me cognizant of the murder, or to implicate me in guilt on account of that cognizance. Above all, *I am known*. The advertiser designates me as the possessor of the beast. I am not sure to what limit his knowledge may extend. Should I avoid claiming a property of so great value, which it is known that I possess, I will render the animal, at least, liable to suspicion. It is not my policy to attract attention either to myself or to the beast. I will answer the advertisement, get the Ourang-Outang, and keep it close until this matter has blown over." '

At this moment we heard a step upon the stairs.

'Be ready,' said Dupin, 'with your pistols, but neither use them nor show them until at a signal from myself.'

The front door of the house had been left open, and the visitor had entered, without ringing, and advanced several steps upon the staircase. Now, however, he seemed to hesitate. Presently we heard him descending. Dupin was moving quickly to the door, when we again heard him coming up. He did not turn back a second time, but stepped up with decision, and rapped at the door of our chamber.

'Come in,' said Dupin, in a cheerful and hearty tone.

A man entered. He was a sailor, evidently,—a tall, stout, and muscular-looking person, with a certain dare-devil expression of countenance, not altogether unprepossessing. His face, greatly sunburnt, was more than half hidden by whisker and *mustachio*. He had with him a huge oaken cudgel, but appeared to be otherwise unarmed. He bowed awkwardly, and bade us 'good evening,' in French accents, which, although somewhat Neufchatelish, were still sufficiently indicative of a Parisian origin.

'Sit down, my friend,' said Dupin. 'I suppose you have called about the Ourang-Outang. Upon my word, I almost envy you the possession of him; a remarkably fine, and no doubt a very valuable animal. How old do you suppose him to be?'

The sailor drew a long breath, with the air of a man relieved of some intolerable burden, and then replied, in an assured tone:

'I have no way of telling—but he can't be more than four or five years old. Have you got him here?'

'Oh no; we had no conveniences for keeping him here. He is at a livery stable in the Rue Dubourg, just by. You can get him in the morning. Of course you are prepared to identify the property?'

'To be sure I am, sir.'

'I shall be sorry to part with him,' said Dupin.

'I don't mean that you should be at all this trouble for nothing, sir,' said the man. 'Couldn't expect it. Am very willing to pay a reward for the finding of the animal—that is to say, anything in reason.'

'Well,' replied my friend, 'that is all very fair, to be sure. Let me think!—what should I have? Oh! I will tell you. My reward shall be this. You shall give me all the information in your power about these murders in the Rue Morgue.'

Dupin said the last words in a very low tone, and very quietly. Just as quietly, too, he walked toward the door, locked it, and put the key in his pocket. He then drew a pistol from his bosom and placed it, without the least flurry, upon the table.

The sailor's face flushed up as if he were struggling with suffocation. He started to his feet and grasped his cudgel; but the next moment he fell back into his seat, trembling violently, and with the countenance of death itself. He spoke not a word. I pitied him from the bottom of my heart.

'My friend,' said Dupin, in a kind tone, 'you are alarming yourself unnecessarily—you are indeed. We mean you no harm whatever. I pledge you the honour of a gentleman, and of a Frenchman, that we intend you no injury. I perfectly well know that you are innocent of the atrocities in the Rue Morgue. It will not do, however, to deny that you are in some measure implicated in them. From what I have already said, you must know that I have had means of information about this matter—means of which you could never have dreamed. Now the thing stands thus. You have done nothing which you could have avoided—nothing, certainly, which renders you culpable. You were not even guilty of robbery, when you might have robbed with impunity. You have nothing to conceal. You have no reason for concealment. On the other hand, you are bound by every principle of honour to confess all you know. An innocent man is now imprisoned, charged with that crime of which you can point out the perpetrator.'

The sailor had recovered his presence of mind, in a great measure, while Dupin uttered these words; but his original boldness of bearing was all gone.

'So help me God,' said he, after a brief pause, 'I *will* tell you all I know about this affair;—but I do not expect you to believe one half I say—I would be a fool indeed if I did. Still, I *am* innocent, and I will make a clean breast if I die for it.'

What he stated was, in substance, this. He had lately made a voyage to the Indian Archipelago. A party, of which he formed one, landed at Borneo, and passed into the interior on an excursion of pleasure. Himself and a companion had captured the Ourang-Outang. This companion dying, the animal fell into his own exclusive possession. After great trouble, occasioned by the intractable ferocity of his captive during the home voyage, he at length succeeded in lodging it safely at his own residence in Paris, where, not to attract toward himself the unpleasant curiosity of his neighbours, he kept it carefully secluded, until such time as it should recover from a wound in the foot, received from a splinter on board ship. His ultimate design was to sell it.

Returning home from some sailors' frolic on the night, or rather in the morning of the murder, he found the beast occupying his own bedroom, into which it had broken from a closet adjoining, where it had been, as was thought, securely confined. Razor in hand, and fully lathered, it was sitting before a looking-glass, attempting the operation of shaving, in which it had no doubt previously watched its master through the key-hole of the closet. Terrified at the sight of so dangerous a weapon in the possession of an animal so ferocious, and so well able to use it, the man, for some moments, was at a loss what to do. He had been accustomed, however, to quiet the creature, even in its fiercest moods, by the use of a whip, and to this he now resorted. Upon sight of it, the Ourang-Outang sprang at once through the door of the chamber, down the stairs, and thence, through a window, unfortunately open, into the street.

The Frenchman followed in despair; the ape, razor still in hand, occasionally stopping to look back and gesticulate at its pursuer, until the latter had nearly come up with it. It then again made off. In this manner the chase continued for a long time. The streets were profoundly quiet, as it was nearly three o'clock in the morning. In passing down an alley in the rear of the Rue Morgue, the fugitive's attention was arrested by a light gleaming from the open window of Madame L'Espanaye's chamber, in the fourth story of her house. Rushing to the building, it perceived the lightning-rod, clambered up with inconceivable agility, grasped the shutter, which was thrown fully back against the wall, and, by its means, swung itself directly upon the headboard of the bed. The whole feat did not occupy a minute. The shutter was kicked open again by the Ourang-Outang as it entered the room.

The sailor, in the meantime, was both rejoiced and perplexed. He had strong hopes of now recapturing the brute, as it could scarcely escape from the trap into which it had ventured, except by the rod, where it might be intercepted as it came down. On the other hand, there was much cause for anxiety as to what it might do in the house. This latter reflection urged the man still to follow the fugitive. A lightning-rod is ascended without difficulty, especially by a sailor; but, when he had arrived as high as the window, which lay far to his left, his career was stopped; the most that he could accomplish was to reach over so as to obtain a glimpse of the interior of the room. At this glimpse he nearly fell from his hold through excess of horror. Now it was that those hideous shrieks arose upon the night, which had startled from slumber the inmates of the Rue Morgue. Madame L'Espanaye and her daughter, habited in their night clothes, had apparently been occupied in arranging some papers in the iron chest already mentioned, which had been wheeled into the middle of the room.

It was open, and its contents lay beside it on the floor. The victims must have been sitting with their backs toward the window; and, from the time elapsing between the ingress of the beast and the screams, it seems probable that it was not immediately perceived. The flapping-to of the shutter would naturally have been attributed to the wind.

As the sailor looked in, the gigantic animal had seized Madame L'Espanaye by the hair (which was loose, as she had been combing it), and was flourishing the razor about her face, in imitation of the motions of a barber. The daughter lay prostrate and motionless; she had swooned. The screams and struggles of the old lady (during which the hair was torn from her head) had the effect of changing the probably pacific purposes of the Ourang-Outang into those of wrath. With one determined sweep of its muscular arm it nearly severed her head from her body. The sight of blood inflamed its anger into frenzy. Gnashing its teeth, and flashing fire from its eyes, it flew upon the body of the girl, and imbedded its fearful talons in her throat, retaining its grasp until she expired. Its wandering and wild glances fell at this moment upon the head of the bed, over which the face of its master, rigid with horror, was just discernible. The fury of the beast, who no doubt bore still in mind the dreaded whip, was instantly converted into fear. Conscious of having deserved punishment, it seemed desirous of concealing its bloody deeds, and skipped about the chamber in an agony of nervous agitation; throwing down and breaking the furniture as it moved, and dragging the bed from the bedstead. In conclusion, it seized first the corpse of the daughter, and thrust it up the chimney, as it was found; then that of the old lady, which it immediately hurled through the window headlong.

As the ape approached the casement with its mutilated burden, the sailor shrank aghast to the rod, and, rather gliding than clambering down it, hurried at once home—dreading the consequences of the butchery, and gladly abandoning, in his terror, all solicitude about the fate of the Ourang-Outang. The words heard by the party upon the staircase were the Frenchman's exclamations of horror and affright, commingled with the fiendish jabberings of the brute.

I have scarcely anything to add. The Ourang-Outang must have escaped from the chamber, by the rod, just before the break of the door. It must have closed the window as it passed through it. It was subsequently caught by the owner himself, who obtained for it a very large sum at the *Jardin des Plantes*. Le Bon was instantly released, upon our narration of the circumstances (with some comments from Dupin) at the *bureau* of the Prefect of Police. This functionary, however well disposed to my friend, could not altogether conceal his chagrin at the turn which affairs had taken, and was fain to indulge in a sarcasm or two, about the propriety of every person minding his own business.

'Let him talk,' said Dupin, who had not thought it necessary to reply. 'Let him discourse; it will ease his conscience, I am satisfied with having defeated him in his own castle. Nevertheless, that he failed in the solution of this mystery is by no means that matter for wonder which he supposes it; for, in truth, our friend the Prefect is somewhat too cunning to be profound. In his wisdom is no *stamen*. It is all head and no body, like the pictures of the Goddess Laverna—or, at best, all head and shoulders, like a codfish. But he is a good creature after all. I like him especially for one master stroke of cant, by which he has attained his reputation for ingenuity. I mean the way he has "*de nier ce qui est, et d'expliquer ce qui n'est pas.*" ' [3]

4
The Mystery of Marie Rogêt[4]

A SEQUEL TO 'THE MURDERS IN THE RUE MORGUE.'

Es giebt eine Reihe idealischer Begebenheiten, die der Wirklichkeit parallel läuft. Selten fallen sie zusammen. Menschen und Zufälle modificiren gewöhnlich die idealische Begebenheit, so dass sie unvollkommen erscheint, und ihre Folgen gleichfalls unvollkommen sind. So bei der Reformation; statt des Protestantismus kam das Lutherthum hervor.

There are ideal series of events which run parallel with the real ones. They rarely coincide. Men and circumstances generally modify the ideal train of events, so that it seems imperfect, and its consequences are equally imperfect. Thus with the Reformation; instead of Protestantism came Lutheranism.

—Novalis.[5] Moral Ansichten.

There are few persons, even among the calmest thinkers, who have not occasionally been startled into a vague yet thrilling half-credence in the supernatural, by coincidences of so seemingly marvellous a character that, as mere coincidences, the intellect has been unable to receive them. Such sentiments—for the half-credences of which I speak have never the full force of thought—such sentiments are seldom thoroughly stifled unless by reference to the doctrine of chance, or, as it is technically termed, the Calculus of Probabilities. Now this Calculus is, in its essence, purely mathematical; and thus we have the anomaly of the most rigidly exact in science applied to the shadow and spirituality of the most intangible in speculation.

The extraordinary details which I am now called upon to make public, will be found to form, as regards sequence of time, the primary branch of a series of scarcely intelligible *coincidences*, whose secondary or concluding branch will be recognised by all readers in the late murder of Mary Cecilia Rogers, at New York.

When, in an article entitled *The Murders in the Rue Morgue*, I endeavoured, about a year ago, to depict some very remarkable features in the mental character of my friend, the Chevalier C. Auguste Dupin, it did not occur to me that I should ever resume the subject. This depicting of character constituted my design; and this design was thoroughly fulfilled in the wild train of circumstances brought to instance Dupin's idiosyncrasy. I might have adduced other examples, but I should have proven no more. Late events, however, in their surprising development, have startled me into some further details, which will carry with them the air of extorted confession. Hearing what I have lately heard, it would be indeed strange should I remain silent in regard to what I both heard and saw so long ago.

Upon the winding up of the tragedy involved in the deaths of Madame L'Espanaye and her daughter, the Chevalier dismissed the affair at once from his attention, and relapsed into his old habits of moody reverie. Prone, at all times, to abstraction, I readily fell in with his humour; and, continuing to occupy our chambers in the Faubourg Saint Germain, we gave the Future to the winds, and slumbered tranquilly in the Present, weaving the dull world around us into dreams.

But these dreams were not altogether uninterrupted. It may

readily be supposed that the part played by my friend, in the drama at the Rue Morgue, had not failed of its impression upon the fancies of the Parisian police. With its emissaries, the name of Dupin had grown into a household word. The simple character of those inductions by which he had disentangled the mystery never having been explained even to the Prefect, or to any other individual than myself, of course it is not surprising that the affair was regarded as little less than miraculous, or that the Chevalier's analytical abilities acquired for him the credit of intuition. His frankness would have led him to disabuse every inquirer of such prejudice; but his indolent humour forbade all further agitation of a topic whose interest to himself had long ceased. It thus happened that he found himself the cynosure of the political eyes; and the cases were not few in which attempt was made to engage his services at the Prefecture. One of the most remarkable instances was that of the murder of a young girl named Marie Rogêt.

This event occurred about two years after the atrocity in the Rue Morgue. Marie, whose Christian and family name will at once arrest attention from their resemblance to those of the unfortunate 'cigar-girl,' was the only daughter of the widow Estelle Rogêt. The father had died during the child's infancy, and from the period of his death, until within eighteen months before the assassination which forms the subject of our narrative, the mother and daughter had dwelt together in the Rue Pavée Saint Andrée;[6] Madame there keeping a *pension*, assisted by Marie. Affairs went on thus until the latter had attained her twenty-second year, when her great beauty attracted the notice of a perfumer, who occupied one of the shops in the basement of the Palais Royal, and whose custom lay chiefly among the desperate adventurers infesting that neighbourhood.

Monsieur Le Blanc[7] was not unaware of the advantages to be derived from the attendance of the fair Marie in his perfumery; and his liberal proposals were accepted eagerly by the girl, although with somewhat more of hesitation by Madame.

The anticipations of the shopkeeper were recognised, and his rooms soon became notorious through the charms of the sprightly *grisette*. She had been in his employ about a year, when her admirers were thrown into confusion by her sudden disappearance from the shop. Monsieur Le Blanc was unable to account for her absence, and Madame Rogêt was distracted with anxiety and terror. The public papers immediately took up the theme, and the police were upon the point of making serious investigations, when, one fine morning, after the lapse of a week, Marie, in good health, but with a somewhat saddened air, made her re-appearance at her usual counter in the perfumery. All inquiry, except that of a private character, was, of course, immediately hushed. Monsieur Le Blanc professed total ignorance, as before. Marie, with Madame, replied to all questions, that the last week had been spent at the house of a relation in the country. Thus the affair died away, and was generally forgotten; for the girl, ostensibly to relieve herself from the impertinence of curiosity, soon bade a final adieu to the perfumer, and sought the shelter of her mother's residence in the Rue Pavée Saint Andrée.

It was about five months after this return home, that her friends were alarmed by her sudden disappearance for the second time. Three days elapsed, and nothing was heard of her. On the fourth her corpse was found floating in the Seine,[8] near the shore which is opposite the Quartier of the Rue Saint Andrée, and at a point not very far distant from the secluded neighbourhood of the Barrière du Roule.[9]

The atrocity of this murder (for it was at once evident that murder had been committed), the youth and beauty of the victim, and, above all, her previous notoriety, conspired to produce intense excitement in the minds of the sensitive Parisians. I can call to mind no similar occurrence producing so general and so intense an effect. For several weeks, in the discussion of this one absorbing theme, even the momentous political topics of the day were forgotten. The Prefect made unusual exertions; and the powers of the whole Parisian police were, of course, tasked to the utmost extent.

Upon the first discovery of the corpse, it was not supposed that the murderer would be able to elude, for more than a very brief period, the inquisition which was immediately set on foot. It was not until the expiration of a week that it was deemed necessary to offer a reward; and even then this reward was limited to a thousand francs. In the meantime the investigation proceeded with vigour, if not always with judgment, and numerous individuals were examined to no purpose; while, owing to the continual absence of all clue to the mystery, the popular excitement greatly increased. At the end of the tenth day it was thought advisable to double the sum originally proposed; and, at length, the second week having elapsed without leading to any discoveries, and the prejudice which always exists in Paris against the Police having given vent to itself in several serious émeutes, the Prefect took it upon himself to offer the sum of twenty thousand francs 'for the conviction of the assassin,' or, if more than one should prove to have been implicated, 'for the conviction of any one of the assassins.' In the proclamation setting forth this reward, a full pardon was promised to any accomplice who should come forward in evidence against his fellow; and to the whole was appended, wherever it appeared, the private placard of a committee of citizens, offering ten thousand francs, in addition to the amount proposed by the Prefecture. The entire reward thus stood at no less than thirty thousand francs, which will be regarded as an extraordinary sum when we consider the humble condition of the girl, and the great frequency, in large cities, of such atrocities as the one described.

No one doubted now that the mystery of this murder would be immediately brought to light. But although, in one or two instances, arrests were made which promised elucidation, yet nothing was elicited which could implicate the parties suspected; and they were discharged forthwith. Strange as it may appear, the third week from the discovery of the body had passed, and passed without any light being thrown upon the subject, before even a rumour of the events which had so agitated the public mind reached the ears of Dupin and myself. Engaged in researches which had absorbed our whole attention, it had been nearly a month since either of us had gone abroad, or received a visitor, or more than glanced at the leading political articles in one of the daily papers. The first intelligence of the murder was brought us by G—, in person. He called upon us early in the afternoon of the thirteenth of July, 18—, and remained with us until late in the night. He had been piqued by the failure of all his endeavours to ferret out the assassins. His reputation—so he said with a peculiarly Parisian air—was at stake. Even his honour was concerned. The eyes of the public were upon him; and there was really no sacrifice which he would not be willing to make for the development of the mystery. He concluded a somewhat droll speech with a compliment upon what he was pleased to term the *tact* of Dupin, and made him a direct and certainly a liberal proposition, the precise nature of which I do not feel myself at liberty to disclose, but which has no bearing upon the proper subject of my narrative.

The compliment my friend rebutted as best he could, but the proposition he accepted at once, although its advantages were altogether provisional. This point being settled, the Prefect broke forth at once into explanations of his own views, interspersing them with long comments upon the evidence; of which latter we were not yet in possession. He discoursed much and, beyond doubt, learnedly; while I hazarded an occasional suggestion as the night wore drowsily away. Dupin, sitting steadily in his accustomed arm-chair, was the embodiment of respectful attention. He wore spectacles, during the whole interview; and an occasional glance beneath their green glasses sufficed to convince me that he slept not the less soundly, because silently, throughout the seven or eight leaden-footed hours which immediately preceded the departure of the Prefect.

In the morning, I procured, at the Prefecture, a full report of all the evidence elicited, and, at the various newspaper offices, a copy of every paper in which, from first to last, had been published any decisive information in regard to this sad affair. Freed from all that was positively disproved, the mass of information stood thus:

Marie Rogêt left the residence of her mother, in the Rue Pavée St. Andrée, about nine o'clock in the morning of Sunday, June the twenty-second, 18—. In going out, she gave notice to a Monsieur Jacques St. Eustache,[10] and to him only, of her intention to spend the day with an aunt, who resided in the Rue des Drômes. The Rue des Drômes is a short and narrow but populous thoroughfare, not far from the banks of the river, and at a distance of some two miles, in the most direct course possible, from the *pension* of Madame Rogôt. St. Eustache was the accepted suitor of Marie, and lodged, as well as took his meals, at the *pension*. He was to have gone for his betrothed at dusk, and to have escorted her home. In the afternoon, however, it came on to rain heavily; and, supposing that she would remain all night at her aunt's (as she had done under similar circumstances before), he did not think it necessary to keep his promise. As night drew on, Madame Rogêt (who was an infirm old lady, seventy years of age) was heard to express a fear 'that she should never see Marie again;' but this observation attracted little attention at the time.

On Monday, it was ascertained that the girl had not been to the Rue des Drômes; and when the day elapsed without tidings of her, a tardy search was instituted at several points in the city and its environs. It was not, however, until the fourth day from the period of her disappearance that anything satisfactory was ascertained respecting her. On this day (Wednesday, the twenty-fifth of June) a Monsieur Beauvais,[11] who, with a friend, had been making inquiries for Marie near the Barrière du Roule, on the shore of the Seine which is opposite the Rue Pavée St. Andrée, was informed that a corpse had just been towed ashore by some fishermen, who had found it floating in the river. Upon seeing the body, Beauvais, after some hesitation, identified it as that of the perfumery-girl. His friend recognised it more promptly.

The face was suffused with dark blood, some of which issued from the mouth. No foam was seen, as in the case of the merely drowned. There was no discolouration in the cellular tissue. About the throat were bruises and impressions of fingers. The arms were bent over on the chest, and were rigid. The right hand was clenched; the left partially open. On the left wrist were two circular excoriations, apparently the effect of ropes, or of a rope in more than one volution. A part of the right wrist, also, was much chafed, as well as the back throughout its extent, but more especially at the shoulder-blades. In bringing the body to the shore the fishermen had attached to it a rope, but none of the excoriations had been effected by this. The flesh of the neck was much swollen. There were no cuts apparent, or bruises which appeared the effect of blows. A piece of lace was found tied so tightly around the neck as to be hidden from sight; it was completely buried in the flesh, and was fasted by a knot which lay just under the left ear. This alone would have sufficed to produce death. The medical testimony spoke confidently of the virtuous character of the deceased. She had been subjected, it said, to brutal violence. The corpse was in such condition when found that there could have been no difficulty in its recognition by friends.

The dress was much torn and otherwise disordered. In the outer garment, a slip, about a foot wide, had been torn upward from the bottom hem to the waist, but not torn off. It was wound three times around the waist, and secured by a sort of hitch in the back. The dress immediately beneath the frock was of fine muslin; and from this a slip eighteen inches wide had been torn entirely out—torn very evenly and with great care. It was found around her neck, fitting loosely, and secured with a hard knot. Over this muslin slip and the slip of lace the strings of a bonnet were attached, the bonnet being appended. The knot by which the strings of the bonnet were fastened was not a lady's, but a slip or sailor's knot.

After the recognition of the corpse, it was not, as usual, taken to the Morgue (this formality being superfluous), but hastily interred not far front the spot at which it was brought ashore. Through the exertions of Beauvais, the matter was industriously hushed up, as far as possible; and several days had elapsed before any public emotion resulted. A weekly paper,[12] however, at length took up the theme; the corpse was disinterred, and a re-examination instituted; but nothing was elicited beyond what has been already noted. The clothes, however, were now submitted to the mother and friends of the deceased, and fully identified as those worn by the girl upon leaving home.

Meantime, the excitement increased hourly. Several individuals were arrested and discharged. St. Eustache fell especially under suspicion; and he failed, at first, to give an intelligible account of his whereabouts during the Sunday on which Marie left home. Subsequently, however, he submitted to Monsieur G—, affidavits, accounting satisfactorily for every hour of the day in question. As time passed and no discovery ensued, a thousand contradictory rumours were circulated, and journalists busied themselves in *suggestions*. Among these, the one which attracted the most notice, was the idea that Marie Rogêt still lived—that the corpse found in the Seine was that of some other unfortunate. It will be proper that I submit to the reader some passages which embody the suggestion alluded to. These passages are *literal* translations from *L'Etoile*,[13] a paper conducted, in general, with much ability.

'Mademoiselle Rogêt left her mother's house on Sunday morning, June the twenty-second, 18—, with the ostensible purpose of going to see her aunt, or some other connection, in the Rue des Drômes. From that hour, nobody is proved to have seen her. There is no trace or tidings of her at all. * * * There has no person, whatever, come forward, so far, who saw her at all, on that day, after she left her mother's door. * * * Now, though we have no evidence that Marie Rogêt was in the land of the living after nine o'clock on Sunday, June the twenty-second, we have proof that, up to that hour, she was alive. On Wednesday noon, at twelve, a female body was discovered afloat on the shore of the Barrière de Roule. This was, even if we presume that Marie Rogêt was thrown into the river within three hours after she left her mother's house, only three days from the time she left her home—three days to an hour. But it is folly to suppose that the murder, if murder was committed on her body, could have been consummated soon enough to have enabled her murderers to throw the body into the river before midnight. Those who are guilty of such horrid crimes choose darkness rather than light. * * * Thus we see that if the body found in the river *was* that of Marie Rogêt, it could only have been in the water two and a half days, or three at the outside. All experience has shown that drowned bodies, or bodies thrown into the water immediately after death by violence, require from six to ten days for sufficient decomposition to take place to bring them to the top of the water. Even where a cannon is fired over a corpse, and it rises before at least five or six days' immersion, it sinks again, if let alone. Now, we ask, what was there in this case to cause a departure from the ordinary course of nature? * * * If the body had been kept in its mangled state on shore until Tuesday night, some trace would be found on shore of the murderers. It is a doubtful point, also, whether the body would be so soon afloat, even were it thrown in after having been dead two days. And, furthermore, it is exceedingly improbable that any villains who had committed such a murder as is here supposed, would have thrown the body in without weight to sink it, when such a precaution could have so easily been taken.'

The editor here proceeds to argue that the body must have been in the water 'not three days merely, but, at least, five times three days,' because it was so far decomposed that Beauvais had great difficulty in recognizing it. This latter point, however, was fully disproved. I continue the translation:

'What, then, are the facts on which M. Beauvais says that he has no doubt the body was that of Marie Rogêt? He ripped up the gown sleeve, and says he found marks which satisfied him of the identity. The public generally supposed those marks to have consisted of some description of scars. He rubbed the arm and found *hair* upon it—something as indefinite, we think, as can readily be imagined—as little conclusive as finding an arm in the sleeve. M. Beauvais did not return that night, but sent word to Madame Rogêt, at seven o'clock, on Wednesday evening, that an investigation was still in progress respecting her daughter. If we allow that Madame Rogêt, from her age and grief, could not go over (which is allowing a great deal), there certainly must have been some one who would have thought it worth while to go over and attend the investigation, if they thought the body was that of Marie. Nobody went over. There was nothing said or heard about the matter in the Rue Pavée St. Andrée, that reached even the occupants of the same building. M. St. Eustache, the lover and intended husband of Marie, who boarded in her mother's house, deposes that he did not hear of the discovery of the body of his intended until the next morning, when M. Beauvais came into his chamber and told him of it. For an item of news like this, it strikes us it was very coolly received.'

In this way the journal endeavoured to create the impression of an apathy on the part of the relatives of Marie, inconsistent with the supposition that these relatives believed the corpse to be hers. Its insinuations amount to this: that Marie, with the connivance of her friends, had absented herself from the city for reasons involving a charge against her chastity; and that these friends upon the discovery of a corpse in the Seine, somewhat resembling that of the girl, had availed themselves of the opportunity to impress the public with the belief of her death. But *L'Etoile* was again over-hasty. It was distinctly proved that no apathy, such as was imagined, existed; that the old lady was exceedingly feeble, and so agitated as to be unable to attend to any duty; that St. Eustache, so far from receiving the news coolly, was distracted with grief, and bore himself so frantically, that M. Beauvais prevailed upon a friend and relative to take charge of him, and prevent his attending the examination at the disinterment. Moreover, although it was stated by *L'Etoile*, that the corpse was re-interred at the public expense, that an advantageous offer of private sepulture was absolutely declined by the family, and that no member of the family attended the ceremonial:—although, I say, all this was asserted by *L'Etoile* in furtherance of the impression it designed to convey—yet *all* this was satisfactorily disproved. In a subsequent number of the paper, an attempt was made to throw suspicion upon Beauvais himself. The editor says:

'Now, then, a change comes over the matter. We are told that, on one occasion, while a Madame B—— was at Madame Rogêt's house, M. Beauvais, who was going out, told her that a *gendarme* was expected there, and that she, Madame B., must not say anything to the *gendarme* until he returned, but let the matter be for him. * * * In the present posture of affairs, M. Beauvais appears to have the whole matter locked up in his head. A single step cannot be taken without M. Beauvais, for, go which way you will, you run against him. * * * For some reason he determined that nobody shall have anything to do with the proceedings but himself, and he has elbowed the male relatives out of the way, according to their representations, in a very singular manner. He seems to have been very much averse to permitting the relatives to see the body.'

By the following fact, some colour was given to the suspicion thus thrown upon Beauvais. A visitor at his office, a few days prior to the girl's disappearance, and during the absence of its occupant, had observed a *rose* in the key-hole of the door, and the name 'Marie' inscribed upon a slate which hung near at hand.

The general impression, so far as we were enabled to glean it from the newspapers, seemed to be, that Marie had been the victim of a *gang* of desperadoes—that by these she had been borne across the river, maltreated and murdered. *Le Commerciel*,[14] however, a print of extensive influence, was earnest in combating this popular idea. I quote a passage or two from its columns:

'We are persuaded that pursuit has hitherto been on a false scent, so far as it has been directed to the Barrière du Roule. It is impossible that a person so well known to thousands as this young woman was, should have passed three blocks without some one having seen her; and any one who saw her would have remembered it, for she interested all who knew her. It was when the streets were full of people, when she went out. * * * It is impossible that she could have gone to the Barrière du Roule, or to the Rue des Drômes, without being recognised by a dozen

persons; yet no one has come forward who saw her outside of her mother's door, and there is no evidence, except the testimony concerning her *expressed intentions*, that she did go out at all. Her gown was torn, bound round her, and tied; and by that the body was carried as a bundle. If the murder had been committed at the Barrière du Roule, there would have been no necessity for any such arrangement. The fact that the body was found floating near the Barrière, is no proof as to where it was thrown into the water. *
* * A piece of one of the unfortunate girl's petticoats, two feet long and one foot wide, was torn out and tied under her chin around the back of her head, probably to prevent screams. This was done by fellows who had no pocket-handkerchief.'

A day or two before the Prefect called upon us, however, some important information reached the police, which seemed to overthrow, at least, the chief portion of *Le Commerciel's* argument. Two small boys, sons of a Madame Deluc, while roaming among the woods near the Barrière du Roule, chanced to penetrate a close thicket, within which were three or four large stones, forming a kind of seat with a back and footstool. On the upper stone lay a white petticoat; on the second, a silk scarf. A parasol, gloves, and a pocket-handkerchief were also here found. The handkerchief bore the name 'Marie Rogêt.' Fragments of dress were discovered on the brambles around. The earth was trampled, the bushes were broken, and there was every evidence of a struggle. Between the thicket and the river, the fences were found taken down, and the ground bore evidence of some heavy burthen having been dragged along it.

A weekly paper, *Le Soleil*,[15] had the following comments upon this discovery—comments which merely echoed the sentiment of the whole Parisian press:

'The things had all evidently been there at least three or four weeks; they were all mildewed down hard with the action of the rain, and stuck together from mildew. The grass had grown around and over some of them. The silk on the parasol was strong, but the threads of it were run together within. The upper part, where it had been doubled and folded, was all mildewed and rotten, and tore on its being opened. * * * The pieces of her frock torn out by the bushes were about three inches wide and six inches long. One part was the hem of the frock, and it had been mended; the other piece was part of the skirt, not the hem. They looked like strips torn off, and were on the thorn bush, about a foot from the ground. * * * There can be no doubt, therefore, that the spot of this appalling outrage has been discovered.'

Consequent upon this discovery, new evidence appeared. Madame Deluc testified that she keeps a roadside inn not far from the bank of the river, opposite the Barrière du Roule. The neighbourhood is secluded—particularly so. It is the usual Sunday resort of blackguards from the city, who cross the river in boats. About three o'clock, in the afternoon of the Sunday in question, a young girl arrived at the inn, accompanied by a young man of dark complexion. The two remained here for some time. On their departure, they took the road to some thick woods in the vicinity. Madame Deluc's attention was called to the dress worn by the girl, on account of its resemblance to one worn by a deceased relative. A scarf was particularly noticed. Soon after the departure of the couple, a gang of miscreants made their appearance, behaved boisterously, ate and drank without making payment, followed in the route of the young man and girl, returned to the inn about dusk, and re-crossed the river as if in great haste.

It was soon after dark, upon this same evening, that Madame Deluc, as well as her eldest son, heard the screams of a female in the vicinity of the inn. The screams were violent but brief. Madame D. recognised not only the scarf which was found in the thicket, but the dress which was discovered upon the corpse. An omnibus driver, Valence,[16] now also testified that he saw Marie Rogêt cross a ferry on the Seine, on the Sunday in question, in company with a young man of dark complexion. He, Valence, knew Marie, and could not be mistaken in her identity. The articles found in the thicket were fully identified by the relatives of Marie.

The items of evidence and information thus collected by myself, from the newspapers, at the suggestion of Dupin, embraced only one more point—but this was a point of seemingly vast consequence. It appears that, immediately after the discovery of the clothes as above described, the lifeless or nearly lifeless body of St. Eustache, Marie's betrothed, was found in the vicinity of what all now supposed the scene of the outrage. A phial labelled 'laudanum,' and emptied, was found near him. His breath gave evidence of the poison. He died without speaking. Upon his person was found a letter, briefly stating his love for Marie, with his design of self-destruction.

'I need scarcely tell you,' said Dupin, as he finished the perusal of my notes, 'that this is a far more intricate case than that of the Rue Morgue; from which it differs in one important respect. This is an *ordinary*, although an atrocious instance of crime. There is nothing peculiarly *outrè* about it. You will observe that, for this reason, the mystery has been considered easy, when, for this reason, it should have been considered difficult, of solution. Thus, at first, it was thought unnecessary to offer a reward. The myrmidons of G— were able at once to comprehend how and why such an atrocity *might have been* committed. They could picture to their imaginations a mode—many modes,—and a motive—many motives; and because it was not impossible that either of these numerous modes and motives *could* have been the actual one, they have taken it for granted that one of them *must.* But the case with which these variable fancies were entertained, and the very plausibility which each assumed, should have been understood as indicative rather of the difficulties than of the facilities which must attend elucidation. I have therefore observed that it is by prominences above the plane of the ordinary, that reason feels her way, if at all, in her search for the true, and that the proper question in cases such as this is not so much "what has occurred?" as "what has occurred that has never occurred before?" In the investigations at the house of Madame L'Espanaye,[17] the agents of G— were discouraged and confounded by that very *unusualness* which, to a properly regulated intellect, would have afforded the surest omen of success; while this same intellect might have been plunged in despair at the ordinary character of all that met the eye in the case of the perfumery-girl, and yet told of nothing but easy triumph to the functionaries of the Prefecture.'

'In the case of Madame L'Espanaye and her daughter, there was, even at the beginning of our investigation, no doubt that murder had been committed. The idea of suicide was excluded at once. Here, too, we are freed, at the commencement, from all supposition of self-murder. The body found at the Barrière du Roule was found under such circumstances as to leave us no room for embarrassment upon this important point. But it has been suggested that the corpse discovered is not that of the Marie Rogêt for the conviction of whose assassin, or assassins, the reward is offered, and respecting whom, solely, our agreement has been arranged with the Prefect. We both know this gentleman well. It will not do to trust him too far. If, dating our inquiries from the body found, and then tracing a murderer, we yet discover this body to be that of some other individual than Marie; or if, starting from the living Marie, we find her, yet find her unassassinated—in either case we lose our labour; since it is Monsieur G— with whom we have to deal. For our own purpose, therefore, if not for the purpose of justice, it is indispensable that our first step should be the determination of the identity of the corpse with the Marie Rogêt who is missing.'

'With the public the arguments of *L'Etoile* have had weight; and that the journal itself is convinced of their importance would appear from the manner in which it commences one of its essays upon the subject—"Several of the morning papers of the day," it says, "speak of the *conclusive* article in Monday's *Etoile*." To me, this article appears conclusive of little beyond the zeal of its inditer. We should bear in mind that, in general, it is the object of our newspapers rather to create a sensation—to make a point—than to further the cause of truth. The latter end is only pursued when it seems coincident with the former. The print which merely falls in with ordinary opinion (however well founded this opinion may be) earns for itself no credit with the mob. The mass of the people regard as profound only him who suggests *pungent contradictions* of the general idea. In ratiocination, not less than in literature, it is the *epigram* which is the most immediately and the most universally appreciated. In both, it is of the lowest order of merit.'

'What I mean to say is, that it is the mingled epigram and melodrama of the idea, that Marie Rogêt still lives, rather than any true plausibility in this idea, which have suggested it to *L'Etoile*, and secured it a favourable reception with the public. Let us examine the heads of this journal's argument; endeavouring to avoid the incoherence with which it is originally set forth.'

'The first aim of the writer is to show, from the brevity of the interval between Marie's disappearance and the finding of the floating corpse, that this corpse cannot be that of Marie. The reduction of this interval to its smallest possible dimension, becomes thus, at once, an object with the reasoner. In the rash pursuit of this object, he rushes into mere assumption at the outset. "It is folly to suppose," he says, "that the murder, if murder was committed on her body, could have been consummated soon enough to have enabled her murderers to throw the body into the river before midnight." We demand at once, and very naturally, *why?* Why is it folly to suppose that the murder was committed *within five minutes* after the girl's quitting her mother's house? Why is it folly to suppose that the murder was committed at any given period of the day? There have been assassinations at all hours. But, had the murder taken place at any moment between nine o'clock in the morning of Sunday and a quarter before midnight, there would still have been time enough "to throw the body into the river before midnight." This assumption, then, amounts precisely to this—that the murder was not committed on Sunday at all—and, if we allow *L'Etoile* to assume this, we may permit it any liberties whatever. The paragraph beginning "It is folly to suppose that the murder, etc.," however it appears as printed in *L'Etoile*, may be imagined to have existed actually *thus* in the brain of its inditer: "It is folly to suppose that the murder, if murder was committed on the body, could have been committed soon enough to have enabled her murderers to throw the body into the river before midnight; it is folly, we say, to suppose all this, and to suppose at the same time (as we are resolved to suppose), that the body was *not* thrown in until *after* midnight"—a sentence sufficiently inconsequential in itself, but not so utterly preposterous as the one printed.'

'Were it my purpose,' continued Dupin, 'merely to make out *a case* against this passage of *L'Etoile's* argument, I might safely leave it where it is. It is not, however, with *L'Etoile* that we have to do, but with the truth. The sentence in question has but one meaning, as it stands; and this meaning I have fairly stated; but it is material that we go behind the mere words, for an idea which these words have obviously intended, and failed to convey. It was the design of the journalists to say that at whatever period of the day or night of Sunday this murder was committed, it was improbable that the assassins would have ventured to bear the corpse to the river before midnight. And herein lies, really, the assumption of which I complain. It is assumed that the murder was committed at such a position, and under such circumstances, that *the bearing it* to the river became necessary. Now, the assassination might have taken place upon the river's brink, or on the river itself; and, thus, the throwing the corpse in the water might have been resorted to at any period of the day or night, as the most obvious and most immediate mode of disposal. You will understand that I suggest nothing here as probable, or as coincident with my own opinion. My design, so far, has no reference to the *facts* of the case. I wish merely to caution you against the whole tone of *L'Etoile's suggestion*, by calling your attention to its *ex-parte* character at the outset.'

'Having prescribed thus a limit to suit its own preconceived notions; having assumed that, if this were the body of Marie, it could have been in the water but a very brief time, the journal goes on to say:

' All experience has shown that drowned bodies, or bodies thrown into the water immediately after death by violence, require from six to ten days for sufficient decomposition to take place to bring them to the top of the water. Even when a cannon is fired over a corpse, and it rises before at least five or six days' immersion, it sinks again if let alone.'

'These assertions have been tacitly received by every paper in Paris, with the exception of *Le Moniteur*.[18] This latter print endeavours to combat that portion of the paragraph which has reference to "drowned bodies" only, by citing some five or six instances in which the bodies of individuals known to be drowned were found floating after the lapse of less time than is insisted upon by *L'Etoile*. But there is something excessively unphilosophical in the attempt, on the part of *Le Moniteur*, to rebut the general assertion of *L'Etoile*, by a citation of particular instances militating against that assertion. Had it been possible to adduce fifty instead of five examples of bodies found floating at the end of two or three days, these fifty examples could still have been properly regarded only as exceptions to *L'Etoile's* rule, until such time as the rule itself should be confuted. Admitting the rule (and this *Le Moniteur* does not deny, insisting merely upon its exceptions), the argument of *L'Etoile* is suffered to remain in full force; for this argument does not pretend to involve more than a question of the *probability* of the body having risen to the surface in less than three days; and this probability will be in favour of *L'Etoile's* position until the instances so childishly adduced shall be sufficient in number to establish an antagonistical rule.'

'You will see at once that all argument upon this head should be urged, if at all, against the rule itself; and for this end we must examine the *rationale* of the rule. Now the human body, in general, is neither much lighter nor much heavier than the water of the Seine; that is to say, the specific gravity of the human body, in its natural condition, is about equal to the bulk of fresh water which it displaces. The bodies of fat and fleshy persons, with small bones, and of women generally, are lighter than those of the lean and large-boned, and of men; and the specific gravity of the water of a river is somewhat influenced by the presence of the tide from the sea. But, leaving this tide out of question, it may be said that *very few human bodies will sink at all, even in fresh water, of their own accord.* Almost any one, falling into a river, will be enabled to float, if he suffer the specific gravity of the water fairly to be adduced in comparison with his own—that is to say, if he suffer his whole person to be immersed, with as little exception as possible. The proper position for one who cannot swim, is the upright position of the walker on land, with the head thrown fully back, and immersed; the mouth and nostrils alone remaining above the surface. Thus circumstanced, we shall find that we float without difficulty and without exertion. It is evident, however, that the gravities of the body, and of the bulk of water displaced, are very nicely balanced, and that a trifle will cause either to preponderate. An arm, for instance, uplifted from the water, and thus deprived of its support, is an additional weight sufficient to immerse the whole head, while the accidental aid of the smallest piece of timber will enable us to elevate the head so as to look about. Now, in the struggles of one unused to swimming, the arms are invariably thrown upwards, while an attempt is made to keep the head in its usual perpendicular position. The result is the immersion of the mouth and nostrils, and the inception, during efforts to breathe while beneath the surface, of water into the lungs. Much is also received into the stomach, and the whole body becomes heavier by the difference between the weight of the air originally distending these cavities, and that of the fluid which now fills them. This difference is sufficient to cause the body to sink, as a general rule; but is insufficient in the cases of individuals with small bones and an abnormal quantity of flaccid or fatty matter. Such individuals float even after drowning.'

'The corpse, being supposed at the bottom of the river, will there remain until, by some means, its specific gravity again becomes less than that of the bulk of water which it displaces. This effect is brought about by decomposition, or otherwise. The result of decomposition is the generation of gas, distending the cellular tissues and all the cavities, and giving the *puffed* appearance which is so horrible. When this distension has so far progressed that the bulk of the corpse is materially increased without a corresponding increase of *mass* or weight, its specific gravity becomes less than that of the water displaced, and it forthwith makes its appearance at the surface. But decomposition is modified by innumerable circumstances—is hastened or retarded by innumerable agencies; for example, by the heat or cold of the season, by the mineral impregnation or purity of the water, by its depth or shallowness, by its currency or stagnation, by the temperament of the body, by its infection or freedom from disease before death. Thus it is evident that we can assign no period, with anything like accuracy, at which the corpse shall rise through decomposition. Under certain conditions this result would be brought about within an hour;

under others it might not take place at all. There are chemical infusions by which the animal frame can be preserved *forever* from corruption; the bichloride of mercury is one. But, apart from decomposition, there may be, and very usually is, a generation of gas within the stomach, from the acetous fermentation of vegetable matter (or within other cavities from other causes) sufficient to induce a distension which will bring the body to the surface. The effect produced by the firing of a cannon is that of simple vibration. This may either loosen the corpse from the soft mud or ooze in which it is embedded, thus permitting it to rise when other agencies have already prepared it for so doing; or it may overcome the tenacity of some putrescent portions of the cellular tissue, allowing the cavities to distend under the influence of the gas.'

'Having thus before us the whole philosophy of this subject, we can easily test by it the assertions of *L'Etoile*. "All experience shows," says this paper, "that drowned bodies, or bodies thrown into the water immediately after death by violence, require from six to ten days for sufficient decomposition to take place to bring them to the top of the water. Even when a cannon is fired over a corpse, and it rises before at least five or six days' immersion, it sinks again if let alone." '

'The whole of this paragraph must now appear a tissue of inconsequence and incoherence. All experience does *not* show that "drowned bodies" *require* from six to ten days for sufficient decomposition to take place to bring them to the surface. Both science and experience show that the period of their rising is, and necessarily must be, indeterminate. If, moreover, a body has risen to the surface through firing of cannon, it will *not* "sink again if let alone," until decomposition has so far progressed as to permit the escape of the generated gas. But I wish to call your attention to the distinction which is made between "drowned bodies," and "bodies thrown into the water immediately after death by violence." Although the writer admits the distinction, he yet includes them all in the same category. I have shown how it is that the body of a drowning man becomes specifically heavier than its bulk of water, and that he would not sink at all, except for the struggle by which he elevates his arms above the surface, and his gasps for breath while beneath the surface—gasps which supply by water the place of the original air in the lungs. But these struggles and these gasps would not occur in the body "thrown into the water immediately after death by violence." Thus, in the latter instance, *the body, as a general rule, would not sink at all*—a fact of which *L'Etoile* is evidently ignorant. When decomposition had proceeded to a very great extent—when the flesh had in a great measure left the bones—then, indeed, but not *till* then, should we lose sight of the corpse.'

'And now what are we to make of the argument, that the body found could not be that of Marie Rogêt, because, three days only having elapsed, this body was found floating? If drowned, being a woman, she might never have sunk; or having sunk, might have re-appeared in twenty-four hours or less. But no one supposes her to have been drowned; and, dying before being thrown into the river, she might have been found floating at any period afterward whatever.'

' "But," says *L'Etoile*, "if the body had been kept in its mangled state on shore until Tuesday night, some trace would be found on shore of the murderers." Here it is at first difficult to perceive the intention of the reasoner. He means to anticipate what he imagines would be an objection to his theory—viz.: that the body was kept on shore two days, suffering rapid decomposition—*more* rapid than if immersed in water. He supposes that, had this been the case, it *might* have appeared at the surface on the Wednesday, and thinks that *only* under such circumstances it could have so appeared. He is, accordingly, in haste to show that it *was not* kept on shore; for, if so, "some trace would be found on shore of the murderers." I presume you smile at the *sequitur*. You cannot be made to see how the mere *duration* of the corpse on the shore could operate to *multiply traces* of the assassins. Nor can I.'

' "And furthermore it is exceedingly improbable," continues our journal, "that any villains who had committed such a murder as is here supposed, would have thrown the body in without weight to sink it, when such a precaution could have so easily been taken." Observe, here, the laughable confusion of thought! No one—not even *L'Etoile*—disputes the murder committed *on the body found*. The marks of violence are too obvious. It is our reasoner's object merely to show that this body is not Marie's. He wishes to prove that *Marie* is not assassinated—not that the corpse was not. Yet his observation proves only the latter point. Here is a corpse without weight attached. Murderers, casting it in, would not have failed to attach a weight. Therefore it was not thrown in by murderers. This is all which is proved, if anything is. The question of identity is not even approached, and *L'Etoile* has been at great pains merely to gainsay now what it has admitted only a moment before. "We are perfectly convinced," it says, "that the body found was that of a murdered female." '

'Nor is this the sole instance, even in this division of his subject, where our reasoner unwittingly reasons against himself.

His evident object, I have already said, is to reduce, as much as possible, the interval between Marie's disappearance and the finding of the corpse. Yet we find him *urging* the point that no person saw the girl from the moment of her leaving her mother's house. "We have no evidence," he says, "that Marie Rogêt was in the land of the living after nine o'clock on Sunday, June the twenty-second." As his argument is obviously an *ex-parte* one, he should, at least, have left this matter out of sight; for had any one been known to see Marie, say on Monday, or on Tuesday, the interval in question would have been much reduced, and, by his own ratiocination, the probability much diminished of the corpse being that of the *grisette*. It is, nevertheless, amusing to observe that *L'Etoile* insists upon its point in the full belief of its furthering its general argument.'

'Re-peruse now that portion of this argument which has reference to the identification of the corpse by Beauvais. In regard to the *hair* upon the arm, *L'Etoile* has been obviously disingenuous. M. Beauvais, not being an idiot, could never have urged in identification of the corpse, simply *hair upon its arm.* No arm is *without* hair. The *generality* of the expression of *L'Etoile* is a mere perversion of the witness' phraseology. He must have spoken of some *peculiarity* in this hair. It must have been a peculiarity of colour, of quantity, of length, or of situation.'

' "Her foot," says the journal, "was small—so are thousands of feet. Her garter is no proof whatever—nor is her shoe—for shoes and garters are sold in packages. The same may be said of the flowers in her hat. One thing upon which M. Beauvais strongly insists is, that the clasp on the garter found had been set back to take it in. This amounts to nothing; for most women find it proper to take a pair of garters home and fit them to the size of the limbs they are to encircle, rather than to try them in the store where they purchase." Here it is difficult to suppose the reasoner in earnest. Had M. Beauvais, in his search for the body of Marie, discovered a corpse corresponding in general size and appearance to the missing girl, he would have been warranted (without reference to the question of habiliment at all) in forming an opinion that his search had been successful. If, in addition to the point of general size and contour, he had found upon the arm a peculiar hairy appearance which he had observed upon the living Marie, his opinion might have been justly strengthened; and the increase of positiveness might well have been in the ratio of the peculiarity, or unusualness, of the hairy mark. If, the feet of Marie being small, those of the corpse were also small, the increase of probability that the body was that of Marie would not be an increase in a ratio merely arithmetical, but in one highly geometrical, or accumulative. Add to all this shoes such as she had been known to wear upon the day of her disappearance, and, although these shoes may be "sold in packages," you so far augment the probability as to verge upon the certain. What, of itself, would be no evidence of identity, becomes, through its corroborative position, proof most sure. Give us, then, flowers in the hat corresponding to those worn by the missing girl, and we seek for nothing further. If only *one* flower, we seek for nothing further—what then if two or three, or more? Each successive one is multiple evidence—proof not *added* to proof, but *multiplied* by hundreds or thousands. Let us now discover, upon the deceased, garters such as the living used, and it is almost folly to proceed. But these garters are found to be tightened, by the setting back of a clasp, in just such a manner as her own had been tightened by Marie shortly previous to her leaving home. It is now madness or hypocrisy to doubt. What *L'Etoile* says in respect to this abbreviation of the garters being an unusual occurrence, shows nothing beyond its own pertinacity in error. The elastic nature of the clasp-garter is self-demonstration of the *unusualness* of the abbreviation. What is made to adjust itself, must of necessity require foreign adjustment but rarely. It must have been by an accident, in its strictest sense, that these garters of Marie needed the tightening described. They alone would have amply established her identity. But it is not that the corpse was found to have the garters of the missing girl, or found to have her shoes, or her bonnet, or the flowers of her bonnet, or her feet, or a peculiar mark upon the arm, or her general size and appearance—it is that the corpse had each, and *all collectively*. Could it be proved that the editor of *L'Etoile* really entertained a doubt, under the circumstances, there would be no need, in his case, of a commission *de lunatico inquirendo*. He has thought it sagacious to echo the small talk of the lawyers, who, for the most part, content themselves with echoing the rectangular precepts of the courts. I would here observe that very much of what is rejected as evidence by a court is the best of evidence to the intellect. For the court, guiding itself by the general principles of evidence— the recognised and *booked* principles—is averse from swerving at particular instances. And this steadfast adherence to principle, with rigorous disregard of the conflicting exception, is a sure mode of attaining the *maximum* of attainable truth, in any long sequence of time. The practice, *en masse*, is therefore philosophical; but it is not the less certain that it engenders vast individual error.'[19]

'In respect to the insinuations levelled at Beauvais, you will be willing to dismiss them in a breath. You have already fathomed the true character of this good gentleman. He is a *busy-body*, with much of romance and little of wit. Any one so constituted will readily so conduct himself, upon occasion of *real* excitement, as to render himself liable to suspicion on the part of the over-acute, or the ill-disposed. M. Beauvais (as it appears from your notes) had some personal interviews with the editor of *L'Etoile*, and offended him by venturing an opinion that the corpse, notwithstanding the theory of the editor, was, in sober fact, that of Marie. "He persists," says the paper, "in asserting the corpse to be that of Marie, but cannot give a circumstance, in addition to those which we have commented upon, to make others believe." Now, without re-adverting to the fact that stronger evidence "to make others believe," could *never* have been adduced, it may be remarked that a man may very well be understood to believe, in a case of this kind, without the ability to advance a single reason for the belief of a second party. Nothing is more vague than impressions of individual identity. Each man recognises his neighbour, yet there are few instances in which any one is prepared *to give a reason* for his recognition. The editor of *L'Etoile* had no right to be offended at M. Beauvais' unreasoning belief.'

'The suspicious circumstances which invest him, will be found to tally much better with my hypothesis of *romantic busy-bodyism*, than with the reasoner's suggestion of guilt. Once adopting the more charitable interpretation, we shall find no difficulty in comprehending the rose in the key-hole; the "Marie" upon the slate; the "elbowing the male relatives out of the way"; the "aversion to permitting them to see the body"; the caution given to Madame B—, that she must hold no conversation with the *gendarme* until his (Beauvais') return; and, lastly, his apparent determination "that nobody should have anything to do with the proceedings except himself." It seems to me unquestionable that Beauvais was a suitor of Marie's; that she coquetted with him; and that he was ambitious of being thought to enjoy her fullest intimacy and confidence. I shall say nothing more upon this point; and, as the evidence fully rebuts the assertion of *L'Etoile*, touching the matter of *apathy* on the part of the mother and other relatives—an apathy inconsistent with the supposition of their believing the corpse to be that of the perfumery-girl—we shall now proceed as if the question of *identity* were settled to our perfect satisfaction.'

'And what,' I here demanded, 'do you think of the opinions of *Le Commerciel?*'

'That, in spirit, they are far more worthy of attention than any which have been promulgated upon the subject. The deductions from the premises are philosophical and acute; but the premises, in two instances, at least, are founded in imperfect observation. *Le Commerciel* wishes to intimate that Marie was seized by some gang of low ruffians not far from her mother's door. "It is impossible," it urges, "that a person so well known to thousands as this young woman was, should have passed three blocks without some one having seen her." This is the idea of a man long resident in Paris—a public man—and one whose walks to and fro in the city have been mostly limited to the vicinity of the public offices. He is aware that he seldom passes so far as a dozen blocks from his own *bureau*, without being recognised and accosted. And, knowing the extent of his personal acquaintance with others, and of others with him, he compares his notoriety with that of the perfumery-girl, finds no great difference between them, and reaches at once the conclusion that she, in her walks, would be equally liable to recognition with himself in his. This could only be the case were her walks of the same unvarying, methodical character, and within the same *species* of limited region as are his own. He passes to and fro, at regular intervals, within a confined periphery, abounding in individuals who are led to observation of his person through interest in the kindred nature of his occupation with their own. But the walks of Marie may, in general, be supposed discursive. In this particular instance, it will be understood as most probable, that she proceeded upon a route of more than average diversity from her accustomed ones. The parallel which we imagine to have existed in the mind of *Le Commerciel* would only be sustained in the event of the two individuals traversing the whole city. In this case, granting the personal acquaintances to be equal, the chances would be also equal that an equal number of personal *rencontres* would be made. For my own part, I should hold it not only as possible, but as far more than probable, that Marie might have proceeded, at any given period, by any one of the many routes between her own residence and that of her aunt, without meeting a single individual whom she knew, or by whom she was known. In viewing this question in its full and proper light, we must hold steadily in mind the great disproportion between the personal acquaintances of even the most noted individual in Paris, and the entire population of Paris itself.'

'But whatever force there may still appear to be in the suggestion of *Le Commerciel*, will be much diminished when we take into consideration *the hour* at which the girl went abroad. "It was when the streets were full of people," says *Le Commerciel*, "that she went out." But not so. It was at nine o'clock in the morning. Now at nine o'clock of every morning in the week, *with the exception of Sunday*, the streets in the city are, it is true, thronged with people. At nine on Sunday, the populace are chiefly within doors *preparing for church*. No observing person can have failed to notice the peculiarly deserted air of the town, from about eight until ten on the morning of every Sabbath. Between ten and eleven the streets are thronged, but not at so early a period as that designated.'

'There is another point at which there seems a deficiency of *observation* on the part of *Le Commerciel*. "A piece," it says, "of one of the unfortunate girl's petticoats, two feet long, and one foot wide, was torn out and tied under her chin, and around the back of her head, probably to prevent screams. This was done by fellows who had no pocket-handkerchiefs." Whether this idea is or is not well founded, we will endeavour to see hereafter; but by "fellows who have no pocket-handkerchiefs," the editor intends the lowest class of ruffians. These, however, are the very description of people who will always be found to have handkerchiefs even when destitute of shirts. You must have had occasion to observe how absolutely indispensable, of late years, to the thorough blackguard, has become the pocket-handkerchief.'

'And what are we to think,' I asked, 'of the article in *Le Soleil?*'

'That it is a vast pity its inditer was not born a parrot—in which case he would have been the most illustrious parrot of his race. He has merely repeated the individual items of the already published opinion; collecting them, with a laudable industry, from this paper and from that. "The things had all evidently been there," he says, "at least three or four weeks, and there can be *no doubt* that the spot of this appalling outrage has been discovered." The facts here re-stated by *Le Soleil* are very far indeed from removing my own doubts upon this subject, and we will examine them more particularly hereafter in connection with another division of the theme.'

'At present we must occupy ourselves with other investigations. You cannot fail to have remarked the extreme laxity of the examination of the corpse. To be sure, the question of identity was readily determined, or should have been; but there were other points to be ascertained. Had the body been in any respect *despoiled*? Had the deceased any articles of jewellry about her person upon leaving home? If so, had she any when found? These are important questions utterly untouched by the evidence; and there are others of equal moment, which have met with no attention. We must endeavour to satisfy ourselves by personal inquiry. The case of St. Eustache must be re-examined. I have no suspicion of this person; but let us proceed methodically. We will ascertain beyond a doubt the validity of the *affidavits* in regard to his whereabouts on the Sunday. Affidavits of this character are readily made matter of mystification. Should there be nothing wrong here, however, we will dismiss St. Eustache from our investigations. His suicide, however corroborative of suspicion, were there found to be deceit in the affidavits, is, without such deceit, in no respect an unaccountable circumstance, or one which need cause us to deflect from the line of ordinary analysis.'

'In that which I now propose, we will discard the interior points of this tragedy, and concentrate our attention upon its outskirts. Not the least usual error in investigations such as this is the limiting of inquiry to the immediate, with total disregard of the collateral or circumstantial events. It is the malpractice of the courts to confine evidence and discussion to the bounds of apparent relevancy. Yet experience has shown, and a true philosophy will always show, that a vast, perhaps the larger, portion of truth arises from the seemingly irrelevant. It is through the spirit of this principle, if not precisely through its letter, that modern science has resolved to *calculate upon the unforeseen*. But perhaps you do not comprehend me. The history of human knowledge has so uninterruptedly shown that to collateral, or incidental, or accidental events we are indebted for the most numerous and most valuable discoveries, that it has at length become necessary, in prospective view of improvement, to make not only large, but the largest, allowances for inventions that shall arise by chance, and quite out of the range of ordinary expectation. It is no longer philosophical to base upon what has been a vision of what is to be. *Accident* is admitted as a portion of the substructure. We make chance a matter of absolute calculation. We subject the unlooked-for and unimagined to the mathematical *formulae* of the schools.

'I repeat that it is no more than fact that the *larger* portion of all truth has sprung from the collateral; and it is but in accordance with the spirit of the principle involved in this fact that I would divert inquiry, in the present case, from the trodden and hitherto unfruitful ground of the event itself to the contemporary circumstances which surround it. While you ascertain the validity of the affidavits, I will examine the newspapers more generally than you have as yet done. So far, we have only reconnoitred the field of investigation; but it will be strange, indeed, if a comprehensive survey, such as I propose, of the public prints will not afford us some minute points which shall establish a *direction* for inquiry.'

In pursuance of Dupin's suggestion, I made scrupulous

examination of the affair of the affidavits. The result was a firm conviction of their validity, and of the consequent innocence of St. Eustache. In the meantime my friend occupied himself, with what seemed to me a minuteness altogether objectless, in a scrutiny of the various newspaper files. At the end of a week he placed before me the following extracts:

'About three years and a half ago, a disturbance very similar to the present was caused by the disappearance of this same Marie Rogêt from the *parfumerie* of Monsieur Le Blanc, in the Palais Royal. At the end of a week, however, she re-appeared at her customary *comptoir*, as well as ever, with the exception of a slight paleness not altogether usual. It was given out by Monsieur Le Blanc and her mother that she had merely been on a visit to some friend in the country; and the affair was speedily hushed up. We presume that the present absence is a freak of the same nature, and that, at the expiration of a week or, perhaps, of a month, we shall have her among us again.'—*Evening Paper*, Monday, June 23.[20]

'An evening journal of yesterday refers to a former mysterious disappearance of Mademoiselle Rogêt. It is well known that, during the week of her absence from Le Blanc's *parfumerie*, she was in the company of a young naval officer much noted for his debaucheries. A quarrel, it is supposed, providentially led to her return home. We have the name of the Lothario in question, who is at present stationed in Paris, but for obvious reasons forbear to make it public.'—*Le Mercurie*, Tuesday Morning, June 24.[21]

'An outrage of the most atrocious character was perpetrated near this city the day before yesterday. A gentleman, with his wife and daughter, engaged, about dusk, the services of six young men, who were idly rowing a boat to and fro near the banks of the Seine, to convey him across the river. Upon reaching the opposite shore the three passengers stepped out, and had proceeded so far as to be beyond the view of the boat, when the daughter discovered that she had left in it her parasol. She returned for it, was seized by the gang, carried out into the stream, gagged, brutally treated, and finally taken to the shore at a point not far from that at which she had originally entered the boat with her parents. The villains have escaped for the time, but the police are upon their trail, and some of them will soon be taken.'—*Morning Paper*, June 25.[22]

'We have received one or two communications, the object of which is to fasten the crime of the late atrocity upon Mennais;[23] but as this gentleman has been fully exonerated by a legal inquiry, and as the arguments of our several correspondents appear to be more zealous than profound, we do not think it advisable to make them public.'—*Morning Paper*, June 28.[24]

'We have received several forcibly written communications, apparently from various sources, and which go far to render it a matter of certainty that the unfortunate Marie Rogêt has become a victim of one of the numerous bands of blackguards which infest the vicinity of the city upon Sunday. Our own opinion is decidedly in favour of this supposition. We shall endeavour to make room for some of these arguments hereafter.'—*Evening Paper*, Tuesday, June 30.[25]

'On Monday, one of the bargemen connected with the revenue service saw an empty boat floating down the Seine. Sails were lying in the bottom of the boat. The bargeman towed it under the barge office. The next morning it was taken from thence without the knowledge of any of the officers. The rudder is now at the barge office.'—*Le Diligence*, Thursday, June 26.[26]

Upon reading these various extracts, they not only seemed to me irrelevant, but I could perceive no mode in which any one of them could be brought to bear upon the matter in hand. I waited for some explanation from Dupin.

'It is not my present design,' he said, 'to *dwell* upon the first and second of those extracts. I have copied them chiefly to show you the extreme remissness of the police, who, as far as I can understand from the Prefect, have not troubled themselves, in any respect, with an examination of the naval officer alluded to. Yet it is mere folly to say that between the first and second disappearance of Marie there is no *supposable* connection. Let us admit the first elopement to have resulted in a quarrel between the lovers, and the return home of the betrayed. We are now prepared to view a second *elopement* (if we *know* that an elopement has again taken place) as indicating a renewal of the betrayer's advances, rather than as the result of new proposals by a second individual—we are prepared to regard it as a "making up" of the old *amour*, rather than as the commencement of a new one. The chances are ten to one, that he who had once eloped with Marie would again propose an elopement, rather than that she to whom proposals of elopement had been made by one individual, should have them made to her by another. And here let me call your attention to the fact, that the time elapsing between the first ascertained and the second supposed elopement is a few months more than the general period of the cruises of our men-of-war. Had the lover been interrupted in his first villainy by the necessity of departure to sea, and had he seized the first moment of his return to renew the base designs not yet altogether accomplished—or not yet altogether accomplished *by him?* Of all these things we know nothing.'

'You will say, however, that, in the second instance, there was *no* elopement as imagined. Certainly not—but are we prepared to say that there was not the frustrated design? Beyond St. Eustache, and perhaps Beauvais, we find no recognised, no open, no honouable suitors of Marie. Of none other is there anything said. Who, then, is the secret lover, of whom the relatives (*at least most of them*) know nothing, but whom Marie meets upon the morning of Sunday, and who is so deeply in her confidence, that she hesitates not to remain with him until the shades of the evening descend, amid the solitary groves of the Barrière du Roule? Who is that secret lover, I ask, of whom, at least, *most* of the relatives know nothing? And what means the singular prophecy of Madame Rogêt on the morning of Marie's departure?—"I fear that I shall never see Marie again." '

'But if we cannot imagine Madame Rogêt privy to the design of elopement, may we not at least suppose this design entertained by the girl? Upon quitting home, she gave it to be understood that she was about to visit her aunt in the Rue des Drômes, and St. Eustache was requested to call for her at dark. Now, at first glance, this fact strongly militates against my suggestion;—but let us reflect. That she *did* meet some companion, and proceed with him across the river, reaching the Barrière du Roule at so late an hour as three o'clock in the afternoon, is known. But in consenting so to accompany this individual (*for whatever purpose—to her mother known or unknown*), she must have thought of her expressed intention when leaving home, and of the surprise and suspicion aroused in the bosom of her affianced suitor, St. Eustache, when, calling for her, at the hour appointed, in the Rue des Drômes, he should find that she had not been there, and when, moreover, upon returning to the *pension* with this alarming intelligence, he should become aware of her continued absence from home. She must have thought of these things, I say. She must have foreseen the chagrin of St. Eustache, the suspicion of all. She could not have thought of returning to brave this suspicion; but the suspicion becomes a point of trivial importance to her, if we suppose her *not* intending to return.'

'We may imagine her thinking thus—"I am to meet a certain person for the purpose of elopement, or for certain other purposes known only to myself. It is necessary that there be no chance of interruption—there must be sufficient time given us to elude pursuit—I will give it to be understood that I shall visit and spend the day with my aunt at the Rue des Drômes—I will tell St. Eustache not to call for me until dark—in this way, my absence from home for the longest possible period, without causing suspicion or anxiety, will be accounted for, and I shall gain more time than in any other manner. If I bid St. Eustache call for me at dark, he will be sure not to call before; but if I wholly neglect to bid him call, my time for escape will be diminished, since it will be expected that I return the earlier, and my absence will the sooner excite anxiety. Now, if it were my design to return at all—if I had in contemplation merely a stroll with the individual in question—it would not be my policy to bid St. Eustache call; for, calling, he will be *sure* to ascertain that I have played him false—a fact of which I might keep him for ever in ignorance, by leaving home without notifying him of my intention, by returning before dark, and by then stating that I had been to visit my aunt in the Rue des Drômes. But, as it is my design *never* to return—or not for some weeks—or not until certain concealments are effected—the gaining of time is the only point about which I need give myself any concern." '

'You have observed, in your notes, that the most general opinion in relation to this sad affair is, and was from the first, that the girl had been the victim of *a gang* of blackguards. Now, the popular opinion, under certain conditions, is not to be disregarded. When arising of itself—when manifesting itself in a strictly spontaneous manner—we should look upon it as analogous with that *intuition* which is the idiosyncrasy of the individual man of genius. In ninety-nine cases from the hundred I would abide by its decision. But it is important that we find no palpable traces of *suggestion*. The opinion must be rigorously *the public's own*; and the distinction is often exceedingly difficult to perceive and to maintain. In the present instance, it appears to me that this "public opinion," in respect to *a gang*, has been superinduced by the collateral event which is detailed in the third of my extracts. All Paris is excited by the discovered corpse of Marie, a girl young, beautiful and notorious. This corpse is found, bearing marks of violence, and floating in the river. But it is now made known that, at the very period, or about the very period, in which it is supposed that the girl was assassinated, an outrage similar in nature to that endured by the deceased, although less in extent, was perpetuated, by a gang of young ruffians, upon the person of a second young female. Is it wonderful that the one known atrocity should influence the popular judgment in regard to the other unknown? This judgment awaited direction, and the known outrage seemed so opportunely to afford it! Marie, too, was found in the river; and upon this very river was this known outrage committed. The connection of the two events had about it so much of the palpable, that the true wonder would have been a *failure* of the populace to appreciate and to seize it. But, in fact, the one atrocity, known to be so committed, is, if anything, evidence that the other, committed at a time nearly coincident, was *not* so committed. It would have been a miracle indeed, if, while a gang of ruffians were perpetrating, at a given locality, a most unheard-of wrong, there should have been another similar gang, in a similar locality, in the same city, under the same circumstances, with the same means and appliances, engaged in a wrong of precisely the same aspect, at precisely the same period of time! Yet in what, if not in this marvellous train of coincidence, does the accidentally *suggested* opinion of the populace call upon us to believe?'

'Before proceeding futher, let us consider the supposed scene of the assassination, in the thicket at the Barrière du Roule. This thicket, although dense, was in the close vicinity of a public road. Within were three or four large stones, forming a kind of seat with a back and a footstool. On the upper stone was discovered a white petticoat; on the second, a silk scarf. A parasol, gloves, and a pocket-handkerchief were also here found. The handkerchief bore the name "Marie Rogêt." Fragments of dress were seen on the branches around. The earth was trampled, the bushes were broken, and there was every evidence of a violent struggle.'

'Notwithstanding the acclamation with which the discovery of this thicket was received by the press, and the unanimity with which it was supposed to indicate the precise scene of the outrage, it must be admitted that there was some very good reason for doubt. That it *was* the scene, I may or I may not believe—but there was excellent reason for doubt. Had the *true* scene been, as *Le Commerciel* suggested, in the neighboyhood of the Rue Pavée St. Andrée, the perpetrators of the crime, supposing them still resident in Paris, would naturally have been stricken with terror at the public attention thus acutely directed into the proper channel; and, in certain classes of minds, there would have arisen, at once, a sense of the necessity of some exertion to redivert this attention. And thus, the thicket of the Barrière du Roule having been already suspected, the idea of placing the articles where they were found, might have been naturally entertained. There is no real evidence, although *Le Soleil* so supposes, that the articles discovered had been more than a few days in the thicket; while there is much circumstantial proof that they could not have remained there, without attracting attention, during the twenty days elapsing between the fatal Sunday and the afternoon upon which they were found by the boys. "They were all *mildewed* down hard," says *Le Soleil*, adopting the opinions of its predecessors, "with the action of the rain and stuck together from *mildew*. The grass had grown around and over some of them. The silk of the parasol was strong, but the threads of it were run together within. The upper part, where it bad been doubled and folded, was all *mildewed* and rotten, and tore on being opened." In respect to the grass having "grown around and over some of them," it is obvious that the fact could only have been ascertained from the words, and thus from the recollections, of two small boys; for these boys removed the articles and took them home before they had been seen by a third party. But the grass will grow, especially in warm and damp weather (such as was that of the period of the murder), as much as two or three inches in a single day. A parasol lying upon a newly turfed ground, might, in a single week, be entirely concealed from sight by the upspringing grass. And touching that *mildew* upon which the editor of *Le Soleil* so pertinaciously insists, that he employs the word no less than three times in the brief paragraph just quoted, is he really unaware of the nature of this mildew? Is he to be told that it is one of the many classes of *fungus*, of which the most ordinary feature is its upspringing and decadence within twenty-four hours?'

'Thus we see, at a glance, that what has been most triumphantly adduced in support of the idea that the articles bad been "for at least three or four weeks" in the thicket, is most absurdly null as regards any evidence of that fact. On the other hand, it is exceedingly difficult to believe that these articles could have remained in the thicket specified for a longer period than a single week—for a longer period than from one Sunday to the next. Those who know anything of the vicinity of Paris, know the extreme difficulty of finding *seclusion*, unless at a great distance from its suburbs. Such a thing as an unexplored or even an unfrequently visited recess, amid its woods or groves, is not for a moment to be imagined. Let any one who, being at heart a lover of nature, is yet chained by duty to the dust and heat of this great metropolis—let any such one attempt, even during the week-days, to slake his thirst for solitude amid the scenes of natural loveliness which immediately surround us. At every second step, he will find the growing charm dispelled by the voice and personal intrusion of some ruffian or party of carousing blackguards. He will seek privacy amid the densest foliage, all in vain. Here are the very nooks where the unwashed most abound—here are the temples most desecrate. With sickness of the heart the wanderer will flee back to the polluted Paris as to a less odious because less incongruous sink of pollution. But if the vicinity of the city is so beset during the working days of the week, how much more so on the Sabbath! It is now especially that, released from the claims of labour, or deprived of the customary opportunities of crime, the town blackguard seeks the precincts of the town, not through love of the rural, which in his heart he despises, but by way of escape from the restraints and conventionalities of society. He desires less the fresh air and the green trees, than the utter *license* of the country. Here, at the road-side inn, or beneath the foliage of the woods, he indulges, unchecked by any eye except those of his boon companions, in all the mad excess of a counterfeit hilarity— the joint offspring of liberty and of rum. I say nothing more than what must be obvious to every dispassionate observer, when I repeat that the circumstance of the articles in question having remained undiscovered, for a longer period than from one Sunday to another, in *any* thicket in the immediate neighbourhood of Paris, is to be looked upon as little less than miraculous.'

'But there are not wanting other grounds for the suspicion that the articles were placed in the thicket with the view of diverting attention from the real scene of the outrage. And, first, let me direct your notice to the *date* of the discovery of the articles. Collate this with the date of the fifth extract made by myself from the newspapers. You will find that the discovery followed, almost immediately, the urgent communications sent to the evening paper. These communications, although various, and apparently from various sources, tended all to the same point—viz., the directing of attention to *a gang* as the perpetrators of the outrage, and to the neighbourhood of the Barrière du Roule as its scene. Now, here, of course, the situation is not that, in consequence of these communications, or of the public attention by them directed, the articles were found by the boys; but the suspicion might and may well have been, that the articles were not *before* found by the boys, for the reason that the articles had not before been in the thicket; having been deposited there only at so late a period as at the date, or shortly prior to the date of the communications by the guilty authors of these communications themselves.'

'This thicket was a singular—an exceedingly singular one. It was unusually dense. Within its naturally walled enclosure were three extraordinary stones, *forming a seat with a back and footstool.* And this thicket, so full of art, was in the immediate vicinity, *within a few rods*, of the dwelling of Madame Deluc, whose boys were in the habit of closely examining the shrubberies about them in search of the bark of the sassafras. Would it be a rash wager—a wager of one thousand to one—that a *day* never passed over the heads of these boys without finding at least one of them ensconced in the umbrageous hall, and enthroned upon its natural throne? Those who would hesitate at such a wager, have either never been boys themselves, or have forgotten the boyish nature. I repeat—it is exceedingly hard to comprehend how the articles could have remained in this thicket undiscovered, for a longer period than one or two days; and that thus there is good ground for suspicion, in spite of the dogmatic ignorance of *Le Soleil*, that they were, at a comparatively late date, deposited where found.'

'But there are still other and stronger reasons for believing them so deposited, than any which I have as yet urged. And, now, let me beg your notice to the highly artificial arrangement of the articles. On the *upper* stone lay a white petticoat; on the *second*, a silk scarf; scattered around, were a parasol, gloves, and a pocket-handkerchief bearing the name "Marie Rogêt." Here is just such an arrangement as would *naturally* be made by a not-over-acute person wishing to dispose the articles *naturally*. But it is by no means a *really* natural arrangement. I should rather have looked to see the things *all* lying on the ground and trampled under foot. In the narrow limits of that bower, it would have been scarcely possible that the petticoat and scarf should have retained a position upon the stones, when subjected to the brushing to and fro of many struggling persons. "There was evidence," it is said, "of a struggle; and the earth was trampled, the bushes were broken,"—but the petticoat and the scarf are found deposited as if upon shelves. "The pieces of the frock torn out by the bushes were about three inches wide and six inches long. One part was the hem of the frock, and it had been mended. They *looked like strips torn off.*" Here, inadvertently, *Le Soleil* has employed an exceedingly suspicious phrase. The pieces, as described, do indeed "look like strips torn off," but purposely and by hand. It is one of the rarest of accidents that a piece is "torn off," from any garment such as is now in question, by the agency *of a thorn.* From the very nature of such fabrics, a thorn or nail becoming tangled in them, tears them rectangularly—divides them into two longitudinal rents, at right angles with each other, and meeting at an apex where the thorn enters—but it is scarcely possible to conceive the piece "torn off." I never so knew it, nor did you. To tear a piece *off* from such fabric, two distinct forces, in different directions, will be, in almost every case, required. If there be two edges to the fabric—if, for example, it be a pocket-handkerchief, and it is desired to tear from it a slip, then, and then only, will the one force serve the purpose. But in the present case the question is of a dress, presenting but one edge. To tear a piece from the interior, where no edge is presented, could only be effected by a miracle through the agency of thorns, and no *one* thorn could accomplish it. But, even where an edge is presented, two thorns will be necessary, operating, the one in two distinct directions, and the other in one. And this in the supposition that the edge is unhemmed. If hemmed, the matter is nearly out of the question. We thus see the numerous and great obstacles in the way of pieces being "torn off" through the simple agency of "thorns;" yet we are required to believe not only that one piece but that many have been so torn. "And one part," too, *was the hem of the frock!*" Another piece was *"part of the skirt, not the hem,"*—that is to say, was torn completely out, through the agency of thorns, from the unedged interior of the dress! These, I say, are things which one may well be pardoned for disbelieving; yet, taken collectedly, they form, perhaps, less of reasonable ground for suspicion, than the one startling circumstance of the articles having been left in this thicket at all, by any *murderers* who had enough precaution to think of removing the corpse. You will not have apprehended me rightly, however, if you suppose it my design to *deny* this thicket as the scene of the outrage. There might have been a wrong *here,* or, more possibly, an accident at Madame Deluc's. But, in fact, this is a point of minor importance. We are not engaged in an attempt to discover the scene, but to produce the perpetrators of the murder. What I have adduced, notwithstanding the minuteness with which I have adduced it, has been with the view, first, to show the folly of the positive and headlong assertions of *Le Soleil,* but secondly and chiefly, to bring you, by the most natural route, to a further contemplation of the doubt whether this assassination has, or has not, been the work of *a gang.*'

'We will resume this question by mere allusion to the revolting details of the surgeon examined at the inquest. It is only necessary to say that his published *inferences*, in regard to the number of ruffians, have been properly ridiculed as unjust and totally baseless, by all the reputable anatomists of Paris. Not that the matter *might not* have been as inferred, but that there was no ground for the inference:—was there not much for another?'

'Let us reflect now upon "the traces of a struggle"; and let me ask what these traces have been supposed to demonstrate. A gang. But do they not rather demonstrate the absence of a gang? What *struggle* could have taken place—what struggle so violent and so enduring as to have left its "traces" in all directions—between a weak and defenceless girl and the *gang* of ruffians imagined? The silent grasp of a few rough arms and all would have been over. The victim must have been absolutely passive at their will. You will here bear in mind that the arguments used against the thicket as the scene, are applicable, in chief part, only against it as the scene of an outrage committed by *more than a single individual*. If we imagine but *one* violator, we can conceive, and thus only conceive, the struggle of so violent and so obstinate a nature as to have left the "traces" apparent.'

'And again. I have already mentioned the suspicion to be excited by the fact that the articles in question were suffered to remain *at all* in the thicket where discovered. It seems almost impossible that these evidences of guilt should have been accidentally left where found. There was sufficient presence of mind (it is supposed) to remove the corpse; and yet a more positive evidence than the corpse itself (whose features might have been quickly obliterated by decay), is allowed to lie conspicuously in the scene of the outrage—I allude to the handkerchief with the *name* of the deceased. If this was accident, it was not the accident *of a gang*. We can imagine it only the accident of an individual. Let us see. An individual has committed the murder. He is alone with the ghost of the departed. He is appalled by what lies motionless before him. The fury of his passion is over, and there is abundant room in his heart for the natural awe of the deed. His is none of that confidence which the presence of numbers inevitably inspires. He is *alone* with the dead. He trembles and is bewildered. Yet there is a necessity for disposing of the corpse. He bears it to the river, but leaves behind him the other evidences of his guilt; for it is difficult, if not impossible, to carry all the burthen at once, and it will be easy to return for what is left. But in his toilsome journey to the water his fears redouble within him. The sounds of life encompass his path. A dozen times he hears or fancies he hears the step of an observer. Even the very lights from the city bewilder him. Yet, in time and by long and frequent pauses of deep agony, he reaches the river's brink, and disposes of his ghastly charge—perhaps through the medium of a boat. But *now* what treasure does the world hold—what threat of vengeance could it hold out—which would have power to urge the return of that lonely murderer over that toilsome and perilous path, to the thicket and its blood-chilling recollections? He returns *not*, let the consequences be what they may. He *could* not return if he would. His sole thought is immediate escape. He turns his back *forever* upon those dreadful shrubberies, and flees as from the wrath to come.'

'But how with a gang? Their number would have inspired them with confidence; if, indeed, confidence is ever wanting in the breast of the arrant blackguard; and of arrant blackguards alone are the supposed *gangs* ever constituted. Their number, I say, would have prevented the bewildering and unreasoning terror which I have imagined to paralyse the single man. Could we suppose an oversight in one, or two, or three, this oversight would have been remedied by a fourth. They would have left nothing behind them; for their number would have enabled them to carry *all* at once. There would have been no need of *return.'*

'Consider now the circumstance that, in the outer garment of the corpse when found, "a slip, about a foot wide, had been torn upward from the bottom hem to the waist, wound three times round the waist, and secured by a sort of hitch in the back." This was done with the obvious design of affording *a handle* by which to carry the body. But would any *number* of men have dreamed of resorting to such an expedient? To three or four, the limbs of the corpse would have afforded not only a sufficient, but the best possible, hold. The device is that of a single individual; and this brings us to the fact that "between the thicket and the river the rails of the fences were found taken down, and the ground bore evident traces of some heavy burden having been dragged along it!" But would a *number* of men have put themselves to the superfluous trouble of taking down a fence, for the purpose of dragging through it a corpse which they might have *lifted over* any fence in an instant? Would a *number* of men have so *dragged* a corpse at all as to have left evident *traces* of the dragging?'

'And here we must refer to an observation of *Le Commerciel*; an observation upon which I have already, in some measure, commented. "A piece," says this journal, "of one of the unfortunate girl's petticoats was torn out and tied under her chin, and around the back of her head, probably to prevent screams. This was done by fellows who had no pocket-handkerchiefs." '

'I have before suggested that a genuine blackguard is never

without a pocket-handkerchief. But it is not to this fact that I now especially advert. That it was not through want of a handkerchief for the purpose imagined by *Le Commerciel*, that this bandage was employed, is rendered apparent by the handkerchief left in the thicket; and that the object was not "to prevent screams" appears, also, from the bandage having been employed in preference to what would so much better have answered the purpose. But the language of the evidence speaks of the strip in question as "found around the neck, fitting loosely, and secured with a hard knot." These words are sufficiently vague, but differ materially from those of *Le Commerciel*. The slip was eighteen inches wide, and therefore, although of muslin, would form a strong band when folded or rumpled longitudinally. And thus rumpled it was discovered. My inference is this. The solitary murderer, having borne the corpse for some distance (whether from the thicket or elsewhere) by means of the bandage *hitched* around its middle, found the weight, in this mode of procedure, too much for his strength. He resolved to drag the burthen—the evidence goes to show that it *was* dragged. With this object in view, it became necessary to attach something like a rope to one of the extremities. It could be best attached about the neck, where the head would prevent its slipping off. And now the murderer bethought him, unquestionably, of the bandage about the loins. He would have used this, but for its volution about the corpse, the *hitch* which embarrassed it, and the reflection that it had not been "torn off" from the garment. It was easier to tear a new slip from the petticoat. He tore it, made it fast about the neck, and so *dragged* his victim to the brink of the river. That this "bandage," only attainable with trouble and delay, and but imperfectly answering its purpose—that this bandage was employed *at all*, demonstrates that the necessity for its employment sprang from circumstances arising at a period when the handkerchief was no longer attainable—that is to say, arising, as we have imagined, after quitting the thicket (if the thicket it was), and on the road between the thicket and the river.'

'But the evidence, you will say, of Madame Deluc (!) points especially to the presence of *a gang* in the vicinity of the thicket, at or about the epoch of the murder. This I grant. I doubt if there were not a *dozen* gangs, such as described by Madame Deluc, in and about the vicinity of the Barrière du Roule at *or about* the period of this tragedy. But the gang which has drawn upon itself the pointed animadversion, although the somewhat tardy and very suspicious evidence of Madame Deluc, is the *only* gang which is represented by that honest and scrupulous old lady as having eaten her cakes and swallowed her brandy, without putting themselves to the trouble of making her payment. *Et hinc illæ iræ?*'

'But what *is* the precise evidence of Madame Deluc? "A gang of miscreants made their appearance, behaved boisterously, ate and drank without making payment, followed in the route of the young man and the girl, returned to the inn *about dusk*, and re-crossed the river as if in great haste."'

'Now this "great haste" very possibly seemed *greater* haste in the eyes of Madame Deluc, since she dwelt lingeringly and lamentingly upon her violated cakes and ale,—cakes and ale for which she might still have entertained a faint hope of compensation. Why, otherwise, since it was *about dusk*, should she make a point of the *haste?* It is no cause for wonder, surely, that even a gang of blackguards should make *haste* to get home, when a wide river is to be crossed in small boats, when storm impends, and when night *approaches.*'

'I say *approaches*; for the night had *not yet arrived.* It was only *about dusk* that the indecent haste of these "miscreants" offended the sober eyes of Madame Deluc. But we are told that it was upon this very evening that Madame Deluc, as well as her eldest son, "heard the screams of a female in the vicinity of the inn." And in what words does Madame Deluc designate the period of the evening at which these screams were heard? "*It was soon after dark*," she says. But "*soon after dark*," is, at least, *dark*; and "*about dusk*" is as certainly daylight. Thus it is abundantly clear that the gang quitted the Barrière du Roule *prior* to the screams overheard (?) by Madame Deluc. And although, in all the many reports of the evidence, the relative expressions in question are distinctly and invariably employed just as I have employed them in this conversation with yourself, no notice whatever of the gross discrepancy has, as yet, been taken by any of the public journals, or by any of the Myrmidons of police.'

'I shall add but one to the arguments against *a gang*; but this *one* has, to my own understanding at least, a weight altogether irresistible. Under the circumstances of large reward offered, and full pardon to any king's evidence, it is not to be imagined, for a moment, that some member of *a gang* of low ruffians, or of any body of men, would not long ago have betrayed his accomplices. Each one of a gang, so placed, is not so much greedy of reward, or anxious for escape, as *fearful of betrayal.* He betrays eagerly and early that *he may not himself be betrayed.* That the secret has not been divulged is the very best of proof that it is, in fact, a secret. The horrors of this dark deed are known only to *one*, or two, living human beings, and to God.'

'Let us sum up now the meagre yet certain fruits of our long analysis. We have attained the idea either of a fatal accident under the roof of Madame Deluc, or of a murder perpetrated, in the thicket at the Barrière du Roule, by a lover, or at least by an intimate and secret associate of the deceased. This associate is of swarthy complexion. This complexion, the "hitch" in the bandage, and the "sailor's knot" with which the bonnet-ribbon is tied, point to a seaman. His companionship with the deceased—a gay but not an abject young girl—designates him as above the grade of the common sailor. Here the well-written and urgent communications to the journals are much in the way of corroboration. The circumstance of the first elopement, as mentioned by *Le Mercurie*, tends to blend the idea of this seaman with that of the "naval officer" who is first known to have led the unfortunate into crime.'

'And here, most fitly, comes the consideration of the continued absence of him of the dark complexion. Let me pause to observe that the complexion of this man is dark and swarthy; it was no common swarthiness which constituted the *sole* point of remembrance, both as regards Valence and Madame Deluc. But why is this man absent? Was he murdered by the gang? If so, why are there only *traces* of the assassinated *girl*? The scene of the two outrages will naturally be supposed identical. And where is his corpse? The assassins would most probably have disposed of both in the same way. But it may be said that this man lives, and is deterred from making himself known, through dread of being charged with the murder. This consideration might be supposed to operate upon him now—at this late period—since it has been given in evidence that he was seen with Marie, but it would have had no force at the period of the deed. The first impulse of an innocent man would have been to announce the outrage, and to aid in identifying the ruffians. This *policy* would have suggested. He had been seen with the girl. He had crossed the river with her in an open ferry-boat. The denouncing of the assassins would have appeared, even to an idiot, the surest and sole means of relieving himself from suspicion. We cannot suppose him, on the night of the fatal Sunday, both innocent himself and incognizant of an outrage committed. Yet only under such circumstances is it possible to imagine that he would have failed, if alive, in the denouncement of the assassins.'

'And what means are ours of attaining the truth? We shall find these means multiplying and gathering distinctness as we proceed. Let us sift to the bottom this affair of the first elopement. Let us know the full history of "the officer," with his present circumstances, and his whereabouts at the precise period of the murder. Let us carefully compare with each other the various communications sent to the evening paper, in which the object was to inculpate *a gang*. This done, let us compare these communications, both as regards style and MS., with those sent to the morning paper, at a previous period, and insisting so vehemently upon the guilt of Mennais. And, all this done, let us again compare these various communications with the known MSS. of the officer. Let us endeavour to ascertain, by repeated questionings of Madame Deluc and her boys, as well as of the omnibus-driver, Valence, something more of the personal appearance and bearing of the "man of dark complexion." Queries, skilfully directed, will not fail to elicit, from some of these parties, information on this particular point (or upon others)—information which the parties themselves may not even be aware of possessing. And let us now trace *the boat* picked up by the bargeman on the morning of Monday the twenty-third of June, and which was removed from the barge-office, without the cognizance of the officer in attendance, and *without the rudder*, at some period prior to the discovery of the corpse. With a proper caution and perseverance we shall infallibly trace this boat; for not only can the bargeman who picked it up identify it, but the *rudder is at hand*. The rudder *of a sail boat* would not have been abandoned, without inquiry, by one altogether at ease in heart. And here let me pause to insinuate a question. There was no *advertisement* of the picking up of this boat. It was silently taken to the barge-office, and as silently removed. But its owner or employer—how *happened* he, at so early a period as Tuesday morning, to be informed, without the agency of advertisement, of the locality of the boat taken up on Monday, unless we imagine some connection with the *navy*—some personal permanent connection leading to cognizance of its minute interests—its petty local news?'

'In speaking of the lonely assassin dragging his burden to the shore, I have already suggested the probability of his availing himself *of a boat*. Now we are to understand that Marie Rogêt *was* precipitated from a boat. This would naturally have been the case. The corpse could not have been trusted to the shallow waters of the shore. The peculiar marks on the back and shoulders of the victim tell of the bottom ribs of a boat. That the body was found without weight is also corroborative of the idea. If thrown from the shore a weight would have been attached. We can only account for its absence by supposing the murderer to have neglected the precaution of supplying himself with it before pushing off. In the act of consigning the corpse to the water, he would unquestionably have noticed his oversight; but then no remedy would have been at hand. Any risk would have been preferred to a return to that accursed shore. Having rid himself of his ghastly charge, the murderer would have hastened to the city. There, at some obscure wharf, he would have leaped on land. But the boat—would he have secured it? He would have been in too great haste for such things as securing a boat. Moreover, in fastening it to the wharf, he would have felt as if securing evidence against himself. His natural thought would have been to cast from him, as far as possible, all that had held connection with his crime. He would not only have fled from the wharf, but he would not have permitted *the boat* to remain. Assuredly he would have cast it adrift. Let us pursue our fancies.—In the morning, the wretch is stricken with unutterable horror at finding that the boat has been picked up and detained at a locality which he is in the daily habit of frequenting—at a locality, perhaps, which his duty compels him to frequent. The next night, *without daring to ask for the rudder*, he removes it. Now *where* is that rudderless boat? Let it be one of our first purposes to discover. With the first glimpse we obtain of it, the dawn of our success shall begin. This boat shall guide us, with a rapidity which will surprise even ourselves, to him who employed it in the midnight of the fatal Sabbath. Corroboration will rise upon corroboration, and the murderer will be traced.'

[For reasons which we shall not specify, but which to many readers will appear obvious, we have taken the liberty of here omitting, from the MSS. placed in our hands, such portion as details the *following up* of the apparently slight clue obtained by Dupin. We feel it advisable only to state, in brief, that the result desired was brought to pass; and that the Prefect fulfilled punctually, although with reluctance, the terms of his compact with the Chevalier. Mr. Poe's article concludes with the following words.—*Eds.*[27]]

It will be understood that I speak of coincidences and *no more*. What I have said above upon this topic must suffice. In my own heart there dwells no faith in præter-nature[28]. That Nature and its God are two, no man who thinks will deny. That the latter, creating the former, can, at will, control or modify it, is also unquestionable. I say "at will"; for the question is of will, and not, as the insanity of logic has assumed, of power. It is not that the Deity *cannot* modify his laws, but that we insult him in imagining a possible necessity for modification. In their origin these laws were fashioned to embrace *all* contingencies which *could* lie in the Future. With God all is *Now*.

I repeat, then, that I speak of these things only as of coincidences. And further: in what I relate it will be seen that between the fate of the unhappy Mary Cecilia Rogers, so far as that fate is known, and the fate of one Marie Rogêt up to a certain epoch in her history, there has existed a parallel in the contemplation of whose wonderful exactitude the reason becomes embarrassed. I say all this will be seen. But let it not for a moment be supposed that, in proceeding with the sad narrative of Marie from the epoch just mentioned, and in tracing to its *dénouement* the mystery which enshrouded her, it is my covert design to hint at an extension of the parallel, or even to suggest that the measures adopted in Paris for the discovery of the assassin of a *grisette*, or measures founded in any similar ratiocination, would produce any similar result.

For, in respect to the latter branch of the supposition, it should be considered that the most trifling variation in the facts of the two cases might give rise to the most important miscalculations, by diverting thoroughly the two courses of events; very much as, in arithmetic, an error which, in its own individuality, may be inappreciable, produces, at length, by dint of multiplication at all points of the process, a result enormously at variance with truth. And, in regard to the former branch, we must not fail to hold in view that the very Calculus of Probabilities to which I have referred, forbids all idea of the extension of the parallel,—forbids it with a positiveness strong and decided just in proportion as this parallel has already been long-drawn and exact. This is one of those anomalous propositions which, seemingly appealing to thought altogether apart from the mathematical, is yet one which only the mathematician can fully entertain. Nothing, for example, is more difficult than to convince the merely general reader that the fact of sixes having been thrown twice in succession by a player at dice, is sufficient cause for betting the largest odds that sixes will not be thrown in the third attempt. A suggestion to this effect is usually rejected by the intellect at once. It does not appear that the two throws which have been completed, and which lie now absolutely in the Past, can have influence upon the throw which exists only in the Future. The chance for throwing sixes seems to be precisely as it was at any ordinary time—that is to say, subject only to the influence of the various other throws which may be made by the dice. And this is a reflection which appears so exceedingly obvious that attempts to controvert it are received more frequently with a derisive smile than with anything like respectful attention. The error here involved—a gross error redolent of mischief—I cannot pretend to expose within the limits assigned me at present; and with the philosophical it needs no exposure. It may be sufficient here to say that it forms one of an infinite series of mistakes which arise in the path of Reason through her propensity for seeking truth *in detail.*

5

The Purloined Letter

Nil sapientiæ odiosius acumine nimio. [29]

—*Seneca*

At Paris, just after dark one gusty evening in the autumn of 18—, I was enjoying the twofold luxury of meditation and a meerschaum, in company with my friend, C. Auguste Dupin, in his little back library, or book-closet, au troisième, No. 33, Rue Dunôt, Faubourg St. Germain. For one hour at least we had maintained a profound silence; while each, to any casual observer, might have seemed intently and exclusively occupied with the curling eddies of smoke that oppressed the atmosphere of the chamber. For myself, however, I was mentally discussing certain topics which had formed matter for conversation between us at an earlier period of the evening; I mean the affair of the Rue Morgue, and the mystery attending the murder of Marie Rogêt. I looked upon it, therefore, as something of a coincidence, when the door of our apartment was thrown open and admitted our old acquaintance, Monsieur G—, the Prefect of the Parisian police.

We gave him a hearty welcome; for there was nearly half as much of the entertaining as of the contemptible about the man, and we had not seen him for several years. We had been sitting in the dark, and Dupin now arose for the purpose of lighting a lamp, but sat down again, without doing so, upon G—'s saying that he had called to consult us, or rather to ask the opinion of my friend, about some official business which had occasioned a great deal of trouble.

'If it is any point requiring reflection,' observed Dupin, as he forbore to enkindle the wick, 'we shall examine it to better purpose in the dark.'

'That is another of your odd notions,' said the Prefect, who had a fashion of calling everything "odd" that was beyond his comprehension, and thus lived amid an absolute legion of "oddities."

'Very true,' said Dupin, as he supplied his visitor with a pipe, and rolled towards him a comfortable chair.

'And what is the difficulty now?' I asked. 'Nothing more in the assassination way, I hope?'

'Oh no; nothing of that nature. The fact is, the business is *very* simple indeed, and I make no doubt that we can manage it sufficiently well ourselves; but then I thought Dupin would like to hear the details of it, because it is so excessively odd.'

'Simple and odd,' said Dupin.

'Why, yes; and not exactly that either. The fact is, we have all been a good deal puzzled because the affair *is* so simple, and yet baffles us altogether.'

'Perhaps it is the very simplicity of the thing which puts you at fault,' said my friend.

'What nonsense you *do* talk!' replied the Prefect, laughing heartily.

'Perhaps the mystery is a little *too* plain,' said Dupin.

'Oh, good heavens! who ever heard of such an idea?'

'A little *too* self-evident.'

'Ha! ha! ha—ha! ha! ha!—ho! ho! ho!' roared our visitor, profoundly amused, 'oh, Dupin, you will be the death of me yet!'

'And what, after all, *is* the matter on hand?' I asked.

'Why, I will tell you,' replied the Prefect, as he gave a long, steady, and contemplative puff, and settled himself in his chair. 'I will tell you in a few words; but, before I begin, let me caution you that this is an affair demanding the greatest secrecy, and that I should most probably lose the position I now hold, were it known that I confided it to any one.'

'Proceed,' said I.

'Or not,' said Dupin.

'Well, then; I have received personal information, from a very high quarter, that a certain document of the last importance has been purloined from the royal apartments. The individual who purloined it is known; this beyond a doubt; he was seen to take it. It is known, also, that it still remains in his possession.'

'How is this known?' asked Dupin.

'It is clearly inferred,' replied the Prefect, 'from the nature of the document, and from the non-appearance of certain results which would at once arise from its passing *out* of the robber's possession—that is to say, from his employing it as he must design in the end to employ it.'

'Be a little more explicit,' I said.

'Well, I may venture so far as to say that the paper gives its holder a certain power in a certain quarter where such power is immensely valuable.' The Prefect was fond of the cant of diplomacy.

'Still I do not quite understand,' said Dupin.

'No? Well; the disclosure of the document to a third person, who shall be nameless, would bring in question the honour of a personage of most exalted station; and this fact gives the holder of the document an ascendancy over the illustrious personage whose honour and peace are so jeopardised.'

'But this ascendancy,' I interposed, 'would depend upon the robber's knowledge of the loser's knowledge of the robber. Who would dare—'

'The thief,' said G—, 'is the Minister D—, who dares all things, those unbecoming as well as those becoming a man. The method of the theft was not less ingenious than bold. The document in question—a letter, to be frank—had been received by the personage robbed while alone in the royal *boudoir*. During its perusal she was suddenly interrupted by the entrance of the other exalted personage from whom especially it was her wish to conceal it. After a hurried and vain endeavour to thrust it in a drawer, she was forced to place it, open as it was, upon a table. The address, however, was uppermost, and, the contents thus unexposed, the letter escaped notice. At this juncture enters the Minister D—. His lynx eye immediately perceives the paper, recognises the handwriting of the address, observes the confusion of the personage addressed, and fathoms her secret. After some business transactions, hurried through in his ordinary manner, he produces a letter somewhat similar to the one in question, opens it, pretends to read it, and then places it in close juxtaposition to the other. Again he converses, for some fifteen minutes, upon the public affairs. At length, in taking leave, he takes also from the table the letter to which he had no claim. Its rightful owner saw, but, of course, dared not call attention to the act, in the presence of the third personage who stood at her elbow. The minister decamped; leaving his own letter—one of no importance—upon the table.'

'Here, then,' said Dupin to me, 'you have precisely what you demand to make the ascendancy complete—the robber's knowledge of the loser's knowledge of the robber.'

'Yes,' replied the Prefect; 'and the power thus attained has, for some months past, been wielded, for political purposes, to a very dangerous extent. The personage robbed is more thoroughly convinced, every day, of the necessity of reclaiming her letter. But this, of course, cannot be done openly. In fine, driven to despair, she has committed the matter to me.'

'Than whom,' said Dupin, amid a perfect whirlwind of smoke, 'no more sagacious agent could, I suppose, be desired, or even imagined.'

'You flatter me,' replied the Prefect; 'but it is possible that some such opinion may have been entertained.'

'It is clear,' said I, 'as you observe, that the letter is still in possession of the minister; since it is this possession, and not any employment of the letter, which bestows the power. With the employment the power departs.'

'True,' said G—; 'and upon this conviction I proceeded. My first care was to make thorough search of the minister's hotel; and here my chief embarrassment lay in the necessity of searching without his knowledge. Beyond all things, I have been warned of the danger which would result from giving him reason to suspect our design.'

'But,' said I, 'you are quite *au fait* in these investigations. The Parisian police have done this thing often before.'

'O yes; and for this reason I did not despair. The habits of the minister gave me, too, a great advantage. He is frequently absent from home all night. His servants are by no means numerous. They sleep at a distance from their master's apartment, and, being chiefly Neapolitans, are readily made drunk. I have keys, as you know, with which I can open any chamber or cabinet in Paris. For three months a night has not passed, during the greater part of which I have not been engaged, personally, in ransacking the D— Hotel. My honour is interested, and, to mention a great secret, the reward is enormous. So I did not abandon the search until I had become fully satisfied that the thief is a more astute man than myself. I fancy that I have investigated every nook and corner of the premises in which it is possible that the paper can be concealed.'

'But is it not possible,' I suggested, 'that although the letter may be in possession of the minister, as it unquestionably is, he may have concealed it elsewhere than upon his own premises?'

'This is barely possible,' said Dupin. 'The present peculiar condition of affairs at court, and especially of those intrigues in which D— is known to be involved, would render the instant availability of the document—its susceptibility of being produced at a moment's notice—a point of nearly equal importance with its possession.'

'Its susceptibility of being produced?' said I.

'That is to say, of being *destroyed*,' said Dupin.

'True,' I observed; 'the paper is clearly then upon the premises. As for its being upon the person of the minister, we may consider that as out of the question.'

'Entirely,' said the Prefect. 'He has been twice waylaid, as if by footpads, and his person rigorously searched under my own inspection.'

'You might have spared yourself this trouble,' said Dupin. 'D—, I presume, is not altogether a fool, and, if not, must have anticipated these waylayings, as a matter of course.'

'Not *altogether* a fool,' said G—, 'but then he's a poet, which I take to be only one remove from a fool.'

'True,' said Dupin, after a long and thoughtful whiff from his meerschaum, 'although I have been guilty of certain doggerel myself.'

'Suppose you detail,' said I, 'the particulars of your search.'

'Why the fact is, we took our time, and we searched *everywhere*. I have had long experience in these affairs. I took the entire building, room by room; devoting the nights of a whole week to each. We examined, first, the furniture of each apartment. We opened every possible drawer; and I presume you know that, to a properly trained police-agent, such a thing as a "*secret*" drawer is impossible. Any man is a dolt who permits a "secret" drawer to escape him in a search of this kind. The thing is *so* plain. There is a certain amount of bulk—of space—to be accounted for in every cabinet. Then we have accurate rules. The fiftieth part of a line could not escape us. After the cabinets we took the chairs. The cushions we probed with the fine long needles you have seen me employ. From the tables we removed the tops.'

'Why so?'

'Sometimes the top of a table, or other similarly arranged piece of furniture, is removed by the person wishing to conceal an article; then the leg is excavated, the article deposited within the cavity, and the top replaced. The bottoms and tops of bedposts are employed in the same way.'

'But could not the cavity be detected by sounding?' I asked.

'By no means, if, when the article is deposited, a sufficient wadding of cotton be placed around it. Besides, in our case, we were obliged to proceed without noise.'

'But you could not have removed—you could not have taken to pieces *all* articles of furniture in which it would have been possible to make a deposit in the manner you mention. A letter may be compressed into a thin spiral roll, not differing much in shape or bulk from a large knitting-needle, and in this form it might be inserted into the rung of a chair, for example. You did not take to pieces all the chairs?'

'Certainly not; but we did better—we examined the rungs of every chair in the hotel, and, indeed the jointings of every description of furniture, by the aid of a most powerful microscope. Had there been any traces of recent disturbance we should not have failed to detect it instantly. A single grain of gimlet-dust, for example, would have been as obvious as an apple. Any disorder in the gluing—any unusual gaping in the joints—would have sufficed to insure detection.'

'I presume you looked to the mirrors, between the boards and the plates, and you probed the beds and the bedclothes, as well as the curtains and carpets.'

'That of course; and when we had absolutely completed every particle of the furniture in this way, then we examined the house itself. We divided its entire surface into compartments, which we numbered, so that none might be missed; then we scrutinised each individual square inch throughout the premises, including the two houses immediately adjoining, with the microscope, as before.'

'The two houses adjoining!' I exclaimed; 'you must have had a great deal of trouble.'

'We had; but the reward offered is prodigious!'

'You include the *grounds* about the houses?'

'All the grounds are paved with brick. They gave us comparatively little trouble. We examined the moss between the bricks, and found it undisturbed.'

'You looked among D—'s papers, of course, and into the books of the library?'

'Certainly; we opened every package and parcel; we not only opened every book, but we turned over every leaf in each volume, not contenting ourselves with a mere shake, according to the fashion of some of our police officers. We also measured the thickness of every book-*cover*, with the most accurate admeasurement, and applied to each the most jealous scrutiny of the microscope. Had any of the bindings been recently meddled with, it would have been utterly impossible that the fact should have escaped observation. Some five or six volumes, just from the hands of the binder, we carefully probed, longitudinally, with the needles.'

'You explored the floors beneath the carpets?'

'Beyond doubt. We removed every carpet, and examined the boards with the microscope.'

'And the paper on the walls?'

'Yes.'

'You looked into the cellars?'

'We did.'

'Then,' I said, 'you have been making a miscalculation, and the letter is *not* upon the premises, as you suppose.'

'I fear you are right there,' said the Prefect. 'And now, Dupin, what would you advise me to do?'

'To make a thorough search of the premises.'

'That is absolutely needless,' replied G—. 'I am not more sure that I breathe than I am that the letter is not at the hotel.'

'I have no better advice to give you,' said Dupin. 'You have, of course, an accurate description of the letter?'

'Oh yes!'—And here the Prefect, producing a memorandum-book, proceeded to read aloud a minute account of the internal, and especially of the external appearance of the missing document. Soon after finishing the perusal of this description, he took his departure, more entirely depressed in spirits than I had ever known the good gentleman before.

In about a month afterwards he paid us another visit, and found us occupied very nearly as before. He took a pipe and a chair and entered into some ordinary conversation. At length I said:

'Well, but G—, what of the purloined letter? I presume you have at last made up your mind that there is no such thing as overreaching the Minister?'

'Confound him, say I—yes; I made the re-examination, however, as Dupin suggested—but it was all labour lost, as I knew it would be.'

'How much was the reward offered, did you say?' asked Dupin.

'Why, a very great deal—a *very* liberal reward—I don't like to say how much, precisely; but one thing I *will* say, that I wouldn't mind giving my individual check for fifty thousand francs to any one who could obtain me that letter. The fact is, it is becoming of more and more importance every day; and the reward has been lately doubled. If it were trebled, however, I could do no more than I have done.'

'Why, yes,' said Dupin, drawlingly, between the whiffs of his meerschaum, 'I really—think, G—, you have not exerted yourself—to the utmost in this matter. You might—do a little more, I think, eh?'

'How?—in what way?'

'Why—puff, puff—you might—puff, puff—employ counsel in the matter, eh?—puff, puff, puff. Do you remember the story they tell of Abernethy?'

'No; hang Abernethy!'

'To be sure! hang him and welcome. But, once upon a time, a certain rich miser conceived the design of spunging upon this Abernethy for a medical opinion. Getting up, for this purpose, an ordinary conversation in a private company, he insinuated his case to the physician as that of an imaginary individual.'

' "We will suppose," said the miser, "that his symptoms are such and such; now, doctor, what would *you* have directed him to take?" '

' "Take!" said Abernethy, "why, take *advice*, to be sure." '

'But,' said the Prefect, a little discomposed, '*I* am *perfectly* willing to take advice, and to pay for it. I would *really* give fifty thousand francs to any one who would aid me in the matter.'

'In that case,' replied Dupin, opening a drawer, and producing a check-book, 'you may as well fill me up a check for the amount mentioned. When you have signed it, I will hand you the letter.'

I was astounded. The Prefect appeared absolutely thunder-stricken. For some minutes he remained speechless and motionless, looking incredulously at my friend with open mouth, and eyes that seemed starting from their sockets; then, apparently recovering himself in some measure, he seized a pen, and after several pauses and vacant stares, finally filled up and signed a check for fifty thousand francs, and handed it across the table to Dupin. The latter examined it carefully and deposited it in his pocket-book; then, unlocking an *escritoire*, took thence a letter and gave it to the Prefect. This functionary grasped it in a perfect agony of joy, opened it with a trembling hand, cast a rapid glance at its contents, and then, scrambling and struggling to the door, rushed at length unceremoniously from the room and from the house, without having uttered a syllable since Dupin had requested him to fill up the check.

When he had gone, my friend entered into some explanations.

'The Parisian police,' he said, 'are exceedingly able in their way.

They are persevering, ingenious, cunning, and thoroughly versed in the knowledge which their duties seem chiefly to demand. Thus, when G— detailed to us his mode of searching the premises at the Hotel D—, I felt entire confidence in his having made a satisfactory investigation—so far as his labours extended.'

'So far as his labours extended?' said I.

'Yes,' said Dupin. 'The measures adopted were not only the best of their kind, but carried out to absolute perfection. Had the letter been deposited within the range of their search, these fellows would, beyond a question, have found it.'

I merely laughed—but he seemed quite serious in all that he said.

'The measures, then,' he continued, 'were good in their kind, and well executed; their defect lay in their being inapplicable to the case and to the man. A certain set of highly ingenious resources are, with the Prefect, a sort of Procrustean bed, to which he forcibly adapts his designs. But he perpetually errs by being too deep or too shallow for the matter in hand; and many a school-boy is a better reasoner than he. I knew one about eight years of age, whose success at guessing in the game of "even and odd" attracted universal admiration. This game is simple, and is played with marbles. One player holds in his hand a number of these toys, and demands of another whether that number is even or odd. If the guess is right, the guesser wins one; if wrong, he loses one. The boy to whom I allude won all the marbles of the school. Of course he had some principle of guessing; and this lay in mere observation and admeasurement of the astuteness of his opponents. For example, an arrant simpleton is his opponent, and, holding up his closed hand, asks, "Are they even or odd?" Our school-boy replies, "odd," and loses; but upon the second trial he wins, for he then says to himself, "the simpleton had them even upon the first trial, and his amount of cunning is just sufficient to make him have them odd upon the second; I will therefore guess odd";—he guesses odd, and wins. Now, with a simpleton a degree above the first, he would have reasoned thus: "This fellow finds that in the first instance I guessed odd, and, in the second, he will propose to himself, upon the first impulse, a simple variation from even to odd, as did the first simpleton; but then a second thought will suggest that this is too simple a variation, and finally he will decide upon putting it even as before. I will therefore guess even";—he guesses even, and wins. Now this mode of reasoning in the school-boy, whom his fellows termed "lucky,"—what, in its last analysis, is it?'

'It is merely,' I said, 'an identification of the reasoner's intellect with that of his opponent.'

'It is,' said Dupin; 'and, upon inquiring, of the boy by what means he effected the *thorough* identification in which his success consisted, I received answer as follows: "When I wish to find out how wise, or how stupid, or how good, or how wicked is any one, or what are his thoughts at the moment, I fashion the expression of my face, as accurately as possible, in accordance with the expression of his, and then wait to see what thoughts or sentiments arise in my mind or heart, as if to match or correspond with the expression." This response of the school-boy lies at the bottom of all the spurious profundity which has been attributed to Rochefoucault, to La Bougive, to Machiavelli, and to Campanella.'

'And the identification,' I said, 'of the reasoner's intellect with that of his opponent, depends, if I understand you aright, upon the accuracy with which the opponent's intellect is admeasured.'

'For its practical value it depends upon this,' replied Dupin; 'and the Prefect and his cohort fail so frequently, first, by default of this identification, and, secondly, by ill-admeasurement, or rather through non-admeasurement, of the intellect with which they are engaged. They consider only their *own* ideas of ingenuity; and, in searching for anything hidden, advert only to the modes in which *they* would have hidden it. They are right in this much—that their own ingenuity is a faithful representative of that of *the mass*; but when the cunning of the individual felon is diverse in character from their own, the felon foils them, of course. This always happens when it is above their own, and very usually when it is below. They have no variation of principle in their investigations; at best, when urged by some unusual emergency—by some extraordinary reward—they extend or exaggerate their old modes of *practice*, without touching their principles. What, for example, in this case of D——, has been done to vary the principle of action? What is all this boring, and probing, and sounding, and scrutinizing with the microscope, and dividing the surface of the building into registered square inches—what is it all but an exaggeration of *the application* of the one principle or set of principles of search, which are based upon the one set of notions regarding human ingenuity, to which the Prefect, in the long routine of his duty, has been accustomed? Do you not see he has taken it for granted that *all* men proceed to conceal a letter, not exactly in a gimlet hole bored in a chair-leg, but, at least, in *some* out-of-the-way hole or corner suggested by the same tenor of thought which would urge a man to secrete a letter in a gimlet-hole bored in a chair-leg? And do you not see also, that such *recherchés* nooks for concealment are adapted only for ordinary occasions, and would be adopted only by ordinary intellects; for, in all cases of concealment, a disposal of the article concealed—a disposal of it in this *recherché* manner,—is, in the very first instance, presumable and presumed; and thus its discovery depends, not at all upon the acumen, but altogether upon the mere care, patience, and determination of the seekers; and where the case is of importance—or, what amounts to the same thing in the political eyes, when the reward is of magnitude,—the qualities in question have *never* been known to fail. You will now understand what I meant in suggesting that, had the purloined letter been hidden anywhere within the limits of the Prefect's examination—in other words, had the principle of its concealment been comprehended within the principles of the Prefect—its discovery would have been a matter altogether beyond question. This functionary, however, has been thoroughly mystified; and the remote source of his defeat lies in the supposition that the Minister is a fool, because he has acquired renown as a poet. All fools are poets; this the Prefect *feels*; and he is merely guilty of a *non distributio medii* in thence inferring that all poets are fools.'

'But is this really the poet?' I asked. 'There are two brothers, I know; and both have attained reputation in letters. The Minister I believe has written learnedly on the Differential Calculus. He is a mathematician, and no poet.'

'You are mistaken; I know him well; he is both. As poet *and* mathematician, he would reason well; as mere mathematician, he could not have reasoned at all, and thus would have been at the mercy of the Prefect.'

'You surprise me,' I said, 'by these opinions, which have been contradicted by the voice of the world. You do not mean to set at naught the well-digested idea of centuries. The mathematical reason has long been regarded as *the* reason *par excellence*.'

' "*Il y a à parier*," ' replied Dupin, quoting from Chamfort, ' "*que toute idée publique, toute convention reçue, est une sottise, car elle a convenue au plus grand nombre*." The mathematicians, I grant you, have done their best to promulgate the popular error to which you allude, and which is none the less an error for its promulgation as truth. With an art worthy a better cause, for example, they have insinuated the term "analysis" into application to algebra. The French are the originators of this particular deception; but if a term is of any importance—if words derive any value from applicability—then "analysis" conveys "algebra" about as much as, in Latin, "*ambitus*" implies "ambition," "*religio*" "religion," or "*homines honesti*" a set of *honourable* men.'

'You have a quarrel on hand, I see,' said I, 'with some of the algebraists of Paris; but proceed.'

'I dispute the availability, and thus the value, of that reason which is cultivated in any special form other than the abstractly logical. I dispute, in particular, the reason educed by mathematical study. The mathematics are the science of form and quantity; mathematical reasoning is merely logic applied to observation upon form and quantity. The great error lies in supposing that even the truths of what is called *pure* algebra, are abstract or general truths. And this error is so egregious that I am confounded at the universality with which it has been received. Mathematical axioms are *not* axioms of general truth. What is true of *relation*— of form and quantity—is often grossly false in regard to morals, for example. In this latter science it is very usually *un*true that the aggregated parts are equal to the whole. In chemistry also the axiom fails. In the consideration of motive it fails; for two motives, each of a given value, have not, necessarily, a value when united, equal to the sum of their values apart. There are numerous other mathematical truths which are only truths within the limits of *relation*. But the mathematician argues from his *finite truths*, through habit, as if they were of an absolutely general applicability—as the world indeed imagines them to be. Bryant, in his very learned *Mythology*, mentions an analogous source of error, when he says that "although the pagan fables are not believed, yet we forget ourselves continually, and make inferences from them as existing realities." With the algebraists, however, who are pagans themselves, the "pagan fables" *are* believed, and the inferences are made, not so much through lapse of memory as through an unaccountable addling of the brains. In short, I never yet encountered the mere mathematician who could be trusted out of equal roots, or one who did not clandestinely hold it as a point of his faith that $x^2 + px$ was absolutely and unconditionally equal to q. Say to one of these gentlemen, by way of experiment, if you please, that you believe occasions may occur where $x^2 + px$ is not altogether equal to q, and, having made him understand what you mean, get out of his reach as speedily as convenient, for, beyond doubt, he will endeavour to knock you down.

'I mean to say,' continued Dupin, while I merely laughed at his last observations, 'that if the Minister had been no more than a mathematician, the Prefect would have been under no necessity of giving me this check. I know him, however, as both mathematician and poet, and my measures were adapted to his capacity, with reference to the circumstances by which he was surrounded. I knew him as a courtier, too, and as a bold *intriguant*. Such a man, I considered, could not fail to be aware of the ordinary policial modes of action. He could not have failed to anticipate—and events have proved that he did not fail to anticipate—the waylayings to which he was subjected. He must have foreseen, I reflected, the secret investigations of his premises. His frequent absences from home at night, which were hailed by the Prefect as certain aids to his success, I regarded only as *ruses*, to afford opportunity for thorough search to the police, and thus the sooner to impress them with the conviction to which G—, in fact, did finally arrive—the conviction that the letter was not upon the premises. I felt, also, that the whole train of thought, which I was at some pains in detailing to you just now, concerning the invariable principle of political action in searches for articles concealed—I felt that this whole train of thought would necessarily pass through the mind of the Minister. It would imperatively lead him to despise all the ordinary *nooks* of concealment. *He* could not, I reflected, be so weak as not to see that the most intricate and remote recess of his hotel would be as open as his commonest closets to the eyes, to the probes, to the gimlets, and to the microscopes of the Prefect. I saw, in fine, that he would be driven, as a matter of course, to *simplicity*, if not deliberately induced to it as a matter of choice. You will remember, perhaps, how desperately the Prefect laughed when I suggested, upon our first interview, that it was just possible this mystery troubled him so much on account of its being so *very* self-evident.'

'Yes,' said I, 'I remember his merriment well. I really thought he would have fallen into convulsions.'

'The material world,' continued Dupin, 'abounds with very strict analogies to the immaterial; and thus some colour of truth has been given to the rhetorical dogma, that metaphor, or simile, may be made to strengthen an argument as well as to embellish a description. The principle of the *vis inertiæ*[30], for example, seems to be identical in physics and metaphysics. It is not more true in the former, that a large body is with more difficulty set in motion than a smaller one, and that its subsequent *momentum* is commensurate with this difficulty, than it is, in the latter, that intellects of the vaster capacity, while more forcible, more constant, and more eventful in their movements than those of inferior grade, are yet the less readily moved, and more embarrassed, and full of hesitation in the first few steps of their progress. Again: have you ever noticed which of the street signs, over the shop doors, are the most attractive of attention?'

'I have never given the matter a thought,' I said.

'There is a game of puzzles,' he resumed, 'which is played upon a map. One party playing requires another to find a given word—the name of town, river, state or empire—any word, in short, upon the motley and perplexed surface of the chart. A novice in the game generally seeks to embarrass his opponents by giving them the most minutely lettered names; but the adept selects such words as stretch, in large characters, from one end of the chart to the other. These, like the over-largely lettered signs and placards of the street, escape observation by dint of being excessively obvious; and here the physical oversight is precisely analogous with the moral inapprehension by which the intellect suffers to pass unnoticed those considerations which are too obtrusively and too palpably self-evident. But this is a point, it appears, somewhat above or beneath the understanding of the Prefect. He never once thought it probable, or possible, that the Minister had deposited the letter immediately beneath the nose of the whole world, by way of best preventing any portion of that world from perceiving it.

'But the more I reflected upon the daring, dashing, and discriminating ingenuity of D—; upon the fact that the document must always have been *at hand*, if he intended to use it to good purpose; and upon the decisive evidence, obtained by the Prefect, that it was not hidden within the limits of that dignitary's ordinary search—the more satisfied I became that, to conceal this letter, the minister had resorted to the comprehensive and sagacious expedient of not attempting to conceal it at all.

'Full of these ideas, I prepared myself with a pair of green spectacles, and called one fine morning, quite by accident, at the Ministerial hotel. I found D— at home, yawning, lounging, and dawdling, as usual, and pretending to be in the last extremity of *ennui*. He is, perhaps, the most really energetic human being now alive—but that is only when nobody sees him.

'To be even with him, I complained of my weak eyes, and lamented the necessity of the spectacles, under cover of which I cautiously and thoroughly surveyed the whole apartment, while seemingly intent only upon the conversation of my host.

'I paid special attention to a large writing-table near which he sat, and upon which lay confusedly, some miscellaneous letters and other papers, with one or two musical instruments and a few books. Here, however, after a long and very deliberate scrutiny, I saw nothing to excite particular suspicion.

'At length my eyes, in going the circuit of the room, fell upon a trumpery filigree card-rack of pasteboard, that hung dangling by a dirty blue ribbon, from a little brass knob just beneath the middle of the mantel-piece. In this rack, which had three or four compartments, were five or six visiting cards and a solitary letter. This last was much soiled and crumpled. It was torn nearly in two, across the middle—as if a design, in the first instance, to tear it entirely up as worthless, had been altered, or stayed, in the second. It had a large black seal, bearing the D— cipher *very* conspicuously, and was addressed, in a diminutive female hand, to D—, the minister, himself. It was thrust carelessly, and even, as it seemed, contemptuously, into one of the uppermost divisions of the rack.

'No sooner had I glanced at this letter, than I concluded it to be that of which I was in search. To be sure, it was, to all appearance, radically different from the one of which the Prefect had read us so minute a description. Here the seal was large and black, with the D— cipher; there it was small and red, with the ducal arms of the S— family. Here, the address, to the minister, diminutive and feminine; there the superscription, to a certain royal personage, was markedly bold and decided; the size alone formed a point of correspondence. But, then, the *radicalness* of these differences, which was excessive; the dirt; the soiled and torn condition of the paper, so inconsistent with the *true* methodical habits of D—, and so suggestive of a design to delude the beholder into an idea of the worthlessness of the document; these things, together with the hyper-obtrusive situation of this document, full in the view of every visitor, and thus exactly in accordance with the conclusions to which I had previously arrived; these things, I say, were strongly corroborative of suspicion, in one who came with the intention to suspect.

'I protracted my visit as long as possible, and, while I maintained a most animated discussion with the minister, upon a topic which I knew well had never failed to interest and excite him, I kept my attention really riveted upon the letter. In this examination, I committed to memory its external appearance and arrangement in the rack; and also fell, at length, upon a discovery which set at rest whatever trivial doubt I might have entertained. In scrutinizing the edges of the paper, I observed them to be more *chafed* than seemed necessary. They presented the *broken* appearance which is manifested when a stiff paper, having been once folded and pressed with a folder, is refolded in a reversed direction, in the same creases or edges which had formed the original fold. This discovery was sufficient. It was clear to me that the letter had been turned, as a glove, inside out, re-directed, and re-sealed. I bade the minister good morning, and took my departure at once, leaving a gold snuff-box upon the table.

'The next morning I called for the snuff-box, when we resumed, quite eagerly, the conversation of the preceding day. While thus engaged, however, a loud report, as if of a pistol, was heard immediately beneath the windows of the hotel, and was succeeded by a series of fearful screams, and the shoutings of a terrified mob. D— rushed to a casement, threw it open, and looked out. In the meantime, I stepped to the card-rack, took the letter, put it in my pocket, and replaced it by a *fac-simile* (so far as regards externals), which I had carefully prepared at my lodgings—imitating the D— cipher, very readily, by means of a seal formed of bread.

'The disturbance in the street had been occasioned by the frantic behaviour of a man with a musket. He had fired it among a crowd of women and children. It proved, however, to have been without ball, and the fellow was suffered to go his way as a lunatic or a drunkard. When he had gone, D— came from the window, whither I had followed him immediately upon securing the object in view. Soon afterwards I bade him farewell. The pretended lunatic was a man in my own pay.'

'But what purpose had you,' I asked, 'in replacing the letter by a *fac-simile*? Would it not have been better, at the first visit, to have seized it openly, and departed?'

'D—,' replied Dupin, 'is a desperate man, and a man of nerve. His hotel, too, is not without attendants devoted to his interests. Had I made the wild attempt you suggest, I might never have left the Ministerial presence alive. The good people of Paris might have heard of me no more. But I had an object apart from these considerations. You know my political prepossessions. In this matter, I act as a partisan of the lady concerned. For eighteen months the Minister has had her in his power. She has now him in hers—since, being unaware that the letter is not in his possession, he will proceed with his exactions as if it was. Thus will he inevitably commit himself, at once, to his political destruction. His downfall, too, will not be more precipitate than awkward. It is all very well to talk about the *facilis descensus Averni*; but in all kinds of climbing, as Catalani said of singing, it is far more easy to get up than to come down. In the present instance I have no sympathy— at least no pity—for him who descends. He is that *monstrum horrendum*, an unprincipled man of genius. I confess, however, that I should like very well to know the precise character of his thoughts, when, being defied by her whom the Prefect terms "a certain personage," he is reduced to opening the letter which I left for him in the card-rack.'

'How? did you put anything particular in it?'

'Why—it did not seem altogether right to leave the interior blank—that would have been insulting. D—, at Vienna once, did me an evil turn, which I told him, quite good-humouredly, that I should remember. So, as I knew he would feel some curiosity in regard to the identity of the person who had outwitted him, I thought it a pity not to give him a clue. He is well acquainted with my MS., and I just copied into the middle of the blank sheet the words—

"———   —Un dessein si funeste,
S'il n'est digne d'Atrée, est digne de Thyeste."

'They are to be found in Crébillon's *Atrée*.'

6

The Fall of the House of Usher

Son cœur est un luth suspendu; Sitôt qu'on le touche il résonne.[31]

—*De Béranger.*

During the whole of a dull, dark, and soundless day in the autumn of the year, when the clouds hung oppressively low in the heavens, I had been passing alone, on horseback, through a singularly dreary tract of country; and at length found myself, as the shades of the evening drew on, within view of the melancholy House of Usher. I know not how it was—but, with the first glimpse of the building, a sense of insufferable gloom pervaded my spirit. I say insufferable; for the feeling was unrelieved by any of that half-pleasurable, because poetic, sentiment, with which the mind usually receives even the sternest natural images of the desolate or terrible. I looked upon the scene before me—upon the mere house, and the simple landscape features of the domain— upon the bleak walls—upon the vacant eye-like windows—upon a few rank sedges—and upon a few white trunks of decayed trees—with an utter depression of soul which I can compare to no earthly sensation more properly than to the after-dream of the reveller upon opium—the bitter lapse into everyday life—the hideous dropping off of the veil. There was an iciness, a sinking, a sickening of the heart—an unredeemed dreariness of thought which no goading of the imagination could torture into aught of the sublime. What was it—I paused to think—what was it that so unnerved me in the contemplation of the House of Usher? It was a mystery all insoluble; nor could I grapple with the shadowy fancies that crowded upon me as I pondered. I was forced to fall back upon the unsatisfactory conclusion, that while, beyond doubt, there are combinations of very simple natural objects which have the power of thus affecting us, still the analysis of this power lies among considerations beyond our depth. It was possible, I reflected, that a mere different arrangement of the particulars of the scene, of the details of the picture, would be sufficient to modify, or perhaps to annihilate its capacity for sorrowful impression; and, acting upon this idea, I reined my horse to the precipitous brink of a black and lurid tarn that lay in unruffled lustre by the dwelling, and gazed down—but with a shudder even more thrilling than before—upon the remodelled and inverted images of the gray sedge, and the ghastly tree-stems, and the vacant and eye-like windows.

Nevertheless, in this mansion of gloom I now proposed to myself a sojourn of some weeks. Its proprietor, Roderick Usher, had been one of my boon companions in boyhood; but many years had elapsed since our last meeting. A letter, however, had lately reached me in a distant part of the country—a letter from him—which, in its wildly importunate nature, had admitted of no other than a personal reply. The MS. gave evidence of nervous agitation. The writer spoke of acute bodily illness—of a mental disorder which oppressed him—and of an earnest desire to see me, as his best, and indeed his only personal friend, with a view of attempting, by the cheerfulness of my society, some alleviation of his malady. It was the manner in which all this, and much more, was said—it was the apparent heart that went with his request—which allowed me no room for hesitation; and I accordingly obeyed forthwith what I still considered a very singular summons.

Although, as boys, we had been even intimate associates, yet I really knew little of my friend. His reserve had been always excessive and habitual. I was aware, however, that his very ancient family had been noted, time out of mind, for a peculiar sensibility of temperament, displaying itself, through long ages, in many works of exalted art, and manifested, of late, in repeated deeds of munificent yet unobtrusive charity, as well as in a passionate devotion to the intricacies, perhaps even more than to the orthodox and easily recognisable beauties, of musical science. I had learned, too, the very remarkable fact, that the stem of the Usher race, all time-honoured as it was, had put forth, at no period, any enduring branch; in other words, that the entire family lay in the direct line of descent, and had always, with very trifling and very temporary variation, so lain. It was this deficiency, I considered, while running over in thought the perfect keeping of the character of the premises with the accredited character of the people, and while speculating upon the possible influence which the one, in the long lapse of centuries, might have exercised upon the other—it was this deficiency, perhaps, of collateral issue, and the consequent undeviating transmission, from sire to son, of the patrimony with the name, which had, at length, so identified the two as to merge the original title of the estate in the quaint and equivocal appellation of the "House of Usher"—an appellation which seemed to include, in the minds of the peasantry who used it, both the family and the family mansion.

I have said that the sole effect of my somewhat childish experiment—that of looking down within the tarn—had been to deepen the first singular impression. There can be no doubt that the consciousness of the rapid increase of my superstition— for why should I not so term it?—served mainly to accelerate the increase itself. Such, I have long known, is the paradoxical law of all sentiments having terror as a basis. And it might have been for this reason only, that, when I again uplifted my eyes to the house itself, from its image in the pool, there grew in my mind a strange fancy—a fancy so ridiculous, indeed, that I but mention it to show the vivid force of the sensations which oppressed me. I had so worked upon my imagination as really to believe that about the whole mansion and domain there hung an atmosphere peculiar to themselves and their immediate vicinity—an atmosphere which had no affinity with the air of heaven, but which had reeked up from the decayed trees, and the gray wall, and the silent tarn—a pestilent and mystic vapour, dull, sluggish, faintly discernible, and leaden-hued.

Shaking off from my spirit what must have been a dream, I scanned more narrowly the real aspect of the building. Its principal feature seemed to be that of an excessive antiquity. The discolouration of ages had been great. Minute fungi overspread the whole exterior, hanging in a fine tangled web-work from the eaves. Yet all this was apart from any extraordinary dilapidation. No portion of the masonry had fallen; and there appeared to be a wild inconsistency between its still perfect adaptation of parts, and the crumbling condition of the individual stones. In this there was much that reminded me of the specious totality of old wood-work which has rotted for long years in some neglected vault, with no disturbance from the breath of the external air. Beyond this indication of extensive decay, however, the fabric gave little token of instability. Perhaps the eye of a scrutinising observer might have discovered a barely perceptible fissure, which, extending from the roof of the building in front, made its way down the wall in a zigzag direction, until it became lost in the sullen waters of the tarn.

Noticing these things, I rode over a short causeway to the house. A servant in waiting took my horse, and I entered the Gothic archway of the hall. A valet, of stealthy step, thence conducted me, in silence, through many dark and intricate passages in my progress to the studio of his master. Much that I encountered on the way contributed, I know not how, to heighten the vague sentiments of which I have already spoken. While the objects around me—while the carvings of the ceilings, the sombre tapestries of the walls, the ebon blackness of the floors, and the phantasmagoric armorial trophies which rattled as I strode, were but matters to which, or to such as which, I had been accustomed from my infancy—while I hesitated not to acknowledge how familiar was all this—I still wondered to find how unfamiliar were the fancies which ordinary images were stirring up. On one of the staircases, I met the physician of the family. His countenance, I thought, wore a mingled expression of low cunning and perplexity. He accosted me with trepidation and passed on. The valet now threw open a door and ushered me into the presence of his master.

The room in which I found myself was very large and lofty. The windows were long, narrow, and pointed, and at so vast a distance from the black oaken floor as to be altogether inaccessible from within. Feeble gleams of encrimsoned light made their way through the trellised panes, and served to render sufficiently distinct the more prominent objects around the eye, however, struggled in vain to reach the remoter angles of the chamber, or the recesses of the vaulted and fretted ceiling. Dark draperies hung upon the walls. The general furniture was profuse, comfortless, antique, and tattered. Many books and musical instruments lay scattered about, but failed to give any vitality to the scene. I felt that I breathed an atmosphere of sorrow. An air of stern, deep, and irredeemable gloom hung over and pervaded all.

Upon my entrance, Usher arose from a sofa on which he had been lying at full length, and greeted me with a vivacious warmth which had much in it, I at first thought, of an overdone cordiality—of the constrained effort of the ennuyé man of the world. A glance, however, at his countenance, convinced me of his perfect sincerity. We sat down; and for some moments, while he spoke not, I gazed upon him with a feeling half of pity, half of awe. Surely, man had never before so terribly altered, in so brief a period, as had Roderick Usher! It was with difficulty that I could bring myself to admit the identity of the wan being before me with the companion of my early boyhood. Yet the character of his face had been at all times remarkable. A cadaverousness of complexion; an eye large, liquid, and luminous beyond comparison; lips somewhat thin and very pallid, but of a surpassingly beautiful curve; a nose of a delicate Hebrew model, but with a breadth of nostril unusual in similar formations; a finely moulded chin, speaking, in its want of prominence, of a want of moral energy; hair of a more than web-like softness and tenuity; these features, with an inordinate expansion above the regions of the temple, made up altogether a countenance not easily to be forgotten. And now in the mere exaggeration of the prevailing character of these features, and of the expression they were wont to convey, lay so much of change that I doubted to whom I spoke. The now ghastly pallor of the skin, and the now miraculous lustre of the eve, above all things startled and even awed me. The silken hair, too, had been suffered to grow all unheeded, and as, in its wild gossamer texture, it floated rather than fell about the face, I could not, even with effort, connect its Arabesque expression with any idea of simple humanity.

In the manner of my friend I was at once struck with an incoherence—an inconsistency; and I soon found this to arise from a series of feeble and futile struggles to overcome an habitual trepidancy—an excessive nervous agitation. For something of this nature I had indeed been prepared, no less by his letter, than by reminiscences of certain boyish traits, and by conclusions deduced from his peculiar physical conformation and temperament. His action was alternately vivacious and sullen. His voice varied rapidly from a tremulous indecision (when the animal spirits seemed utterly in abeyance) to that species of energetic concision—that abrupt, weighty, unhurried, and hollow-sounding enunciation—that leaden, self-balanced and perfectly modulated guttural utterance, which may be observed in the lost drunkard, or the irreclaimable eater of opium, during the periods of his most intense excitement.

It was thus that he spoke of the object of my visit, of his earnest desire to see me, and of the solace he expected me to afford him. He entered, at some length, into what he conceived to be the nature of his malady. It was, he said, a constitutional and

a family evil, and one for which he despaired to find a remedy—
a mere nervous affection, he immediately added, which would
undoubtedly soon pass off. It displayed itself in a host of unnatural
sensations. Some of these, as he detailed them, interested and
bewildered me; although, perhaps, the terms, and the general
manner of the narration had their weight. He suffered much from
a morbid acuteness of the senses; the most insipid food was alone
endurable; he could wear only garments of certain texture; the
odours of all flowers were oppressive; his eyes were tortured by
even a faint light; and there were but peculiar sounds, and these
from stringed instruments, which did not inspire him with horror.

To an anomalous species of terror I found him a bounden
slave. "I shall perish," said he, "I must perish in this deplorable
folly. Thus, thus, and not otherwise, shall I be lost. I dread the
events of the future, not in themselves, but in their results. I
shudder at the thought of any, even the most trivial, incident,
which may operate upon this intolerable agitation of soul. I have,
indeed, no abhorrence of danger, except in its absolute effect—
in terror. In this unnerved—in this pitiable condition—I feel that
the period will sooner or later arrive when I must abandon life
and reason together, in some struggle with the grim phantasm,
FEAR."

I learned, moreover, at intervals, and through broken and
equivocal hints, another singular feature of his mental condition.
He was enchained by certain superstitious impressions in regard
to the dwelling which he tenanted, and whence, for many years,
he had never ventured forth—in regard to an influence whose
supposititious force was conveyed in terms too shadowy here
to be re-stated—an influence which some peculiarities in the

mere form and substance of his family mansion, had, by dint of long sufferance, he said, obtained over his spirit-an effect which the physique of the gray walls and turrets, and of the dim tarn into which they all looked down, had, at length, brought about upon the morale of his existence.

He admitted, however, although with hesitation, that much of the peculiar gloom which thus afflicted him could be traced to a more natural and far more palpable origin—to the severe and long-continued illness—indeed to the evidently approaching dissolution—of a tenderly beloved sister—his sole companion for long years—his last and only relative on earth. "Her decease," he said, with a bitterness which I can never forget, "would leave him (him the hopeless and the frail) the last of the ancient race of the Ushers." While he spoke, the lady Madeline (for so was she called) passed slowly through a remote portion of the apartment, and, without having noticed my presence, disappeared. I regarded her with an utter astonishment not unmingled with dread—and yet I found it impossible to account for such feelings. A sensation of stupor oppressed me, as my eyes followed her retreating steps. When a door, at length, closed upon her, my glance sought instinctively and eagerly the countenance of the brother—but he had buried his face in his hands, and I could only perceive that a far more than ordinary wanness had overspread the emaciated fingers through which trickled many passionate tears.

The disease of the lady Madeline had long baffled the skill of her physicians. A settled apathy, a gradual wasting away of the person, and frequent although transient affections of a partially cataleptical character, were the unusual diagnosis. Hitherto she had steadily borne up against the pressure of her malady, and had not betaken herself finally to bed; but, on the closing in of the evening of my arrival at the house, she succumbed (as her brother told me at night with inexpressible agitation) to the prostrating power of the destroyer; and I learned that the glimpse I had obtained of her person would thus probably be the last I should obtain—that the lady, at least while living, would be seen by me no more.

For several days ensuing, her name was unmentioned by either Usher or myself: and during this period I was busied in earnest endeavours to alleviate the melancholy of my friend. We painted and read together; or I listened, as if in a dream, to the wild improvisations of his speaking guitar. And thus, as a closer and closer still intimacy admitted me more unreservedly into the recesses of his spirit, the more bitterly did I perceive the futility of all attempt at cheering a mind from which darkness, as if an inherent positive quality, poured forth upon all objects of the moral and physical universe, in one unceasing radiation of gloom.

I shall ever bear about me a memory of the many solemn hours I thus spent alone with the master of the House of Usher. Yet I should fail in any attempt to convey an idea of the exact character of the studies, or of the occupations, in which he involved me, or led me the way. An excited and highly distempered ideality threw a sulphureous lustre over all. His long improvised dirges will ring forever in my ears. Among other things, I hold painfully in mind a certain singular perversion and amplification of the wild air of the last waltz of Von Weber. From the paintings over which his elaborate fancy brooded, and which grew, touch by touch, into vaguenesses at which I shuddered the more thrillingly, because I shuddered knowing not why;—from these paintings (vivid as their images now are before me) I would in vain endeavour to educe more than a small portion which should lie within the compass of merely written words. By the utter simplicity, by the nakedness of his designs, he arrested and overawed attention. If ever mortal painted an idea, that mortal was Roderick Usher. For me at least— in the circumstances then surrounding me—there arose out of the pure abstractions which the hypochondriac contrived to throw upon his canvas, an intensity of intolerable awe, no shadow of which felt I ever yet in the contemplation of the certainly glowing yet too concrete reveries of Fuseli.

One of the phantasmagoric conceptions of my friend, partaking not so rigidly of the spirit of abstraction, may be shadowed forth, although feebly, in words. A small picture presented the interior of an immensely long and rectangular vault or tunnel, with low walls, smooth, white, and without interruption or device. Certain accessory points of the design served well to convey the idea that this excavation lay at an exceeding depth below the surface of the earth. No outlet was observed in any portion of its vast extent, and no torch, or other artificial source of light was discernible; yet a flood of intense rays rolled throughout, and bathed the whole in a ghastly and inappropriate splendour.

I have just spoken of that morbid condition of the auditory nerve which rendered all music intolerable to the sufferer, with the exception of certain effects of stringed instruments. It was, perhaps, the narrow limits to which he thus confined himself upon the guitar, which gave birth, in great measure, to the fantastic character of his performances. But the fervid facility of his impromptus could not be so accounted for. They must have been, and were, in the notes, as well as in the words of his wild fantasias (for he not unfrequently accompanied himself with rhymed verbal improvisations), the result of that intense mental collectedness and concentration to which I have previously alluded as observable only in particular moments of the highest artificial excitement. The words of one of these rhapsodies I have easily remembered. I was, perhaps, the more forcibly impressed with it, as he gave it, because, in the under or mystic current of its meaning, I fancied that I perceived, and for the first time, a full consciousness on the part of Usher, of the tottering of his lofty reason upon her throne. The verses, which were entitled "The Haunted Palace," ran very nearly, if not accurately, thus:

I.

In the greenest of our valleys,
By good angels tenanted,
Once a fair and stately palace—
Radiant palace—reared its head.
In the monarch Thought's dominion—
It stood there!
Never seraph spread a pinion
Over fabric half so fair

II.

Banners yellow, glorious, golden,
On its roof did float and flow;
(This—all this—was in the olden
Time long ago);
And every gentle air that dallied,
In that sweet day,
Along the ramparts plumed and pallid,
A winged odour went away.

III.

Wanderers in that happy valley
Through two luminous windows saw
Spirits moving musically
To a lute›s well-tunèd law;
Round about a throne, where sitting
(Porphyrogene!)
In state his glory well befitting,
The ruler of the realm was seen.

IV.

And all with pearl and ruby glowing
Was the fair palace door,
Through which came flowing, flowing, flowing
And sparkling evermore,
A troop of Echoes whose sweet duty
Was but to sing,
In voices of surpassing beauty,
The wit and wisdom of their king.

V.

But evil things, in robes of sorrow,
Assailed the monarch's high estate;
(Ah, let us mourn, for never morrow
Shall dawn upon him, desolate!)
And, round about his home, the glory
That blushed and bloomed
Is but a dim-remembered story
Of the old time entombed.

VI.

And travellers now within that valley,
Through the red-litten windows see
Vast forms that move fantastically
To a discordant melody;
While, like a rapid ghastly river,
Through the pale door,
A hideous throng rush out forever,
And laugh—but smile no more.

I well remember that suggestions arising from this ballad
led us into a train of thought wherein there became manifest an
opinion of Usher's which I mention not so much on account of
its novelty, (for other men have thought thus,) as on account of
the pertinacity with which he maintained it. This opinion, in its
general form, was that of the sentience of all vegetable things.
But, in his disordered fancy, the idea had assumed a more daring
character, and trespassed, under certain conditions, upon the
kingdom of inorganization. I lack words to express the full extent,
or the earnest abandon of his persuasion. The belief, however, was
connected (as I have previously hinted) with the gray stones of
the home of his forefathers. The conditions of the sentience had
been here, he imagined, fulfilled in the method of collocation of
these stones—in the order of their arrangement, as well as in that
of the many fungi which overspread them, and of the decayed
trees which stood around—above all, in the long undisturbed
endurance of this arrangement, and in its reduplication in the still
waters of the tarn. Its evidence—the evidence of the sentience—
was to be seen, he said, (and I here started as he spoke,) in the

gradual yet certain condensation of an atmosphere of their own about the waters and the walls. The result was discoverable, he added, in that silent, yet importunate and terrible influence which for centuries had moulded the destinies of his family, and which made him what I now saw him—what he was. Such opinions need no comment, and I will make none.

Our books—the books which, for years, had formed no small portion of the mental existence of the invalid—were, as might be supposed, in strict keeping with this character of phantasm. We pored together over such works as the Ververt et Chartreuse of Gresset; the Belphegor of Machiavelli; the Heaven and Hell of Swedenborg; the Subterranean Voyage of Nicholas Klimm by Holberg; the Chiromancy of Robert Flud, of Jean D'Indaginé, and of De la Chambre; the Journey into the Blue Distance of Tieck; and the City of the Sun of Campanella. One favourite volume was a small octavo edition of the Directorium Inquisitorum, by the Dominican Eymeric de Gironne; and there were passages in Pomponius Mela, about the old African Satyrs and Ægipans, over which Usher would sit dreaming for hours. His chief delight, however, was found in the perusal of an exceedingly rare and curious book in quarto Gothic—the manual of a forgotten church—the Vigilae Mortuorum secundum Chorum Ecclesiae Maguntinae.

I could not help thinking of the wild ritual of this work, and of its probable influence upon the hypochondriac, when, one evening, having informed me abruptly that the lady Madeline was no more, he stated his intention of preserving her corpse for a fortnight, (previously to its final interment,) in one of the numerous vaults within the main walls of the building. The worldly reason, however, assigned for this singular proceeding, was one which I did not feel at liberty to dispute. The brother had been led to his resolution (so he told me) by consideration of the unusual character of the malady of the deceased, of certain obtrusive and eager inquiries on the part of her medical men, and of the remote and exposed situation of the burial-ground of the family. I will not deny that when I called to mind the sinister countenance of the person whom I met upon the staircase, on the day of my arrival at the house, I had no desire to oppose what I regarded as at best but a harmless, and by no means an unnatural, precaution.

At the request of Usher, I personally aided him in the arrangements for the temporary entombment. The body having been encoffined, we two alone bore it to its rest. The vault in which we placed it (and which had been so long unopened that our torches, half smothered in its oppressive atmosphere, gave us little opportunity for investigation) was small, damp, and entirely without means of admission for light; lying, at great depth, immediately beneath that portion of the building in which was my own sleeping apartment. It had been used, apparently, in remote feudal times, for the worst purposes of a donjon-keep, and, in later days, as a place of deposit for powder, or some other highly combustible substance, as a portion of its floor, and the whole interior of a long archway through which we reached it, were carefully sheathed with copper. The door, of massive iron, had been, also, similarly protected. Its immense weight caused an unusually sharp grating sound, as it moved upon its hinges.

Having deposited our mournful burden upon tressels within this region of horror, we partially turned aside the yet unscrewed lid of the coffin, and looked upon the face of the tenant. A striking similitude between the brother and sister now first arrested my attention; and Usher, divining, perhaps, my thoughts, murmured out some few words from which I learned that the deceased and himself had been twins, and that sympathies of a scarcely intelligible nature had always existed between them. Our glances, however, rested not long upon the dead—for we could not regard her unawed. The disease which had thus entombed the lady in the maturity of youth, had left, as usual in all maladies of a strictly cataleptical character, the mockery of a faint blush upon the bosom and the face, and that suspiciously lingering smile upon the lip which is so terrible in death. We replaced and screwed down the lid, and, having secured the door of iron, made our way, with toil, into the scarcely less gloomy apartments of the upper portion of the house.

And now, some days of bitter grief having elapsed, an observable change came over the features of the mental disorder of my friend. His ordinary manner had vanished. His ordinary occupations were neglected or forgotten. He roamed from chamber to chamber with hurried, unequal, and objectless step. The pallor of his countenance had assumed, if possible, a more ghastly hue—but the luminousness of his eye had utterly gone out. The once occasional huskiness of his tone was heard no more; and a tremulous quaver, as if of extreme terror, habitually characterised his utterance. There were times, indeed, when I thought his unceasingly agitated mind was labouring with some oppressive secret, to divulge which he struggled for the necessary courage. At times, again, I was obliged to resolve all into the mere inexplicable vagaries of madness, for I beheld him gazing upon vacancy for long hours, in an attitude of the profoundest attention, as if listening to some imaginary sound. It was no wonder that his condition terrified—that it infected me. I felt creeping upon me, by slow yet certain degrees, the wild influences of his own fantastic yet impressive superstitions.

It was, especially, upon retiring to bed late in the night of the seventh or eighth day after the placing of the lady Madeline within the don-jon, that I experienced the full power of such feelings. Sleep came not near my couch—while the hours waned and waned away. I struggled to reason off the nervousness which had dominion over me. I endeavoured to believe that much, if not all of what I felt, was due to the bewildering influence of the gloomy furniture of the room—of the dark and tattered draperies, which, tortured into motion by the breath of a rising tempest, swayed fitfully to and fro upon the walls, and rustled uneasily about the decorations of the bed. But my efforts were fruitless. An irrepressible tremour gradually pervaded my frame; and, at length, there sat upon my very heart an incubus of utterly causeless alarm. Shaking this off with a gasp and a struggle, I uplifted myself upon the pillows, and, peering earnestly within the intense darkness of the chamber, hearkened—I know not why, except that an instinctive spirit prompted me—to certain low and indefinite sounds which came, through the pauses of the storm, at long intervals, I knew not whence. Overpowered by an intense sentiment of horror, unaccountable yet unendurable, I threw on my clothes with haste (for I felt that I should sleep no more during the night), and endeavoured to arouse myself from the pitiable condition into which I had fallen, by pacing rapidly to and fro through the apartment.

I had taken but few turns in this manner, when a light

step on an adjoining staircase arrested my attention. I presently recognised it as that of Usher. In an instant afterward he rapped, with a gentle touch, at my door, and entered, bearing a lamp. His countenance was, as usual, cadaverously wan—but, moreover, there was a species of mad hilarity in his eyes—an evidently restrained hysteria in his whole demeanour. His air appalled me—but anything was preferable to the solitude which I had so long endured, and I even welcomed his presence as a relief.

"And you have not seen it?" he said abruptly, after having stared about him for some moments in silence—"you have not then seen it?—but, stay! you shall." Thus speaking, and having carefully shaded his lamp, he hurried to one of the casements, and threw it freely open to the storm.

The impetuous fury of the entering gust nearly lifted us from our feet. It was, indeed, a tempestuous yet sternly beautiful night, and one wildly singular in its terror and its beauty. A whirlwind had apparently collected its force in our vicinity; for there were frequent and violent alterations in the direction of the wind; and the exceeding density of the clouds (which hung so low as to press upon the turrets of the house) did not prevent our perceiving the lifelike velocity with which they flew careering from all points against each other, without passing away into the distance. I say that even their exceeding density did not prevent our perceiving this—yet we had no glimpse of the moon or stars—nor was there any flashing forth of the lightning. But the under surfaces of the huge masses of agitated vapour, as well as all terrestrial objects immediately around us, were glowing in the unnatural light of a faintly luminous and distinctly visible gaseous exhalation which hung about and enshrouded the mansion.

"You must not—you shall not behold this!" said I, shudderingly, to Usher, as I led him, with a gentle violence, from the window to a seat. "These appearances, which bewilder you, are merely electrical phenomena not uncommon—or it may be that they have their ghastly origin in the rank miasma of the tarn. Let us close this casement;—the air is chilling and dangerous to your frame. Here is one of your favourite romances. I will read, and you shall listen;—and so we will pass away this terrible night together."

The antique volume which I had taken up was the "Mad Trist" of Sir Launcelot Canning; but I had called it a favourite of Usher's more in sad jest than in earnest; for, in truth, there is little in its uncouth and unimaginative prolixity which could have had interest for the lofty and spiritual ideality of my friend. It was, however, the only book immediately at hand; and I indulged a vague hope that the excitement which now agitated the hypochondriac, might find relief (for the history of mental disorder is full of similar anomalies) even in the extremeness of the folly which I should read. Could I have judged, indeed, by the wild over-strained air of vivacity with which he hearkened, or apparently hearkened, to the words of the tale, I might well have congratulated myself upon the success of my design.

I had arrived at that well-known portion of the story where Ethelred, the hero of the Trist, having sought in vain for peaceable admission into the dwelling of the hermit, proceeds to make good an entrance by force. Here, it will be remembered, the words of the narrative run thus:

"And Ethelred, who was by nature of a doughty heart, and who was now mighty withal, on account of the powerfulness of the wine which he had drunken, waited no longer to hold parley with the hermit, who, in sooth, was of an obstinate and maliceful turn, but, feeling the rain upon his shoulders, and fearing the rising of the tempest, uplifted his mace outright, and, with blows, made quickly room in the plankings of the door for his gauntleted hand; and now pulling there-with sturdily, he so cracked, and ripped, and tore all asunder, that the noise of the dry and hollow-sounding wood alarumed and reverberated throughout the forest."

At the termination of this sentence I started, and for a moment, paused; for it appeared to me (although I at once concluded that my excited fancy had deceived me)—it appeared to me that, from some very remote portion of the mansion, there came, indistinctly, to my ears, what might have been, in its exact similarity of character, the echo (but a stifled and dull one certainly) of the very cracking and ripping sound which Sir Launcelot had so particularly described. It was, beyond doubt, the coincidence alone which had arrested my attention; for, amid the rattling of the sashes of the casements, and the ordinary commingled noises of the still increasing storm, the sound, in itself, had nothing, surely, which should have interested or disturbed me. I continued the story:

"But the good champion Ethelred, now entering within the door, was sore enraged and amazed to perceive no signal of the maliceful hermit; but, in the stead thereof, a dragon of a scaly and prodigious demeanour, and of a fiery tongue, which sate in guard before a palace of gold, with a floor of silver; and upon the wall there hung a shield of shining brass with this legend enwritten—

Who entereth herein, a conqueror hath bin;
Who slayeth the dragon, the shield he shall win.

And Ethelred uplifted his mace, and struck upon the head of the dragon, which fell before him, and gave up his pesty breath, with a shriek so horrid and harsh, and withal so piercing, that Ethelred had fain to close his ears with his hands against the dreadful noise of it, the like whereof was never before heard."

Here again I paused abruptly, and now with a feeling of wild amazement—for there could be no doubt whatever that, in this instance, I did actually hear (although from what direction it proceeded I found it impossible to say) a low and apparently distant, but harsh, protracted, and most unusual screaming or grating sound—the exact counterpart of what my fancy had already conjured up for the dragon's unnatural shriek as described by the romancer.

Oppressed, as I certainly was, upon the occurrence of the second and most extraordinary coincidence, by a thousand conflicting sensations, in which wonder and extreme terror were predominant, I still retained sufficient presence of mind to avoid exciting, by any observation, the sensitive nervousness of my companion. I was by no means certain that he had noticed the sounds in question; although, assuredly, a strange alteration had, during the last few minutes, taken place in his demeanour. From a position fronting my own, he had gradually brought round his chair, so as to sit with his face to the door of the chamber; and thus I could but partially perceive his features, although I saw that his lips trembled as if he were murmuring inaudibly. His head had dropped upon his breast—yet I knew that he was not asleep, from the wide and rigid opening of the eye as I caught a glance of it in profile. The motion of his body, too, was at variance with this idea—for he rocked from side to side with a gentle yet constant and uniform sway. Having rapidly taken notice of all this, I resumed the narrative of Sir Launcelot, which thus proceeded:

"And now, the champion, having escaped from the terrible fury of the dragon, bethinking himself of the brazen shield, and of the breaking up of the enchantment which was upon it, removed the carcass from out of the way before him, and approached valorously over the silver pavement of the castle to where the shield was upon the wall; which in sooth tarried not for his full coming, but fell down at his feet upon the silver floor, with a mighty great and terrible ringing sound."

No sooner had these syllables passed my lips, than—as if a shield of brass had indeed, at the moment, fallen heavily upon a floor of silver became aware of a distinct, hollow, metallic, and clangorous, yet apparently muffled reverberation. Completely unnerved, I leaped to my feet; but the measured rocking movement of Usher was undisturbed. I rushed to the chair in which he sat. His eyes were bent fixedly before him, and throughout his whole countenance there reigned a stony rigidity. But, as I placed my hand upon his shoulder, there came a strong shudder over his whole person; a sickly smile quivered about his lips; and I saw that he spoke in a low, hurried, and gibbering murmur, as if unconscious of my presence. Bending closely over him, I at length drank in the hideous import of his words.

"Not hear it?—yes, I hear it, and have heard it. Long—long—long—many minutes, many hours, many days, have I heard it—yet I dared not—oh, pity me, miserable wretch that I am!—I dared not—I dared not speak! We have put her living in the tomb! Said I not that my senses were acute? I now tell you that I heard her first feeble movements in the hollow coffin. I heard them—many, many days ago—yet I dared not—I dared not speak! And now—to-night—Ethelred—ha! ha!—the breaking of the hermit's door, and the death-cry of the dragon, and the clangour of the shield!—say, rather, the rending of her coffin, and the grating of the iron hinges of her prison, and her struggles within the coppered archway of the vault! Oh whither shall I fly? Will she not be here anon? Is she not hurrying to upbraid me for my haste? Have I not heard her footstep on the stair? Do I not distinguish that heavy and horrible beating of her heart? Madman!" here he sprang furiously to his feet, and shrieked out his syllables, as if in the effort he were giving up his soul—"Madman! I tell you that she now stands without the door!"

As if in the superhuman energy of his utterance there had

been found the potency of a spell—the huge antique panels to which the speaker pointed, threw slowly back, upon the instant, ponderous and ebony jaws. It was the work of the rushing gust—but then without those doors there did stand the lofty and enshrouded figure of the lady Madeline of Usher. There was blood upon her white robes, and the evidence of some bitter struggle upon every portion of her emaciated frame. For a moment she remained trembling and reeling to and fro upon the threshold, then, with a low moaning cry, fell heavily inward upon the person of her brother, and in her violent and now final death-agonies, bore him to the floor a corpse, and a victim to the terrors he had anticipated.

From that chamber, and from that mansion, I fled aghast. The storm was still abroad in all its wrath as I found myself crossing the old causeway. Suddenly there shot along the path a wild light, and I turned to see whence a gleam so unusual could we have issued; for the vast house and its shadows were alone behind me. The radiance was that of the full, setting, and blood-red moon which now shone vividly through that once barely-discernible fissure of which I have before spoken as extending from the roof of the building, in a zigzag direction, to the base. While I gazed, this fissure rapidly widened—there came a fierce breath of the whirlwind—the entire orb of the satellite burst at once upon my sight—my brain reeled as I saw the mighty walls rushing asunder—there was a long tumultuous shouting sound like the voice of a thousand waters—and the deep and dank tarn at my feet closed sullenly and silently over the fragments of the "HOUSE OF USHER."

7
The Masque of the Red Death

The "Red Death" had long devastated the country. No pestilence had ever been so fatal, or so hideous. Blood was its Avatar and its seal—the redness and the horror of blood. There were sharp pains, and sudden dizziness, and then profuse bleeding at the pores, with dissolution. The scarlet stains upon the body and especially upon the face of the victim, were the pest ban which shut him out from the aid and from the sympathy of his fellow-men. And the whole seizure, progress, and termination of the disease, were the incidents of half an hour.

But the Prince Prospero was happy and dauntless and sagacious. When his dominions were half depopulated, he summoned to his presence a thousand hale and light-hearted friends from among the knights and dames of his court, and with these retired to the deep seclusion of one of his castellated abbeys. This was an extensive and magnificent structure, the creation of the prince's own eccentric yet august taste. A strong and lofty wall girdled it in. This wall had gates of iron. The courtiers, having entered, brought furnaces and massy hammers and welded the bolts. They resolved to leave means neither of ingress or egress to the sudden impulses of despair or of frenzy from within. The abbey was amply provisioned. With such precautions the courtiers might bid defiance to contagion. The external world could take care of itself. In the meantime it was folly to grieve, or to think. The prince had provided all the appliances of pleasure. There were buffoons, there were improvisatori, there were ballet-dancers, there were musicians, there was Beauty, there was wine. All these and security were within. Without was the 'Red Death.'

It was toward the close of the fifth or sixth month of his seclusion, and while the pestilence raged most furiously abroad, that the Prince Prospero entertained his thousand friends at a masked ball of the most unusual magnificence.

It was a voluptuous scene, that masquerade. But first let me tell of the rooms in which it was held. There were seven—an imperial suite. In many palaces, however, such suites form a long and straight vista, while the folding doors slide back nearly to the walls on either hand, so that the view of the whole extent is scarcely impeded. Here the case was very different; as might have been expected from the duke's love of the *bizarre*. The apartments were so irregularly disposed that the vision embraced but little more than one at a time. There was a sharp turn at every twenty or thirty yards, and at each turn a novel effect. To the right and left, in the middle of each wall, a tall and narrow Gothic window looked out upon a closed corridor which pursued the windings of the suite. These windows were of stained glass whose colour varied in accordance with the prevailing hue of the decorations of the chamber into which it opened. That at the eastern extremity was hung, for example, in blue—and vividly blue were its windows. The second chamber was purple in its ornaments and tapestries, and here the panes were purple. The third was green throughout, and so were the casements. The fourth was furnished and lighted with orange—the fifth with white—the sixth with violet. The seventh apartment was closely shrouded in black velvet tapestries that hung all over the ceiling and down the walls, falling in heavy folds upon a carpet of the same material and hue. But in this chamber only, the colour of the windows failed to correspond with the decorations.

The panes here were scarlet—a deep blood colour. Now in no one of the seven apartments was there any lamp or candelabrum, amid the profusion of golden ornaments that lay scattered to and fro or depended from the roof. There was no light of any kind emanating from lamp or candle within the suite of chambers. But in the corridors that followed the suite, there stood, opposite to each window, a heavy tripod, bearing a brazier of fire that projected its rays through the tinted glass and so glaringly illumined the room. And thus were produced a multitude of gaudy and fantastic appearances. But in the western or black chamber the effect of the fire-light that streamed upon the dark hangings through the blood-tinted panes was ghastly in the extreme, and produced so wild a look upon the countenances of those who entered, that there were few of the company bold enough to set foot within its precincts at all.

It was in this apartment, also, that there stood against the western wall, a gigantic clock of ebony. Its pendulum swung to and fro with a dull, heavy, monotonous clang; and when the minute-hand made the circuit of the face, and the hour was to be stricken, there came from the brazen lungs of the clock a sound which was clear and loud and deep and exceedingly musical, but of so peculiar a note and emphasis that, at each lapse of an hour, the musicians of the orchestra were constrained to pause, momentarily, in their performance, to hearken to the sound; and thus the waltzers perforce ceased their evolutions; and there was a brief disconcert of the whole gay company; and, while the chimes of the clock yet rang, it was observed that the giddiest grew pale, and the more aged and sedate passed their hands over their brows as if in confused reverie or meditation. But when the echoes had fully ceased, a light laughter at once pervaded the assembly; the musicians looked at each other and smiled as if at their own nervousness and folly, and made whispering vows, each to the other, that the next chiming of the clock should produce in them no similar emotion; and then, after the lapse of sixty minutes (which embrace three thousand and six hundred seconds of the Time that flies), there came yet another chiming of the clock, and then were the same disconcert and tremulousness and meditation as before.

But, in spite of these things, it was a gay and magnificent revel. The tastes of the duke were peculiar. He had a fine eye for colours and effects. He disregarded the *decora* of mere fashion. His plans were bold and fiery, and his conceptions glowed with barbaric lustre. There are some who would have thought him mad. His followers felt that he was not. It was necessary to hear and see and touch him to be *sure* that he was not.

He had directed, in great part, the moveable embellishments of the seven chambers, upon occasion of this great *fête*; and it was his own guiding taste which had given character to the masqueraders. Be sure they were grotesque. There were much glare and glitter and piquancy and phantasm—much of what has been since seen in 'Hernani.' There were arabesque figures with unsuited limbs and appointments. There were delirious fancies such as the madman fashions. There was much of the beautiful, much of the wanton, much of the *bizarre*, something of the terrible, and not a little of that which might have excited disgust. To and fro in the seven chambers there stalked, in fact, a multitude of dreams. And these— the dreams—writhed in and about, taking hue from the rooms, and causing the wild music of the orchestra to seem as the echo of their steps. And, anon, there strikes the ebony clock which stands in the hall of the velvet. And then, for a moment, all is still, and all is silent save the voice of the clock. The dreams are stiff-frozen as they stand. But the echoes of the chime die away—they have endured but an instant—and a light, half-subdued laughter floats after them as they depart. And now again the music swells, and the dreams live, and writhe to and fro more merrily than ever, taking hue from the many-tinted windows through which stream the rays from the tripods. But to the chamber which lies most westwardly of the seven there are now none of the maskers who venture; for the night is waning away; and there flows a ruddier light through the blood-coloured panes; and the blackness of the sable drapery appals; and to him whose foot falls upon the sable carpet, there comes from the near clock of ebony a muffled peal more solemnly emphatic than any which reaches *their* ears who indulge in the more remote gaieties of the other apartments.

But these other apartments were densely crowded, and in them beat feverishly the heart of life. And the revel went whirlingly on, until at length there commenced the sounding of midnight upon the clock. And then the music ceased, as I have told; and the evolutions of the waltzers were quieted; and there was an uneasy cessation of all things as before. But now there were twelve strokes to be sounded by the bell of the clock; and thus it happened, perhaps, that more of thought crept, with more of time, into the meditations of the thoughtful among those who revelled. And thus too, it happened, perhaps, that before the last echoes of the last chime had utterly sunk into silence, there were many individuals in the crowd who had found leisure to become aware of the presence of a masked figure which had arrested the attention of no single individual before. And the rumour of this new presence having spread itself whisperingly around, there arose at length from the whole company a buzz, or murmur, expressive of disapprobation and surprise—then, finally, of terror, of horror, and of disgust.

In an assembly of phantasms such as I have painted, it may well be supposed that no ordinary appearance could have excited such sensation. In truth the masquerade license of the night was nearly unlimited; but the figure in question had out-Heroded Herod, and gone beyond the bounds of even the prince's indefinite decorum. There are chords in the hearts of the most reckless which cannot be touched without emotion. Even with the utterly lost, to whom life and death are equally jests, there are matters of which no jest can be made. The whole company, indeed, seemed now deeply to feel that in the costume and bearing of the stranger neither wit nor propriety existed. The figure was tall and gaunt, and shrouded from head to foot in the habiliments of the grave. The mask which concealed the visage was made so nearly to resemble the countenance of a stiffened corpse that the closest scrutiny must have had difficulty in detecting the cheat. And yet all this might have been endured, if not approved, by the mad revellers around. But the mummer had gone so far as to assume the type of the Red Death. His vesture was dabbled in *blood*—and his broad brow, with all the features of the face, was besprinkled with the scarlet horror.

When the eyes of Prince Prospero fell upon this spectral image (which with a slow and solemn movement, as if more fully to sustain its *rôle*, stalked to and fro among the waltzers) he was seen to be convulsed, in the first moment with a strong shudder either of terror or distaste; but, in the next, his brow reddened with rage.

'Who dares?'—he demanded hoarsely of the courtiers who stood near him—'who dares insult us with this blasphemous mockery? Seize him and unmask him—that we may know whom we have to hang at sunrise, from the battlements!'

It was in the eastern or blue chamber in which stood the Prince Prospero as he uttered these words. They rang throughout the seven rooms loudly and clearly—for the prince was a bold and robust man, and the music had become hushed at the waving of his hand.

It was in the blue room where stood the prince, with a group of pale courtiers by his side. At first, as he spoke, there was a slight rushing movement of this group in the direction of the intruder, who at the moment was also near at hand, and now, with deliberate and stately step, made closer approach to the speaker. But from a certain nameless awe with which the mad assumptions of the mummer had inspired the whole party, there were found none who put forth hand to seize him; so that, unimpeded, he passed within a yard of the prince's person; and, while the vast assembly, as if with one impulse, shrank from the centres of the rooms to the walls, he made his way uninterruptedly, but with the same solemn and measured step which had distinguished him from the first, through the blue chamber to the purple—through the purple to the green—through the green to the orange—through this again to the white—and even thence to the violet, ere a decided movement had been made to arrest him. It was then, however, that the Prince Prospero, maddening with rage and the shame of his own momentary cowardice, rushed hurriedly through the six chambers, while none followed him on account of a deadly terror that had seized upon all. He bore aloft a drawn dagger, and had approached, in rapid impetuosity, to within three or four feet of the retreating figure, when the latter, having attained the extremity of the velvet apartment, turned suddenly and confronted his pursuer. There was a sharp cry—and the dagger dropped gleaming upon the sable carpet, upon which, instantly afterwards, fell prostrate in death the Prince Prospero. Then, summoning the wild courage of despair, a throng of the revellers at once threw themselves into the black apartment, and, seizing the mummer, whose tall figure stood erect and motionless within the shadow of the ebony clock, gasped in unutterable horror at finding the grave cerements and corpse-like mask, which they handled with so violent a rudeness, untenanted by any tangible form.

And now was acknowledged the presence of the Red Death. He had come like a thief in the night. And one by one dropped the revellers in the blood-bedewed halls of their revel, and died each in the despairing posture of his fall. And the life of the ebony clock went out with that of the last of the gay. And the flames of the tripods expired. And Darkness and Decay and the Red Death held illimitable dominion over all.

8

The Premature Burial

There are certain themes of which the interest is all-absorbing, but which are too entirely horrible for the purposes of legitimate fiction. These the mere romanticist must eschew, if he do not wish to offend, or to disgust. They are with propriety handled only when the severity and majesty of truth sanctify and sustain them. We thrill, for example, with the most intense of "pleasurable pain" over the accounts of the Passage of the Beresina, of the Earthquake at Lisbon, of the Plague at London, of the Massacre of St. Bartholomew, or of the stifling of the hundred and twenty-three prisoners in the Black Hole at Calcutta. But, in these accounts, it is the fact—it is the reality—it is the history which excites. As inventions, we should regard them with simple abhorrence.

I have mentioned some few of the more prominent and august calamities on record; but in these it is the extent, not less than the character of the calamity, which so vividly impresses the fancy. I need not remind the reader that, from the long and weird catalogue of human miseries, I might have selected many individual instances more replete with essential suffering than any of these vast generalities of disaster. The true wretchedness, indeed,—the ultimate woe,—is particular, not diffuse. That the ghastly extremes of agony are endured by man the unit, and never by man the mass—for this let us thank a merciful God!

To be buried while alive is, beyond question, the most terrific of these extremes which has ever fallen to the lot of mere mortality. That it has frequently, very frequently, so fallen will scarcely be denied by those who think. The boundaries which divide Life from Death are at best shadowy and vague. Who shall say where the one ends, and where the other begins? We know that there are diseases in which occur total cessations of all the apparent functions of vitality, and yet in which these cessations are merely suspensions, properly so called. They are only temporary pauses in the incomprehensible mechanism. A certain period elapses, and some unseen mysterious principle again sets in motion the magic pinions and the wizard wheels. The silver cord was not for ever loosed, nor the golden bowl irreparably broken. But where, meantime, was the soul?

Apart, however, from the inevitable conclusion, *a priori* that such causes must produce such effects,—that the well-known occurrence of such cases of suspended animation must naturally give rise, now and then, to premature interments,—apart from this consideration, we have the direct testimony of medical and ordinary experience to prove that a vast number of such interments have actually taken place. I might refer at once, if necessary, to a hundred well-authenticated instances. One of very remarkable character, and of which the circumstances may be fresh in the memory of some of my readers, occurred, not very long ago, in the neighbouring city of Baltimore, where it occasioned a painful, intense, and widely-extended excitement. The wife of one of the most respectable citizens—a lawyer of eminence and a member of Congress—was seized with a sudden and unaccountable illness, which completely baffled the skill of her physicians. After much suffering she died, or was supposed to die. No one suspected, indeed, or had reason to suspect, that she was not actually dead. She presented all the ordinary appearances of death. The face assumed the usual pinched and sunken outline. The lips were of the usual marble pallor. The eyes were lustreless. There was no warmth. Pulsation had ceased. For three days the body was preserved unburied, during which it had acquired a stony rigidity. The funeral, in short, was hastened, on account of the rapid advance of what was supposed to be decomposition.

The lady was deposited in her family vault, which, for three subsequent years, was undisturbed. At the expiration of this term it was opened for the reception of a sarcophagus;—but, alas! how fearful a shock awaited the husband, who, personally, threw open the door! As its portals swung outwardly back, some white-apparelled object fell rattling within his arms. It was the skeleton of his wife in her yet unmoulded shroud.

A careful investigation rendered it evident that she had revived within two days after her entombment; that her struggles within the coffin had caused it to fall from a ledge, or shelf, to the floor, where it was so broken as to permit her escape. A lamp which had been accidentally left, full of oil, within the tomb, was found empty; it might have been exhausted, however, by evaporation. On the uppermost of the steps which led down into the dread chamber was a large fragment of the coffin, with which, it seemed that she had endeavoured to arrest attention by striking the iron door. While thus occupied, she probably swooned, or possibly died, through sheer terror; and, in failing, her shroud became entangled in some iron-work which projected interiorly. Thus she remained, and thus she rotted, erect.

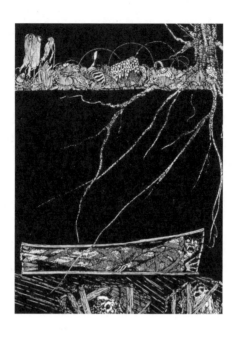

In the year 1810, a case of living inhumation happened in France, attended with circumstances which go far to warrant the assertion that truth is, indeed, stranger than fiction. The heroine of the story was a Mademoiselle Victorine Lafourcade, a young girl of illustrious family, of wealth, and of great personal beauty. Among her numerous suitors was Julien Bossuet, a poor *litterateur*, or journalist of Paris. His talents and general amiability had recommended him to the notice of the heiress, by whom he seems to have been truly beloved; but her pride of birth decided her, finally, to reject him, and to wed a Monsieur Renelle, a banker and a diplomatist of some eminence. After marriage, however, this gentleman neglected, and, perhaps, even more positively ill-treated her. Having passed with him some wretched years, she died— at least her condition so closely resembled death as to deceive every one who saw her. She was buried—not in a vault, but in an ordinary grave in the village of her nativity. Filled with despair, and still inflamed by the memory of a profound attachment, the lover journeys from the capital to the remote province in which the village lies, with the romantic purpose of disinterring the corpse, and possessing himself of its luxuriant tresses. He reaches the grave. At midnight he unearths the coffin, opens it, and is in the act of detaching the hair, when he is arrested by the unclosing of the beloved eyes. In fact, the lady had been buried alive. Vitality had not altogether departed, and she was aroused by the caresses of her lover from the lethargy which had been mistaken for death. He bore her frantically to his lodgings in the village. He employed certain powerful restoratives suggested by no little medical learning. In fine, she revived. She recognised her preserver. She remained with him until, by slow degrees, she fully recovered her original health. Her woman's heart was not adamant, and this last lesson of love sufficed to soften it. She bestowed it upon Bossuet. She returned no more to her husband, but, concealing from him her resurrection, fled with her lover to America. Twenty years afterward, the two returned to France, in the persuasion that time had so greatly altered the lady's appearance that her friends would be unable to recognise her. They were mistaken, however, for, at the first meeting, Monsieur Renelle did actually recognise and make claim to his wife. This claim she resisted, and a judicial tribunal sustained her in her resistance, deciding that the peculiar circumstances, with the long lapse of years, had extinguished, not only equitably, but legally, the authority of the husband.

The *Chirurgical Journal* of Leipsic—a periodical of high

authority and merit, which some American bookseller would do well to translate and republish, records in a late number a very distressing event of the character in question.

An officer of artillery, a man of gigantic stature and of robust health, being thrown from an unmanageable horse, received a very severe contusion upon the head, which rendered him insensible at once; the skull was slightly fractured, but no immediate danger was apprehended. Trepanning was accomplished successfully. He was bled, and many other of the ordinary means of relief were adopted. Gradually, however, he fell into a more and more hopeless state of stupor, and, finally, it was thought that he died.

The weather was warm, and he was buried with indecent haste in one of the public cemeteries. His funeral took place on Thursday. On the Sunday following, the grounds of the cemetery were, as usual, much thronged with visitors, and about noon an intense excitement was created by the declaration of a peasant that, while sitting upon the grave of the officer, he had distinctly felt a commotion of the earth, as if occasioned by some one struggling beneath. At first little attention was paid to the man's asseveration; but his evident terror, and the dogged obstinacy with which he persisted in his story, had at length their natural effect upon the crowd. Spades were hurriedly procured, and the grave, which was shamefully shallow, was in a few minutes so far thrown open that the head of its occupant appeared. He was then seemingly dead; but he sat nearly erect within his coffin, the lid of which, in his furious struggles, he had partially uplifted.

He was forthwith conveyed to the nearest hospital, and there pronounced to be still living, although in an asphytic condition. After some hours he revived, recognised individuals of his acquaintance, and, in broken sentences spoke of his agonies in the grave.

From what he related, it was clear that he must have been conscious of life for more than an hour, while inhumed, before lapsing into insensibility. The grave was carelessly and loosely filled with an exceedingly porous soil; and thus some air was necessarily admitted. He heard the footsteps of the crowd overhead, and endeavoured to make himself heard in turn. It was the tumult within the grounds of the cemetery, he said, which appeared to awaken him from a deep sleep, but no sooner was he awake than he became fully aware of the awful,horrors of his position.

This patient, it is recorded, was doing well, and seemed to be in a fair way of ultimate recovery, but fell a victim to the quackeries of medical experiment. The galvanic battery was applied, and he suddenly expired in one of those ecstatic paroxysms which, occasionally, it superinduces.

The mention of the galvanic battery, nevertheless, recalls to my memory a well-known and very extraordinary case in point, where its action proved the means of restoring to animation a young attorney of London, who had been interred for two days. This occurred in 1831, and created, at the time, a very profound sensation wherever it was made the subject of converse.

The patient, Mr. Edward Stapleton, had died, apparently of typhus fever, accompanied with some anomalous symptoms which had excited the curiosity of his medical attendants. Upon his seeming decease, his friends were requested to sanction a *post-mortem* examination, but declined to permit it. As often happens, when such refusals are made, the practitioners resolved to disinter the body and dissect it at leisure, in private. Arrangements were easily effected with some of the numerous corps of body-snatchers with which London abounds; and, upon the third night after the funeral, the supposed corpse was unearthed from a grave eight feet deep, and deposited in the opening chamber of one of the private hospitals.

An incision of some extent had been actually made in the abdomen, when the fresh and undecayed appearance of the subject suggested an application of the battery. One experiment succeeded another, and the customary effects supervened, with nothing to characterise them in any respect, except, upon one or two occasions, a more than ordinary degree of life-likeness in the convulsive action.

It grew late. The day was about to dawn; and it was thought expedient, at length, to proceed at once to the dissection. A student, however, was especially desirous of testing a theory of his own, and insisted upon applying the battery to one of the pectoral muscles. A rough gash was made, and a wire hastily brought in contact, when the patient, with a hurried but quite unconvulsive movement, arose from the table, stepped into the middle of the floor, gazed about him uneasily for a few seconds, and then— spoke. What he said was unintelligible; but words were uttered; the syllabification was distinct. Having spoken, he fell heavily to the floor.

For some moments all were paralysed with awe—but the urgency of the case soon restored them their presence of mind. It was seen that Mr. Stapleton was alive, although in a swoon. Upon exhibition of ether he revived and was rapidly restored to health, and to the society of his friends—from whom, however, all knowledge of his resuscitation was withheld, until a relapse was no longer to be apprehended. Their wonder—their rapturous astonishment—may be conceived.

The most thrilling peculiarity of this incident, nevertheless, is involved in what Mr. S. himself asserts. He declares that at no period was he altogether insensible—that, dully and confusedly, he was aware of everything which happened to him, from the moment in which he was pronounced *dead* by his physicians, to that in which he fell swooning to the floor of the hospital. 'I am alive,' were the uncomprehended words which, upon recognizing the locality of the dissecting-room, he had endeavoured, in his extremity, to utter.

It were an easy matter to multiply such histories as these— but I forbear—for, indeed, we have no need of such to establish the fact that premature interments occur. When we reflect how very rarely, from the nature of the case, we have it in our power to detect them, we must admit that they may *frequently* occur without our cognizance. Scarcely, in truth, is a graveyard ever encroached upon, for any purpose, to any great extent, that skeletons are not found in postures which suggest the most fearful of suspicions.

Fearful indeed the suspicion—but more fearful the doom! It may be asserted, without hesitation, that *no* event is so terribly well adapted to inspire the supremeness of bodily and of mental distress, as is burial before death. The unendurable oppression of the lungs—the stifling fumes from the damp earth—the clinging to the death garments—the rigid embrace of the narrow house— the blackness of the absolute Night—the silence like a sea that overwhelms—the unseen but palpable presence of the Conqueror Worm—these things, with the thoughts of the air and grass above, with memory of dear friends who would fly to save us if but informed of our fate, and with consciousness that of this fate they can *never* be informed—that our hopeless portion is that of the really dead—these considerations, I say, carry into the heart, which still palpitates, a degree of appalling and intolerable horror from which the most daring imagination must recoil. We know of nothing so agonizing upon Earth—we can dream of nothing half so hideous in the realms of the nethermost Hell. And thus all narratives upon this topic have an interest profound; an interest, nevertheless, which, through the sacred awe of the topic itself, very properly and very peculiarly depends upon our conviction of the *truth* of the matter narrated. What I have now to tell is of my own actual knowledge—of my own positive and personal experience.

For several years I had been subject to attacks of the singular disorder which physicians have agreed to term catalepsy, in default of a more definitive title. Although both the immediate and the predisposing causes, and even the actual diagnosis, of this disease are still mysterious, its obvious and apparent character is sufficiently well understood. Its variations seem to be chiefly of degree. Sometimes the patient lies, for a day only, or even for a shorter period, in a species of exaggerated lethargy. He is senseless and externally motionless; but the pulsation of the heart is still faintly perceptible; some traces of warmth remain; a slight colour lingers within the centre of the cheek; and, upon application of a mirror to the lips, we can detect a torpid, unequal, and vacillating action of the lungs. Then again the duration of the trance is for weeks—even for months; while the closest scrutiny, and the most rigorous medical tests, fail to establish any material distinction between the state of the sufferer and what we conceive of absolute death. Very usually he is saved from premature interment solely by the knowledge of his friends that he has been previously subject to catalepsy, by the consequent suspicion excited, and, above all, by the non-appearance of decay. The advances of the malady are, luckily, gradual. The first manifestations, although marked, are unequivocal. The fits grow successively more and more distinctive, and endure each for a longer term than the preceding. In this lies the principal security from inhumation. The unfortunate whose *first* attack should be of the extreme character which is occasionally seen, would almost inevitably be consigned alive to the tomb.

My own case differed in no important particular from those mentioned in medical books. Sometimes, without any apparent cause, I sank, little by little, into a condition of semi-syncope, or half swoon; and, in this condition, without pain, without ability to stir, or, strictly speaking, to think, but with a dull lethargic consciousness of life and of the presence of those who surrounded my bed, I remained, until the crisis of the disease restored me, suddenly, to perfect sensation. At other times I was quickly and impetuously smitten. I grew sick, and numb, and chilly, and dizzy, and so fell prostrate at once. Then, for weeks, all was void, and black, and silent, and Nothing became the universe. Total annihilation could be no more. From these latter attacks I awoke, however, with a gradation slow in proportion to the suddenness of the seizure. Just as the day dawns to the friendless and houseless beggar who roams the streets throughout the long desolate winter night—just so tardily—just so wearily—just so cheerily came back the light of the Soul to me.

Apart from the tendency to trance, however, my general health appeared to be good; nor could I perceive that it was at all affected by the one prevalent malady—unless, indeed, an idiosyncrasy in my ordinary *sleep* may be looked upon as superinduced. Upon awaking from slumber, I could never gain, at once, thorough possession of my senses, and always remained, for many minutes, in much bewilderment and perplexity—the mental faculties in general, but the memory in especial, being in a condition of absolute abeyance.

In all that I endured there was no physical suffering, but of moral distress an infinitude. My fancy grew charnel. I talked 'of worms, of tombs, and epitaphs.' I was lost in reveries of death, and the idea of premature burial held continual possession of my brain. The ghastly Danger to which I was subjected haunted me day and night. In the former, the torture of meditation was excessive; in the latter, supreme. When the grim Darkness overspread the Earth, then, with every horror of thought, I shook—shook as the quivering plumes upon the hearse. When Nature could endure wakefulness no longer, it was with a struggle that I consented to sleep—for I shuddered to reflect that, upon awaking, I might find myself the tenant of a grave. And when, finally, I sank into slumber, it was only to rush at once into a world of phantasms, above which, with vast, sable, overshadowing wing, hovered, predominant, the one sepulchral Idea.

From the innumerable images of gloom which thus oppressed me in dreams, I select for record but a solitary vision. Methought I was immersed in a cataleptic trance of more than usual duration and profundity. Suddenly there came an icy hand upon my forehead, and an impatient, gibbering voice whispered the word 'Arise!' within my ear.

I sat erect. The darkness was total. I could not see the figure of him who had aroused me. I could call to mind neither the period at which I had fallen into the trance, nor the locality in which I then lay. While I remained motionless, and busied in endeavours to collect my thought, the cold hand grasped me fiercely by the wrist, shaking it petulantly, while the gibbering voice said again:

'Arise! did I not bid thee arise?'

'And who,' I demanded, 'art thou?'

'I have no name in the regions which I inhabit,' replied the voice, mournfully; 'I was mortal, but am fiend. I was merciless, but am pitiful. Thou dost feel that I shudder. My teeth chatter as I speak, yet it is not with the chilliness of the night—of the night without end. But this hideousness is insufferable. How canst *thou* tranquilly sleep? I cannot rest for the cry of these great agonies. These sights are more than I can bear. Get thee up! Come with me into the outer Night, and let me unfold to thee the graves. Is not this a spectacle of woe?—Behold!'

I looked; and the unseen figure, which still grasped me by the wrist, had caused to be thrown open the graves of all mankind; and from each issued the faint phosphoric radiance of decay; so that I could see into the innermost recesses, and there view the shrouded bodies in their sad and solemn slumbers with the worm. But alas! the real sleepers were fewer, by many millions, than those who slumbered not at all; and there was a feeble struggling; and there was a general sad unrest; and from out the depths of the countless pits there came a melancholy rustling from the garments of the buried. And of those who seemed tranquilly to repose, I saw that a vast number had changed, in a greater or less degree, the rigid and uneasy position in which they had originally been entombed. And the voice again said to me as I gazed:

'Is it not—oh! is it *not* a pitiful sight?' But, before I could find words to reply, the figure had ceased to grasp my wrist, the phosphoric lights expired, and the graves were closed with a sudden violence, while from out them arose a tumult of despairing cries, saying again, 'Is it not—O, God, is it *not* a very pitiful sight?'

Phantasies such as these, presenting themselves at night, extended their terrific influence far into my waking hours. My nerves became thoroughly unstrung, and I fell a prey to perpetual horror. I hesitated to ride, or to walk, or to indulge in any exercise that would carry me from home. In fact, I no longer dared trust myself out of the immediate presence of those who were aware of my proneness to catalepsy, lest, falling into one of my usual fits, I should be buried before my real condition could be ascertained. I doubted the care, the fidelity of my dearest friends. I dreaded that, in some trance of more than customary duration, they might be prevailed upon to regard me as irrecoverable. I even went so far as to fear that, as I occasioned much trouble, they might be glad to consider any very protracted attack as sufficient excuse for getting rid of me altogether. It was in vain they endeavoured to reassure me by the most solemn promises. I exacted the most sacred oaths, that under no circumstances they would bury me until decomposition had so materially advanced as to render further preservation impossible. And, even then, my mortal terrors would listen to no reason—would accept no consolation. I entered into a series of elaborate precautions. Among other things, I had the family vault so remodelled as to admit of being readily opened from within. The slightest pressure upon a long lever that extended far into the tomb would cause the iron portal to fly back. There were arrangements also for the free admission of air and light, and convenient receptacles for food and water, within immediate reach of the coffin intended for my reception. This coffin was warmly and softly padded, and was provided with a lid, fashioned upon the principle of the vault-door, with the addition of springs so contrived that the feeblest movement of the body would be sufficient to set it at liberty. Besides all this, there was suspended from the roof of the tomb, a large bell, the rope of which, it was designed, should extend through a hole in the coffin, and so be fastened to one of the hands of the corpse. But, alas! what avails the vigilance against the Destiny of man? Not even these well-contrived securities sufficed to save from the uttermost agonies of living inhumation, a wretch to these agonies foredoomed!

There arrived an epoch—as often before there had arrived—in which I found myself emerging from total unconsciousness into the first feeble and indefinite sense of existence. Slowly—with a tortoise gradation—approached the faint gray dawn of the psychal day. A torpid uneasiness. An apathetic endurance of dull pain. No care—no hope—no effort. Then, after a long interval, a ringing in the ears; then, after a lapse still longer, a pricking or tingling sensation in the extremities; then a seemingly eternal period of pleasurable quiescence, during which the awakening feelings are struggling into thought; then a brief re-sinking into non-entity; then a sudden recovery. At length the slight quivering of an eyelid, and immediately thereupon, an electric shock of a terror, deadly and indefinite, which sends the blood in torrents from the temples to the heart. And now the first positive effort to think. And now the first endeavour to remember. And now a partial and evanescent success. And now the memory has so far regained its dominion, that, in some measure, I am cognizant of my state. I feel that I am not awaking from ordinary sleep. I recollect that I have been subject to catalepsy. And now, at last, as if by the rush of an ocean, my shuddering spirit is overwhelmed by the one grim Danger—by the one spectral and ever-prevalent idea.

For some minutes after this fancy possessed me, I remained without motion. And why? I could not summon courage to move. I dared not make the effort which was to satisfy me of my fate— and yet there was something at my heart which whispered me *it was sure*. Despair—such as no other species of wretchedness ever calls into being—despair alone urged me, after long irresolution, to uplift the heavy lids of my eyes. I uplifted them. It was dark— all dark. I knew that the fit was over. I knew that the crisis of my disorder had long passed. I knew that I had now fully recovered the use of my visual faculties—and yet it was dark—all dark— the intense and utter raylessness of the Night that endureth for evermore.

I endeavoured to shriek; and my lips and my parched tongue moved convulsively together in the attempt—but no voice issued from the cavernous lungs, which, oppressed as if by the weight of some incumbent mountain, gasped and palpitated, with the heart, at every elaborate and struggling inspiration.

The movement of the jaws, in this effort to cry aloud, showed me that they were bound up, as is usual with the dead. I felt, too, that I lay upon some hard substance; and by something similar my sides were, also, closely compressed. So far, I had not ventured to stir any of my limbs—but now I violently threw up my arms, which had been lying at length, with the wrists crossed. They struck a solid wooden substance, which extended above my person at an elevation of not more than six inches from my face. I could no longer doubt that I reposed within a coffin at last.

And now, amid all my infinite miseries, came sweetly the cherub Hope—for I thought of my precautions. I writhed, and made spasmodic exertions to force open the lid: it would not move. I felt my wrists for the bell-rope: it was not to be found. And now the Comforter fled for ever, and a still sterner Despair reigned triumphant; for I could not help perceiving the absence of the paddings which I had so carefully prepared—and then, too, there came suddenly to my nostrils the strong peculiar odour of moist earth. The conclusion was irresistible. I was *not* within the vault. I had fallen into a trance while absent from home—while among strangers—when, or how, I could not remember—and it was they who had buried me as a dog—nailed up in some common coffin—and thrust deep, deep, and for ever, into some ordinary and nameless *grave*.

As this awful conviction forced itself, thus, into the innermost chambers of my soul, I once again struggled to cry aloud. And in this second endeavour I succeeded. A long, wild, and continuous shriek, or yell, of agony, resounded through the realms of the subterranean Night.

'Hillo! hillo, there!' said a gruff voice, in reply.

'What the devil's the matter now!' said a second.

'Get out o' that!' said a third.

'What do you mean by yowling in that ere kind of style, like a catty-mount?' said a fourth; and hereupon I was seized and shaken without ceremony, for several minutes, by junto of very rough-looking individuals. They did not arouse me from my slumber—for I was wide-awake when I screamed—but they restored me to the full possession of my memory.

This adventure occurred near Richmond, in Virginia.

Accompanied by a friend, I had proceeded, upon a gunning expedition, some miles down the banks of the James River. Night approached, and we were overtaken by a storm. The cabin of a small sloop lying at anchor in the stream, and laden with garden mould, afforded us the only available shelter. We made the best of it, and passed the night on board. I slept in one of the only two berths in the vessel—and the berths of a sloop of sixty or seventy tons need scarcely be described. That which I occupied had no bedding of any kind. Its extreme width was eighteen inches. The distance of its bottom from the deck overhead was precisely the same. I found it a matter of exceeding difficulty to squeeze myself in. Nevertheless, I slept soundly; and the whole of my vision—for it was no dream, and no nightmare—arose naturally from the circumstances of my position—from my ordinary bias of thought—and from the difficulty, to which I have alluded, of collecting my senses, and especially of regaining my memory, for a long time after awaking from slumber. The men who shook me were the crew of the sloop, and some labourers engaged to unload it. From the load itself came the earthly smell. The bandage about the jaws was a silk handkerchief in which I had bound up my head, in default of my customary nightcap.

The tortures endured, however, were indubitably quite equal, for the time, to those of actual sepulture. They were fearfully— they were inconceivably hideous; but out of Evil proceeded Good; for their very excess wrought in my spirit an inevitable revulsion. My soul acquired tone—acquired temper. I went abroad. I took vigorous exercise. I breathed the free air of Heaven. I thought upon other subjects than Death. I discarded my medical books. *Buchan* I burned. I read no *Night Thoughts*—no fustian about church-yards—no bugaboo tales—*such as this*. In short, I became a new man, and lived a man's life. From that memorable night, I dismissed forever my charnel apprehensions, and with them vanished the cataleptic disorder, of which, perhaps, they had been less the consequence than the cause.

There are moments when, even to the sober eye of Reason, the world of our sad Humanity may assume the semblance of a Hell—but the imagination of man is no Carathis, to explore with impunity its every cavern. Alas! the grim legion of sepulchral terrors cannot be regarded as altogether fanciful—but, like the Demons in whose company Afrasiab made his voyage down the Oxus, they must sleep, or they will devour us—they must be suffered to slumber, or we perish.

9

The Pit and the Pendulum

Impia tortorum longos hic turba furores Sanguinis innocui, non satiata, aluit. Sospite nunc patria, fracto nunc funeris antro, Mors ubi dira fuit vita salusque patent.[32]

(Quatrain composed for the gates of a market to be erected upon the site of the Jacobin Club House at Paris.)

I was sick—sick unto death with that long agony; and when they at length unbound me, and I was permitted to sit, I felt that my senses were leaving me. The sentence—the dread sentence of death—was the last of distinct accentuation which reached my ears. After that, the sound of the inquisitorial voices seemed merged in one dreamy indeterminate hum. It conveyed to my soul the idea of revolution—perhaps from its association in fancy with the burr of a mill wheel. This only for a brief period; for presently I heard no more. Yet, for a while, I saw; but with how terrible an exaggeration! I saw the lips of the black-robed judges. They appeared to me white—whiter than the sheet upon which I trace these words—and thin even to grotesqueness; thin with the intensity of their expression of firmness—of immoveable resolution—of stern contempt of human torture. I saw that the decrees of what to me was Fate, were still issuing from those lips. I saw them writhe with a deadly locution. I saw them fashion the syllables of my name; and I shuddered because no sound succeeded. I saw, too, for a few moments of delirious horror, the soft and nearly imperceptible waving of the sable draperies which enwrapped the walls of the apartment. And then my vision fell upon the seven tall candles upon the table. At first they wore the aspect of charity, and seemed white and slender angels who would save me; but then, all at once, there came a most deadly nausea over my spirit, and I felt every fibre in my frame thrill as if I had touched the wire of a galvanic battery, while the angel forms became meaningless spectres, with heads of flame, and I saw that from them there would be no help. And then there stole into my fancy, like a rich musical note, the thought of what sweet rest there must be in the grave. The thought came gently and stealthily, and it seemed long before it attained full appreciation; but just as my spirit came at length properly to feel and entertain it, the figures of the judges vanished, as if magically, from before me; the tall candles sank into nothingness; their flames went out utterly; the blackness of darkness supervened; all sensations appeared swallowed up in a mad rushing descent as of the soul into Hades. Then silence, and stillness, and night were the universe.

I had swooned; but still will not say that all of consciousness was lost. What of it there remained I will not attempt to define, or even to describe; yet all was not lost. In the deepest slumber— no! In delirium—no! In a swoon—no! In death—no! even in the grave all is not lost. Else there is no immortality for man. Arousing from the most profound of slumbers, we break the gossamer web of some dream. Yet in a second afterward, (so frail may that web have been) we remember not that we have dreamed. In the return to life from the swoon there are two stages; first, that of the sense of mental or spiritual; secondly, that of the sense of physical, existence. It seems probable that if, upon reaching the second stage, we could recall the impressions of the first, we should find these impressions eloquent in memories of the gulf beyond. And that gulf is—what? How at least shall we distinguish its shadows from those of the tomb? But if the impressions of what I have termed the first stage, are not, at will, recalled, yet, after long interval, do they not come unbidden, while we marvel whence they come? He who has never swooned, is not he who finds strange palaces and wildly familiar faces in coals that glow; is not he who beholds floating in mid-air the sad visions that the many may not view; is not he who ponders over the perfume of some novel flower—is not he whose brain grows bewildered with the meaning of some musical cadence which has never before arrested his attention.

Amid frequent and thoughtful endeavors to remember; amid earnest struggles to regather some token of the state of seeming nothingness into which my soul had lapsed, there have been moments when I have dreamed of success; there have been brief, very brief periods when I have conjured up remembrances which the lucid reason of a later epoch assures me could have had reference only to that condition of seeming unconsciousness. These shadows of memory tell, indistinctly, of tall figures that lifted and bore me in silence down—down—still down—till a hideous dizziness oppressed me at the mere idea of the interminableness of the descent. They tell also of a vague horror at my heart, on account of that heart's unnatural stillness. Then comes a sense of sudden motionlessness throughout all things; as if those who bore me (a ghastly train!) had outrun, in their descent, the limits of the limitless, and paused from the wearisomeness of their toil.

After this I call to mind flatness and dampness; and then all is madness—the madness of a memory, which busies itself among forbidden things.

Very suddenly there came back to my soul motion and sound—the tumultuous motion of the heart, and, in my ears, the sound of its beating. Then a pause in which all is blank. Then again sound, and motion, and touch—a tingling sensation pervading my frame. Then the mere consciousness of existence, without thought—a condition which lasted long. Then, very suddenly, thought, and shuddering terror, and earnest endeavor to comprehend my true state. Then a strong desire to lapse into insensibility. Then a rushing revival of soul and a successful effort to move. And now a full memory of the trial, of the judges, of the sable draperies, of the sentence, of the sickness, of the swoon. Then entire forgetfulness of all that followed; of all that a later day and much earnestness of endeavor have enabled me vaguely to recall.

So far, I had not opened my eyes. I felt that I lay upon my back, unbound. I reached out my hand, and it fell heavily upon something damp and hard. There I suffered it to remain for many minutes, while I strove to imagine where and what I could be. I longed, yet dared not to employ my vision. I dreaded the first glance at objects around me. It was not that I feared to look upon things horrible, but that I grew aghast lest there should be nothing to see. At length, with a wild desperation at heart, I quickly unclosed my eyes. My worst thoughts, then, were confirmed. The blackness of eternal night encompassed me. I struggled for breath. The intensity of the darkness seemed to oppress and stifle me. The atmosphere was intolerably close. I still lay quietly, and made effort to exercise my reason. I brought to mind the inquisitorial proceedings, and attempted from that point to deduce my real condition. The sentence had passed; and it appeared to me that a very long interval of time had since elapsed. Yet not for a moment did I suppose myself actually dead. Such a supposition, notwithstanding what we read in fiction, is altogether inconsistent with real existence;—but where and in what state was I? The condemned to death, I knew, perished usually at the autos-da-fe, and one of these had been held on the very night of the day of my trial. Had I been remanded to my dungeon, to await the next sacrifice, which would not take place for many months? This I at once saw could not be. Victims had been in immediate demand. Moreover, my dungeon, as well as all the condemned cells at Toledo, had stone floors, and light was not altogether excluded.

A fearful idea now suddenly drove the blood in torrents upon my heart, and for a brief period, I once more relapsed into insensibility. Upon recovering, I at once started to my feet, trembling convulsively in every fibre. I thrust my arms wildly above and around me in all directions. I felt nothing; yet dreaded to move a step, lest I should be impeded by the walls of a tomb. Perspiration burst from every pore, and stood in cold big beads upon my forehead. The agony of suspense grew at length intolerable, and I cautiously moved forward, with my arms extended, and my eyes straining from their sockets, in the hope of catching some faint ray of light. I proceeded for many paces; but still all was blackness and vacancy. I breathed more freely. It seemed evident that mine was not, at least, the most hideous of fates.

And now, as I still continued to step cautiously onward, there came thronging upon my recollection a thousand vague rumors of the horrors of Toledo. Of the dungeons there had been strange things narrated—fables I had always deemed them—but yet strange, and too ghastly to repeat, save in a whisper. Was I left to perish of starvation in this subterranean world of darkness; or what fate, perhaps even more fearful, awaited me? That the result would be death, and a death of more than customary bitterness, I knew too well the character of my judges to doubt. The mode and the hour were all that occupied or distracted me.

My outstretched hands at length encountered some solid obstruction. It was a wall, seemingly of stone masonry—very smooth, slimy, and cold. I followed it up; stepping with all the careful distrust with which certain antique narratives had inspired me. This process, however, afforded me no means of ascertaining the dimensions of my dungeon; as I might make its circuit, and return to the point whence I set out, without being aware of the fact; so perfectly uniform seemed the wall. I therefore sought the knife which had been in my pocket, when led into the inquisitorial chamber; but it was gone; my clothes had been exchanged for a wrapper of coarse serge. I had thought of forcing the blade in some minute crevice of the masonry, so as to identify my point of departure. The difficulty, nevertheless, was but trivial; although, in the disorder of my fancy, it seemed at first insuperable. I tore a part of the hem from the robe and placed the fragment at full length, and at right angles to the wall. In groping my way around the prison, I could not fail to encounter this rag upon completing the circuit. So, at least I thought: but I had not counted upon the extent of the dungeon, or upon my own weakness. The ground was moist and slippery. I staggered onward for some time, when I stumbled and fell. My excessive fatigue induced me to remain prostrate; and sleep soon overtook me as I lay.

Upon awaking, and stretching forth an arm, I found beside me a loaf and a pitcher with water. I was too much exhausted to reflect upon this circumstance, but ate and drank with avidity. Shortly afterward, I resumed my tour around the prison, and with much toil came at last upon the fragment of the serge. Up to the period when I fell I had counted fifty-two paces, and upon resuming my walk, I had counted forty-eight more;—when I arrived at the rag. There were in all, then, a hundred paces; and, admitting two paces to the yard, I presumed the dungeon to be fifty yards in circuit. I had met, however, with many angles in the wall, and thus I could form no guess at the shape of the vault; for vault I could not help supposing it to be.

I had little object—certainly no hope these researches; but a vague curiosity prompted me to continue them. Quitting the wall, I resolved to cross the area of the enclosure. At first I proceeded with extreme caution, for the floor, although seemingly of solid material, was treacherous with slime. At length, however, I took courage, and did not hesitate to step firmly; endeavoring to cross in as direct a line as possible. I had advanced some ten or twelve paces in this manner, when the remnant of the torn hem of my robe became entangled between my legs. I stepped on it, and fell violently on my face.

In the confusion attending my fall, I did not immediately apprehend a somewhat startling circumstance, which yet, in a few seconds afterward, and while I still lay prostrate, arrested my attention. It was this—my chin rested upon the floor of the prison, but my lips and the upper portion of my head, although seemingly at a less elevation than the chin, touched nothing. At the same time my forehead seemed bathed in a clammy vapor, and the peculiar smell of decayed fungus arose to my nostrils. I put forward my arm, and shuddered to find that I had fallen at the very brink of a circular pit, whose extent, of course, I had no means of ascertaining at the moment. Groping about the masonry just below the margin, I succeeded in dislodging a small fragment, and let it fall into the abyss. For many seconds I hearkened to its reverberations as it dashed against the sides of the chasm in its descent; at length there was a sullen plunge into water, succeeded by loud echoes. At the same moment there came a sound resembling the quick opening, and as rapid closing of a door overhead, while a faint gleam of light flashed suddenly through the gloom, and as suddenly faded away.

I saw clearly the doom which had been prepared for me, and congratulated myself upon the timely accident by which I had escaped. Another step before my fall, and the world had seen me no more. And the death just avoided, was of that very character which I had regarded as fabulous and frivolous in the tales respecting the Inquisition. To the victims of its tyranny, there was the choice of death with its direst physical agonies, or death with its most hideous moral horrors. I had been reserved for the latter. By long suffering my nerves had been unstrung, until I trembled at the sound of my own voice, and had become in every respect a fitting subject for the species of torture which awaited me.

Shaking in every limb, I groped my way back to the wall; resolving there to perish rather than risk the terrors of the wells, of which my imagination now pictured many in various positions about the dungeon. In other conditions of mind I might have had courage to end my misery at once by a plunge into one of these abysses; but now I was the veriest of cowards. Neither could I forget what I had read of these pits—that the sudden extinction of life formed no part of their most horrible plan.

Agitation of spirit kept me awake for many long hours; but at length I again slumbered. Upon arousing, I found by my side, as before, a loaf and a pitcher of water. A burning thirst consumed me, and I emptied the vessel at a draught. It must have been drugged; for scarcely had I drunk, before I became irresistibly drowsy. A deep sleep fell upon me—a sleep like that of death. How long it lasted of course, I know not; but when, once again, I unclosed my eyes, the objects around me were visible. By a wild sulphurous lustre, the origin of which I could not at first determine, I was enabled to see the extent and aspect of the prison.

In its size I had been greatly mistaken. The whole circuit of its walls did not exceed twenty-five yards. For some minutes this fact occasioned me a world of vain trouble; vain indeed! for what could be of less importance, under the terrible circumstances which environed me, then the mere dimensions of my dungeon? But my soul took a wild interest in trifles, and I busied myself in endeavors to account for the error I had committed in my measurement. The truth at length flashed upon me. In my first attempt at exploration I had counted fifty-two paces, up to the period when I fell; I must then have been within a pace or two of the fragment of serge; in fact, I had nearly performed the circuit of the vault. I then slept, and upon awaking, I must have returned upon my steps—thus supposing the circuit nearly double what it actually was. My confusion of mind prevented me from observing that I began my tour with the wall to the left, and ended it with the wall to the right.

I had been deceived, too, in respect to the shape of the

enclosure. In feeling my way I had found many angles, and thus deduced an idea of great irregularity; so potent is the effect of total darkness upon one arousing from lethargy or sleep! The angles were simply those of a few slight depressions, or niches, at odd intervals. The general shape of the prison was square. What I had taken for masonry seemed now to be iron, or some other metal, in huge plates, whose sutures or joints occasioned the depression. The entire surface of this metallic enclosure was rudely daubed in all the hideous and repulsive devices to which the charnel superstition of the monks has given rise. The figures of fiends in aspects of menace, with skeleton forms, and other more really fearful images, overspread and disfigured the walls. I observed that the outlines of these monstrosities were sufficiently distinct, but that the colours seemed faded and blurred, as if from the effects of a damp atmosphere. I now noticed the floor, too, which was of stone. In the centre yawned the circular pit from whose jaws I had escaped; but it was the only one in the dungeon.

All this I saw indistinctly and by much effort: for my personal condition had been greatly changed during slumber. I now lay upon my back, and at full length, on a species of low framework of wood. To this I was securely bound by a long strap resembling a surcingle. It passed in many convolutions about my limbs and body, leaving at liberty only my head, and my left arm to such extent that I could, by dint of much exertion, supply myself with food from an earthen dish which lay by my side on the floor. I saw, to my horror, that the pitcher had been removed. I say to my horror; for I was consumed with intolerable thirst. This thirst it appeared to be the design of my persecutors to stimulate: for the food in the dish was meat pungently seasoned.

Looking upward, I surveyed the ceiling of my prison. It was some thirty or forty feet overhead, and constructed much as the side walls. In one of its panels a very singular figure riveted my whole attention. It was the painted figure of Time as he is commonly represented, save that, in lieu of a scythe, he held what, at a casual glance, I supposed to be the pictured image of a huge pendulum such as we see on antique clocks. There was something, however, in the appearance of this machine which caused me to regard it more attentively. While I gazed directly upward at it (for its position was immediately over my own) I fancied that I saw it in motion. In an instant afterward the fancy was confirmed. Its sweep was brief, and of course slow. I watched it for some minutes, somewhat in fear, but more in wonder. Wearied at length with observing its dull movement, I turned my eyes upon the other objects in the cell.

A slight noise attracted my notice, and, looking to the floor, I saw several enormous rats traversing it. They had issued from the well, which lay just within view to my right. Even then, while I gazed, they came up in troops, hurriedly, with ravenous eyes, allured by the scent of the meat. From this it required much effort and attention to scare them away.

It might have been half an hour, perhaps even an hour, (for I could take but imperfect note of time) before I again cast my eyes upward. What I then saw confounded and amazed me. The sweep of the pendulum had increased in extent by nearly a yard. As a natural consequence, its velocity was also much greater. But what mainly disturbed me was the idea that had perceptibly descended. I now observed—with what horror it is needless to say—that its nether extremity was formed of a crescent of glittering steel, about a foot in length from horn to horn; the horns upward, and the under edge evidently as keen as that of a razor. Like a razor also, it seemed massy and heavy, tapering from the edge into a solid and broad structure above. It was appended to a weighty rod of brass, and the whole hissed as it swung through the air.

I could no longer doubt the doom prepared for me by monkish ingenuity in torture. My cognizance of the pit had become known to the inquisitorial agents—the pit whose horrors had been destined for so bold a recusant as myself—the pit, typical of hell, and regarded by rumor as the Ultima Thule of all their punishments. The plunge into this pit I had avoided by the merest of accidents, I knew that surprise, or entrapment into torment, formed an important portion of all the grotesquerie of these dungeon deaths. Having failed to fall, it was no part of the demon plan to hurl me into the abyss; and thus (there being no alternative) a different and a milder destruction awaited me. Milder! I half smiled in my agony as I thought of such application of such a term.

What boots it to tell of the long, long hours of horror more than mortal, during which I counted the rushing vibrations of the steel! Inch by inch—line by line—with a descent only appreciable at intervals that seemed ages—down and still down it came! Days passed—it might have been that many days passed—ere it swept so closely over me as to fan me with its acrid breath. The odour of the sharp steel forced itself into my nostrils. I prayed—I wearied heaven with my prayer for its more speedy descent. I grew frantically mad, and struggled to force myself upward against the sweep of the fearful scimitar. And then I fell suddenly calm, and lay smiling at the glittering death, as a child at some rare bauble.

There was another interval of utter insensibility; it was brief; for, upon again lapsing into life there had been no perceptible descent in the pendulum. But it might have been long; for I knew there were demons who took note of my swoon, and who could have arrested the vibration at pleasure. Upon my recovery, too, I felt very—oh, inexpressibly sick and weak, as if through long inanition. Even amid the agonies of that period, the human nature craved food. With painful effort I outstretched my left arm as far as my bonds permitted, and took possession of the small remnant which had been spared me by the rats. As I put a portion of it within my lips, there rushed to my mind a half formed thought of joy—of hope? Yet what business had I with hope? It was, as I say, a half formed thought—man has many such which are never completed. I felt that it was of joy—of hope; but felt also that it had perished in its formation. In vain I struggled to perfect—to regain it. Long suffering had nearly annihilated all my ordinary powers of mind. I was an imbecile—an idiot.

The vibration of the pendulum was at right angles to my length. I saw that the crescent was designed to cross the region of the heart. It would fray the serge of my robe—it would return and repeat its operations—again—and again. Notwithstanding its terrifically wide sweep (some thirty feet or more) and the hissing vigor of its descent, sufficient to sunder these very walls of iron, still the fraying of my robe would be all that, for several minutes, it would accomplish. And at this thought I paused. I dared not go farther than this reflection. I dwelt upon it with a pertinacity of attention—as if, in so dwelling, I could arrest here the descent of the steel. I forced myself to ponder upon the sound of the crescent as it should pass across the garment—upon the peculiar thrilling sensation which the friction of cloth produces on the nerves. I pondered upon all this frivolity until my teeth were on edge.

Down—steadily down it crept. I took a frenzied pleasure in contrasting its downward with its lateral velocity. To the right—to the left—far and wide—with the shriek of a damned spirit; to my heart with the stealthy pace of the tiger! I alternately laughed and howled as the one or the other idea grew predominant.

Down—certainly, relentlessly down! It vibrated within three inches of my bosom! I struggled violently, furiously, to free my left arm. This was free only from the elbow to the hand. I could reach the latter, from the platter beside me, to my mouth, with great effort, but no farther. Could I have broken the fastenings above the elbow, I would have seized and attempted to arrest the pendulum. I might as well have attempted to arrest an avalanche!

Down—still unceasingly—still inevitably down! I gasped and struggled at each vibration. I shrunk convulsively at its every sweep. My eyes followed its outward or upward whirls with the eagerness of the most unmeaning despair; they closed themselves spasmodically at the descent, although death would have been a relief, oh! how unspeakable! Still I quivered in every nerve to think how slight a sinking of the machinery would precipitate that keen, glistening axe upon my bosom. It was hope that prompted the nerve to quiver—the frame to shrink. It was hope—the hope that triumphs on the rack—that whispers to the death-condemned even in the dungeons of the Inquisition.

I saw that some ten or twelve vibrations would bring the steel in actual contact with my robe, and with this observation there suddenly came over my spirit all the keen, collected calmness of despair. For the first time during many hours—or perhaps days— I thought. It now occurred to me that the bandage, or surcingle, which enveloped me, was unique. I was tied by no separate cord. The first stroke of the razorlike crescent athwart any portion of the band, would so detach it that it might be unwound from my person by means of my left hand. But how fearful, in that case, the proximity of the steel! The result of the slightest struggle how deadly! Was it likely, moreover, that the minions of the torturer had not foreseen and provided for this possibility! Was it probable that the bandage crossed my bosom in the track of the pendulum? Dreading to find my faint, and, as it seemed, in last hope frustrated, I so far elevated my head as to obtain a distinct view of my breast. The surcingle enveloped my limbs and body close in all directions—save in the path of the destroying crescent.

Scarcely had I dropped my head back into its original position, when there flashed upon my mind what I cannot better describe than as the unformed half of that idea of deliverance to which I have previously alluded, and of which a moiety only floated indeterminately through my brain when I raised food to my burning lips. The whole thought was now present—feeble, scarcely sane, scarcely definite,—but still entire. I proceeded at once, with the nervous energy of despair, to attempt its execution.

For many hours the immediate vicinity of the low framework upon which I lay, had been literally swarming with rats. They were wild, bold, ravenous; their red eyes glaring upon me as if they waited but for motionlessness on my part to make me their prey. "To what food," I thought, "have they been accustomed in the well?"

They had devoured, in spite of all my efforts to prevent them, all but a small remnant of the contents of the dish. I had fallen into an habitual seesaw, or wave of the hand about the platter: and, at length, the unconscious uniformity of the movement deprived it of effect. In their voracity the vermin frequently fastened their sharp fangs in my fingers. With the particles of the oily and spicy viand which now remained, I thoroughly rubbed the bandage wherever I could reach it; then, raising my hand from the floor, I lay breathlessly still.

At first the ravenous animals were startled and terrified at the change—at the cessation of movement. They shrank alarmedly back; many sought the well. But this was only for a moment. I had not counted in vain upon their voracity. Observing that I remained without motion, one or two of the boldest leaped upon the frame-work, and smelt at the surcingle. This seemed the signal for a general rush. Forth from the well they hurried in fresh troops. They clung to the wood—they overran it, and leaped in hundreds upon my person. The measured movement of the pendulum disturbed them not at all. Avoiding its strokes they busied themselves with the anointed bandage. They pressed—they swarmed upon me in ever accumulating heaps. They writhed upon my throat; their cold lips sought my own; I was half stifled by their thronging pressure; disgust, for which the world has no name, swelled my bosom, and chilled, with a heavy clamminess, my heart. Yet one minute, and I felt that the struggle would be over. Plainly I perceived the loosening of the bandage. I knew that in more than one place it must be already severed. With a more than human resolution I lay still.

Nor had I erred in my calculations—nor had I endured in vain. I at length felt that I was free. The surcingle hung in ribands from my body. But the stroke of the pendulum already pressed upon my bosom. It had divided the serge of the robe. It had cut through the linen beneath. Twice again it swung, and a sharp sense of pain shot through every nerve. But the moment of escape had arrived. At a wave of my hand my deliverers hurried tumultuously away. With a steady movement—cautious, sidelong, shrinking, and slow—I slid from the embrace of the bandage and beyond the reach of the scimitar. For the moment, at least, I was free.

Free!—and in the grasp of the Inquisition! I had scarcely stepped from my wooden bed of horror upon the stone floor of the prison, when the motion of the hellish machine ceased and I beheld it drawn up, by some invisible force, through the ceiling. This was a lesson which I took desperately to heart. My every motion was undoubtedly watched. Free!—I had but escaped death in one form of agony, to be delivered unto worse than death in some other. With that thought I rolled my eyes nervously around on the barriers of iron that hemmed me in. Something unusual—some change which, at first, I could not appreciate distinctly—it was obvious, had taken place in the apartment. For many minutes of a dreamy and trembling abstraction, I busied myself in vain, unconnected conjecture. During this period, I became aware, for the first time, of the origin of the sulphurous light which illumined the cell. It proceeded from a fissure, about half an inch in width, extending entirely around the prison at the base of the walls, which thus appeared, and were, completely separated from the floor. I endeavored, but of course in vain, to look through the aperture.

As I arose from the attempt, the mystery of the alteration in the chamber broke at once upon my understanding. I have observed that, although the outlines of the figures upon the walls were sufficiently distinct, yet the colours seemed blurred and indefinite. These colours had now assumed, and were momentarily assuming, a startling and most intense brilliancy, that gave to the spectral and fiendish portraitures an aspect that might have thrilled even firmer nerves than my own. Demon eyes, of a wild and ghastly vivacity, glared upon me in a thousand directions, where none had been visible before, and gleamed with the lurid lustre of a fire that I could not force my imagination to regard as unreal.

Unreal!—Even while I breathed there came to my nostrils the breath of the vapour of heated iron! A suffocating odour pervaded the prison! A deeper glow settled each moment in the eyes that glared at my agonies! A richer tint of crimson diffused itself over the pictured horrors of blood. I panted! I gasped for breath! There could be no doubt of the design of my tormentors—oh! most unrelenting! oh! most demoniac of men! I shrank from the glowing metal to the centre of the cell. Amid the thought of the fiery destruction that impended, the idea of the coolness of the well came over my soul like balm. I rushed to its deadly brink. I threw my straining vision below. The glare from the enkindled roof illumined its inmost recesses. Yet, for a wild moment, did my spirit refuse to comprehend the meaning of what I saw. At length it forced—it wrestled its way into my soul—it burned itself in upon my shuddering reason.—Oh! for a voice to speak!—oh! horror!—oh! any horror but this! With a shriek, I rushed from the margin, and buried my face in my hands—weeping bitterly.

The heat rapidly increased, and once again I looked up, shuddering as with a fit of the ague. There had been a second change in the cell—and now the change was obviously in the form. As before, it was in vain that I, at first, endeavoured to appreciate or understand what was taking place. But not long was I left in doubt. The Inquisitorial vengeance had been hurried by my twofold escape, and there was to be no more dallying with the King of Terrors. The room had been square. I saw that two of its iron angles were now acute—two, consequently, obtuse. The fearful difference quickly increased with a low rumbling or moaning sound. In an instant the apartment had shifted its form into that of a lozenge. But the alteration stopped not here-I neither hoped nor desired it to stop. I could have clasped the red walls to my bosom as a garment of eternal peace. "Death," I said, "any death but that of the pit!" Fool! might I have not known that into the pit it was the object of the burning iron to urge me? Could I resist its glow? or, if even that, could I withstand its pressure And now, flatter and flatter grew the lozenge, with a rapidity that left me no time for contemplation. Its centre, and of course, its greatest width, came just over the yawning gulf. I shrank back—but the closing walls pressed me resistlessly onward. At length for my seared and writhing body there was no longer an inch of foothold on the firm floor of the prison. I struggled no more, but the agony of my soul found vent in one loud, long, and final scream of despair. I felt that I tottered upon the brink—I averted my eyes—

There was a discordant hum of human voices! There was a loud blast as of many trumpets! There was a harsh grating as of a thousand thunders! The fiery walls rushed back! An outstretched arm caught my own as I fell, fainting, into the abyss. It was that of General Lasalle. The French army had entered Toledo. The Inquisition was in the hands of its enemies.

10
The Tell-Tale Heart

True!—nervous—very, very dreadfully nervous I had been and am; but why will you say that I am mad? The disease had sharpened my senses—not destroyed—not dulled them. Above all was the sense of hearing acute. I heard all things in the heaven and in the earth. I heard many things in hell. How, then, am I mad? Hearken! and observe how healthily—how calmly I can tell you the whole story.

It is impossible to say how first the idea entered my brain; but once conceived, it haunted me day and night. Object there was none. Passion there was none. I loved the old man. He had never wronged me. He had never given me insult. For his gold I had no desire. I think it was his eye! yes, it was this! He had the eye of a vulture—a pale blue eye, with a film over it. Whenever it fell upon me, my blood ran cold; and so by degrees—very gradually— I made up my mind to take the life of the old man, and thus rid myself of the eye forever.

Now this is the point. You fancy me mad. Madmen know nothing. But you should have seen *me*. You should have seen how wisely I proceeded—with what caution—with what foresight— with what dissimulation I went to work! I was never kinder to the old man than during the whole week before I killed him. And every night, about midnight, I turned the latch of his door and opened it—oh, so gently! And then, when I had made an opening sufficient for my head, I put in a dark lantern, all closed, closed, so that no light shone out, and then I thrust in my head. Oh, you would have laughed to see how cunningly I thrust it in! I moved it slowly—very, very slowly, so that I might not disturb the old man's sleep. It took me an hour to place my whole head within the opening so far that I could see him as he lay upon his bed. Ha!—would a madman have been so wise as this? And then, when my head was well in the room, I undid the lantern cautiously—oh, so cautiously—cautiously (for the hinges creaked)—I undid it just so much that a single thin ray fell upon the vulture eye. And this I did for seven long nights—every night just at midnight—but I found the eye always closed; and so it was impossible to do the work; for it was not the old man who vexed me, but his Evil Eye. And every morning, when the day broke, I went boldly into the chamber, and spoke courageously to him, calling him by name in a hearty tone, and inquiring how he had passed the night. So you see he would have been a very profound old man, indeed, to suspect that every night, just at twelve, I looked in upon him while he slept.

Upon the eighth night I was more than usually cautious in opening the door. A watch's minute hand moves more quickly than did mine. Never before that night had I *felt* the extent of my own powers—of my sagacity. I could scarcely contain my feelings of triumph. To think that there I was, opening the door, little by little, and he not even to dream of my secret deeds or thoughts. I fairly chuckled at the idea; and perhaps he heard me; for he moved on the bed suddenly, as if startled. Now you may think that I drew back—but no. His room was as black as pitch with the thick darkness (for the shutters were close fastened, through fear of robbers), and so I knew that he could not see the opening of the door, and I kept pushing it on steadily, steadily.

I had my head in, and was about to open the lantern, when my thumb slipped upon the tin fastening, and the old man sprang up in bed, crying out—'Who's there?'

I kept quite still and said nothing. For a whole hour I did not move a muscle, and in the meantime I did not hear him lie down. He was still sitting up in the bed listening;—just as I have done, night after night, hearkening to the death watches in the wall.

Presently I heard a slight groan, and I knew it was the groan of mortal terror. It was not a groan of pain or of grief—oh, no!—it was the low stifled sound that arises from the bottom of the soul when overcharged with awe. I knew the sound well. Many a night, just at midnight, when all the world slept, it has welled up from my own bosom, deepening, with its dreadful echo, the terrors that distracted me. I say I knew it well. I knew what the old man felt, and pitied him, although I chuckled at heart. I knew that he had been lying awake ever since the first slight noise, when he had turned in the bed. His fears had been ever since growing upon him. He had been trying to fancy them causeless, but could not. He had been saying to himself—'It is nothing but the wind in the chimney—it is only a mouse crossing the floor,' or 'it is merely a cricket which has made a single chirp.' Yes, he had been trying to comfort himself with these suppositions: but he had found all in vain. *All in vain*; because Death, in approaching him had stalked with his black shadow before him, and enveloped the victim. And it was the mournful influence of the unperceived shadow that caused him to feel—although he neither saw nor heard—to *feel* the presence of my head within the room.

When I had waited a long time, very patiently, without hearing him lie down, I resolved to open a little—a very, very little crevice in the lantern. So I opened it—you cannot imagine how stealthily, stealthily—until, at length a single dim ray, like the thread of the spider, shot from out the crevice and fell full upon the vulture eye.

It was open—wide, wide open—and I grew furious as I gazed upon it. I saw it with perfect distinctness—all a dull blue, with a hideous veil over it that chilled the very marrow in my bones;

but I could see nothing else of the old man's face or person: for I had directed the ray as if by instinct, precisely upon the damned spot.

And have I not told you that what you mistake for madness is but over-acuteness of the senses?—now, I say, there came to my ears a low, dull, quick sound, such as a watch makes when enveloped in cotton. I knew *that* sound well, too. It was the beating of the old man's heart. It increased my fury, as the beating of a drum stimulates the soldier into courage.

But even yet I refrained and kept still. I scarcely breathed. I held the lantern motionless. I tried how steadily I could maintain the ray upon the eye. Meantime the hellish tattoo of the heart increased. It grew quicker and quicker, and louder and louder every instant. The old man's terror *must* have been extreme! It grew louder, I say, louder every moment!—do you mark me well? I have told you that I am nervous: so I am. And now at the dead hour of the night, amid the dreadful silence of that old house, so strange a noise as this excited me to uncontrollable terror. Yet, for some minutes longer I refrained and stood still. But the beating grew louder, louder! I thought the heart must burst. And now a new anxiety seized me— the sound would be heard by a neighbour! The old man's hour had come! With a loud yell, I threw open the lantern and leaped into the room. He shrieked once—once only. In an instant I dragged him to the floor, and pulled the heavy bed over him. I then smiled gaily, to find the deed so far done. But, for many minutes, the heart beat on with a muffled sound. This, however, did not vex me; it would not be heard through the wall. At length it ceased. The old man was dead. I removed the bed and examined the corpse. Yes, he was stone, stone dead. I placed my hand upon the heart and held it there many minutes. There was no pulsation. He was stone dead. His eye would trouble me no more.

If still you think me mad, you will think so no longer when I describe the wise precautions I took for the concealment of the body. The night waned, and I worked hastily, but in silence. First of all I dismembered the corpse. I cut off the head and the arms and the legs.

I then took up three planks from the flooring of the chamber, and deposited all between the scantlings. I then replaced the boards so cleverly, so cunningly, that no human eye—not even *his*—could have detected any thing wrong. There was nothing to wash out—no stain of any kind—no blood-spot whatever. I had been too wary for that. A tub had caught all—ha! ha!

When I had made an end of these labours, it was four o'clock—still dark as midnight. As the bell sounded the hour, there came a knocking at the street door. I went down to open it with a light heart,—for what had I *now* to fear? There entered three men, who introduced themselves, with perfect suavity, as officers of the police. A shriek had been heard by a neighbour during the night; suspicion of foul play had been aroused; information had been lodged at the police office, and they (the officers) had been deputed to search the premises.

I smiled,—for *what* had I to fear? I bade the gentlemen welcome. The shriek, I said, was my own in a dream. The old man, I mentioned, was absent in the country. I took my visitors all over the house. I bade them search—search *well*. I led them, at length, to *his* chamber. I showed them his treasures, secure, undisturbed. In the enthusiasm of my confidence, I brought chairs into the room, and desired them *here* to rest from their fatigues, while I myself, in the wild audacity of my perfect triumph, placed my own seat upon the very spot beneath which reposed the corpse of the victim.

The officers were satisfied. My *manner* had convinced them. I was singularly at ease. They sat, and while I answered cheerily, they chatted of familiar things. But, ere long, I felt myself getting pale and wished them gone. My head ached, and I fancied a ringing in my ears: but still they sat and still chatted. The ringing became more distinct:—it continued and became more distinct: I talked more freely to get rid of the feeling: but it continued and gained definiteness—until, at length, I found that the noise was *not* within my ears.

No doubt I now grew very pale;—but I talked more fluently, and with a heightened voice. Yet the sound increased—and what could I do? It was *a low, dull, quick sound—much such a sound as a watch makes when enveloped in cotton.* I gasped for breath—and yet the officers heard it not. I talked more quickly—more vehemently; but the noise steadily increased. I arose and argued about trifles, in a high key and with violent gesticulations; but the noise steadily increased. Why *would* they not be gone? I paced the floor to and fro with heavy strides, as if excited to fury by the observations of the men—but the noise steadily increased. Oh God! what *could* I do? I foamed—I raved—I swore! I swung the chair upon which I had been sitting, and grated it upon the boards, but the noise arose over all and continually increased. It grew louder—louder—

louder! And still the men chatted pleasantly, and smiled. Was it possible they heard not? Almighty God!—no, no! They heard!—they suspected!—they *knew*!—they were making a mockery of my horror!—this I thought, and this I think. But anything was better than this agony! Anything was more tolerable than this derision! I could bear those hypocritical smiles no longer! I felt that I must scream or die!—and now—again!—hark! louder! louder! louder! *louder*!

'Villains!' I shrieked, 'dissemble no more! I admit the deed!—tear up the planks! here, here!—it is the beating of his hideous heart!'

THE END

Notes

1   Some versions use 'especial' for 'special' instead.

2   Equivalent to the English word 'preternatural'.

3   Rousseau, *Nouvelle Héloïse.*

4   Upon the original publication of 'Marie Rogêt,' the foot-notes now appended were considered unnecessary; but the lapse of several years since the tragedy upon which the tale is based, renders it expedient to give them, and also to say a few words in explanation of the general design. A young girl, Mary Cecilia Rogers, was murdered in the vicinity of New York; and although her death occasioned an intense and long-enduring excitement, the mystery attending it had remained unsolved at the period when the present paper was written and published (November, 1842). Herein, under pretence of relating the fate of a Parisian grisette, the author has followed, in minute detail, the essential, while merely paralleling the inessential, facts of the real murder of Mary Rogers. Thus all argument founded upon the fiction is applicable to the truth: and the investigation of the truth was the object.

The *Mystery of Marie Rogêt* was composed at a distance from the scene of the atrocity, and with no other means of investigation than the newspapers afforded. Thus much escaped the writer of which he could have availed himself had he been upon the spot and visited the localities. It may not be improper to record, nevertheless, that the confessions of *two* persons (one of them the Madame Deluc of the narrative), made, at different periods, long subsequent to the publication, confirmed, in full, not only the general conclusion, but absolutely *all* the chief hypothetical details by which that conclusion was attained.

5   The *nom de plume* of Von Hardenburg.

6   Nassau Street.

7   Anderson.

8   The Hudson.

9   Weehawken.

10 Payne.

11 Crommelin.

12 The New York *Mercury*.

13 The New York *Brother Jonathan*, edited by H. Hastings Weld, Esq.

14 New York *Journal of Commerce*.

15 Philadelphia *Saturday Evening Post*, edited by C. I. Peterson, Esq.

16 Adam.

17 See *Murders in the Rue Morgue*.

18 The New York *Commercial Advertiser*, edited by Col. Stone.

19 'A theory based on the qualities of an object, will prevent its being unfolded according to its objects; and he who arranges topics in reference to their causes, will cease to value them according to their results. Thus the jurisprudence of every nation will show that, when law becomes a science and a system, it ceases to be justice. The errors into which a blind devotion to *principles* of classification has led the common law, will be seen by observing how often the legislature has been obliged to come forward to restore the equity its scheme had lost.'—*Landor*.

20 New York *Express*.

21 New York *Herald*.

22 New York *Courier and Inquirer*.

23 Mennais was one of the parties originally suspected and arrested, but discharged through total lack of evidence.

24 New York *Courier and Inquirer*.

25 New York *Evening Post*.

26 New York *Standard*.

27 Of the Magazine in which the article was originally published.

28 Equivalent to the English word 'preter-nature'.

29 Latin expressions.

30 Latin expressions.

31 French epigraph: His/her heart is a suspended lute; as soon as one touches it, it resonates.

32 Latin epigraph: Here the wicked mob, unappeased, long cherished a hatred of innocent blood. Now that the fatherland is saved, and the cave of death demolished, where grim death has been, life and health appear.

黑貓

Preface to the Chinese Translation
中文譯本序

這本選集選譯了愛倫・坡的小說中較有代表性的作品，以期為無法讀完他全部作品的讀者提供一個相對精當的選本。其中，《金甲蟲》、《摩格街謀殺案》、《瑪麗・羅傑疑案》及《被竊的信》可認為是愛倫・坡的推理小說典範，其影響仍可見於當今各國的推理小說中；《厄舍屋的倒塌》、《紅死病假面》、《過早埋葬》、《陷坑與鐘擺》表現了愛倫・坡作品的一個常見題材：極度的身體和心智病態、腐朽和死亡，以及作家對恐怖效果的刻意追求；《黑貓》和《泄密之心》在一定程度上繼續了前一組小說的題材，但更將筆觸探及人的內心深處，涉及到心理的和無意識、下意識的層面，雖然作品中的主人公大多帶有狂人瘋漢的特徵。

愛倫・坡的作品，譯來決非易事，雖竭盡全力，錯漏恐依然難免，所以任何批評都會受到歡迎。只希望這一譯本在"為賦新詞"的無奈之餘，多少能給讀者提供一點與已有的譯本不太一樣的東西。不一定更好，有點不同而已，畢竟，總有時代、讀者、譯者的不同在裏面。

1
黑貓

對於我要寫的這個最瘋狂也是最樸實的故事，我從沒指望或希望有人會相信它。若是我期望別人相信有時連我自己的理智都拒絕接受的這種事實，那我就真是瘋了。不過，我並沒有發瘋 —— 而且很肯定也沒有在做夢。可是，我明天就將死去，今天我要卸掉靈魂的重負。我最迫切的目的是明白地、簡潔地、不加評論地向世界展示一系列純屬於家庭瑣事的事件。因為這些事件震驚了 —— 折磨了 —— 而且毀滅了我。但是我不打算對它們進行詳細說明。對我來說，它們帶來的僅僅是恐懼 —— 對很多人而言，它們也許並不那麼恐怖，倒是很有些巴羅克式的古怪色彩。將來，或許會有人來把我的幻覺歸結為某種普通的心理現象 —— 某種更加平和、更有邏輯性，而且比我的更不易激動的心理狀況，它可以在我懷着敬畏心情來詳細描述的情境中，看出那不過是起因自然和效果普通的事件。

從我孩提時，我就以脾性乖順和厚道而出名。我的心善良溫柔得連夥伴們都拿這當笑柄。我特別喜歡動物，父母便給我弄來了各種各樣的寵物。我大多數的時間就是和動物們在一起，給牠們餵食和撫摸牠們時，我無比開心。這種癖好隨着年紀的增長而加劇，於是，我成年時的主要樂趣，就是從寵物中獲得的。對於那些對忠誠敏捷的狗獨具好感的人來說，我無需費力解釋那種快樂的性質和強度。我已多次嘗到那徒有虛名的人吝嗇的友誼和易變的忠誠，倒是從這些獸類的愛中，體會到某種刻骨銘心的無私和忘我。

我很早就結婚了，而且很高興地發現妻子的脾氣與我很相配。看到我對寵物的偏愛，她就不錯過任何能弄到那些最可愛品種的機會。我們養了一些鳥、金魚、一條可愛的狗、幾隻兔子、一隻小猴子，還有一隻貓。

那隻貓是個體形龐大十分美麗的動物，牠渾身漆黑，敏捷得令人驚訝。說到牠的智力，我那內心充滿迷信思想的妻子常常會提到古老而流行的說法，認為所有黑貓都是女巫偽裝成的。她倒不是對這說法有多認真 —— 我提到這事，完全是因為此時我恰好記了起來。

普魯托 —— 這是那隻貓的名字 —— 是我寵愛的動物和玩伴。我單獨餵牠，而且無論我走到屋子哪裏，牠都跟着我。我上街時也很難不讓牠跟着。

就這樣，我們的友誼持續了幾年，這期間我通常的脾氣和個性 —— 由於嗜酒成癖 —— 已（我得羞愧地承認）從本質上趨向惡化。我日益憂悒、易怒，更加不在乎旁人的感情。我任自己對妻子惡言相向，最後，我甚至對她動粗。當然了，我的寵物們都察覺了我脾性的改變。我不僅忽視牠們，而且虐待牠們。不過，對普魯托我還是控制自己不去虐待牠，而對那些偶然或是出於親情朝我跑來的兔子、猴子，甚至是狗，我都肆無忌憚地粗暴相待。

這樣的惡疾日益加深——還有甚麼病比得上嗜酒！最後，連普魯托——牠正日趨衰老，因此多少有些暴躁——都開始感受到我那惡脾氣了。

一天晚上，我從城裏一個常去之處喝得醉醺醺地回家，便覺得那隻貓在躲我。我一把抓住牠；牠對我的暴力很是害怕，就用牙齒在我手上輕輕咬了一口。我心裏騰起一種邪惡的憤怒，立刻失去了理智，原初的靈魂似乎在一瞬間飛離了軀殼，一陣更加殘忍的暴虐在烈酒的催化下刺激着我身體的每根纖維。我從背心口袋裏掏出一把小刀，打開它，抓住了那可憐畜生的脖子，不慌不忙地從牠的眼窩裏挖出了一隻眼珠！在寫下這該詛咒的殘酷行為時，我漲紅着臉，渾身發燙，戰慄着。

早晨，我的理智恢復了——睡眠消退了夜晚那恣意的憤怒——對於那罪惡的行為，我有種半是恐懼半是自責的感覺；不過，那至多是一種微弱而模糊的感覺，而我的靈魂依然無動於衷。我再次縱酒，把這事的記憶淹沒在酒精中。

同時，那隻貓慢慢復原了。真的，那失去眼珠的眼窩看上去很可怕，但是那貓不再顯出感到疼痛的樣子。牠像往常一樣在屋子周圍走動，不過，正如我所預料的，我一靠近，牠就極其驚慌地逃開。我當時的舊情尚未完全泯滅，眼見這曾經如此喜愛我的動物對我明顯表露出厭惡，我開始還感到傷心，但是那感覺很快就變成憤怒。然後，仿佛是要導致我最終不可改變的滅亡，那乖戾之魔出現了。對於這種乖戾，哲學上尚未有解釋。然而，就像我相信自己的靈魂存在，我也相信這乖戾是人內心最原始的衝動之一——是最基本的資質，或者說是情感之一，它決定了人的個性。誰沒有過一百次地發現，正是因為自己知道不該為之，才偏偏幹了可恥或是愚蠢的行徑呢？難道我們沒有正因為知道法規是怎麼回事，卻偏要最不顧理智地以身試法嗎？我認為，徹底擊垮了我的就是這種乖戾。正是這種深不可測的要違背本性的靈魂渴望——想糟踐自身的天性——明知故犯，才促使我繼續並最終完成自己對這不加反抗的畜生的傷害。一天早晨，我冷酷地在那隻貓的脖子上打了個套索，並將牠吊在一棵樹的樹杈上——我吊起牠，一邊淚水縱橫，內心充斥着最苦澀的自責——我把牠吊起來是因為我知道牠愛過我，因為我覺得牠不給我施用暴力的理由；——我吊起牠是因為我知道這樣做是犯罪——那可怕的罪行會威脅我那不朽的靈魂，將它置於——如果這事可能的話——甚至最萬能的上帝那無盡的憐憫都觸及不到的地方。

在犯下這罪行的夜裏，我被起火了的喊叫聲從睡夢中喚醒。我牀上的帷幔都着火了，整個房子也在燃燒。妻子、僕人、我自己千辛萬苦地從大火中逃出來。大火把一切燒個精光。我的全部財產都被它吞噬了，我沉浸在絕望中。

現在我並不企圖查找災難和殘忍之間的因果關係，但我要詳細敘述這一系列的事件——並希望沒有任何遺漏。在大火發生的次日，我查看了廢墟。除了一道牆，其餘的都坍倒了。這道倖存的牆壁是一道隔牆，它並不太厚，站立在房子中央，我的牀頭正靠着這堵牆。牆上的泥灰在很大程度上阻止了大火——我把這事實歸結為那牆最近剛粉刷過。一大羣人圍攏在這堵牆跟前，很多人似乎在細緻地檢查它的某個部分。那些諸如"奇怪！""少有！"以及其他類似的表述刺激了我的好奇心。我靠近牆壁，看了看，白色牆壁上似乎淺浮雕般地刻着一隻巨大的貓的身形。形象確實精細逼真，貓的脖子上還繞着一根繩子。

我一看到這幽靈——因為我只能這樣來稱呼它——便驚愕和恐懼到了極點。但是，回憶最終幫了我。我記得，那隻貓是在房子附近的花園裏被吊死的。火警發出時，那花園已經迅速擠滿了人羣——肯定有人砍了樹上的繩套，把貓從敞開的窗戶扔了進來，扔進了我的房間。這樣做可能是為了喚醒我。在其他牆壁倒塌時，這隻受我殘害的貓就被壓進了剛刷過的石灰裏；石灰在火焰及動物屍體的氨水的作用下，完成了我所看見的那張肖像畫。

儘管我就這樣輕鬆地對我的理性（如果不完全是對我的良心）解釋了剛才所詳述的那個驚人事實，但那事實給我的想像力留下了深刻的印象。幾個月來，我無法擺脫那隻貓的幻影；而且，這期間，我的靈魂中恢復了一種含混的，似乎是卻又不是悔恨的感覺。我竟然對失去牠感到後悔，並到時常光顧的下等場所去尋找另一隻同樣種類、長得多少有些相像的寵物，來替代那隻貓。

一天夜裏，我懵懵懂懂地坐在一家臭名昭著的下等酒館裏，注意力突然被某樣黑色的東西吸引了，那東西靜靜地趴在一隻巨大的杜松子酒或是朗姆酒的酒桶上。這隻桶是房間裏主要的擺設。我一直盯着桶上的東西看了好幾分鐘，令我吃驚的是，剛才怎麼沒有馬上看出上面的東西。我靠近牠，用手摸了摸。那是一隻黑貓——一隻巨大的貓——和普魯托一樣大，幾乎每一處都很像牠，除了一個地方。普魯托身上沒有一根白毛，但這隻貓卻一塊大大的、雖然是很模糊的白斑，幾乎蓋住了整個胸部。

我一摸牠，牠就站起身來，大聲地咕嚕着，擦着我的手，顯得很高興引起我的注意。這就是我一直在找尋的動物了，我立刻向店主買這隻貓；但是那人說貓不是他的 —— 也不知道牠的來龍去脈 —— 而且從沒見過牠。

我繼續撫摸着牠，當我準備回家時，這傢伙顯出願意跟着我的樣子。我就讓牠跟着，一路走，一邊不時地俯下身子拍拍牠。牠一進家裏，馬上就熟悉了那裏，並立刻贏得我妻子的寵愛。

可是我很快就發現，自己內心裏產生了對牠的一種厭惡，這恰好與我期待的正相反；我不知道這是怎麼回事，也不明白是為甚麼 —— 牠對我明顯的喜愛反而令我噁心和生氣。慢慢地，這種厭惡的感覺和惱火的情緒變成一種仇恨的痛苦。我避開那隻貓；一種羞辱感，以及對我過去殘酷行為的回憶使我沒有對牠施虐。好幾個星期，我沒有打過牠，也沒有虐待過牠，但是漸漸地 —— 很緩慢地 —— 我開始用無法言說的厭惡眼光來看待牠，並且悄悄地從牠那可惡的存在現場，以及從那瘟疫般的氣息中逃開。

毫無疑問，一個發現加重了我對那畜生的仇恨。把牠帶回家的次日早晨，我發現牠和普魯托一樣，也被挖掉了一隻眼睛。不過，這情況反而增加了妻子對牠的憐愛，正如我早已說過的，她天性高尚仁慈，而這種情操曾經是我卓越的品行，也是我許多最樸實最純粹的快樂的源泉。

然而，我對那隻貓日益厭惡，牠對我的喜愛卻似乎與日俱增。我到哪裏牠跟到哪裏，那執着勁讀者也許難以理解。無論我坐在哪裏，牠就蜷縮在我椅子下面，或者攀上我的雙膝，用牠那可惡的撫摸侵擾我。如果我起身走開，牠就會跑到我的雙腿間，差點要把我推倒，或者把那又長又尖銳的爪子扣在我衣服上，爬上我的胸口。這種時候，儘管我很想一拳揍扁了牠，但還是忍住沒那麼幹，這多少有點出於對以往罪行的回憶，但是主要的原因是——讓我立刻承認了吧——我真的很害怕這畜生。

這恐懼不完全因具體的邪惡而起——可是我又不知道此外還能用甚麼來形容。我幾乎羞於承認——是的，即使是在這死牢裏我都幾乎羞於承認——這畜生在我心裏引起的驚慌和恐懼，被我想像中最純粹的狂想所激化。我妻子不止一次地提醒我注意牠那白毛的特徵，我已經描述過那白毛了，它是唯一可見的使這奇怪的傢伙和那隻被我毀了的貓之間的區別。讀者會記得，這塊白斑雖然很大，但是本來很模糊；可是，慢慢地——慢得令人幾乎察覺不到，而且很長時間裏我的理智也拼命抵抗，認為這只是幻覺——它最終顯出了清晰的輪廓。現在，那形狀令我說起來都要顫慄——尤其，我覺得厭惡，而且害怕，如果我有膽量的話，我早就除掉這妖怪了——現在，我是說，那可怕的形象——是一樣恐怖的東西——是個絞刑架！——哦，那恐懼和罪惡的機器，它是如此令人悲哀而驚慌——那痛苦和死亡的引擎！

當時，我真是悲慘到常人無法忍受的地步。這殘忍的畜生——我已經將牠的夥伴輕蔑地毀滅了——這殘忍的畜生是來折磨我的——折磨我，一個被塑造成高高在上的上帝形象的人——那痛苦是如此難以忍受！唉！我晝夜不能安寧！在白天，這畜生不讓我有片刻獨處時間，在夜裏我不時地從無以名狀的噩夢中驚醒，發現那傢伙朝我臉上呼熱氣，感受到牠巨大的重量——牠是一個我無力驅除的噩夢的化身——是我心頭永遠的重負！

在這些折磨之下，我那所剩無幾的善性也屈服了。惟有邪惡的念頭親密地陪伴着我——那是最黑暗、最惡毒的念頭。我慣有的陰鬱積聚着，變成了對所有事物所有人的仇恨；在驟然、頻繁、失控的怒火噴發中，我盲目地放任自我，而我那默默忍受着痛苦的妻子，唉！她成為了最經常、最寬容的受害者。

一天，為家事之故，她陪我走進了那古老建築的地窖裏。因為貧窮，我們被迫居住在那幢老房子裏。那隻貓跟着我走下了陡峭的樓梯，並且差點將我絆倒在地，把我惹得要瘋狂了。我舉起一把斧子，在憤怒中竟忘了那種使我一直未能下手的幼稚的恐懼，朝着那畜生揮過去。當然，如果真如我希望的那樣劈下去，這畜生會在瞬間斃命。不過我那一揮手的動作被妻子的手攔住了。我被這種干擾刺激得更加氣憤，變得比狂暴的瘋子還要激動，我使勁掙脫她的手，一斧子向她的頭部劈下去。她沒哼一聲就倒地死了。

幹完這可怕的謀殺後，我立刻開始仔細考慮藏匿屍體的事。我知道，無論白天黑夜，我都不能將它移出房子，鄰居會看見的。我的腦海裏出現了很多計劃。一會想到把屍體剁成碎塊，用火來銷毀它們，一會又決定在地窖的地裏挖一個坑埋了它。我還仔細考慮過把它丟進院子中的井裏——又考慮按兇手通常的做法，把屍體像貨物一樣裝進箱子，找一個搬運工抬出房子。最後，我有了個比其他這些都更可行的主意。我決定將它砌進地窖的牆壁裏——就像書中所説的中世紀僧侶們把受害者砌到牆裏一樣。

這地窖很適合派這種用場。它的牆壁建構得很疏鬆，最近還全部塗了層石灰，石灰很粗糙，潮濕的空氣使它還沒有變硬。另外，其中一堵牆上還有個凸起，這是因為裏面有一個假煙囱，或是假壁爐，後來那牆被填補抹平，其表面和周圍很相像。我相信自己可以輕易地移開這裏的磚頭，把屍體塞進去，並把牆壁砌得和原先一樣，這樣，就沒人能看出甚麼值得懷疑的東西了。

我的估計沒有錯。我用一根撬杠就輕鬆地移開了那些磚頭，小心地把屍體靠在內牆上，讓它保持這個樣子，不太費力地又把牆壁照原樣砌回去。我弄到了灰泥、沙土，還有毛髮，儘量小心翼翼地把它們調成了與舊的無法分辨的灰泥，並細心地把它抹在新砌好的牆面上。完工後，我對所做的一切很滿意。牆面沒有顯出一絲被破壞過的痕跡。地板上的垃圾也被我謹慎細緻地堆起來。我不無得意地四處看了看，自言自語道——"至少，我的努力沒有白費。"

下一步，我要去找那個畜生，是牠導致了這場邪惡事件；我終於堅定決心要將牠處死。如果當時我能找到牠，牠的宿命無疑是注定了；但是這狡猾的畜生好像早已對我剛才的憤怒暴行有了警覺，牠避免在我當時的情緒下出現。我無法形容或想像，這可惡的傢伙消失後，我心中感到的那種深深的、欣然的輕鬆。在夜裏，牠也沒有出現——因此，從牠走進這房子以來，我終於有一個夜晚可以睡得酣暢安寧了；是的，即使我還帶着心頭那謀殺的重負，我還是入睡了。

第二天，第三天過去了，那個折磨人的東西還是沒出現。我又一次像自由人一般呼吸了。那可怕的妖魔永遠從這裏消失了！我再也不會見到牠了！我感到無上歡樂！我那陰險的罪行並沒有讓我感到甚麼不安。警方來進行了幾次詢問，但是我很輕鬆地回答了他們。他們甚至還進行了搜查——不過當然不會發現甚麼了。我覺得未來的幸福已安然無憂了。

　　謀殺妻子後的第四天，一夥警察來了，他們出乎意料地進了房子，又開始對房子進行嚴格的搜查。然而，我藏匿屍體的位置十分安全，誰也猜不到，我根本不覺得慌張。警官們讓我陪着他們查找。他們任何角落都不放過。最後，他們第三或者是第四次地進入地窖。我連肌肉都沒有顫抖一下，心臟跳動得和一個純真入睡的人一樣平穩。我從地窖這頭走到那頭，雙臂交叉抱在胸前，悠閒地踱來踱去。警察的疑慮徹底消除了，並準備離開。我內心的喜悅強烈到無法控制。得意洋洋中，我興奮地想，哪怕只說一個詞，讓他們加倍確信我是清白的。

　　"先生們，"我終於說了，這時他們正走上階梯，"我很高興打消了你們的疑慮，希望你們健康，並再次向諸位表示我微薄的敬意。順便提一下，先生們，這—— 這是一間結構很不錯的房子，"（在我急切地想說得輕鬆點時，我幾乎不知道自己到底說了甚麼）——"可以說是一間結構非常精良的房子。這些牆壁—— 先生們，你們要走了嗎？—— 這些牆壁砌得很牢固"；這時，純粹是出於虛張聲勢的狂熱，我用手裏的手杖重重地敲了敲，正好敲在裏面藏了我愛妻屍體的那部分牆壁上。

　　可是—— 願上帝將我從大惡魔的利牙中保護和解救出來！—— 沒等敲擊牆壁的回聲停下來，我就聽到那墓穴中有聲音在回答！—— 那是一聲喊叫，起初很壓抑，斷斷續續的，就像孩子的抽泣聲，很快，那聲音就增強了，變成了一聲長長的、響亮的、持續的尖叫，完全是異樣的、非人的—— 那是一聲嚎叫—— 一聲哀歎般的尖叫，它半是恐懼半是得意，好像只有地獄才能升起這樣的聲音，而且是由下了地獄的痛苦的靈魂，以及由那因毀滅而歡呼的惡魔共同從喉嚨裏發出來的聲音。

就不必再形容我當時的想法了。我大驚失色，踉蹌地走向對面的牆壁。在那一瞬間，那夥站在樓梯上的人因為極度的恐慌和敬畏而靜止不動。接着，十幾條粗壯的胳膊用力推着那堵牆。牆徹底倒塌了。那屍體 —— 它早已腐爛，血塊凝結在上面 —— 站立在大家面前。在屍體頭上，坐着那隻可怕的野獸，牠張大着血紅的嘴，獨眼裏噴着怒火，就是牠的詭計誘惑我犯下了謀殺的罪行，也是牠泄密的聲音將我交到了絞刑吏手裏。我竟把那妖怪也砌進了墳墓。

（張瓊譯）

2
金甲蟲

天哪！天哪！這傢伙正瘋狂地舞蹈！

他遭那毒蜘蛛咬了。

——《一切皆錯》

多年以前，我和威廉姆·勒格朗先生建立了友誼。他出生於一個名望悠久的法國新教家族，曾經很富有，但是一系列不幸使他淪落到經濟窘迫的地步。為了避免那些災難所引發的羞辱，他離開了新奧爾良這個父輩們一直生活的城市，在南卡羅來納州查爾斯頓附近的沙利文島居住下來。

這是個很孤立的島嶼，盡是海邊的沙石，大約有三英里長，寬度也超不過四分之一英里。島嶼和陸地之間被一條不太明顯的支流隔開，那水流蜿蜒地穿越一片茫茫的蘆葦叢和泥灘，那是沼澤雞樂於棲息之地。人們可能會料想，那裏的植物稀少，而且身形都十分矮小，根本看不到任何高大的樹種。在島的最西端附近，是莫爾特里堡。夏天，那裏有一些簡陋的框架房屋被出租，房客都是從查爾斯頓的喧囂和炎熱中逃來的難民。在那裏，確實有可能會發現葉子又短又硬的矮棕櫚；但是，除了西端，以及海岸邊的一道堅硬、白色的海灘，整個島嶼都被茂密而芳香的香桃木叢覆蓋着，英國的園藝師們倒是很珍視這類植物。這些灌木叢通常高十五或二十英尺，它們形成了幾乎是密不可透的矮木林，並且籠罩在馥郁芳香的氛圍中。

在這片叢林的最深處，離東部或者說離島嶼那荒涼的盡頭不遠的地方，勒格朗為自己修築了一間小屋。在我第一次、純屬偶然地和他相識之時，他就住在那裏。這相識立刻發展成了我們之間的友誼——因為隱居者身上有許多令人感興趣和可尊敬之處。我發現他受過很好的教育，有非凡的思維能力，但是他厭倦了與人交往，沉溺於乖張的情緒，喜怒無常。他藏書豐富，卻很少閱讀。他主要的興趣在於狩獵和垂釣，或者沿着海灘漫步，穿越那片香桃木叢林，並尋找貝殼或是昆蟲標本——他對昆蟲標本的收集或許連斯瓦姆默丹[1]都會眼紅。他在這些短途旅行中，常有一個名叫丘必特的老黑人陪伴着。老人在他家族沒落之前就被釋放了，可是無論是威脅，還是利誘，都沒法說服他放棄他所認為的跟隨年輕"主子"足跡的權利。也許勒格朗的親戚們在考慮到他多少有些思維混亂的情況下，努力使丘必特懷着這種固執，讓他監督和照料這個流浪者。

在沙利文島所處的緯度上，冬天罕有酷寒天氣，而且秋天通常無需生火。然而，在 18×× 年的十月中旬的某一天，天氣突然變得異常寒冷。日落之前，我從那片常綠叢林向朋友的小屋跋涉，我已經好幾個星期沒有拜訪他了——當時我住在查爾斯頓，那裏離島有九英里的路，而往返的交通工具又遠比今天落後。到達小屋時，我照常敲響了他的門，但是沒人應。於是我就在自己知道的藏鑰匙的地方找到鑰匙，打開門，走了進去。壁爐裏的火在熊熊燃燒着，這可真罕見，但是倒不令人反感。我脱掉外套，在一張靠背椅上坐下，靠着那堆劈啪作響地在燃燒的木柴，耐心地等着主人回來。

天黑後不久，他們就回來了，並且給了我最熱情的歡迎。丘必特咧嘴笑着，四下張羅着要燒沼澤雞當晚餐。勒格朗處於一種熱情狀態中 —— 除此我還能怎麼來形容他們呢？他發現了一種不知名的雙殼貝，它是一個新的種類，而且，不僅如此，他還繼續追蹤下去，並在丘必特的協助下獲得了一種聖甲蟲，他確信那是全新的種類，不過在這方面，他希望我能在次日發表一下見解。

"幹嘛不在今晚呢？"我問道，一邊在火上搓着雙手，希望整個聖甲蟲種類都滾蛋。

"啊，如果我早知道你在這裏就好了！"勒格朗説道，"我們好久沒見面了；我怎麼想得到你會偏偏在這麼個夜晚來看我？在我回來的路上，我遇到了從堡壘來的 G 中尉，而且，很愚蠢的是，我把甲蟲借給了他；因此你只有明天一早才能見到牠了。今晚就住這裏吧，日出時，我就會派丘必特去拿。牠可是最可愛的生靈了！"

"甚麼？ —— 日出？"

"胡説！不！ —— 我指的是甲蟲。牠有着燦爛的黃金色 —— 大約有大核桃那麼大 —— 在背的一端有兩個墨黑的點，另一端的黑點似乎要大長一些。牠的觸角是 —— "

"牠可不摻雜質，主人，我不斷地告訴過你，"丘必特插進話來，"牠是金甲蟲，每個部分都是黃金，從裏到外，除了翅膀 —— 我這輩子還從沒掂過這麼重的甲蟲。"

"行，就算是吧，丘必特，"勒格朗說着，顯得更加熱切了，在我看來，他似乎沒必要如此認真的；"可難道這就是你要讓雞燒糊的理由嗎？那顏色"—— 這時他轉向我 ——"真的幾乎能證明丘必特的看法。你一定沒見過比那表面發散出來的金屬光澤更絢麗的了 —— 不過你得等到明天才能有結論。現在，我還可以給你講講牠的形狀。"說着，他在一張小桌子旁落座，桌上放着一支鋼筆和一瓶墨水，但是沒有紙張。他想從抽屜裏找些紙，可是沒找到。

"沒關係，"他最後這麼說道，"有這就行。"然後他從背心口袋裏抽出了一張令我覺得髒兮兮的紙，並用鋼筆在上頭畫起了草圖。他這麼做時，我由於仍然覺得寒冷，還是靠在火邊的椅子上。他畫完圖形，沒站起身就交給了我。我接過來時，聽到一聲響亮的咆哮，接着門上傳來了刮擦聲。丘必特打開門，勒格朗那隻巨大的紐芬蘭犬竄了進來，牠跳上我的肩膀，親昵地撫摸舔舐並壓在我身上，因為我前幾次拜訪時對牠很是關注。等牠嬉戲夠了，我看看那張紙，實話說，我對朋友所描繪的東西感到莫名其妙。

"不錯！"凝視了片刻後，我說道，"不得不承認，這是一種奇怪的聖甲蟲，很新穎，我從沒見過類似的 —— 除非說牠是顱骨，或者是死人的腦殼，在我所觀察到的事物中，還沒比這更像的了。"

"死人的腦殼！"勒格朗重複着，"哦 —— 是的 —— 沒錯，毫無疑問，從紙上看，外形倒有些相像。上頭的那兩個黑點就像眼睛，呃？底部那個稍長一些的就像嘴巴 —— 而且整個形狀是橢圓形的。"

"也許是吧，"我說，"但是，勒格朗，恐怕你不是個畫家，必須得等我親眼見過那隻甲蟲，我才能對牠的外形有所了解。"

　　"呃，我也不知道自己算不算個畫家，"他說着，有點慍惱，"可我畫得還不錯——至少應該這麼畫——我拜過一些名師，也自信並不算笨。"

　　"可是，親愛的，那你是在開玩笑了，"我說，"這是一個非常像樣的腦殼——真的，根據生理學標本的一般概念，可以說這是一個相當漂亮的腦殼——如果你說的聖甲蟲與之相像的話，那牠一定是這世上最奇怪的聖甲蟲了。哎呀，從這一點看，我們可以來一點令人毛骨悚然的興奮。我想你可以把牠稱作人頭甲蟲，或者類似的——博物學中有許多相似的名稱。可是你所說的觸角在哪裏呢？"

　　"牠的觸角！"勒格朗說着，顯得對此話題有種莫名的熱衷，"你一定得看看這個觸角。我畫得和真的蟲子上的一樣清晰，而且覺得足夠逼真了。"

　　"好，好，"我說，"也許是這樣——可我還是沒見到呀；"於是，我把紙遞給他，沒再作任何評價，我不想惹火他；不過我對這些轉變感到很驚訝，他的惱火令我不解——而且，從那張甲蟲畫裏，也確實看不到觸角，而且整張畫真的和普通的死人頭骨的線條非常相像。

　　他很生氣地接過了那張紙，準備團皺它，顯然是要把它扔進火裏去，這時，他不經意地瞥了一下那個圖形，忽然，他似乎猛一凝神，只一瞬間，臉色就緋紅了——可刹那，它又變得出奇蒼白。過了幾分鐘，他在座位上繼續仔細地觀察着那畫。最後，他站起身，從桌上拿起一支蠟燭，走過去坐在了房間最深角落的一個水手櫃上。在那裏，他又一次很熱切地凝視着那張紙，把它轉成各個方向。不過，他沒說一句話，這舉動把我嚇壞了；可是我覺得謹慎起見，還是別發表意見以激化他不斷喜怒無常的脾氣為好。這時，他從外套口袋裏掏出一隻皮夾，把那張紙小心翼翼地放進去，並把皮夾放置在書桌裏，還上了鎖。現在他鎮靜多了，不過他最初的熱情已完全消失了，他看上去與其說是在發怒，毋寧說是在出神。當夜晚漸深時，他在幻想中越陷越深，對我的俏皮話毫無反應。我原本打算像往常一樣在小屋裏過夜，可是，看到主人這樣的情緒，我覺得還是告辭的好。他也沒有強留我，不過，在我離開時，他甚至比以往更加熱誠地握了握我的手。

大約一個月之後（這期間我再沒見過勒格朗），勒格朗的僕人丘必特到查爾斯頓來找我。我從沒見過這好心的老黑人這樣沮喪過，於是我擔心朋友有糟糕的事情發生了。

"你好，丘必特，有甚麼事嗎？—— 主人怎麼樣了？"我問他。

"哎呀，說真的，先生，主人可不太好。"

"不太好？我真的很難過。他有甚麼難處嗎？"

"唉！問題就在這裏！—— 他從來不說 —— 可是他的病真的很重。"

"病很重？丘必特？—— 你幹嘛不早說？他臥牀不起了？"

"不，不是這樣！—— 他不是這樣子 —— 問題就在這裏 —— 主人這樣子我的心裏沉重極了。"

"丘必特，我得弄清楚你剛才說的話。你說主人生病了，他告訴你哪裏不舒服了嗎？"

"唉，先生，為這個我都要發瘋了——主人根本不會説哪裏難受——可是那又是甚麼使他到處走動，這裏看看，那裏瞧瞧，低着頭，聳着肩膀，像鬼一樣蒼白的呢？而且他整天拿着一張紙——"

"拿着甚麼，丘必特？"

"拿着紙，那上頭有畫——畫着我見過的最古怪的東西。告訴你，我看了都害怕。我非得留神死死盯着他。可那天他在太陽出來前逃走了，然後這好好的一整天都消失了。我早讓人削好了一根大棍子，要等他回來好好揍他一頓——可是我那麼笨，根本沒這個膽量——他看上去可真是虛弱。"

"呃？——甚麼？——哦對了！——總的説，我覺得你最好別對那可憐的傢伙太嚴厲了——別揍他了，丘必特——他會受不了的——不過你能想想是甚麼導致他這樣的，或者説改變了他的？上次我見了你之後，有甚麼不開心的事情發生過嗎？"

"沒有，先生，沒有甚麼不開心的事——我擔心是在那之前——就是你來的那天。"

"怎麼？你這是甚麼意思？"

"唉，先生，我指的是那隻甲蟲——牠還在那裏。"

"甚麼？"

"那隻甲蟲——我敢肯定主人的腦袋瓜被那隻金甲蟲給咬過了。"

"丘必特，你是怎麼才會有這種猜測的？"

"先生，那蟲子有好多腳，還有嘴。我從沒見過這樣厲害的蟲子——牠對任何接近牠的東西都又踢又咬。主人好不容易抓住了牠，但馬上又讓牠給跑了，告訴你 —— 他肯定是那時候被咬的。不知怎麼的，我自己就很討厭那蟲子的嘴巴，所以我不願意用手指去抓牠，不過我找到一張紙去抓。我把牠包在紙裏面，還把紙片塞進了牠的嘴巴 —— 就是這樣子。"

"這麼說你認為主人真的被那甲蟲咬了，覺得咬過後他就生病了？"

"我不是認為 —— 是知道。他要不是給那隻金甲蟲咬了，那他幹嘛滿腦子想着黃金？我以前聽說過金甲蟲的事。"

"你怎麼知道他癡迷黃金的？"

"我怎麼知道的？哎，因為他在夢裏還念叨它 —— 所以我知道了。"

"好吧，丘必特，也許你是對的；可是承蒙你今天的拜訪，我怎樣才能幫你呢？"

"你說甚麼，先生？"

"勒格朗讓你帶甚麼口信沒？"

"有，先生，我把這張紙給帶來了，"接着，丘必特遞給我一封短信，上面是這樣寫的：

親愛的 —— 怎麼這麼長時間不見你？我希望你不至於蠢到對我的些許不雅而感到惱火；不過，不，這是不可能的。

自從見你之後，我就頗為焦慮。我有要事相告，可又不知從何說起，到底該不該說。

幾天來，我的身體一直欠佳，而且可憐的老丘必特還總煩我，他好心的照料幾乎令我無法忍受了。你能相信嗎？

——有一天，他還準備了一根巨大的棍子，要懲罰我，說我趁他不防悄悄溜走，而且還花整天的時間獨自呆在陸地的山丘裏。我真的相信，因為我病歪歪的樣子，才得以免去痛打的。

自我們見面之後，我的陳列櫃裏沒再增添新的標本。

無論如何，如果可以的話，請你抽空隨丘必特一起過來。來吧，我希望今晚能見到你，我有要事相告。我保證這事極其重要。

你永遠的

威廉姆·勒格朗

此信的某種語調令我十分不安。整封信的風格和勒格朗所固有的有着本質上的不同。他在想些甚麼？是甚麼新的奇思怪想在刺激他呢？他會有甚麼"極其重要"的事要辦呢？丘必特所描述的他可不怎麼妙。我擔心，那種不幸而持續的精神壓力會把朋友的理智折磨垮了。因此，我毫不猶豫地就準備和那個黑人一同前往。

到了碼頭，我看到了一把長柄鐮刀和三把鐵鍬，顯然都是簇新的，躺在我們將要登上的那隻船的底部。

"這是甚麼意思，丘必特？"我問道。

"是鐮刀和鐵鍬，先生。"

"沒錯，可是它們放在這裏有啥用？"

"主人硬要我到鎮上買鐮刀和鐵鍬，我花了很多錢才買來的呢。"

"可是，你'主人'神祕兮兮地要鐮刀和鐵鍬做甚麼呀？"

"我也不清楚，要是我相信他自己清楚要幹甚麼的話，讓我出門撞見鬼好了。不過這都是為了那隻蟲子。"

我發現從丘必特那裏問不出甚麼來，他整個人的思想都在"那蟲子"上。於是，我上了船，出發了。風勢強勁順利，我們很快就駛入了去莫爾特里堡北邊的海灣。接着，我們走了大約兩英里的路，就到了小屋。我們到達時大概是下午三點，勒格朗一直在急切地盼着我們。他抓住我的一隻手，有一種神經質的熱情，這使我驚慌起來，更肯定了先前的疑慮。他的面色蒼白得可怕，深陷的眼睛閃爍着異樣的光。我詢問了他的健康狀況，在不知該說些甚麼才好的情況下，我問他是否從 G 中尉那裏拿到了那隻聖甲蟲。

"哦，是的，"他回答說，臉色發生了劇烈的變化，"我第二天上午就拿到了，甚麼都無法讓我和那隻聖甲蟲分開了。你知道丘必特對牠的評價很正確嗎？"

"哪方面？"我問，心裏有一種悲哀的不祥之兆。

"即他認為那是一隻真正黃金質地的甲蟲。"他說這話時態度非常嚴肅深沉，我有種說不出來的震驚。

"這甲蟲給我帶來了財富，"他繼續說着，帶着勝利的微笑；"可以讓我的家產得以恢復。因此，我這樣珍視牠有甚麼奇怪的呢？既然我命該得到財富，我就只能妥善利用了，牠是我找到黃金的指引者。丘必特，把那隻聖甲蟲給我拿過來！"

"甚麼蟲子，先生？我可不願意去拿；你自己拿給他吧。"於是，勒格朗站起身，莊重而嚴肅地把那隻甲蟲從一個關着牠的玻璃盒裏拿出來，交給我。牠是隻很漂亮的聖甲蟲，而且，當時的博物學家還不知道牠 —— 當然了，從科學的角度來看，牠很有價值。牠的背上的一端有兩個黑圓點，另一端的黑點長一些。甲蟲殼極其堅硬光滑，和打磨過的黃金一模一樣。那蟲子的重量也令人吃驚，從所有這些來看，我幾乎沒法挑剔丘必特的描述；可是我這輩子都沒法解釋勒格朗為甚麼會贊同這樣的觀點。

在我好好地觀察了那隻甲蟲後，他說，"我派人叫你來，"語氣顯得很誇張，"我派人叫你來，這樣我就可以聽聽你的評價，得到你的支持，並進一步考慮命運和這隻蟲子——"

"親愛的勒格朗，"我叫起來，打斷了他，"你準是病了，最好有點防範措施。你該臥牀的，我會陪你住幾天，直到你恢復為止。你在發燒，而且——"

"搭搭我的脈搏，"他説。

我搭了搭，説實話，我沒發現絲毫發燒的跡象。

"可是，儘管你沒發燒，你也許病了。這一次你就聽我的吩咐吧，首先你得臥牀，然後——"

"你弄錯了，"他插話了，"我身體現在好得甚至能指望承受這種我正在經歷的興奮。如果你真希望我好，你應該幫我緩解這種興奮。"

"那我怎麼做呢？"

"很簡單，丘必特和我本人打算到大陸的山裏去勘探一下，而且，在考察的過程中，我們會需要某位我們能夠信任的人士的協助。你就是我們唯一能信任的人。無論我們成功或是失敗，你現在感覺到的我身上的興奮就會得到相應地緩解。"

"我很願意幫你，"我回答説，"但是你的意思是説你們到山裏去考察和這隻可惡的甲蟲有關嗎？"

“是的。”

“那麼，勒格朗，對這樣荒唐的舉止，我就愛莫能助了。”

“我很難過——非常難過——因為我們只好自己去試試了。”

“你們自己去試試！你簡直是瘋了——慢着！——你打算去多久？”

“也許整個夜晚。我們會立刻開始行動，無論如何，日出前就回來。”

“那你能向我保證，以你的名譽起誓，等這怪念頭結束後，等關於這蟲子的事（老天！）忙完後，你就回家，好好地採納我的建議，就像照醫生所說的做嗎？”

“好的，我保證，那現在我們走吧，因為不能再耽誤了。”

懷着沉重的心情，我陪伴着朋友出發了。我們是四點走的——包括勒格朗，丘必特，狗，還有我本人。丘必特帶着鐮刀和鐵鍬——他堅持一個人扛這些東西——在我看來，這更多是因為他生怕主人拿到這些工具中的任何一件，而不是因為他極度的吃苦耐勞或殷勤。他的行為固執透了，而且“這可惡的蟲子”是他一路上唯一說出來的話。我拎着兩個黑燈籠，而勒格朗則全心顧及那隻聖甲蟲，把牠拴在一根鞭繩繩端，一路走一路反復讓牠打轉，像變戲法似的。當我看到朋友這種最後的、明顯的神志不清跡象，我幾乎忍不住要哭。不過，我想最好還是順着他的怪念頭，至少目前得這樣做，直到我能採用甚麼更有效的措施來獲得成功的機會。我一邊想着，一邊努力打探他此次考察的目的，不過一無所獲。一旦他說服了我陪着他，就似乎不再願意討論那些次要問題了。對我所有的疑問，他只是回答：“我們等着瞧吧！”

我們乘着船穿越了島嶼頂端的溪流，然後登上了大陸海岸上的高地，並繼續向西北方向穿過一片非常荒涼和杳無人煙的鄉村。勒格朗堅定地領着路，不時地，他只作瞬間的停頓，以查看那些顯然是他上次經過時親手留下的路標。

就這樣，我們大約走了兩小時，日落時分，我們進入了一個區域，那裏比我至今見過的任何地方都荒涼得多。那是一片平台般的地方，靠近一座幾乎難以攀登的小山之峯頂，小山從底部到頂端盡是茂密的樹林，間或有巨石峭壁，插在沙土裏看上去很不牢固，許多巨石之所以未從峭壁墜入下面的山谷，全憑着它們斜靠於其上的樹木的支撐。峽谷深邃，縱橫交錯，透出嚴峻的莊重。

我們所攀登的台階荊棘密佈。穿越其中之際，我們馬上發現不用鐮刀幾乎寸步難行；丘必特在主人的指引下，為我們開路，於是大家來到了一棵巨大的鵝掌楸下。那樹屹立着，一旁簇擁着八九棵橡樹。但是後者，以及我所見過的其他樹木，在樹葉和樹形的優美，枝杈的繁茂修長和氣勢巍峨上，都遠不及那棵鵝掌楸。當我們走到鵝掌楸旁，勒格朗轉向丘必特，問他能否爬上去。那老人對這問題顯得有點驚愕，好久都沒答話。最後，他走到巨大的樹幹前，緩緩地繞着它走，仔細地觀察着。詳細檢查完畢，他只是説：

"行，主人，任何丘必特見過的樹，他都能爬。"

"那就馬上爬上去吧，否則天太黑我們就看不清周圍了。"

"要爬多高，主人？"丘必特問。

"先爬主幹，然後我會告訴再爬哪裏——現在——慢着！把這隻甲蟲帶上。"

"這蟲子，主人！——這金甲蟲！"黑人叫着，驚慌地倒退着——"幹嘛一定要帶這蟲子上樹？——我不幹！"

"丘必特，如果像你這樣的大個子黑人還害怕帶上一隻不會傷人的死甲蟲，那你可以用這繩子把牠弄上去——不過，假如你不想辦法帶牠上去的話，我就非得用鐵鍬打碎你的腦袋了。"

"你這是幹嘛，主人？"丘必特説道，顯然被羞辱得順從起來，"你總想對你的老黑人大聲嚷嚷，我不過説句笑話罷了。我害怕這隻蟲子！我怕牠幹嘛？"於是，他小心地抓住了繩子一端，儘量讓身子離開蟲子遠一些，準備上樹了。

這鵝掌楸，或者叫木蘭鵝掌楸，是美洲森林中最高大的樹種。在成長初期，它的樹幹特別光滑，經常長到很高都沒有橫向的枝杈；不過，到了成熟期，樹皮就會變得粗糙不平，這時，樹幹上會長出很多短小的分支。因此，在目前的情況下，爬樹的困難事實上並沒有表面所看到的那麼難。丘必特抱住了粗大的樹幹，並把雙臂和雙膝儘量貼緊。他的兩隻手抓住了一些突節，光着的腳趾頭停在另外的突節上。有一兩次，他差點沒掉下來。他終於扭動着攀上了第一個分叉，看上去似乎認為自己已經完成了整個任務。事實上，這時，攀爬的危險過去了，儘管爬樹的人離開地面已經有六、七十英尺。

"現在再從哪裏上去，主人？"他問道。

"順着最大的樹杈上——在這邊，"勒格朗説。那黑人立刻遵從他，不過現在麻煩明顯小了；他越爬越高，直到透過茂密的樹葉，我們已經看不到他矮胖的身影。不一會，傳來了他的喊聲。

"還得爬多高？"

"你到多高了？"勒格朗問。

"不能再高了，"黑人回答道，"都能從樹頂看到天空了。"

"別管甚麼天空，照我說的做。往樹幹下面看，數一下你這邊的樹杈數目，你爬過了多少樹杈？"

"一、二、三、四、五——我爬過了這邊的五個大樹杈，主人。"

"那就再爬高一個。"

過了幾分鐘，又傳來了他的聲音，他告訴我們他爬過第七個了。

"聽着，丘必特，"勒格朗喊着，顯然很興奮，"我要你沿這根樹杈往外爬，越遠越好，如果你看到甚麼奇怪的東西的話，就告訴我。"

這時，我對這可憐朋友發生了精神錯亂的猜疑終於被確定了。我只能把它歸結為精神失常，並非常急切地要把他弄回家。當我考慮怎麼做才最好時，丘必特的聲音又傳來了。

"我很害怕，爬這根樹杈太危險了——它整個就是根枯樹枝。"

"丘必特，你說它是一根枯樹枝？"勒格朗用顫抖的聲音叫道。

"是的，主人，全枯了——全朽了——早死透了。"

"我到底該怎麼辦？"勒格朗問，顯得非常沮喪。

"行！"我說着，很高興有機會插話，"幹嘛不回家，躺上牀。現在就走！——好夥計，天要黑了，而且，你得記住自己的諾言。"

"丘必特，"他喊着，根本不理會我，"你聽得到我的話嗎？"

"聽到了，主人，聽得清清楚楚。"

"那麼，用你的刀試試那木頭，看看是不是枯朽。"

"是枯了，主人，我肯定，"過了一會，黑人回答着，"不過沒我想得那麼枯。也許我可以獨自再冒險爬一點點，真的。"

"獨自！—— 你甚麼意思？"

"哎，我說的是那蟲子。牠太重了，如果我把牠扔下來，也許我一個黑人的重量還不會把樹枝壓斷。"

"你這可惡的混蛋！"勒格朗喊道，顯然是如釋重負的樣子，"你告訴我這些廢話是啥意思？你要是把那甲蟲扔下來，我就擰斷你的脖子。往這兒瞧，丘必特，你聽見了沒？"

"聽見了，主人，你不用這樣對着可憐的黑鬼吼。"

"好了！你給我聽着！—— 在你認為安全的範圍內，如果你試着儘量往外爬，並且不扔掉那甲蟲的話，等你一下來，我就送你一塊銀幣。"

"好吧，主人 —— 我試試，"那黑人立刻回答 ——"我就要到頂端了。"

"到頂端了！"這時勒格朗厲聲喊道，"你說你到樹杈頂端了？"

"馬上到了，主人 —— 哦—啊—哎喲！上帝！這上頭是甚麼呀？"

"哎！"勒格朗叫着，情緒高漲，"是甚麼？"

"唉，不過是一個骷髏頭 —— 有人把自己的頭吊在了樹上，而烏鴉把腦袋上的肉都吃光了。"

"甚麼，骷髏頭！—— 太好了，—— 它是怎麼被繫在樹杈上的？—— 是用甚麼固定住的？"

"知道了，主人，我得看看。我敢説，這可真古怪 —— 骷髏頭上有一個很大的釘子，這釘子把它固定在了樹上。"

"好了，丘必特，就照我説的做 —— 聽見了嗎？"

"聽見了，主人。"

"那麼，留心一下，找到頭顱左邊的那隻眼睛。"

"啊！哦！好的！可根本就沒有剩下甚麼眼睛呀。"

"蠢蛋！你能把你的右手和左手區分開來嗎？"

"哦，我知道了 —— 完全明白了 —— 我是用左手來劈木頭的。"

"對了！你是左撇子；你的左眼和左手在一個方向。現在，我想你能找到骷髏頭上的左眼了吧，或者説，就是左眼曾經在的位置，找到了嗎？"

過了好長一會那黑人問道：

"骷髏的左手和左眼也是在一個方向嗎？ —— 可是那骷髏頭根本沒有手 —— 不過沒關係！我找到左眼了 —— 就是它！我該怎麼做？"

"把那隻甲蟲穿過它垂下去，儘量把繩子放完 —— 不過小心點，別讓繩子脱了手。"

"我已經照做了，主人；把蟲子放進去可容易了 —— 瞧牠在下面！"

説話時，我們根本看不到丘必特，卻在繩子的頂端看到了那隻讓他如此費力放下來的甲蟲，牠熠熠閃光，在夕陽的餘暉中，就像一團打磨過的黃金，最後一線陽光還照亮了我們站着的這片高出的地面。聖甲蟲完全穿出了樹杈間的所有枝葉，如果讓牠往下落，都會掉在我們腳邊。勒格朗立刻拿起鐮刀，在甲蟲的正下方劈開了一塊直徑大約三四碼的圓形空地。幹完這事，他命令丘必特放掉繩子下樹來。

朋友又細緻地在甲蟲掉下來的位置打了個樁，然後從口袋裏掏出一個卷尺，把一頭繫在最靠近木樁的樹幹上。他打開卷尺，直到它碰到木樁，接着他沿着樹幹到木樁的方向繼續放卷尺，拉出了五十英尺的距離——丘必特則用鐮刀劈開了荊棘。在那裏，第二個樁子被打下了，朋友以它為中心點，大致畫了一個直徑大約四英尺的圓。最後，勒格朗拿起一把鐵鍬，並將另外兩把分別交給了丘必特和我，請我們儘快地着手挖土。

實話說，任何時候我都不太愛幹這活，而在這種特殊的情況下，我更是恨不得立刻就拒絕他的請求；因為夜晚要降臨了，這一番折騰讓我覺得很疲乏；可是我一時想不出逃避的辦法，而且也害怕自己的拒絕會攪亂了我那可憐朋友的平靜。當然，如果我能依賴丘必特的支持的話，我早就毫不猶豫地試圖強迫這個瘋子回家了；可是我太清楚這老黑人的脾性了，知道不管怎樣他都不會幫我去和主人發生個人衝突的。我能肯定後者已經被無數的關於發現藏寶地的南方迷信所迷惑，而且發現聖甲蟲一事更推波助瀾了他的幻想，或者說，丘必特堅持說那是“一隻足金甲蟲”的固執勁兒也激發了他的胡思亂想。有瘋狂傾向的思想很容易就能被這些暗示左右——尤其它又被一些令人中意的預想所促發着——於是我回憶起那可憐的傢伙所説的關於這隻甲蟲是他“財富的指引者”。想到所有這些，我又是悲傷着急，又是惱火不解，不過，最後，我決定先爽快地去做這些非做不可的事——即懷着美好願望去挖地，並儘快地以眼見為實來證明這是謬誤的空想。

燈籠點亮了，我們都帶着不太理智的熱情開始工作，當光線
照在我們身上和勞動工具上時，我禁不住想，對任何偶爾從這裏
經過的旁人來說，我們這夥人顯得太怪誕了，手裏做的事簡直令
人奇怪和疑惑。

　　我們奮力做了兩個小時，幾乎沒説話，而且，主要是狗的吠叫
讓我們覺得很尷尬，那狗對這工作饒有興趣。終於，牠鬧得太過
分了，我們都擔心牠會讓附近遊蕩的人產生警覺──或者毋寧説
這是勒格朗的擔憂。對我來說，我巴不得有人來打擾，這或許可
以幫我把這昏頭昏腦的人弄回家。終於，那叫聲被丘必特給有效
地制止了，他不慌不忙、不屈不撓地從坑裏爬出來，把那畜生的
嘴巴用一條吊褲帶綁了起來，然後低沉地笑着，又回來繼續幹活。

　　這兩個小時之後，我們已經挖了五英尺深，可是沒有任何財
寶的跡象。一陣停歇後，我開始希望這鬧劇該結束了。然而，
儘管勒格朗明顯很失望的樣子，他沉思着，擦了擦額頭的汗水，
又動手挖了起來。我們已經挖了個直徑為四英尺的完整圓圈，現
在，我們又慢慢地擴大這個範圍，並繼續又挖深了兩英尺。還是
一無所獲。那個我打心底同情的探寶者最終從坑裏爬上來，渾身
帶着極其苦澀的失望情緒，然後他緩慢而不情願地穿上了幹活前
曾丟在一邊的外套。這時，我甚麼話也沒說。丘必特則在主人舉
動的示意之下，也開始收拾工具。這以後，狗嘴巴上綁着的帶子
也被解開了，我們一邊回家，一邊陷入了深深的沉默。

　　往回大概走了十幾步路，勒格朗大聲詛咒，大步走到丘必特
面前，一把抓住他的領子。大吃一驚的黑人睜大了眼睛和嘴巴，
手裏的鐵鍬也掉落在地，他雙膝跪到地上。

"你這混蛋！"勒格朗說着，從緊咬的牙縫裏嘶嘶地發出幾個音節——"你這可惡的黑鬼！——說，快說！——別支吾，馬上回答我！——哪隻——哪隻是你的左眼？"

"哦，上帝啊，主人！這不是我那該死的左眼嗎？"驚愕的丘必特嚎叫着，把手放到他右邊的視覺器官上，拼命地捂着它，好像主人立刻會挖掉它似的。

"我就知道！——我明白了！哦！"勒格朗狂叫着，鬆開了黑人，又是跳，又是旋轉，僕人很震驚，他站起身，看看主人，又看看我，不作聲，又將視線從我身上移到主人那裏。

"走！我們必須得回去，"後者說道，"還沒完事呢，"他又朝那棵鵝掌楸走去。

我們來到樹下時，"丘必特，"他說，"到這裏來！那釘在樹杈上的骷髏頭是臉朝外的，還是朝着樹杈的？"

"臉是朝外的，主人，這樣烏鴉就能很輕鬆地啄到眼睛。"

"行，那麼，你把甲蟲從這隻眼睛還是那隻眼睛放下來的？"說着，他碰了碰丘必特的兩隻眼睛。

"是這隻，主人——左眼——正如你告訴我的，"而那黑人卻指着自己的右眼。

"夠了——我們必須再試一次。"

於是，朋友把標誌着甲蟲落地點的木椿由原來位置向西移動了三英吋，現在我可真見識了，或者說我相信自己看出了他的瘋狂中顯然有一些有條不紊的跡象。此刻，像前一次一樣，他用卷尺從離木椿最近的樹幹上拉到了木椿，並繼續沿着同一個方向拉到了五十英尺距離的位置，由此，把原來我們挖過的地點移動了幾碼距離。

在新的位置畫出了一個似乎比前面一次更大的圓圈，於是我們又開始拿鐵鍬幹活了。我累極了，不過，我幾乎無法理解自己思想發生了甚麼變化，對這強行要幹的活不再覺得太反感了。不知為甚麼，我對此充滿興趣——不，甚至是興奮。也許，在勒格朗所有誇張的舉動中有點甚麼——有點甚麼預見性的意味，或者是深思熟慮打動了我。我熱切地挖着地，不時發現自己懷着類似期待的心情，在等着發現寶藏。這種對寶藏的幻想都使我不幸的夥伴要瘋狂了。有那麼一陣子，我沉浸在這些奇思怪想中。大概幹了一個半小時的活，我們又被狗的猛烈嚎叫騷擾了。很明顯，牠上一次的焦躁不過是因為頑皮和任性，但是這一次，那叫聲有了種痛苦和嚴肅的意味。當丘必特再次試圖捆住牠的嘴巴時，牠劇烈地掙扎反抗，並跳進了坑裏面，用爪子狂亂地刨土。過了一會，牠刨出了一堆人的骷髏，那是兩具完整的骨架，裏面混合着幾個金屬紐扣，還有顯然是羊毛腐爛後的粉塵。我們用鐵鍬鏟了一兩下，翻上了一把大號西班牙刀的刀刃，當我們再鏟下去時，三四個散亂着的金幣和銀幣出現了。

看到這些，丘必特忍不住一陣高興，但是他主人的臉上帶着一種極端失望的表情。不過，他催促我們繼續鏟，而他話音未落，我靴子的腳趾處被一個半掩在泥土裏的鐵圈鈎住，踉蹌着往前摔倒了。

我們這下幹得更起勁了，我還從沒有經歷過比這更緊張而興奮的十分鐘。在這期間，我們順利地挖出了一個長方形的木頭箱子，它保存完好，硬度很高，顯然經歷了礦化處理——也許是經過二氯化汞的處理。那箱子有三英尺半長，三英尺寬，以及兩英尺半深。它被幾條精煉過的鐵條牢牢地綁着，還上了鉚釘，整體上形成了一種格狀結構。在箱子的每一側，靠近頂上的部分，是三個鐵圈——兩邊一共六個——這樣就能有六個人來抓穩它。我們三人使出全身力氣也只是稍稍搖動了一下箱子。我們立刻就明白要移開這麼重的東西是不可能的。好在，箱蓋子上只固定着兩個滑動的插銷。於是，我們拉起插銷——焦急地顫抖着，喘息着。在瞬間，無數的寶藏在我們面前閃亮着。當燈籠的光線照在坑裏時，從一堆令人迷惑的黃金和珠寶裏射出了眩目的光，真的把我們都晃暈了。

我不敢誇口說自己能描述出盯着財寶看時的心情，當然，那是一種撼動人心的驚訝。勒格朗似乎被興奮耗得筋疲力盡了，他幾乎不說話。有那麼一會，丘必特的表情僵死蒼白，當然了，這是從黑人臉部特徵的角度來看的。他好像被震住了——呆呆的。不久，他跪倒在坑裏面，齊肘深地把裸露的雙臂埋在黃金裏，並保持着那個樣子，好像在享受這奢華的沐浴。最後，他深深地歎了口氣，彷彿獨白似地感歎着：

"這都是那隻金甲蟲帶來的！那隻好心的金甲蟲！可憐的小甲蟲，我卻那麼粗魯地對待牠！黑鬼，你害臊嗎？——告訴我！"

最後，我覺得很有必要提醒主僕二人趕緊把這財寶搬走。夜色漸深，我們非得振作精神，在天亮之前把所有東西運回家。很難說該做甚麼，為此花了不少時間來討論，因為三個人的想法都那麼亂紛紛的。最後，我們把箱子裏的東西拿出三分之二，使箱子輕了許多，才費力地將它從坑裏抬了出來。我們把那些拿出來的財寶藏在荊棘裏，丘必特對狗下了嚴厲的命令，讓牠留下來看守財寶，在我們返回前不能藉故離開，也不能發出聲音。於是，我們趕緊抬着箱子回家，並安全地回到小屋，不過費了無數氣力，到達時已經凌晨一點了。我們都累垮了，根本不可能立刻幹活。休息到兩點，吃了飯，我們馬上又向山裏進發，還帶了三個恰巧在屋子裏找出來的結實的袋子。快到四點時，我們到達坑邊，儘量將餘下的財寶均量分攤背負，沒有填坑就再次上了返回小屋的路。第二次到家將金子放下時，黎明的第一道曙光剛從東方的樹梢上射下來。

此刻，我們徹底累癱了，不過那強烈的興奮使我們無法平靜。經過三四小時的淺睡，我們起了牀，彷彿約定好了似的，開始清點那些財寶。

那個箱子裝得滿滿的，我們花了一整天和大半個夜晚才清點完那些東西。箱子裏凌亂無章，每樣東西都雜亂地堆放着。我們細心地歸類後，發現自己擁有了比預料的更多的財富。從錢幣的價值推算來看 —— 我們儘量精確地按當時的兌換率來估算其價值 —— 它們超過了四五十萬元。那裏沒有一個銀幣，全都是古董的金幣，種類繁多 —— 有法國、西班牙、德國的錢幣，還有少量英國的舊金幣，另外一些我們從未見過。那裏還有幾個又大又重的錢幣，它們舊得使我們無法辨認其外形。倒是沒有美國錢。我們發現珠寶的價值很難估計，有寶石 —— 有些極其巨大精美 —— 一共有一百一十顆，每顆都不小；還有十八顆無比璀璨的紅寶石；—— 三百一十顆祖母綠，都很漂亮；以及二十一顆藍寶石，還有一顆貓眼石。這些石頭都和鑲座分離了，在箱子裏散亂地分佈着。那些鑲座被我們從其他的黃金裏揀出來，它們看上去被錘子擊打過，似乎要防止被人辨認出。除了這些，那裏還有數量眾多的黃金飾品；大約有兩百個碩大的戒指和耳環；如果沒記錯的話，有三十根華貴的金鏈；八十三個又大又重的金十字架；五個價值不菲的黃金香爐；一個容量很大的黃金質地的酒缽，上面鑲着精工細雕的葡萄葉和諸酒神圖案；此外還有兩把鑲飾得非常精致的劍柄，以及許多我已記不清楚的小物件。這些寶物的重量超過了三百五十磅；而且在估算中還沒包括一百九十七隻名貴的金錶。其中有三隻錶各自都值五百美元價。它們大多的年代都很老，從計時功能看已經沒有價值；部件多少已經遭受腐蝕——不過它們都鑲有貴重珠寶，價值昂貴。那晚，我們估算整箱子財寶值一百五十萬美元。在處理了那些小飾品和珠寶後（有一些我們自己留下了），我們發現自己大大低估了這些財寶的價值。

當我們終於把財寶清點完畢，當那種強烈的興奮多少平息了些時，勒格朗見我迫不及待地想解開這個最奇異的謎底，就詳細地說起這事的來龍去脈。

"你記得，"他說道，"我讓你看我畫的甲蟲草圖的那個晚上，你也能記起，當時我很氣惱，因為你堅持說那畫像一個骷髏頭。你最初這麼說時，我認為你在開玩笑；不過後來，我想起蟲子背上那些奇怪的點，就私下承認你的話有些道理。不過，你對我繪畫能力的嘲笑令我不快——因為我被認為是位不錯的藝術家——因此，當你把那張羊皮紙片遞給我時，我都想把它搏揉起來，扔進火堆了。"

"你說的是那張紙吧，"我說道。

"不是；它很像紙，一開始我也這麼認為，但是當我在上面畫畫時，立刻就發現那是一張很薄的羊皮紙。你記得吧，它很髒。唉，當我正準備將它揉成一團時，我瞥到你當時看的那個草圖了，你沒法想像我的驚訝程度，我一看，發現我畫甲蟲的地方竟然是一幅骷髏的圖像。有那麼一會兒，我驚得無法好好思考。我明白自己的設想在細節上和這圖形有很大差異 —— 儘管從總的輪廓來看它們真的有相像處。我馬上拿起一支蠟燭，坐在房間的另一端，繼續更仔細地查看那張羊皮紙。當我把它翻過來時，立刻從反面看見了自己的草圖，和我先前畫它時完全一樣。當時，我最先感到的只是驚訝，因為那很相像的輪廓 —— 是奇異的巧合，我驚訝自己竟然不知道在羊皮紙的另一面，就在我畫的聖甲蟲的背面，本來就有一個骷髏頭，而且這個頭骨不僅在外形，而且在尺寸上也很像我的畫。有一會兒，那奇異的巧合讓我真的很驚愕。對這種巧合來說，這樣的反應很正常。我努力地把起因和結果聯繫起來，可是想不出甚麼來，於是產生了一種暫時的痲痺感。但是，當我從這種恍惚中恢復過來時，我逐漸有了某種確信，而這念頭比那巧合更令我震驚。我開始清晰地、確切地想起，當我在羊皮紙上畫聖甲蟲時，上面並沒有甚麼圖畫。我對此很肯定，因為我記得先翻到一面，又翻到另一面，想找最乾淨的地方下筆。如果那骷髏頭早先就在的話，我當然不會忽視它的，這裏真有一種我當時覺得無法解釋的神祕。不過，即使是在最初的時刻，我們昨晚的冒險所昭然揭示的真相似乎就像螢光一般在我內心最祕密的深處隱隱地閃爍着。當時我立刻站起身，把羊皮紙放好，留待我獨處時，才進一步地思考這個問題。

"當你離開，當丘必特熟睡後，我就開始對這件事進行更系統的研究。我首先想到那張羊皮紙是怎麼到我這裏的。我們發現那隻聖甲蟲的地方是在大陸的海岸邊，大抵是在島偏東邊一英里的地方，離漲潮的水位線只有很短的距離。剛抓住這隻蟲子時，牠狠狠地咬了我一口，於是我馬上鬆手。丘必特則向來很謹慎，當蟲子向他飛去時，他四下張望想找葉子或是類似的東西，然後用它來抓蟲子。這時，他和我的目光都落在了那張羊皮紙上，當時我以為是普通的紙，它就半埋在沙土裏，一隻角露在外面。在紙旁邊，我看到船體的殘骸，它顯然曾經是航海商船上的一條救生艇。那殘骸似乎已經在那裏有很長時間了，因為船的木質外表已經模糊難辨。

"於是，丘必特揀起了那張羊皮紙，用它包起了甲蟲，並交給我。不久，我們就回家了，在路上，我們遇到了 G 中尉。我給他看了那隻蟲子，於是他請求我讓他把蟲子帶去查爾斯頓堡。我剛答應他，他就立刻把蟲子丟進了背心的口袋裏，沒有要那張包裹蟲子的羊皮紙。因為在他看蟲子時，我一直把那張紙拿在手裏。他或許是害怕我改變主意，認為自己最好能馬上識貨 —— 你知道他對跟博物學有關的所有話題有多熱衷。我準是在那個時候不知不覺地把那羊皮紙塞進了自己的口袋。

"你還記得，當我走向桌子要畫甲蟲的草圖時，我沒在通常放紙的地方發現紙張。我往抽屜裏看看，沒有發現紙。我就從口袋裏找，希望能找到一封舊信，於是我的手就碰到了那張羊皮紙。我就這樣準確地想起了這紙到我手裏的經過，因為當時的環境給我留下了特別深的印象。

"當然，你會認為我是在瞎想 —— 可是我早已在其間找到了一種聯繫。我把兩個環節連在一起，形成了一個重要的連鎖系列。那個海岸邊有一條船，船附近又有一張羊皮紙 —— 不是普通的紙張 —— 上面畫着一個頭骨。自然，你就會問‘這裏面有甚麼聯繫？’我會這樣回答，那頭骨，或者說是骷髏頭，就是著名的海盜徽章。那面有着骷髏頭的旗幟在所有的交戰中都會被升起來。

“我說過那張東西是羊皮紙，不是普通紙張。羊皮紙很耐用 —— 幾乎不會磨損，它上面的東西不會是瑣事；因為，如果單單是用作普通的繪畫或寫字目的，它還不如紙張受用。想到這一點，我覺得那個骷髏頭有一些暗示 —— 有某種關聯。而且，我也沒忽略那張羊皮紙的形狀。儘管，出於某種原因，它的一個角被損壞了，但我還是看出那裏原先是長方形的。實際上人們可能正是用這片東西來作便箋的 —— 用來記錄一些需要長久記憶並小心保留的東西。”

“可是，”我插話了，“你說在你畫那隻甲蟲時，這個骷髏頭並不在那張羊皮紙上。那後來你怎麼把那條船和骷髏頭聯繫起來呢？ —— 既然你自己也承認，後者肯定是在你畫了那隻聖甲蟲之後才有的（上帝才知道是誰，是怎樣才弄出來的）。”

“啊，這就是整個神祕所在了；儘管我解決這關鍵的一點相對說來並沒費多大力氣。我的步驟很明確，而且它只有一個結果。比如，我是這樣推論的：當我畫那隻聖甲蟲時，羊皮紙上並沒有骷髏頭。當我畫完，遞給了你，並且在你交還給我前，我很仔細地觀察了你。因此，不是你把骷髏頭畫上去的，而且在場也沒有別人能畫。那麼，它就不是人畫的，可是，畫卻在那裏了。

“想到這裏，我努力回憶着，真的清晰地記起了這期間的發生的每一個細節。當時天很冷（哦，這真是難得的幸運），火在壁爐裏熊熊燃燒。我因為走熱了，就坐在桌子旁。然而你卻把椅子拉在爐火旁。當我把羊皮紙交到你手裏，你正要仔細看時，那隻紐芬蘭犬沃爾夫進來了，並跳到了你的肩頭。你用左手撫摸牠，並讓牠走開，而你的右手則拿着那張羊皮紙，一邊隨意而懶散地垂在膝蓋間，離火堆非常近。當時我都擔心那火苗會燒到紙張，並正要提醒你，不過，沒等我說話，你把紙抽了回來，並認真看起來。想到這所有的細節，我再也不懷疑我在羊皮紙上看到的那個骷髏頭是因為熱度而顯現出來的。你很清楚有一種化學藥劑，而且自古以來就存在這種東西，它們可以被寫在紙上或皮紙上，只有經過火烤後，那些字才會露出來。人們有時將鈷藍釉置於王水裏加熱浸提，然後用四倍於浸提物重量的水加以稀釋，這樣就得到一種綠色的溶劑。若是鈷的金屬砂溶解在硝酸鉀溶劑中，則會顯出紅色。這些書寫溶劑冷卻之後，其顏色就會在或長或短的時間裏消失，但是再用火的話，字跡又會清晰起來。

"於是我就仔細觀察起那個骷髏頭來。它的外邊緣 —— 即最靠近皮紙邊緣的線條 —— 比其他的都要清晰。很明顯，熱效作用不完全，或者是不均勻。於是我立刻燃起一堆火，把羊皮紙上的每一部分都烤到熾熱的程度。最初，只是骷髏頭的模糊線條變清晰了；但是，當熱效繼續時，在與畫骷髏頭處成對角線的另一頭皮紙的一角的圖形開始顯現出來。開始，我以為那是一隻山羊。然而，再仔細一看，我很肯定那畫的是一隻小山羊[2]。"

"哈！哈！"我笑了，"我明白自己沒有權利嘲笑你 —— 這一百五十萬的財富可是嚴肅到不能嘲笑的 —— 可是你不能在這系列中再建立第三個環節了 —— 你不能在你的海盜和山羊間找到特

別的聯繫 —— 你知道，海盜與山羊無關；牠們只與農業有關。"

"可我剛説過那圖形不是山羊。"

"行，就算是小山羊吧 —— 也差不到哪兒去。"

"差不多，但不完全是這樣，"勒格朗説，"你也許聽説過有一個叫基德的船長。我馬上就把那畫看作是一種雙關或是象形文字的簽名。我説簽名，因為它在皮紙上的位置給我這樣的想法。同樣道理，那個對角線對面角落的骷髏頭也像是一個圖章，或者是封印。但是令我惱火的是除此之外別的甚麼也沒有 —— 沒有我想像的契約檔內容 —— 或是讓我可以推測的文字等，這很令我苦惱。"

"我想你希望在圖章和簽名中間發現一封信。"

"就是類似的東西。實際上，我不可壓制地產生了一種預感，覺得即將發現大筆的寶藏。我説不出原因。或許，這根本就是一種渴望，而不是真實的信心 —— 可是你知道嗎，丘必特的那些關於那甲蟲是金屬質地的蠢話激化了我的想像力。然後就發生了一系列的事件與巧合 —— 這些事是那麼地不同凡響。你留心到了嗎？所有這些事居然會發生在同一天內是一個多麼純粹的巧合，而那天碰巧又是一整年中冷得必須，或是可以生火的唯一一天，而沒有火的話，或者説沒有這狗恰巧在這時走進來，我根本不會知道有這個骷髏頭，也就不會擁有這筆財富。"

"快説下去 —— 我等不及了。"

"好吧，當然，你也聽説過許多流傳着的故事 —— 那些無數的有關基德和他的手下們在大西洋岸邊的某地埋藏了財寶的傳説。這些傳説肯定會有一些事實基礎，它們存在了那麼長久的時間，而且繼續被流傳着，對我來説，這就意味着，那些埋藏的財寶依然沒有被挖掘出來。如果基德真把這些戰利品藏了起來，過後再去取回來，那麼這些傳言就不會以目前這種千篇一律的形式傳到我們耳朵裏。你會發現，這些傳説都是關於探寶，而不是找到寶藏的。倘若那海盜真找到了財寶，那這事就不會被繼續探究了。我覺得，由於某種意外——例如藏寶圖丟失了——那海盜就失去了發現財寶的途徑，而這意外又被他的手下們聽説了，否則他們可能根本就不會聽説有藏寶這回事。而且，因為沒有路徑，他們白忙活了一場，而他們尋寶的消息又不脛而走，成了今天家喻戶曉的傳聞。你聽説過在海岸附近挖掘出重要的寶藏嗎？"

"從沒聽説過。"

"不過大家都知道，基德的寶藏數量巨大。因此，我理所當然地認為它們仍然被埋在地裏；我説出來你也許還不至於被嚇一跳，當時我感到了一種希望，那希望幾乎是一種確信，我希望來歷如此奇怪的羊皮紙和那失散的藏寶圖有關。"

"可是你怎麼繼續探究下去的呢？"

"我把那張皮紙又拿到火邊，將火加旺後，發現它沒有再顯現甚麼。於是我認為，也許是它蒙了灰塵，才顯不出東西來。因此，我倒了溫水仔細地擦洗了一下，做完這事，我把羊皮紙放在一個平底鍋裏，將骷髏頭的一面朝下，並把鍋放在一個燒着木炭的爐子上。我又拿起那張紙，欣喜若狂地發現有幾個地方出現了似乎是排列着的數字。我再次將紙放在鍋裏，又烤了一分鐘。等我再拿起來時，它就顯出了你現在看到的這個樣子。"

這時，勒格朗已經將羊皮紙再次加熱過了，他將紙遞過來讓我看。在骷髏頭和山羊中間是一些字跡粗糙的文字，顏色是紅的：

'53‡‡†305))6*;4826)4‡.)4‡);806*;48†8¶60))85;1‡

(::‡*8†83(88)5*†

　　;46(;88*96*?;8)*‡(;485);5*†2:*‡(;4956*2(5*—4)8¶8*;40692

　　85);)6†8)4‡‡;　1 (‡9;4808 1 ;8:8‡ 1 ;48†85;4)485†528806*

8 1 (‡9;48;

　　(88;4(‡?34;48)4‡;161:: 1 88;‡?;'

　　"可是，"我説着把紙遞還給他，"我還是一頭霧水。如果得
解開這個謎才能得到那巨大的寶藏，我很明白自己是無法擁有它
們的。"

　　"不過，"勒格朗説，"解謎並沒有你剛才首次粗粗一看所想
像的那麼難。正如人們可以輕鬆地預想到的，那些符號形成了一
組密碼——也就是説，它們傳達了一個意思；但是就我對基德的
了解來説，我不覺得他能編出任何更為深奧的密文來。我立刻就
認為這密碼會很簡單——不過，對粗魯愚頑的水手來説，沒有方
法的話，它肯定是無法破解的。"

　　"你真的破解了它？"

　　"這不難，我還破解過比這艱澀上萬倍的東西呢。具體的生
活境況，以及思想上的偏好使我對解謎很有興趣。而且，這也能
對一個問題進行質疑，即人類的智慧是否能構設出一種憑藉人類
智慧和適當的工具都無法破解的謎？事實上，一旦我發現了這些
有關聯的，而且清晰的符號後，我幾乎不認為進一步解謎會有甚
麼難度了。

　　"在目前這件事上——其實也就是所有關於祕密書寫的事
——首要的問題是關於密碼所採用的語言；因為迄今為止，尤其

是針對這些比較容易的密碼，破解的方法往往依其獨有的語言特徵而定，並且隨其特徵的變化而變化。總的來說，解碼人除了對自己了解的各種語言進行實驗（憑偶然），直到找到確切的那種語言外，別無選擇。但是，對於我們面前的密碼，所有的難度都被那個簽名消除了。那個雙關語"基德"只有在英語裏才有意義。要不是想到這個，我說不定會從西班牙語和法語開始試起，因為出沒於西班牙一帶的海盜編寫密碼最有可能會用那兩種語言。像現在這樣的情況，我就假設那密碼是用英語編的。

你注意到了，那些字符間沒有間隔。如果有間隔的話，破解任務就會相對容易些。如果是那樣的情況，我就可以從整理和分析短詞開始，而且，最有可能的是，如果碰到一個字母的詞（例如，a 或者 I[3]），那麼解碼的方法就得到了肯定。可是，這些符號間沒有間隔，所以我首先得確定最頻繁出現的符號，依次一直到最少出現的。我全部數了一下，列了這樣一張表：

一共有 33 個 8

26 個 ;

19 個 4

16 個 ‡ 和)

13 個 *

12 個 5

11 個 6

8 個 † 和 1

6 個 0

5 個 9 和 2

4 個 : 和 3

3 個 ?

2 個 ¶

1 個 — 和 .

　　"在英語中，最常出現的字母是 e，隨後依次為：a o i d h n
r s t u y c f g l m w b k p q x z。e 的優勢很明顯，在任何長
度的單句中，很少有這個字母不是出現頻率最高的情況。

　　"那麼，我們首先有了不僅僅是單純猜測的推論前提。這張
表的大體用處很明顯 —— 但是，對於這個特殊的密碼，這張表只
起了很有限的作用。既然最頻繁出現的是 8，我們就可以猜測 8
代表的就是字母中的 e。要證實這個猜測，先讓我們來看看是否
8 經常成對地出現 —— 因為 e 在英語中成對出現的幾率很高 ——
例如，有 meet，fleet，speed，seen，been，agree 等這樣一
些詞。我們看到，在這個密碼中，成對出現多達五次，儘管這個
密碼很簡短。

　　"那就讓我們把 8 當成 e。另外，在這種語言的所有詞語中，
the 是最常見的；因此，讓我們來看一下，這裏是否有三個符號
以同樣排列次序重複出現的情況，而且最後一個符號為 8。如果
我們發現了這樣重複的字母組合的話，那麼，它們很有可能就代
表了 the 這個詞。 我們檢查一下，至少有七個這樣的組合，符號

為；48。因此，可以這麼認為，；代表了 t，4 代表 h，而 8 代表 e —— 最後這個假定已被充分證實。這樣，我們就跨出了重要的一步。

"不過，一個詞被確定後，我們就能確立至關重要的環節；也就是說，確立其他一些詞的首字母和尾字母。例如，就說這倒數第二個排列為；48 的詞 —— 它離密碼最末尾不遠處。我們知道緊接着的 ' ; ' 是詞的首字母，那麼，在這個 the 後，有連着六個符號的組合，這六個符號中有五個是我們認識的。讓我們將這些符號用我們所知道的字母記下來，那個不知道代表甚麼字母的符號先空着 ——

是 t eeth

"這樣，我們就能馬上把 th 撇開，因為我們用字母表中所有能適用的字母來填補那個空缺，發現這裏放 th 就無法形成一個首字母為 t 的詞，該兩個字母不可能是詞的組成部分。這樣，我們就把原排列縮短為

t ee

如果有必要，我們可以像前面一樣檢查一下字母表，單詞 tree 是唯一符合的。於是，我們就得到了另一個字母 r，它是由 ' (' 來替代的，這樣前後單詞連起來就是 the tree。

"跳過這些單詞，在不遠處，我們又看到了；48 這樣的組合，將這兩個 the 首尾相連，我們就得到了這樣的組合：

the tree ;4(‡?34 the，

或者，若將已知字母替代進去，就得到了：

the tree thr‡?3h the 。

"那麼，如果把這些未知的符號留空，或者用點來替代，那麼就得到了：

the tree thr...h the，

於是單詞 through 就立刻浮現出來。這個發現就又使我們找到了 o，u 和 g 三個新字母，它們分別由 ‡, ? 和 3 來表示。

"現在，可以詳細來看看密碼中已知符號的組合，這樣我們就發現在開頭不遠處，有一個組合是這樣的：

83(88，或者也是 egree，

很明顯，這形成的是單詞 degree，這樣就讓我們知道了另一個字母 d，它由 † 表示。

"在 degree 一詞的四個符號之後，我們還可以找到一個組合：

;46(;88* 。

"照前面的方法，把已知的字母代入，並用點來替代未知的符號，我們就得到：

th.rtee，

這個組合立刻就令人想到了單詞 thirteen，於是我們又破解了兩個新的符號，即 6 和 * 分別代表 i 和 n。

"現在，我們再來看密碼的最初部分，它形成了這樣一個組合

53‡‡†。

"按照前面的方法，我們得到了

.good，

這就使我們確信，第一個字母應該是 A，所以最初的兩個單詞就是 A good。

"現在，為了避免混淆，我們應該把所有知道的符號列成一張表，該表如下：

5 代表 a

† 代表 d

8 代表 e

3 代表 g

4 代表 h

6 代表 i

* 代表 n

‡ 代表 o

（代表 r

；代表 t

？代表 u

　　"因此，我們至少知道了十個最重要的字母，這樣就沒有必要繼續交代破解細節了。我想這已足夠讓你相信這類密碼是不難破解的，並且讓你對破譯密碼的基本原理有了了解。不過，我敢說，我們面前的例子屬於最簡單的一類密碼。現在唯一要做的就是讓你看根據羊皮紙上密碼所破譯的全文，內容如下：

　　"'A good glass in the bishop's hostel in the devil's seat forty-one degrees and thirteen minutes northeast and by north main branch seventh limb east side shoot from the left eye of the death's head a bee line from the tree through the shot fifty feet out. （一塊好鏡子在主教客棧在惡魔座椅東北偏北 41 度 13 分並在主樹幹東面第七分枝從骷髏頭左眼射出一條直線從樹上穿過射落點五十英尺外。）'"

　　"可是，"我說道，"這個謎似乎依然很難破，我們怎麼可能從這樣的行話，如'惡魔的座位'，'骷髏頭'，和'主教住所'中得出真正的意思來呢？"

　　"得承認，"勒格朗回答，"粗粗一看，這段話還是很費解。我得先將句子分隔成設密者想表達的各段意思。"

　　"你是說，要標上標點嗎？"

　　"差不多是這樣的意思。"

"可是怎麼來做呢？"

"我想到，寫這段話的人是有意要將這些詞沒有分隔地連在一起，這樣就增加了破解的難度。一個不太敏銳的人在看到這樣的話時，很可能會矯枉過正。在他組織這段話的過程中，在碰到常常需要停頓的主語或某一處時，他就會過分傾向於將一些詞在此處聯繫起來。例如，在這段話中，你就很容易發現五個這樣連接不正常的例子。根據剛才的提示，我做了這樣的分隔："

> "'A good glass in the Bishop's hostel in the Devil's seat—forty-one degrees and thirteen minutes—northeast and by north—main branch seventh limb east side—shoot from the left eye of the death's-head—a bee-line front the tree through the shot fifty feet out.（一塊好鏡子在主教客棧在惡魔座椅——41度13分——東北偏北——主樹幹東面第七分枝——從骷髏頭左眼射出——一條直線從樹上穿過射落點五十英尺外。）'"

"就是這樣分隔，"我說，"我還是沒法理解。"

"我也不理解，"勒格朗回答說，"這樣過了幾天，期間我努力地調查了沙利文島附近一帶，詢問了所有名為'主教客棧'的建築；當然了，我沒用'住所'（hostel）這個過氣的詞。我沒有得到關於它的任何信息，於是我擴大了調查範圍，更加系統性地展開了調查。一天上午，突然，一個念頭出現在我腦海，即'主教客棧'或許和某個古老家族有關，而該家族名號叫'貝索普'（Bessop）[4]，它在很久以前，擁有一個古老的莊園，莊園在這島向北的大約四英里處。於是我就去了那地方，並多次向那裏較為年長的黑人打聽。最後，其中一個最年長的女人說她曾經聽到過有個叫'貝索普城堡'的地方，並認為可以給我指路，不過那並不是一個城堡，也不是客棧，而是一塊高高的岩石。

"我答應付一筆可觀的酬勞給她，讓她帶路，她猶豫了一會，同意陪我一起去。我們沒費太多周折就找到那裏了。讓她走後，我繼續檢查那個地方。那個'城堡'是由一些不規則的峭壁和岩石構成——其中一塊岩石很顯眼，因為它很高大，而且與周圍隔絕，樣子很不自然。我爬到了那石頭頂上，對下一步該怎麼做感到很迷惘。

"當我正在思考時，我的目光落在了那石頭東面的一道狹窄的凸起上，大概在我站立的頂端以下一碼的距離。這塊凸起向外突出了大概十八英吋，還不足一尺寬，而且在它正上方的一個小凹使它粗略地看上去很像是一把古人使用的後背鏤空的椅子。毫無疑問，我覺得這就是那段話中所說的那把'惡魔的座位'。這樣，我似乎就發現了這個謎語的全部祕密。

"我知道，那塊'好鏡子'指的肯定就是望遠鏡，因為'鏡子'一詞在海員那裏很少有別的意思。這樣，我立刻就明白，得使用一架望遠鏡，將它擺在一個確定的視點，並且該視點不能有變動，就從那個角度看望遠鏡。於是，我毫不猶豫地相信，那個'41度13分'，以及'東北偏北'指的就是望遠鏡應調整的方向。對於這些發現，我非常興奮，就立刻趕回家，拿到了一架望遠鏡，並返回那塊岩石。

"我爬下那塊凸起的部分，發現除了用一個特定的姿勢外，那裏不可能讓人坐上去。這個事實證明了我的理解沒有錯。接着，我就用了那架望遠鏡。當然，'41度13分'指的就是地平線向上的仰角，因為‘東北偏北’清楚地指出了地平方向。我立刻就用便攜式指南針找到了這方向；然後，我儘量精確地把望遠鏡調整到我所估計的水準 41 度角，並小心翼翼地上下移動它，直到我注意到遠方一棵大樹的樹葉中有一個圓形的縫隙或是裂口，這棵大樹比周圍其他的樹都高大。在這縫隙的中間，我看到一個白點，不過，最初，我看不清那是甚麼。我調整了望遠鏡的焦距，再觀察了一下，發現這是一個人的骷髏頭。

　　"有了這個發現，我就很樂觀地認為這個謎可以破解了；因為‘主樹幹東面第七個分杈’指的正是骷髏頭在樹上的位置，而‘從骷髏頭左眼射出’也只能有一個解釋，它和找尋被埋葬的財寶有關。我認為它指的是將一個子彈從骷髏頭的左眼射出，而那條蜜蜂線，或者，也稱作直線，是樹幹到‘射落點’（或者稱是子彈落下的點）的最近點，接着，再沿着這個方向伸展五十英尺，這樣就能標出一個確定的點 —— 至少我認為，在這個點下面也許就是藏匿寶藏的地方。"

　　"所有這些，"我說，"都清楚不過了，而且，儘管它很精妙，但還是很簡單明瞭。當你離開這主教客棧後，又是怎麼做的呢？"

　　"哦，我仔細地記住了大樹的方位，然後就往家走了。然而，我一離開‘惡魔座椅’，那個圓形縫隙就消失了；我轉了方位，可還是沒看見它。這可能是所有這些中最重要的巧妙處，即（經過多次實驗，我確信這是事實）這個圓形縫隙除了在岩石表面的這個狹窄的凸起位置可被看見，無論在其他的任何角度都是不可見的。

　　"在那次去‘主教客棧’的探測中，丘必特陪着我。毫無疑問，幾星期來，他一直看到我舉動上很心不在焉，就特別留心地不讓我單獨行事。但是，第二天，我起得很早，設法躲開他，進山找那棵樹去了。費了好大力氣，我找到了它。晚上，當我回家時，我那僕人竟然打算揍我一頓。餘下的冒險經歷我相信你就和我一樣熟知了。"

"我想，"我說道，"在第一次掘地時，你找錯了位置，因為丘必特很愚蠢地將甲蟲從骷髏頭的右眼，而不是左眼扔了下來。"

"沒錯，這導致了'射落點'有大概兩英吋半的誤差——也就是說，那個離樹幹最近距離的樁點有了這樣的誤差；如果寶藏是在'射落點'下面，那麼這個誤差就不重要了；但是那個'射落點'和它離樹最近距離的樹幹點只是兩個形成方向線的點；因此，無論那個誤差有多小，卻會使錯誤隨着我們將線連接伸長而加劇，當我們由此延伸了五十英尺後，地點就完全不對了。要不是我深信那寶藏確實埋在這附近，我們也許就白幹了。"

"但是你誇張的言辭，以及你擺動甲蟲的舉止——都古怪到了極點！我都肯定你瘋了呢。那麼，你幹嘛堅持要讓甲蟲從骷髏頭上掉下來，而不是用子彈代替呢？"

"呃，坦率地說，我對你明顯表露出來的對我智力的懷疑感到惱火，於是決定要用我自己的方式，通過鎮定地故弄玄虛來悄悄地懲罰你。為此，我搖擺着甲蟲，並因此讓甲蟲從樹上掉下來。我想到這後一個主意還是因為聽你說那甲蟲很重。"

"哦，我明白了。現在，還有一個問題困惑着我，我們怎麼理解坑裏的那些殘骸？"

"對這問題我和你一樣困惑。不過，似乎有一個唯一還講得

通的解釋 —— 但是要相信我這個解釋所指的那種殘忍就真的太可怕了。很顯然，基德 —— 如果真是基德藏了這些寶物，這我並不懷疑 —— 他顯然得有人協助來幹這活。可是當這事完成後，他也許覺得最好除掉所有知道這祕密的人。當幫工們正在坑裏埋頭苦幹時，他也許用尖嘴鋤砸幾下就能完事；也許要砸十幾下 —— 誰知道呢？"

（張瓊譯）

3

摩格街謀殺案

女妖們唱的是甚麼歌，當阿基里斯隱身於女人中，他使用的是甚麼名字，儘管這都是些令人困惑的問題，但也並非不能猜想。

—— 托馬斯 • 布朗爵士

被論述為具有分析性的心理特徵，其自身很難被分析。我們只感受到心理特徵帶來的效果。除此，我們還知道，在過度擁有這些心理特徵的情況下，它們對其主體而言，總是一種最為活躍的快樂源泉。正如一個健壯的男人為他的體能感到自豪，很樂於做那些肌肉運動，善分析者也為這樣的心理活動而驕傲。他甚至能從最瑣碎的活動中獲取快樂，如果這些活動能使他的才華得以體現。他喜歡神祕的謎、費解的難題、象形文字；在他對此的一一破解中，展示出在常人看來具有超自然性的某種智慧。事實上，他的這些由方法所特有的實質和精髓而給予的解答，完全是一種直覺。

數學研究也許能有效地增強解決問題的才能，尤其在數學最高深的學科分支中；不公平的是，僅僅由於其逆向運算能力，這種學科分支，就似乎顯得非常出類拔萃，被稱為解析學。不過計算在本質上並不是分析。例如，一個象棋手算棋時就無須分析。這表明，象棋在對心理特點產生作用方面，是被大大誤解了的。

我並不是在寫論文，只是想通過非常隨意的觀察來進行某種特殊的開場白；因此，我趁此機會聲明一下，深思熟慮在樸實的國際跳棋中要比在所有精巧輕薄的象棋中更能果斷而有效地得以運用。在後者中，各個棋子都有不同的、怪異的走法，並有各種不定的價值，這僅僅只是複雜，卻被誤認為（錯誤並不少見）是深刻。此間，需要凝神靜氣，稍不留神，就會疏忽，會導致損傷或失敗。可走的棋步不僅是多樣的，而且錯綜複雜，這樣的疏忽幾率就很大；下象棋時，十有八九是更為專心的，而不是更為敏銳的棋手勝出。反之，在國際跳棋中，棋步是唯一的，幾乎沒有變化，粗心的可能性就降低了，純粹的專心就相對不太起作用，棋手贏棋就更取決於哪方具有較高一籌的敏銳。為了減少抽象性，讓我們以一場跳棋比賽為假設，雙方棋子只剩有四個國王，當然了，也不出現疏忽的情況。很顯然，勝利只取決於（棋手是勢均力敵的）某種妙招，那是對智力有效運用的結果。在一般棋招已然無效的情況下，分析者就投身於對對手的心理分析中，於此驗明自己的觀點，他往往發現，只一瞥，就能找到那些唯一的方法（有時候，很荒唐的是，實際只是些非常簡單的方法），通過這些方法，對方也許就誤入歧途，或是草率地作出錯誤判斷。

長期以來，惠斯特牌[5] 因其對計算能力產生影響而負有盛名；人們認為具有最高深智慧的人顯然會對此牌有着解釋不清的愛好，並且，他們避開象棋，覺得它膚淺。毋庸置疑，在此類遊戲中沒有甚麼能比玩惠斯特更需要分析能力。基督教世界中最優秀的象棋手也許只不過是最好的象棋手；但是對惠斯特牌的精通卻意味着具備了在所有那些更重要的工作中的成功能力，這些工作是腦力之間的競爭。我所說的精通，是指在比賽中的一種完美，這完美包括對所有信息的領會，從而獲得合理有效的優勢。這些領會不僅具有多種性，而且形式多樣，常常存在於思想深處，不是常人智力所能企及的。專心觀察意味着要清晰地記憶；因此，迄今，只要紙牌遊戲規則（它們本身是建立在純粹的遊戲機制的基礎上）能被充分和總體地理解，那麼專心的象棋手都擅長玩惠斯特牌。因此，具備持久的記憶力，並依照"慣例"，就通常被認為擁有了擅長此道的資本。但是，在純粹規則之外，就需要運用分析者的技巧了。他會靜靜地作一系列的觀察和推論。因此，或許他的同夥也如此；他們所獲取信息的不同，更多是取決於觀察的細緻，而非推論的正確性。關鍵在於觀察甚麼。棋手根本不限制自己；也不因為遊戲是目的，就拒絕從遊戲之外的事物中進行推論。他觀察同夥的表情，細心地把它與每個對手進行比較。他留心洗牌時每隻手的動作；經常通過持牌者看每張牌的眼光，猜測算計一張張王牌和大牌。在遊戲的發展中，他注意着臉部的每一個變化，從確定、驚訝、勝利，或是苦惱的表情變化中汲取信息。他從對手收攏贏牌的方式判斷收牌人是否會再贏同樣花色的牌。從牌被擲向桌子的氣勢中，他辨別得出甚麼是虛招。一個隨意或粗心的詞，一張偶然掉落或翻轉的牌，以及牌被暴露後伴隨而來的焦慮或是無所謂，計點贏牌的墩數以及那幾墩牌的擺法，還有期間的尷尬、猶豫、急切，或是顫抖 —— 所有這些，都把對真實情況的暗示提供給了他看似直覺性的感知。兩三個回合之後，他對大局瞭如指掌，於是就精確恰當地把自己的牌放出，好像其他參與者的牌都已經擺在了他面前一般。

分析能力不能和單純的機靈相混淆；因為分析者必須要機靈，而機靈的人往往對分析非常不在行。那種推斷或歸納能力，通常表現為機靈，而且顧相學者（錯誤地）把其歸結為是因為一種個別器官，並推測它是一種原始能力，在那些智力在其他方面瀕臨白癡狀態的人身上尤為多見，因此，這些人吸引了心理學者的普遍關注。事實上，在機靈和分析能力之間存在着的區別，遠比幻想和想像之間的要大，但是有一個特徵又十分相似。實際上，人們會發現，機靈的人往往是好幻想的，而真正富有想像力的人常常又是有分析能力的。

以下的敍述對讀者而言，多少是對剛才所提出的命題予以評說。

一八××年的整個春天和部分的夏季，我居住在巴黎，在那裏，我和C·奧古斯特·杜潘先生相識了。這個年輕的紳士來自一個高雅，事實上是顯赫的家族。但是，由於各種不幸事件，這個家族沒落到如此貧困境地，使他個性中的熱情屈服於貧窮之下，他消沉避世，不再對恢復家產有任何興趣。承蒙他債權人的好意，在他的財產中依然保留着一小部分遺產；而且，根據從中獲取的收益，他竭力通過極度節儉來維持生活的必需，並從來不奢求甚麼。事實上，書籍是他唯一的奢侈品，而且在巴黎也很容易獲得。

我們的初次見面是在蒙馬特大街的一家冷僻的圖書館裏，在那裏，我們碰巧都在尋找同一本非常罕見和著名的著作，這使我們的交流更密切了些。此後，我們頻頻會面，我對他所詳細講述的那一段瑣碎家族史很感興趣，在敍述中，他有着法國人只要一說起與己有關的話題就放任情感的坦率。我也對他廣博的閱讀感到很吃驚；而且，尤其是，我覺得自己的靈魂被這狂烈的熱情，以及他想像力的生動清新所感染。在巴黎尋找着我所要探詢的目標時，我感到此人的社會圈子對我來說是無價的財富；而且我也把這種感受坦白地告訴了他。最終，我們決定，在我逗留於這個城市的這段日子裏，我們可以生活在一起；由於我的物質狀況多少還不像他那樣窘迫，他就答應由我出錢在聖熱爾曼區的一個遁世而荒涼的地帶租下了一座年代久遠的古怪官邸，由於人們的迷信想法，它已經荒蕪了很久，搖搖欲墜，我們並沒有去打探這個迷信，我花錢將房子裝修了一番，使它的風格符合我們共有的古怪和陰鬱的脾性。

如果我們在那裏的日常生活被世人所知的話，我們就會被人們看成是瘋子——儘管，或許是那種不會傷害人的瘋子。我們徹底與世隔絕，從不見任何人。事實上，我們隱居的地點被我作為祕密小心地保守着，不為自己以往結交的朋友所知；而且，杜潘好多年前就停止了社交，在巴黎一直不為人知。於是我們就生活在只有兩個人的世界中。

我的朋友有一種怪異的奇想（我還能稱它為其他甚麼嗎），他認為夜晚有其自身的魅力，令人着迷；而且，當我進入了這種怪異之中，就像進入了他所有其他的怪念頭中，我靜靜地感受；徹底放棄了自我，把自己交付給他狂野的幻想。那幽暗的神性並不是總與我們同在；但是我們能營造她在的氣氛。當黎明的第一道曙光出現時，我們關閉了那座古宅裏每一扇厚重的百葉窗；點燃了兩根蠟燭，它們散發着濃郁的香味，僅僅發出最慘淡與微弱的光線。在燭光中，我們任自己的靈魂沉浸在夢幻中 —— 閱讀、寫作，或是交談，直到時鐘提醒我們黑暗的真正來臨。然後我們走上街頭，手拉着手，繼續着白天的話題，或者到處漫遊着，直到深夜，一邊在喧囂城市的燈影中尋找着精神亢奮的無限性，這種極限只有通過平靜的觀察才能企及。

在那樣的時刻，我禁不住要評論和欽佩（儘管因為他豐富的想像力，我對此已有所準備和期待）杜潘所具備的那種獨特的分析能力。他也似乎很熱切、愉悅地運用着它 —— 如果這不能完全算作是炫耀的話 —— 並且毫不猶豫地承認從中可以獲取快樂。他向我誇耀着，一邊低聲咯咯地笑，說大多數人在他看來，內心都有窗戶，隨即他常常說出我當時的所思所想，作為那個論斷直接而驚人的證據。此間，他的樣子是冷漠而抽象的，目光空洞；而他往日洪亮的男高音則拔高到了一種顫音，若不是他發音時的有意控制和完全的清晰，聽上去就會顯得很暴躁。當我觀察他的這些神態時，我經常會陷入對雙心論這一古老的哲學的沉思中，並通過對雙重杜潘 —— 富有創造力的他和擅長分析的他的想像來自娛。

請不要根據我前面的話，就以為我是在詳細地敍述甚麼神祕之事，或是在描寫甚麼浪漫的故事。對這個法國人，我所要描述的只不過是一種亢奮的，或許是病態的才智產生的效果，不過我最好舉一個例子來說明他在那一時期的觀察特點。

有一個晚上，我們在王宮附近沿着一條又髒又長的路漫步走着，兩人顯然都沉浸在思考中，至少在一刻鐘的時間裏，我們誰都沒說一句話。突然，杜潘冒出了下面這句話：

"他是個小個子傢伙，真的，更適合去雜耍劇院。"

"毫無疑問，"我不自覺地回答道，最初並沒注意到（我是那麼專注於自己的思考）說話人進入我沉思的插話竟如此離奇巧合。我立刻回過神來，並感到一種深深的驚訝。

"杜潘，"我嚴肅地說，"我沒法理解這個，可以毫不遲疑地說，我很吃驚，並且幾乎不能相信自己的感覺。你怎麼可能知道我正在想着 —— ？"我在這裏停頓了一下，為了明白無疑地確定他是否真的知道我思考的是誰。

"—— 想着尚蒂耶，"他說，"你為何停下來？你在對自己說他的小身材不適合悲劇。"

這恰好就是我思考的內容。尚蒂耶曾經是聖德尼街的補鞋匠，他瘋狂地迷上了舞台劇，想嘗試扮演克雷比雍悲劇中的薛西斯[6]，結果弄得聲名狼藉，一番苦心卻遭受大家的冷嘲熱諷。

"看在上帝份上，請告訴我，"我喊道，"這個方法 —— 如果真有方法的話 —— 你是怎麼用它來看穿我內心的。"事實上，我甚至比我原本想表示出來的要更為驚訝。

"是那個賣水果的人，"我的朋友回答說，"他使你作出了這樣的結論，即那個修鞋匠沒有足夠的高度來扮演薛西斯 et id genus omne[7]。"

"那水果商！—— 你可真讓我吃驚 —— 我從不認識甚麼水果商。"

"就是我們走上這條街時那個撞到你身上的人 —— 這可能是一刻鐘之前。"

我記起來了，確實有一個水果商，他頭頂着一大筐的蘋果，在無意中幾乎要把我撞倒了，那時我們正從 C —— 街穿過來，走進了這條大街；可是我沒法理解這與尚蒂耶有甚麼關係。

杜潘沒有絲毫假充內行的意思。"我會解釋的，"他說道，"然後你就會清楚地理解這一切了，我們先要回顧你沉思的過程，從我對你說話開始，直到遭遇那個被提及的水果商。這條鏈子中各個重要環節是這樣排列的——尚蒂耶、獵戶星座、尼科爾斯博士、伊壁鳩魯[8]、石頭切割術、街上的石頭、水果商。"

很少有人在他們生活中會沒有過這樣的消遣，即回顧自己的思路是怎樣一步步地到達某個特殊結論的。這種推溯充滿樂趣；初次嘗試的人會對最初的念頭和結論之間明顯有着無限大的距離和毫不相干感到吃驚。因此，當我聽到這個法國人所說的話，就當然感到了驚訝，而且，我不得不承認，他所說的就是事實。他接着又說：

"如果我沒記錯的話，在離開 C —— 街時，我們一直在談論馬。這是我們談的最後一個話題。當我們走到這條街時，一個水果商頭頂着一個大筐，飛快地從我們身邊擦身而過，把你撞向一堆鋪路石上，這些石頭堆在正在修建的人行道上。你踩在其中一塊亂石上，滑了一下，膝蓋輕微扭傷了，你顯得有些惱火或是悶悶不樂，嘀咕了一些話，轉頭看了看那堆石頭，然後就沉默向前走。我並不是特別關注你的舉動；但是最近，觀察已經成了我的一種需要。"

"你的目光停留在地面上 —— 帶着一種暴躁的情緒注視着道路上的洞眼和車轍，（因此我覺得你依然在想着這些石頭，）直到我們到達了那條叫拉馬丁的小巷，正試驗着把石塊交疊鉚接起來。那時你的表情開朗起來，而後，我注意到你的嘴唇動了，我可以肯定你在咕噥着'石頭切割術'這個詞，這是一個常運用於這種類型的人行道的術語。我知道當你自言自語地說'石頭切割術'時，你準會想到原子，繼而聯想起伊壁鳩魯的理論；接着，由於我們不久前曾談及這個話題，我還向你說起過這個希臘人的這些模糊猜測在後來的星原學中得到證實，這是如此怪異，卻少有人知道。當時我覺得你會忍不住地將目光投向獵戶星座的那團大星雲，而且我也料到你會這麼做。你確實往上看了；於是當時我很肯定自己準確地跟隨了你的思維。但是在昨天的《博物館報》中，那個諷刺家對尚蒂耶進行了尖銳、激烈的長篇攻擊性演說，並對這個修鞋匠想憑藉着厚底靴改頭換面作了一些有失其名譽的影射，並引用了一句拉丁語詩句，我們還經常討論它，就是這一句話：

Perdidit antiquum litera prima sonum.[9]

我告訴過你這句詩說的是獵戶星座，它以前被拼作是Urion，而且從某些與此解釋有關的言論的尖刻性來看，我意識到你是不會忘掉這事的。很顯然，你準會把獵戶星座和尚蒂耶這兩者聯繫起來。我從漫過你嘴唇的微笑中就發現你確實將它們結合了。你想到了那可憐的修鞋匠成了犧牲品。到那時為止，你一直彎着腰行走着；但是現在我看到你挺直了身體。因此，我確信你當時是在回想尚蒂耶瘦小的身材。就在這個時候，我打斷了你的沉思，告訴你，事實上，他確實是個小個子傢伙 —— 即那個尚蒂耶 —— 他更合適去雜耍劇院。"

這以後不久，我們翻閱一本夜版的《法庭公報》，下面的一段話引起了我們的注意。

"離奇的兇殺——今天凌晨三點鐘左右，聖羅克區的居民被一陣持續的淒厲慘叫從睡夢中驚醒，這叫聲顯然是從摩格街的一幢房子的四樓傳出的，據說那裏只住着姓萊斯巴拉葉的夫人和她的女兒卡米耶·萊斯巴拉葉小姐。過了一會，由於正常途徑進入房間的嘗試未果，人們用鐵撬棍砸開了大門，在兩位警察的陪同下，八九個鄰居走進屋子。這時，叫聲停住了；但是，當這羣人衝上一樓樓梯時，他們聽到了兩三聲刺耳的、憤怒的爭執聲，這聲音似乎是從樓上傳來的。當人們到達第二層時，這些聲音也消失了，一切又變得悄然無聲了。人羣分散開來，從一個屋子搜尋到另一個屋子。當他們抵達四樓的一個靠後的大套間時，（大家發現大門是反鎖着的，鑰匙在裏面，就奮力推開了它，）裏面呈現的景象使在場的每一個人又驚又怕。

"屋子異常凌亂——家具破碎了，散得到處都是。那裏只有一個牀架；牀墊已經被人從牀架上移開了，並被扔在地板中央。椅子上放着一把剃刀，那上面血跡斑斑。壁爐上有兩三綹又長又密的灰色頭髮，它們也沾着血，似乎是被連根拔起的。人們在地板上發現了四個拿破崙金幣[10]，一個黃玉耳環，三個大銀勺，三個小一些的銅匙，以及兩個包，裏面大約裝有四千法郎的金幣。在房間的一個角落裏，櫃子的抽屜都開着，顯然是遭受了搶劫，儘管許多東西還留在裏面。人們還發現在牀墊下（不是在牀架下）有一個小小的鐵質保險箱。箱子被打開了，鑰匙依然在門上面。除了一些舊的信件，以及其他不太重要的文件，別無他物。

"人們沒有發現萊斯巴拉葉夫人的蹤影；但是在壁爐裏有着數量非同尋常的煙灰，於是大家開始搜尋煙囪內部，然後（説出來太可怕了）發現了萊斯巴拉葉小姐的屍體，她被人們頭朝下地拖了出來；屍體是被人用大力推進這狹窄孔隙的，而且被往上推了相當高的一截距離。屍體尚存一絲暖氣。經過檢查，人們發現皮膚上有多處擦傷，這無疑是因為向上推的猛力，以及後來屍體從煙囪裏拉出來時刮擦所致。她臉上有許多嚴重的抓痕，而且在脖子處有烏黑的瘀傷和深深的指甲凹痕，彷彿死者是被掐死的。

"人們對房間每一部位進行了徹底的檢查，沒再獲得進一步的發現，大家就走進了這幢房子後面的一個鋪砌過的小院子，並在那裏發現了老夫人的屍體，她的脖子整個被砍了，所以在努力將她抬起時，頭掉了下來。她的身體和頭部一樣，毀壞得非常厲害 —— 前者幾乎不成人形了。

"我們相信，至今，對這一可怕的神祕事件，人們還沒有任何線索可尋。"

次日的報紙附加了這樣一些細節：

"摩格街慘案 —— 許多和這個異常與恐怖事件有關的個人都受到了調查，"（"事件"一詞在法國不像在我們這裏那樣有輕浮之意，）"可是案情沒有任何突破。以下，是我們獲得的所有重要證詞。

"波利娜・迪布爾，洗衣女工，她證實自己與兩位死者認識了三年，在此期間一直為她們清洗衣服。老夫人和她女兒的關係看來不錯 —— 彼此很親切。她們給工錢很公道。關於她們的謀生方式或手段，她也說不出甚麼，不過她相信萊斯巴拉葉夫人是靠給人算命維生的，據說很有些積蓄。在夫人讓她去拿衣服或是她送衣服時，她從沒在那裏遇到任何旁人。她能肯定她們沒有僱用人。這棟房子除了四樓，其他樓層都沒擺家具。

"皮埃爾·莫羅，煙草商，他透露說自己常常賣給萊斯巴拉葉夫人少量的煙絲和鼻煙，這已經差不多有四年時間了。他就是在附近出生的，也一直住在那裏。屍體被發現時，死者和她的女兒已經在這房子裏住了六年多。此房過去住的是一個珠寶商，他將上面的房間轉租給三教九流。房子是萊斯巴拉葉夫人的財產，她對房客濫用房屋感到很不滿，於是自己搬進了這些房間，拒絕出租任何部分。那老夫人很孩子氣。證人曾在六年中見過她女兒五六次。她們兩人過着極其隱蔽的生活——據說有些錢。他曾聽鄰居說萊斯巴拉葉夫人會算命——他不相信這個。除了老夫人和她的女兒之外，一個行李搬運工露了一兩次面，還有一個醫生出現了八九次，他就再沒見其他人進過那家的門。

"其他許多人，均是鄰居，都證實了相同的情況。他們都說沒見有誰常去那裏。大家也不知道萊斯巴拉葉夫人和她的女兒是否有任何健在的親朋。她們前面的百葉窗很少被打開過，後窗的也一直關閉着，除了四樓那個大套間。那房子很不錯——不是太舊。

"伊西多爾·米塞，警官，他陳述說自己大約是凌晨三點被召到現場的，並發現有二三十個人站在門口，想努力走進去。最後，門終於被用力打開了，人們用的是一把刺刀——不是鐵撬棍。用它開門沒甚麼難度，因為門是雙層或是摺疊的，底下和頂上沒有上插銷。尖叫一直持續着，直到門被奮力打開後——聲音是頓時停止的，它們聽上去似乎是某個人（或是不止一人）在極其痛苦地喊叫——聲音很響，拖得很長，不是那種短促的類型。證人帶大家上了樓。上了第一個樓梯平台時，大家聽到兩個聲音在大聲而憤怒地爭吵着——其中一個聲音是嘶啞的，另一個是更尖厲的——非常奇怪的聲音。他可以辨認出前者說的一些詞，那是一個法國男人的聲音。他能肯定這不是女性的音質。他聽出了‘該死’和‘見鬼’兩個詞。那個尖厲的聲音聽上去是一個外國人發出的，但他不能肯定這究竟是男人還是女人的聲音，也聽不出說的是甚麼，但是他相信是西班牙語。證人所描述的房間和屍體的情況與我們昨天報道的相同。

"亨利·迪瓦爾，鄰居之一，從事銀匠行業，他作證說自己是最初進入房子的那羣人之一。他大致上證實了米塞的話。當他們剛奮力闖入大門後，就又關閉了大門，把人羣擋在外面，當時人聚攏得很快，雖然當時已深更半夜。這個證人認為那個尖厲的喊聲是個義大利人發出的，並確定這肯定不會是法國人的，但是不確定是否是男人的聲音，它或許是女聲。他對義大利語不熟，不能辨認出詞語，但是聽音調，他確信說話者是個義大利人。他認識萊斯巴拉葉夫人和她的女兒，並經常和二者交談。他很肯定那尖厲的聲音不是兩個死者的。

"奧登赫梅爾，餐館老闆。該證人自願提供證詞。他不會講法語，是通過翻譯被詢問的。他是阿姆斯特丹人，當叫喊聲開始時，他正經過那房子，聲音持續了幾分鐘——也許是十分鐘。它們又長又響——非常可怕，令人悲傷。他也是進入房子的人之一，並證實了前面證人的所有敍述，除了一個地方有出入。他確信那個尖厲的聲音是一個男人——一個法國男人發出的，但是聽不出裏面的詞語。聲音很響，很短促——不太穩定——顯然是在驚慌與憤怒中發出的。那聲音很刺耳——與其說是尖厲，還不如說是刺耳，它不能被稱為是尖厲的聲音。那嘶啞的聲音重複着'該死'、'見鬼'，還有一次是'老天'。

"儒勒·米諾，德洛林大街米諾父子公司銀行家，他是老米諾。萊斯巴拉葉夫人是有一些財產，那年（八年前）春天，她在他的銀行開了一個賬戶，以小金額頻繁地進行儲蓄。直到她死前的第三天，她才第一次開了支票，她親自領了四千法郎。這筆錢是用金幣支付的，一個職員護送她和這筆錢到的家。

"阿道夫·勒邦，米諾父子銀行的職員，他作證說，領錢的當天，大約是中午，他陪同萊斯巴拉葉夫人帶着四千法郎回到她的住處，錢被放在兩個包裏面。當門被打開時，萊斯巴拉葉小姐出現了，並從他的手裏拿走了其中一個包，而那個老夫人拿掉了他手裏的另一隻。然後他鞠躬告退。他當時沒有在街上看見任何人。這是一條小街——很偏僻。

"威廉·伯德，裁縫，他作證說自己是進入房子的人之一，是個英國人。他在巴黎住了兩年，是最早上樓梯的人之一。他聽到了爭吵聲，那個嘶啞的聲音是一個法國男人發出的，他能聽出幾個詞，但是現在記不全了。他清楚地聽到'該死'和'老天'兩個詞。當時有一個聲音，好像幾個人在搏鬥——那是刮擦和扭打聲。那個尖厲的聲音很響——比嘶啞的聲音響。他確信那不是英國人的聲音，好像是一個德國人的，可能是女聲。他聽不懂德語。

"以上四個證人又被傳訊，證實當人們到達時，萊斯巴拉葉夫人屍體所在套間的大門是從裏面被鎖上的。當時那裏寂靜無聲——沒有呻吟，也沒有任何雜音。門被用力推開時，大家沒看到裏面有人。外屋和裏屋的百葉窗都被拉下了，兩扇窗子都從裏面被緊閉着。兩個屋子之間的門是關着的，但是沒上鎖。從外屋通向過道的大門被鎖着，鑰匙掛在門裏面。在房子四樓的前面有一間小屋，它位於走道的頭上，門微微地開着。這間屋子擠滿了舊的牀鋪、箱子等等的東西。這些都被人們仔細地移開並搜尋過了。整幢樓沒有一寸地方被忽略過。大家還派人上下掃了所有煙囱。這是一幢四層樓的房子，帶有閣樓（房子是雙重斜坡屋頂的）。屋頂的活板門被牢牢地用釘子釘住了——看上去有好幾年沒被打開過。證人們敍述的聽到爭吵聲和房門被撞開的時間間隔各不相同，有的短到三分鐘——有的長到五分鐘。打開門頗費了點周折。

"阿方索·加西奧，殯儀事務承辦人，他闡述説自己住在摩格街，是西班牙人，也是進入房子的其中一人。他沒有上樓梯，當時感到很緊張，擔心着這騷動的後果。他聽到了爭吵聲。那嘶啞的聲音是個法國男人發出來的，他無法聽出那人在説啥。那尖厲的聲音來自一個英國男人——他能肯定。他不懂英語，但是能從語調來判斷。

"阿爾貝托·蒙塔尼，糖果店老闆，他作證説自己是最初上了樓梯的人之一。他聽到了爭吵聲，那嘶啞的聲音來自一個法國男人，他能聽出幾個詞。説話的人似乎在規勸甚麼。他聽不出尖厲聲音中的詞。那人説得又快又不穩定，他覺得發那聲音是個俄國人的。他的話大體與其他人的證詞相同。他是個義大利人，從沒和俄國人講過話。

"幾個證人再經傳訊，都證實四樓的所有煙囪都太狹窄，沒法進一個人。'掃煙囪'指的是用圓筒狀的刷子刷煙囪，即用那些掃煙囪工人用的工具來刷。這些刷子上下地刷了房子裏的每一個煙道。該樓房沒有後樓梯，大家上樓時不可能有人下樓。萊斯巴拉葉小姐的屍體被牢牢地卡在煙囪裏，直到四、五個人一起用力才把她拉下來。

"保羅·迪馬，內科醫生，他作證說自己是在黎明時分被叫去檢查屍體的。兩具屍體都躺在牀架的帆布上，並放在萊斯巴拉葉小姐被人發現的那個房間。年輕小姐的屍體上有很多瘀傷，皮膚也被擦破了。這些表面特徵充分説明了屍體是被猛推上煙囪的，她的脖子被重重地掐傷過，下巴下面有幾處深深的抓痕，還有一連串的烏青塊，這顯然是手指的壓痕。她的臉是可怕的慘白色，眼球突出。部分舌頭被咬過了。死者胸口有大片的瘀傷，很明顯，這是由膝蓋的重壓造成的。根據迪馬先生的觀點，萊斯巴拉葉小姐是被一人或數人勒死的。萊斯巴拉葉夫人的屍體也被毀壞得很厲害，她右腿和右手臂的所有骨頭都或多或少地碎裂了。左脛骨骨裂，左邊的所有肋骨也都如此。整具屍體滿是瘀傷，完全變色了。他無法描述這些傷是怎樣造成的。或許是一條重重的木棍，或許是一大塊鐵——一把椅子——或者任何巨大、沉重以及鈍頭的武器都有可能造成這樣的結果，只要揮動它們的是健壯有力的男人之手。女人用任何器械都造成不了這樣的傷害。據證人目擊，死者的頭部完全脱離了身體，也碎得很厲害。她的脖子顯然被某樣鋒利的工具砍過 —— 也許是一把剃刀。

"亞歷山大・艾蒂安,外科醫生,他是和迪馬先生一起被叫來檢查屍體的。他的陳述證實了迪馬先生的觀點。

"雖然其他一些人也被傳訊過了,但是沒有得到其他更重要的信息。這場謀殺如此神祕,在所有細節上又如此複雜,這在巴黎是史無前例的 —— 倘若這真是一件謀殺案的話。警察們完全被它困惑住了 —— 在此類案件中,這是一個非同尋常的事件。不管怎麼樣,沒有找到一絲線索。"

該報的夜版報道說,在聖羅克區,極端的興奮騷動正在持續 —— 作為事發現場,那幢房子又被仔細地搜查了一遍,有關證人再次被警方傳訊,可依然毫無結果。不過,該報道在附言中提到,阿道夫・勒邦被逮捕並監禁了 —— 不過,除了這些早已被詳述過的事實,沒有甚麼可以定他的罪。

杜潘似乎對此事件的發展尤其感興趣 —— 至少這是我從他的態度中判斷出來的,因為他未作任何評價。只有在報紙宣佈說勒邦被捕了,他才問及我對此謀殺案的看法。

我只能同意所有巴黎人的觀點,即認為這是一個解不開的謎。我看不出有甚麼方法可能找到元兇。

"我們一定不能憑藉搜索的表面信息來進行判斷,"杜潘說,"巴黎的警察素以敏銳著稱,他們很機靈,可是僅此而已。除了現場搜索外,他們在辦案進程中沒有甚麼方法可言。他們炫耀了所採取的各種措施;但是,他們常常用得不那麼恰如其分,以至於讓人想到儒爾丹先生要睡衣 —— 以便更清楚地聽音樂。[11] 他們所獲得的結果並非不常常令人驚訝,可是它們大多數靠的是純粹的勤奮和苦幹。當這一切都無計可施時，他們的方案就失敗了。例如，維多克 [12] 很會猜測，而且也很堅韌不拔。但是，沒有訓練有素的思維，他就會不斷地因過分的調查而頻頻出錯。並且，由於太關注細節，他對事物的把握也會發生偏頗。他或許會異常清晰地發現一兩處問題，可是一旦拘泥於此，他必然會失卻對整體情況的洞察。這樣，事情往往顯得過於深刻。真相並不總在深井中，事實上，對越是重要的真知，我倒是相信它越顯而易見。其深度在於我們探詢真相時所去的山谷，而不是真相被發現時的山巔。這種錯誤的形式和起源在人們對天體的注視中非常多見。匆匆地掃視一顆星星——給予它斜視的一瞥，將視網膜的表層（對微弱的光線，表層比內部更加敏感）轉向它，即清晰地看到了那顆星——即充分地欣賞了它的光澤——這光澤與我們所投諸視線的充分程度成反比。實際上，大部分的光線是落在凝視星星的眼睛上，但是匆匆掃視的眼睛卻擁有更敏銳的把握能力。由於不恰當的深刻，我們使思維混亂衰弱；而且，太持久、太集中，或是太直接的細緻觀察甚至可能讓金星自身從蒼穹消失。

　　"至於這個謀殺案，在沒有對此形成觀念前，讓我們自己來進行一些調查。有一個詢問會給我們帶來些樂趣，"（我認為這個詞用得很古怪，但是沒說甚麼）"此外，勒邦曾幫過我一個令我頗為領情的忙。我們可以前往那裏親自觀察一下現場。我認識警察局長 G，應該不難獲得這必要的准許。"

　　得到准許之後，我們立刻前往摩格街。這是介於舍利厄街和聖羅克街之間的眾多破落的街道之一。由於這個區域離我們的住所很遠，我們到那裏時已是傍晚時分。那幢房子很好找；因為仍然有許多人帶着漫無目的的好奇心,從對面注視着那關閉的百葉窗。那是一幢普通的巴黎房屋,有一條通道,道的一邊是一間裝有玻璃的小屋,小屋窗上的一個滑動的窗格表明這是間門房。在進入房子前,我們沿着街走,轉入了一條小巷,然後又轉彎經過了房子的後面 —— 期間,杜潘觀察了整個周圍地帶,包括這所房子,他看得非常細緻,我看不出這有甚麼目的。

我們原路折回,再次走到了房子的前面,按了門鈴,然後出示了我們的證件,並在值勤警察的允許下進入了。我們走上樓梯 —— 進入萊斯巴拉葉小姐被發現的那個套間,那裏還停放着兩具屍體。按慣例,房間凌亂依舊。我看不出任何超乎《法庭公報》報道的東西。杜潘仔細檢查了每樣東西 —— 也包括被害者的屍體。然後我們走進了其他房間,還有院子;一個警官一直陪着我們。我們查看完現場要告辭時,天已黑了。在回家的途中,我的同伴走進了其中一家日報社的辦公室,逗留了片刻。

我曾說過,我朋友的怪念頭很多,對這些奇想,Je les ménageais[13] —— 因為我找不出英文的措辭來表達。那時,依照他的性情,他拒絕談論這個謀殺案,直到次日中午,他才突然問我有否注意到兇殺現場的特殊細節。

他說話時對"特殊"一詞有些強調,這引起了我莫名的戰慄。

"沒有,沒有甚麼特殊的,"我說,"至少,沒有超過我們讀過的報紙所報道的信息。"

"那報紙,"他回答說,"恐怕並沒有領會到事件中異常的恐怖之處。可是,拋卻這報紙的這些散漫無用的觀點,我發現,這慘案被認為是無法破解的,可這正是讓人覺得好解決的原因 ——

我指的是事件的超常特徵。警察感到困惑的是表面上的動機缺乏——不是謀殺本身——而是兇手的殘忍。人們聽到的爭吵聲和樓上除了被謀殺的萊斯巴拉葉小姐外沒有發現任何人的事實，以及沒有能不被上樓的人發現的出口這一事實似乎根本無法統一，這讓警方大惑不解。那凌亂的房間，屍體被倒着硬插入煙囪，老夫人屍體遭到了令人恐懼的傷害；這些現象，以及剛才所提及的事實，還有我無須提及的事，都足以使警察當局癱瘓無力，並使他們所吹噓的敏銳徹底陷入困惑之中。他們掉入了嚴重的卻又是普通的錯誤中，即把異常與深奧混淆了。可是，正是由於這些對常規的偏離，推論才摸索着找尋真相，如果這推論真的存在的話。在諸如我們目前進行的調查中，與其說是經常問‘發生了甚麼’，還不如問‘發生了甚麼過去從未有過的事’。事實上，我將會做到的或已經做到的解決這個神祕事件的敏捷，是與它在警察眼裏明顯的不可解決性成正比的。”

我沉默而驚訝地盯着說話的人。

“我正在等待着，”他繼續說着，一邊望着我們公寓的房門——“我正在等待着一個人，雖然，他也許並不是殺人兇手，但他一定多少與這些罪行有關聯。至於那最殘忍的罪孽，或許他對此一無所知。我希望自己的推測沒有錯；因為我把自己解構整個謎的期望建立在這個推測之上了。我在此期待着這個人——來這間屋子——每時每刻。誠然，他也許不會來；但是他也很可能會來。倘若他來了，就有必要拖延他。這裏有手槍；而且我們都知道，一旦需要時該如何使用。”

我拿過了槍，不明白自己做了甚麼，也不相信自己所聽到的，而杜潘繼續着，講了一大堆話，好像在獨白似的。我早就說過他在這樣的時刻中的令人費解的神態。他的話是對着我說的；可是他的聲音，雖然不響，卻有着一種對某個在遠處的人說話的語調。他的眼睛盯着牆壁，顯得很空洞。

"那爭吵的聲音，"他說，"即被走上樓梯的那羣人所聽到的聲音，不是那兩個女人自己的，這個事實已經充分證實了。這讓我們消除了那個老夫人可能先殺害了女兒再自殺的嫌疑。我這麼說主要是出於對謀殺方法的考慮；因為萊斯巴拉葉夫人的力氣根本不可能將女兒的屍體推上煙囱，推到屍體被發現時的位置；而且她自己身上的傷口性質也完全排除了自殺的想法。那麼，謀殺是第三者進行的；並且，第三者是其中一個爭吵者。現在讓我來說說——不是說關於這些爭吵聲的全部證詞——而是那證詞中有甚麼特殊的東西。你注意到它的特殊性了嗎？"

我對他說，所有的證人都一致推測那個嘶啞的聲音是發自一個法國男人的，而針對那個尖厲的聲音，或者照其中一個證人所說的刺耳的聲音，則有許多不同的意見。

"那本身就是證據，"杜潘說道，"但是它不是證據的特殊所在。你沒有注意到特殊之處。但是確實有東西值得留意。照你說的，那些證人在嘶啞的聲音上意見相同；這一點上是一致的。但是在尖厲的聲音上，特殊之處在於——不是在於他們意見不同——而是，當一個義大利人、英國人、西班牙人、荷蘭人以及法國人試圖要描述它時，每個人都把它說成是外國人的聲音。每個人都很確信那人不是自己的同胞。大家都把它比成——不是比成自己精通該語言的那國人——而是恰恰相反。法國人推測這聲音是西班牙人的，而且'如果他懂西班牙語的話，他可能會分辨出幾個詞。'荷蘭人認為這是法國人的聲音；但是我們發現報導中說'他不會講法語，是通過翻譯被詢問的'。英國人則認為聲音是德國人的，而且他'不懂德語'。那個西班牙人則'確信'那是英國人的聲音，但他完全'憑語調斷定，因為他根本不懂英語'。義大利人相信這是俄國人的聲音，但是他'從沒和俄國人講過話'。還有，第二個法國人與第一個不同，而且他很肯定那聲音是一個義大利人的；但是他對義大利語不熟，就像那西班牙人，靠'憑語調'。看來，那聲音真的是又奇怪又特殊，居然會引出這樣的證詞！——這人的語調，甚至是歐洲五個重要區域的居民都不太熟悉！你會說也許它是亞洲人的——非洲人的話。巴黎很少有亞洲人或非洲人；但是，在不否定推論的情況下，我現在只是請你注意以下三點。這聲音被一個證人表述為'與其說是尖厲，還不如說是刺耳'。它被另外兩人認為是'短促而不穩定的'。沒有詞語——沒有像詞語的聲音——被任何證人提到是可辨別的。"

"我不知道，"杜潘接着說，"到此為止，根據你的理解，我這樣講給了你怎樣的印象；但是我可以毫不猶豫地說，正是這些從證詞中獲得的合理推論——我指的是有關嘶啞和尖厲聲音的證詞——它們自身就足以引出一個疑問，這個疑問將為對此神祕事件的所有更進一步的調查指明方向。我說的是'合理推論'；但是我的意思並沒有因此而被充分表達。我的意圖是要暗示，這些推論是唯一正確的，而且從中產生的必然的疑問也是唯一的結果。然而，這疑問是甚麼，我現在還不會說。我只是希望你記住，對於我，那懷疑足以讓我在對那房間進行調查時，有一種確定的形式——一種明確的傾向。

"讓我們把想像轉到這個房間。我們首先該在這裏找尋甚麼呢？找兇手逃離的途徑。應該說我們都不太相信超自然的事。萊斯巴拉葉夫人和小姐不會是被幽靈殺害的。罪犯是個物質化的肉身，也通過物質化的方式逃離。那麼他是如何做到的呢？幸虧這一點上只有一種解釋，這種解釋必然會引導我們找到明確的結論。讓我們來一一探討可能的逃離方法。很明顯，當大家上樓梯的時候，兇手正在後來萊斯巴拉葉小姐被發現的房間裏，或者，至少是在隔壁的房間。因此，我們只須從這兩個房間來尋找線索。警察已經四處搜索了地板、天花板，以及牆上的磚砌，沒有甚麼隱祕的出口會逃過他們的警惕。但是，我信不過他們的眼睛，親自檢查了一下。那裏的確沒有甚麼隱祕的出口。從兩個房間通向過道的兩扇門都被牢牢地鎖上了，鑰匙在裏面。讓我們再轉到煙囪。這些煙囪的寬度很尋常，壁爐上方位置寬達八、九英尺，但也容不下一隻大點的貓的身體。這早就說明了不存在從這裏逃走的可能性，那我們就把線索範圍縮小到窗戶上。若從前面屋子的窗戶逃跑，就肯定會被街上的人發現。那麼，兇手必須得從裏面屋子的窗口逃走。現在，既然我們對結論是如此確定，那麼，作為推理者，我們就不能因為其看似的不可能性來推翻這個結論。我們只有來證明，事實上，這些明顯的'不可能性'並非如此。

"房間有兩扇窗。一扇沒有被家具擋住，是完全看得見的。另一扇的下面部分被笨重的牀架頂部遮住了，牀架靠窗很近。第一扇窗從裏面被牢牢鎖上了，再怎麼用力抬，它都抵擋得住。窗戶左邊有一個大大的手鑽的孔，一顆很結實的釘子插在孔內，孔外幾乎只露出釘頭。再檢查另一扇窗，那裏也以類似的方式插着釘子；因此再大力氣也抬不動窗子。於是警察就完全肯定出口不會在這些地方。因此，他們就認為拔出釘子打開窗是多此一舉。

"我的調查多少有點特別，而且正是為此，我才去調查的 —— 因為，我知道，所有明顯的不可能性必將被證明事實並非如此。

"於是我接着思考 —— 追溯下去。兇手肯定是從其中的一扇窗戶逃跑的。照此說，他們不能在裏面重新鎖上窗戶，無法做到像人們發現時那樣被鎖着 —— 出於這樣的考慮，在明白的事實面前，警察就不再檢查這個部位了。可是窗架是鎖上的，那麼，它們就必然有力氣來鎖住自己。這是個不能被回避的論斷。我走到不被遮擋的窗扉前，費了些周折地拔掉了釘子，並試圖抬起窗框。不出我所料，它抵住了我所有的努力。於是，我明白了，一定有一個隱藏着的彈簧；這個念頭使我確信，至少我的假設是沒錯的，儘管釘子問題依然顯得有些神祕。經過仔細檢查，我很快發現了那隱藏的彈簧。我按了它一下，於是，令我滿意的是，窗框向上移動了。

"於是我把釘子插回原處，並仔細地研究它。一個從這扇窗穿過的人也許能重新關上窗，並且彈簧會自動碰上 —— 但是釘子是不可能被插回去的。這個結論是很明顯的，我的調查範圍再一次地縮小了。兇手一定是從另一扇窗逃離的。現在，假設每個窗框上的彈簧都是一樣的，這是可能的，那麼，釘子之間一定會有不同，或者，至少它們的固定方式是不同的。當我走到牀架上的帆布前，我細細地檢查了第二個窗扉旁的牀頭板。我把手放在板後面，很容易地就發現並按下了彈簧，這些，正如我所料想的，與剛才那扇窗的特點一樣。於是我看了看釘子，它也和剛才那扇窗的一樣結實，而且明顯地是以同一種方式給插上的——幾乎被插得深及頂部。

"你會說我這下子感到困惑了；但是，如果你這麼想，就一定是誤解了歸納的本質。套用一個打獵術語，我還從沒'失卻嗅跡'過。嗅跡絲毫沒有消失過，這條鏈子上的任何環節都沒有丟失。我已經把祕密推溯到了它最終的癥結上——這個癥結就是那個釘子。我說這個釘子的外形在每個方面都和另一扇窗上的釘子一致；但是，從現在的推論來看，這個事實完全是無效的（儘管它或許顯得很無可置疑），尤其是這推論會於此將線索終結。我曾說過，'這釘子一定有不尋常之處'。我碰了碰它，釘子的頂部和下面長約四分之一英吋的部分斷在了我的手中。釘子的其他部分沒入了手鑽的孔裏面，在那裏斷開了。釘子的斷裂部分很破舊（因為它的邊緣覆蓋着鐵銹），而且很明顯地被鐵錘敲擊過，釘子頂上的一部分被敲進了窗框的底部上方。於是我小心地把這釘子頂部放回我拿出釘子的凹陷處，使它看上去像一個完好的釘子——斷裂處是看不見的。我按了一下彈簧，輕輕地把窗框抬高幾英吋；釘子頭部隨之被抬起，剩餘部分還牢牢地在原處。我關上窗，釘子又顯得完好無損了。

"至此，這個謎就被破解了。兇手是從這個牀上方的窗戶逃跑的。在他離開後，窗子自動歸位（或者是有意被關上的），並靠彈簧被鎖住了；正是這個彈簧的保持力，警察才誤以為這是釘子的力量——這樣，他們就認為沒必要對此進行深入的調查。

　　"下一個疑問是兇手下樓的方式。就這一疑點，我在和你一起繞着房子走時已經弄清楚了。離那扇窗戶大約五英尺半的地方有一個避雷針。沒有人可能從這個避雷針到達窗戶，更不用說進入房間了。然而，據我觀察，四樓的百葉窗屬很特殊的那種，巴黎的木匠稱之為"火印窗"——那是一種目前少見的類型，但是它在里昂和波爾多地區的老房子中較為多見。它們外形上是普通的門（是單一的門，而不是摺疊門），只是門的上半部分是格子的，或是開放的格子結構的——這樣就能使手很好地攀抓。目前，這種百葉窗全寬為三英尺半。當我們從房子後面看它們時，它們都是半開着的——這就是說，它們與牆壁成直角。也許，除了我，警察也檢查過了房子的背面部分；但是，如果是這樣，他們在看到這些火印窗的寬度時（他們肯定會看），就不會感覺到它實際幅度的寬闊，或者，無論如何，他們不會把它當一回事。事實上，一旦他們令自己相信這塊地方是沒有進出可能的，他們就自然會對此處的檢查做得較為粗略。但是，在我看來很明確的是，這扇牀架上方窗戶的百葉窗，假如完全轉回牆壁的話，就離避雷針不到兩英尺。同樣明顯的是，人若憑藉異常的矯健和勇氣，或許就可以從避雷針進入窗戶。只要越過兩英尺半的距離（現在我們假設百葉窗是完全打開的），盜賊就可能一隻手牢牢地抓住窗格子。然後，他鬆開抓住避雷針的另一隻手，將雙腿平穩地頂在牆上，並果敢地從牆上一蹬，就可以轉動百葉窗，使它關閉，而且，如果我們想像這時窗戶是開着的，那他甚至就順勢轉進了屋子。

　　"我希望你特別要記住的是，我剛才講到了需要異常的矯健才能成功地完成如此危險和困難的技藝。我這樣是想讓你明白，第一，從窗戶進入房間也許是可能的——但是，第二，同時也是更關鍵的，我希望讓你理解這種十分不同尋常——幾乎是不可思議的敏捷，惟有它，才能完成這一動作。

"毫無疑問，你會套用法律用語說，'為了證明我是有理的'，我應該寧願低估，而不是堅持最大限度地估算做到這事所需要的敏捷。這或許是法律的慣例，但是這不是理性的作用。我的最終目的只是真相。我的直接目的是讓你把我剛才說過的那十分不同尋常的敏捷和那非常怪異的尖厲（或嘶啞）而不穩定的聲音並列放置，而且那說話人的國籍沒有人的意見相同，在他的整個說話中，沒人能分辨出他的音節劃分。"

聽到杜潘的這些話，我腦海裏掠過了一個模糊而隱約的概念。我似乎快要理解了，卻沒有力量去領會——就像人們有時候發現自己馬上要記起甚麼了，而最終也沒能想起。我的朋友繼續往下說着。

"你看得出，"他說，"我已經把問題從出口轉到了入口。我就是在設法傳達這個想法，即兩個方法是一樣的，地點也相同。讓我們回到房間內部，來調查那裏的情況。據報導，櫃子的抽屜已經被搶劫過了，不過許多衣物仍然在裏面。這個結論是荒謬的。這只有猜測——一種非常愚蠢的猜測——僅此而已。我們憑甚麼知道那些在抽屜裏發現的衣物並不全是抽屜原來就有的？萊斯巴拉葉夫人和小姐過着異常隱居的生活——不拜訪親朋——很少出門——幾乎不需要常換服飾。至少那些被發現的衣物料子與這些女士們身份相符。如果竊賊要偷走的話，他為甚麼不帶走

最好的呢 —— 為甚麼不全都偷走呢？總之，為何他要放棄了四千法郎的金幣，拿這堆面料來麻煩自己呢？金幣被捨棄了。人們發現，米尼亞爾先生，那個銀行家提到過的全部金額幾乎都在地板上，被放在包裹裏面。因此，我希望你能從那些關於動機的浮躁想法中掙脫出來，警察只有送錢上門這些證據，才產生了這些想法的。比這事（遞交錢，然後收到錢的三天之內發生謀殺）奇怪十倍的巧合在我們生活中每時每刻都發生着，它們並沒有引起哪怕是短暫的注意。大體上説，對這一類的思想者來説，巧合是巨大的絆腳石，這些人雖然受過教育卻不懂概率論 —— 人類對一些最輝煌的目標的探究就得益於這一理論，因為它給予了最輝煌的例證。在這個例子中，如果金幣消失了，那麼三天前送交的錢財就不僅僅是一個巧合了，它就能證實這個關於動機的想法。但是，在這個案件的真實情況下面，如果我們假設金幣是這場暴行的動機，我們必然會認為這個罪犯是個如此猶豫不決的白癡，居然會放棄了黃金和他的犯罪動機。

"現在，請將這些引起了你注意的要點好好琢磨一下 —— 那怪異的聲音，異常的敏捷，還有在這個如此古怪、殘忍的兇殺案中令人驚訝的動機缺失 —— 讓我們來看看這場殘殺本身。此間，一個女人被人力勒死了，並頭朝下地被推上了煙囪。普通的謀殺不會採用這樣的殺人方式，尤其不會對死者進行如此的處理。你得承認，如此這般地將屍體推上煙囪，總有些過分之嫌 —— 這與我們通常所謂的行為常規完全是格格不入的，哪怕行為者是最喪失人性的。而且，再想想，能把屍體硬推入這樣的孔徑中，該需要怎樣巨大的力量，幾個人合力使勁都幾乎無法把屍體拽下來！

"現在，再轉到關於這個巨大力量的其他跡象上。在壁爐上面有濃密的卷髮 —— 非常濃密 —— 是灰色的人的頭髮。這些頭髮是被連根拔起的。現在你明白，哪怕是這樣地從頭上一起拔掉二三十根頭髮都需要巨大的力量。你和我一樣清楚地看到了這幾綹頭髮，它們的根部（看着太讓人害怕了）凝結着幾塊頭皮上的血肉 —— 這明顯就是用了猛力，或許這股力量一次就能連根拔出五十萬根頭髮。那老婦人的脖子不僅被砍了，而且那頭顱還完全地從身體脱落：兇器僅僅是一把剃刀。我希望你也看到了這些行為中殘忍的獸性。我就不用說萊斯巴拉葉夫人身上的那些傷痕了，迪馬先生和他能幹的助手艾蒂安先生已經説過它們是某種鈍頭兇器所致；照此看來，這些先生們的論斷是正確的。這鈍頭兇器顯然是院子裏的鋪路石材，受害者是從牀上的那扇窗墜落在它上面的。儘管這個想法現在看來也許有些簡單，但是警察疏忽於此的原因與他們由於百葉窗的寬度而發生疏忽同出一轍 —— 因為，由於釘子的緣故，警察根本排除了窗戶是曾被打開過的可能性。

　　"補充了上述的這些信息，如果此刻你恰恰已經想到了房間的凌亂，那麼迄今我們就可以把那驚人的敏捷、超人的力量、殘忍的獸性、缺失動機的謀殺、完全喪失了人性的怪異恐怖、許多不同國家的人聽來是異國的語調，以及含混或是費解的音節劃分等信息結合起來。那麼，接着會產生甚麼結果呢？這又給你留下了怎樣的印象呢？"

　　在杜潘問這個問題時，我有一種毛骨悚然的感覺。於是我説，"這是一個瘋子幹的 —— 是某個從附近的療養院逃出來的瘋瘋發狂者。"

"從某些方面來看，"他回答道，"你的觀點不無道理。但是瘋子的聲音，即使是在最癲狂的發作中，也不會和人們在樓上聽到的怪異聲音一樣。瘋子是有族裔的，儘管他們的語言在表達上會語無倫次，但是音節的劃分總是有連貫性的。另外，瘋子的頭髮是不會像我現在握在手中的那樣的。我從萊斯巴拉葉夫人緊緊捏着的手指中解下了一小撮頭髮。告訴我，你對此作何解釋？"

　　"杜潘！"我非常驚慌失措地說道，"這頭髮太古怪了 —— 這不是人的頭髮。"

　　"我並沒說過它是，"他說，"但是，在我們解決這一點前，我希望你看一看我畫在這張紙上的草圖。這幅畫是描摹其中一段證詞中所謂萊斯巴拉葉小姐的脖子上有'烏黑的瘀傷和深深的指甲抓痕'，也就是其他人（迪馬先生和艾蒂安先生）的證詞中'一連串烏青塊，顯然是手指的壓痕'的現象。"

　　"你會覺得，"我的朋友繼續說着，把紙在我們面前的桌子上展開，"這張畫使人想到緊緊而牢固的一握，很顯然沒有任何打滑。每一根手指都保持着 —— 也許直到受害者死去 —— 那可怕的緊握，最初連它們自己都深陷進肉裏了。現在，請你努力將所有的手指都同時放在你看到的每個壓痕上。"

　　我企圖這麼做，可是無濟於事。

　　"我們的嘗試也許不太恰當，"他說道，"這張紙是鋪放在一個平面上的；但是人的脖子是圓柱形的。這裏有一條木塊，它的周長與脖子差不多。用畫紙包捲它，然後再嘗試一遍。"

　　於是我依此做了；但是難度甚至明顯比前一次更大。"這不是人手留下的印子。"我說道。

杜潘回答說:"那麼讀一下這段居維埃教授講的話。"

這是一份關於東印度羣島上巨大的黃褐色猩猩的從解剖學和一般習性角度進行的詳細報道。那巨大的身材、超常的力量和敏捷、野性的兇殘以及這些哺乳動物的模仿習性都是廣為人知的。我立刻就明白了這個謀殺的可怕之處。

閱讀完後,我說:"在足趾的描寫上,這與那幅畫是一致的。我知道除了這裏提到的大猩猩種羣,沒有甚麼動物能留下你所描摹的壓痕。這一撮黃褐色的頭髮也和居維埃寫的動物有着同樣的特徵。但是我還是不可能理解這恐怖之謎中的一些細節。另外,人們聽到在爭吵中有兩個聲音,而且其中一個毫無疑問是法國人的聲音。"

"沒錯;而且你會記得,根據實情,這聲音有一種大家意見一致的語調 —— 是'我的天哪'的表達。在此情況下,這種語調的特徵已經被其中一個證人(即蒙塔尼,糖果店老闆)恰當地表述為指責或是規勸。因此,就是這兩個詞,我才充分擁有了徹底解開這個謎團的信心。那個法國人知道這個慘案。這是可能的 —— 事實上非常有可能 —— 即他在這場血腥慘案中是無罪的。那個猩猩也許是從他那裏逃跑的。他也許追逐到了那個房間窗下;但是,在隨後的混亂局面中,他沒法抓住牠,那畜生現在依然逍遙自在。我不想再追溯這些猜想了 —— 因為我沒有權利把它們稱作是別的甚麼 —— 既然它們所基於的思考幾乎沒有足夠的深度能令我自己賞識,而且,我也沒法自認為可以讓它們在別人的理解中變得好懂些。那麼,我們就權且稱它們為猜想,並這樣來談及它們吧。如果這個法國人真的如我所猜想的,在此暴行中是無罪的話，那麼這個啟事，即我昨夜回家路上在《世界報》報館刊登的（是一張關於航海方面，常常被水手關注的報紙）啟事，會將他帶到我們的住所。"

他遞給我一張報紙，我讀到如下信息：

招領——某日清晨（即謀殺發生的那個清晨），在布洛涅樹林捕獲了一隻巨大的黃褐色婆羅洲猩猩。失主（據説是一艘馬耳他商船上的水手）若能驗證辨明，並支付抓捕和豢養的少量費用，就可以將其領回。認領處在聖熱爾曼區 ×× 街 ×× 號，上四樓即可。

"這怎麼可能，"我問道，"你怎麼知道那人是個水手，並屬馬耳他商船？"

"我並不知道，"杜潘説，"我並不肯定。然而，這是一小段帶子，從它的形狀和油膩的外表看，很明顯，它是用來繫那些水手們很喜愛的長辮子的。另外，這個結是那種除了水手，很少有人能打的，而且這結是馬爾他商船所特有的。我是在避雷針的腳下撿起這條帶子的。它不可能屬於其中的任何一位死者。這樣，如果我對這條帶子的推論，即那個法國人是馬爾他商船上的水手的推測根本就是錯誤的，我在啟事中所説的話依然是無害的。如果我的推測是正確的，那麼我就得到了要點。如果這個法國人見證了謀殺，儘管他是無罪的，他自然會對啟事的答覆持猶豫態度——即認領那隻猩猩。他會這樣説服自己：'我對此毫不知情；我很貧窮；我的猩猩很值錢——對我這種處境的人來説，牠算得上是一筆財富——我幹嘛要因為這種無聊的憂慮危險而失去牠呢？牠就在這裏，伸手可及。牠是在布洛涅樹林裏被發現的 —— 與謀殺的現場有很遠的距離。人們怎麼會懷疑這事是一個殘忍的畜生幹的呢？警察對此茫然無知 —— 他們沒有抓住絲毫線索。他們哪怕是查出了是這頭畜生，也不可能證明我見證了謀殺，或是因為我見證了而把我牽連到罪行中去。重要的是，我被人知道了。登啟事的人認為我是這畜生的主人，我不太確定他到底對此有多少了解。如果我放棄認領這價值昂貴之物，而眾所周知我對此有所有權，那麼我至少就會使牠遭受懷疑。我是不會以此來吸引公眾對我或對這動物的關注的。我會答覆這條啟事，並領走那隻猩猩的，在這陣風波過去前好好地看着牠。'"

正在這時，我們聽到有上樓的腳步聲。

"準備好手槍，"杜潘說，"但是在我給你信號前別用它，也別讓別人看見。"

房子的前門一直開着，拜訪者沒有按鈴就走了進來，他往樓梯上走了幾步。然而，這時他似乎有些猶豫，接着我們就聽到他下樓的聲音。杜潘迅速地移到門邊，這時我們又聽到他上樓了。這次他沒有再折回，而是毅然地走上了樓梯，並叩響了我們房間的門。

"進來，"杜潘愉快而熱情地說道。

一個男人走了進來。顯然，他就是一名水手 —— 個子高高的，健壯，而且肌肉發達，臉上有一種蠻勇無畏的表情，倒不是太令人討厭。他的臉被太陽曬得黝黑，一大半被絡腮鬍子和髭髮掩蓋着。他帶着一根巨大的橡木棍，但是似乎除此沒有其他的武裝。他笨拙地鞠了個躬，並用法語問候我們"晚上好"，這語調雖然多少有點新夏特勒口音，但是仍然很明顯能聽出他是巴黎本地人。

"請坐，朋友，"杜潘説着，"我想你是為那隻猩猩而來的。真的，我幾乎要嫉妒你擁有牠了。牠是一頭非常不錯的、毫無疑問也是很珍貴的動物。你認為牠有多大了？"

那個水手長長地吸了口氣，有一種如釋重負的感覺，然後，他很放心地回答道：

"我也不清楚 —— 但是牠至多四、五歲。牠在你這裏嗎？"

"哦，不；我們沒法把牠養在這裏。牠在迪布爾街的馬房，就在附近。你可以明天一早就領走牠，當然，你打算領牠走了？"

"那是肯定的，先生。"

"我會很捨不得離開牠的 ，"杜潘説。

"先生，我不會讓您勞而無功的，"那人説道，"我不會這麼做，我很願意酬謝你找到了牠 —— 也就是説，只要合理，甚麼都行。"

"啊，"我的朋友回答説，"我確信這倒是相當公道的。讓我想想！—— 我該要甚麼呢？哦！我會告訴你。我要的是這個，你應該盡你所能告訴我所有關於摩格街兒殺案的信息。"

杜潘説最後幾個字時聲調很低，也很平靜。同樣地，他很平靜地走向大門，鎖上了它，並把鑰匙放進了口袋。然後他從胸口掏出一把手槍，並不慌不忙地將它放在桌上。

那水手的臉刷地紅了，好像在窒息中掙扎着。他猛地站起身，抓住了棍棒，但隨後又坐了回去，猛烈地顫抖着，臉色如死灰一般。他沒説一句話。我從心底裏同情他。

"朋友，"杜潘説着，語氣友善，"你不必如此驚嚇自己 —— 真的沒這必要。我們怎麼也不會害你的。我以一個紳士，也是一個法國人的榮譽向你保證，我們對你沒有惡意。我完全清楚在摩格街的殘殺中，你是無罪的。然而，這並不是説你與此就沒有任何牽連了。正如我早已説過的，你肯定知道我對此事件的情況有着了解的途徑——這途徑你做夢都想不到的。現在事情擺在那裏了，對於你能避免不做的事，你確實甚麼也沒做——很確定的是，沒甚麼事能判定你有罪。甚至當你可以泰然地搶劫時，你也沒有盜竊甚麼。你沒甚麼可掩藏的，也沒有理由要掩藏。另一方面，你得遵從道義坦陳所有你知道的事。現在一個無罪的人被監禁了，你能説清那兇殺的真正兇手。"

在杜潘説出上述話時，那個水手的情緒恢復了大半；但是他最初的蠻勇無畏不脛而走。

"老天幫幫我！"他停了一會，如此説道，"我會告訴你關於此事件我所知道的一切——但是我不指望你能相信我説的一半的話——我這麼指望的話，就真的很蠢了。可是，我是無罪的，我即便為此送命也得説個明白。"

他所説的大致如下：他最近航海去了印度羣島。一夥人，包括他在內，在婆羅洲登陸，他們投入了其間的愉快旅行中。他和一個夥伴捕獲了這隻猩猩。夥伴死了，這隻動物就歸他一人所有。在返程中他領教了捕獲物難馴的野性，頗費了一些周折後，他終於成功地將牠安頓在自己巴黎的住所中。為了不招致鄰居們令人不快的好奇，他細心地把牠隔離起來，想一直等到牠腿上的傷口痊癒，那傷口是船上的尖鋭碎片導致的。他最終的目的是想把牠賣了。

謀殺發生的那天晚上，或者説，那時已經是凌晨了，他從某個水手的嬉鬧聚會返回家中，他發現那畜生佔據了他自己的臥室，牠是從臨近的儲藏室掙脫出來，進入房間的。他曾以為那儲藏室能穩當地禁錮住這畜生。牠手裏拿着剃刀，滿臉塗着肥皂泡，坐在鏡子前，試圖要刮臉，很顯然，牠以前從儲藏室的鑰匙孔裏看到主人這麼做過。看到一個這麼兇狠的動物手裏拿着如此危險的武器，而且還用得那麼得心應手，他非常驚恐，有那麼一會，他一直是驚慌失措的。然而，他已經習慣於用鞭子使那畜生鎮定下來，哪怕是在牠最殘暴的狀態中，於是，他就又借助於此。看到鞭子，那猩猩立刻躍出了房門，跑下樓梯，然後，穿過了一扇不巧正開啟着的窗戶，跑到了街上。

那個法國人絕望地跟隨着；那隻猩猩的手裏仍然拿着剃刀，偶爾停下來回頭看看，對着追牠的人做着手勢，直到後者幾乎要趕上牠。然後牠又匆忙跑開了。就這樣，這場追捕繼續了很長時間。在將近凌晨三點鐘時，街道上寂靜無聲。當跑進摩格街後面的小巷時，那亡命之徒被四樓萊斯巴拉葉夫人房間那開啟着的窗戶所發出的亮光吸引。牠衝向那幢房子，看到了避雷針，用令人難以置信的敏捷攀了上去，抓住了百葉窗，窗子被完全地甩向牆面，然後，靠這個途徑，牠把自己徑直地旋在牀頭板上。整個舉動不到一分鐘，在猩猩進入房間時，那扇百葉窗被牠再次踢開。

這時候，那個水手又高興又為難。他強烈地希望能夠馬上就抓住這隻野獸，因為牠幾乎無法從牠冒險陷入的困境中逃離，除了從避雷針那裏逃，也許牠從那裏下來時就能被劫獲。另一方面，他感到萬分焦慮，生怕牠會在房子裏做出點甚麼。後一種想法促使他依然跟隨着那個逃亡者。爬上避雷針並不困難，尤其對一個水手而言，但是當他爬到窗戶的高度時，那窗在左邊很遠處，他的行進就停止了，他至多只能伸過去瞥一眼房間的內部。

這一瞥幾乎嚇得他要鬆手跌下去。此時，那些淒厲可怕的叫聲穿破了黑夜，驚醒了摩格街正在沉睡的居民。萊斯巴拉葉夫人和她的女兒穿着睡衣，顯然正專注於整理那曾被提及的鐵箱子裏的某些票據，這隻箱子被拖滾到房間的中央，它是開着的，裏面的東西被放到了一旁的地板上。被害者準是背對着窗戶坐着；而且，從這畜生進入房間到尖叫的時間間隔來看，似乎她們並非立刻看到猩猩，並自然而然地以為那百葉窗的拍打聲是風造成的。

　　當那水手往裏看時，那巨大的野獸已經抓住了萊斯巴拉葉夫人的頭髮（她的頭髮已經鬆了，因為她方才一直在梳理它），並用剃刀在她的臉上揮舞，模仿着理髮師的動作。萊斯巴拉葉小姐則俯臥着，一動不動；她已經暈厥過去了。那老夫人的尖叫和掙扎（這期間她的頭髮也被扯落了）使這猩猩或許是平和的目的轉變為那些憤怒之舉。牠只消用肌肉發達的手臂斷然地一摑，幾乎就將她的頭從身體上切斷開來。一看到血，牠的憤怒就被激發成了瘋狂。他咬牙切齒，眼睛冒着火，目光中的火勢蔓延到了那姑娘的身體上，於是牠將那可怕的爪子深深地嵌入她的脖子，緊捏不放，直到她斷了氣。然後，牠恍惚而狂野的目光又落在牀頭，那上面是牠主人的臉，那臉因為驚懼而僵硬着，正好落入了牠的視線。由於牠腦海中依然停留着那可怕的鞭子的記憶，那野獸的怒火立刻轉化成了恐懼。牠意識到要遭受懲罰，似乎很想掩蓋自己的血腥暴行，就在房間裏到處亂蹦，處於一種緊張焦慮的痛苦中；在移動中，牠推倒並摧毀了家具，還把牀從牀板上拖了下來。總之，牠先抓住了女兒的屍體，然後把她塞上了煙囪，就像屍體被發現時的樣子；接着，牠就來對付那老夫人了，牠迅速地把她向窗外頭朝下地猛擲去。

當這隻猩猩拖着那具殘骸靠近窗扉時，那水手嚇得縮到了避雷針上，與其說他是爬下去的，毋寧說是滑下杆子的，而且，他立即趕回家——生怕自己被牽扯進這場殘殺中，並在恐慌中主動放棄了對這猩猩命運的一切關注。那羣人在樓梯上聽到的話就是這個法國人驚駭和恐懼的感歎，其間混雜着這頭野獸殘忍而含混不清的咕噥聲。

我幾乎沒有甚麼可補充的了。那隻猩猩準是在大家破門而入前，從那個房間，通過那個避雷針逃走的。當牠穿過窗子時，一定將窗戶關閉了。後來，牠被主人親手抓住了，主人以一個很高的價格將牠賣給了巴黎動物園。我們去警務局長辦公室講述了事件的真相（還有杜潘的一些評論），於是勒邦立刻獲得釋放。不過，儘管警察局長對我的朋友態度友好，他還是沒法真正掩飾起自己對事態的變化所持有的懊惱態度，只好一味地諷刺着，說任何人都摻和進他的公務這不太合適。

"讓他說，"杜潘說道，他認為沒必要作出答覆。"讓他講吧；這樣可以讓他心裏好受些。我很滿意自己在他的地盤打贏了他。不過，他是輸在對這個謎的解答上，這並非是他所料想的奇跡之類的事；因為，事實上，我們的局長朋友多少有些太過機靈，反而不夠深刻了。他的智慧之花中沒有雄蕊，就像拉威耳娜女神的畫像，只有頭腦，沒有身體——或者，最多不過像鱈魚一樣只有頭腦和肩膀。但是他畢竟還是個好人。我尤其欣賞他的能言善辯，就因為這個，他贏得了靈巧機敏的聲響。我說的是他那種 'de nier ce qui est, et d'expliquer ce qui n'est pas' [14] 的本領。"

（張瓊譯）

4

瑪麗·羅傑疑案 [15]

Es giebt eine Reihe idealischer Begebenheiten, die der Wirklichkeit parallel läuft. Selten fallen sie zusammen. Menschen und Zufälle modificiren gewöhnlich die idealische Begebenheit, so dass sie unvollkommen erscheint, und ihre Folgen gleichfalls unvollkommen sind. So bei der Reformation; statt des Protestantismus kam das Lutherthum hervor.

理想中的一系列事件會與真實情況相似。它們很少能完全一致。人和環境會在總體上改動理想中的一連串事情，使之顯得不盡完美，從而其結果也同樣無法盡善盡美。宗教改革亦是如此；想的是新教，來的卻是路德教。

——諾瓦利斯 [16]《精神論》

即使是最鎮定的思想者，都很少有人不曾對超自然事物陷入一種模糊的、令人毛骨悚然的、半信半疑的驚訝中，那事物又似乎恰巧具備一種不可思議的特性，而這種純粹的巧合是具備才智之人無法接受的。這樣的情緒——因為我所說的半信半疑絕不具備充分的思維能力——這些情緒很少被徹底地壓制住，除非借助機會學說，或者，用科學的術語來說，即概率演算。從實質上說，這個演算純粹是數學性的；因此我們就把科學中的極盡嚴格與精確作為異例，運用於思維中最不可捉摸的幻象與精神性之中。

依據時間的順序，我要應約公之於眾的那些不可思議的細節，起初的發展是一系列令人費解的巧合，其後，或者說最終的進展會讓所有讀者認出，這是在隱射不久前瑪麗·塞西莉亞·羅傑斯在紐約被謀殺的事件。

大約在一年前，在一篇題名為《摩格街謀殺案》的文章中，我曾竭力描述了我的朋友，C·奧古斯特·杜潘先生在思維特性上的一些非凡之處，我沒曾想到自己還會繼續這個話題。當時，我對這種特性的描述形成了文章的構思；而且這構思在例證杜潘特性的一連串混亂的事實中得到了充分證實。我還可以引證其他的事例，但是我不想再贅言了。不過，最近一些事件的發展很令人驚訝，促使我進一步地描述了一些詳情，這些細節會帶有一種強制性的招供意味。在了解了我最近所聽說的事之後，如果我依然對很久以前的所見所聞保持沉默的話，我就會真的感到不安了。

在萊斯巴拉葉夫人和她的女兒之死的悲劇結束之際，杜潘爵士立刻從心中擯除了此事件，又回到了他所固有的變化無常的幻想中。我向來喜歡抽象概念，就很樂於順應他的心情；並繼續住在我們位於聖熱爾曼區的居所中，我們不考慮未來，寧靜地安睡於現在，將周圍沉悶的世界編織成夢幻。

但是這些夢並非完全不受干擾。我早就說過，杜潘在摩格街戲劇性事件中的表現在巴黎的警察的想像中留下了不可磨滅的印象。在這些密探中，杜潘的大名膾炙人口。除了我之外，他從不對其他任何人解釋破案時那些推論上簡潔利落的特點，甚至連警察局長也不了解。難怪這事件理所當然地被認為幾乎是奇跡，或者說他所具備的分析能力被歸結為直覺。他的直率原本會打消任何質疑者持有的這種偏見；但是他懶散的脾性卻終止了人們對這一他早已不感興趣的話題做進一步的爭議。就這樣，他才發現自己成了警方眼中的焦點人物；並且，轄區中的案件也沒少麻煩他。其中最引起關注的案子就是那個名叫瑪麗·羅傑的年輕女子的謀殺事件。

此事件大約是在摩格街慘案發生的兩年之後。瑪麗是寡婦埃斯特爾·羅傑的獨生女，她的教名及家姓和那不幸的"雪茄女郎"很相近，讀者一看就會引起注意。她自幼喪父，從她父親的死一直到被我們所論及的那場謀殺的前十八個月，她和母親一直共同住在聖安德列街[17]；夫人在那裏經營一個膳宿公寓，由瑪麗幫着照料。就這樣，一些事情在女兒二十二歲時發生了，她非凡的美麗吸引了一位香料商，他在王宮的底層開了一家店鋪，主顧主要是附近大批滋生的一些流氓惡棍。勒布朗先生[18]意識到漂亮的瑪麗來光顧他的香料店會帶來諸多好處；他那慷慨的供職提議被這姑娘欣然接受了，儘管夫人多少還是有些顧慮。

那位店老闆如願以償，他的店鋪頓時因為這個活潑動人的女店員而變得眾所周知。她被他僱用了大約一年時間，然後突然失蹤了，這令她的崇拜者們感到無比困惑。勒布朗先生也無法對她的離開作出解釋，羅傑夫人為此心煩意亂，驚惶焦慮。報紙立刻抓住這個話題，警察正準備着手進行嚴格的調查。然後，在一個風和日麗的早晨，在失蹤了一個星期後，瑪麗健健康康地又出現在了她往常站的那個香料櫃台，只是她多少有些憂鬱。除了帶有私人性質的詢問，所有的調查自然都停止了。勒布朗先生像以往那樣，表明自己對此事一無所知。瑪麗和母親一起回答了所有的問題，説上一週她是在鄉下的親戚家度過的。於是這事件就平息下來，基本上被人淡忘了。至於那個姑娘，她藉口要從人們的好奇心所導致的無禮中擺脱出來，就向香料商提出了辭呈，然後在聖安德列街她母親的住所隱居起來。

她回家後大約過了五個月，朋友們又為她第二次突然失蹤感到震驚。三天過去了，她依然杳無音信。第四天，有人發現她的屍體漂浮在塞納河 [19] 裏，就在聖安德列區對岸離魯爾門 [20] 那片僻靜地區不遠的河邊。

這場謀殺的兇殘（因為一看就明白這是一場謀殺），受害者的年輕與美麗，尤其是她以往的風流名聲，這些都引起了敏感的巴黎民眾心中的強烈震動。在我記憶中，我從沒見過其他類似事件引發過如此廣泛而強烈的反響。幾週時間裏，人們談論着這一引人注目的話題，甚至連當日重大的政治事件都忘卻了。警察局長盡了不同一般的努力，當然了，整個巴黎的警察們都在竭力調查。

在屍體剛被發現時，人們認為兇手無法逃脱，因為在最短的時間內就展開了調查。直到一週快結束時，人們才認為有必要對此案提供酬金；即使在那時，酬金也僅限於一千法郎。同時，人們對案情的調查充滿熱情，不過總是沒有甚麼論斷，無數的人都被審訊過了，依然毫無收穫。而且，由於一直缺乏疑案的各條線索，公眾的激情急劇高漲。在第十天末，人們認為應該將原先提議的數額增加一倍。於是，當第二週過去時，案情依然沒有甚麼進展，巴黎人民一直以來就對警察懷有的偏見就在幾次嚴重的暴動中爆發出來，警察局長就毅然提出將“緝拿兇手”的酬金增至兩萬法郎，如果不止一人被證實與案件有牽連，那麼“每緝拿一名兇手”就獲得一筆這樣的酬金。這份酬金聲明還説，一旦任何同謀犯能站出來以事實揭發同夥，那麼他就能保證獲得完全的赦免。和這份聲明貼在一起的，還有一個市民委員會的非官方告示，表示在警察局給予的酬金數額之外，願意再給予一萬法郎。那麼，這筆酬金的總額就不低於三萬法郎，當我們考慮到那個姑娘的卑微境遇，以及在大城市中像這種慘案的高發率，這筆錢的數額就相當可觀了。

那時沒有人懷疑這個謀殺疑案會立即昭明天下。可是，在一兩個實例中，那些保證能闡明案情的逮捕卻沒能拿出任何能讓被捕者與此案有所牽連的證據，嫌疑犯即刻就被釋放了。奇怪的是，屍體發現後的第三週也過去了，還是沒有絲毫進展，而我和杜潘甚至對人們津津樂道的此案傳聞沒有甚麼察覺。我們兩人正潛心專注於自己的研究，幾乎一個月都沒有外出，也沒有會客，哪怕是多看一眼日報上的標題性政論也沒有。對此謀殺案的最初了解是由 G 個人告知的。他在 18×× 年 7 月 13 日午後來拜訪我們，和我們一起直到深夜。他竭力想查出兇手卻一直沒有結果，為此他一直感到悶悶不樂。他的名聲 —— 談及它時他帶着特有的巴黎人的腔調 —— 岌岌可危了，甚至連榮譽都受到了威脅。公眾的目光正落在他身上，而他也確實不遺餘力地為這個疑案的進展在努力着。在結束這次有些滑稽離奇的談話時，他恭維杜潘，並樂意稱之為機智老練，而且直截了當地而確切地給予杜潘一個慷慨的提議，這提議的基本實質我不便透露，不過它對我此文所敍述的主題沒有任何影響。

我的朋友很得體地婉拒了這樣的溢美之詞，不過倒是很快接受了他的提議，儘管總的來說這好處只是暫時的。提議達成後，警察局長立刻滔滔不絕地解釋自己的觀點，並散佈長篇的例證論述，我們對此並沒太專注。那人說了很多，而且毫無疑問，顯得很淵博。當夜晚漸漸逝去時，我斗膽提了個不經意的暗示。杜潘穩穩地坐在他常用的那把扶手椅中，對他的談話表示着尊重與關注。在整個交談中，他戴着眼鏡；我不時地朝他那綠色鏡片瞥上幾眼，這足以令我確信他睡得不算差，因為警察局長立即起身告辭前，他在七、八個小時緩慢而沉重的整段時間中一直很安靜。

早晨，我從轄區拿到了一份對所有已取得證據的完整報告，而且，我從不同的報社網羅了已出版的從最初到最近的所有有關此慘案明確報道的報紙。除去所有那些被證明是肯定錯誤的信息，大體的情況報道如下：

18××年6月22日，星期天，瑪麗·羅傑大約是早上九點鐘離開她聖安德列街母親的住所的。在離開時，她只通知了雅克·聖厄斯塔什先生[21]，告訴他自己打算陪一位住在德羅梅街的姨媽過一天。德羅梅街是條又短又狹窄的街道，不過人口眾多，離河岸不遠，從羅傑夫人的公寓到那裏大約是兩英里的直線距離。聖厄斯塔什是被瑪麗接受的求婚者，他食宿在那間公寓裏。他得在黃昏時分去未婚妻那裏，並陪她回家。然而，那天下午，下了場大雨；他估計瑪麗整個晚上會在姨媽家（因為曾有類似的先例），就認為沒有必要遵照諾言。當夜晚來臨時，羅傑夫人（她是個虛弱的老太太，有七十歲了）表示她害怕"再也見不到瑪麗了"；但是當時這並沒引起別人的注意。

星期一，那姑娘被證實並沒有去過德羅梅街，當一天過去後都沒有她的消息時，人們才着手對城市和鄰近地區進行已被拖延了的搜索。然而直到她失蹤後的第四天，人們仍未打聽到任何關於她的下落。在這天（6 月 25 日，星期三），一位名叫博章的先生 [22] 和他的朋友在魯爾門附近，在正對着聖安德列街的塞納河邊詢問了有關瑪麗的事，並被告知一具屍體剛被某個漁夫拖上岸，該漁夫發現屍體漂浮在河面上。看到這具屍體後，博章遲疑了一會兒，辨認出她就是那個香料店的姑娘。他的朋友比他更快地就認出是她。

那張臉滿是黑色的血跡，有些是從嘴部流出來的，沒有發現在純粹淹死的情況下通常可見的白沫。細胞組織尚未變色。在脖子部位有瘀傷和手指印。屍體雙臂彎曲在胸口上，已經僵硬了。右手緊握着；左手是部分打開的。在左手腕上有兩個環形的皮膚擦傷痕跡，顯然是幾條繩子所致，或是一條繩子被綁了好幾圈。右手腕部分及整個背部也有嚴重擦傷，但是在肩胛處尤其嚴重。漁夫在把屍體拖上岸時，是用繩子繫上拉的，但是那些擦傷不是由此造成。屍體脖子處很腫，身上沒有明顯的刀痕，也沒有明顯的被擊打過的瘀傷。一條緞帶緊緊地繫在脖子上，似乎不易被人發現，它完全地陷入肌肉中，並恰好在左耳朵下繫了個結。光這個結就足以導致她的死亡。驗屍報告確認死者死前有過性行為，還說她遭受了兇殘的暴力。屍體被發現時就是這樣的狀況，朋友們不費太大困難就辨認出她了。

她的衣服被撕得很破，或者說是非常凌亂。外套上從底邊向上一直到腰部被撕開大約一尺來長，但是碎片並沒有被扯下來。它圍着腰部繞了三圈，並被背後搭鈎狀的東西固定住。緊貼着外衣的衣服質地是精紡的棉布；從這上面完全撕扯下了一條十八吋長的布 —— 撕得很均勻很小心。那條布被纏繞在脖子上，纏得鬆鬆的，並被打了個死結。在這條布帶和那根飾帶上還繫着兩端連着一頂無簷女帽的帽帶。那個帽子的細繩上的結不是女士風格的，而是一個活結，或是一個水手結。

在屍體被辨認後，人們並沒有像往常一樣把它送到停屍間（這個形式是多餘的），而是很草率地將它埋葬在離屍體被拖上岸處不遠的地方。通過博韋先生的努力，這件事儘量被努力掩蓋起來，所以幾天過去了，一直未引起公眾的騷動。然而，一份週報[23]最終披露了這個事件，於是屍體被挖掘出來，再次進行調查；可是除了已經得到的信息，沒有甚麼新的收穫。不過，那些衣服被交給了死者的母親和朋友們，並被確認為是那姑娘離家時所穿之物。

同時，對此事的騷動持續增長。已有幾人被捕，而後又被釋放。其中聖厄斯塔什最值得懷疑；他最初無法明確地交代星期日瑪麗離家那天自己的行蹤。然而，後來他向 G 先生遞交了一份書面陳述，對這一天每一時間段進行了令人信服而詳細的說明。隨着時間的過去，因為沒有任何新發現，許多自相矛盾的傳言被散佈開了，於是記者們都忙於提出假設。在這些假設中，最引人注意的是關於瑪麗·羅傑依然活着的說法 —— 即在塞納河裏被發現的屍體是別的不幸之人。我覺得有必要將幾段包含這種想法的話讓讀者一讀。這些片段是照原話從《星報》[24]上翻譯過來的，總的來說，這報紙具有較高的水準。

"羅傑小姐於一八××年六月二十二日，星期天的早晨離開其母親家，她藉口是要去拜訪姨媽，或是在羅德梅街的其他親戚。從離開後，證實沒有人再見到過她，也根本沒有其他與她相關的消息和音訊……不管怎麼說，迄今沒有人自願出來表明自己曾在那天她離開母親家後見過她……現在，儘管我們沒有任何證據認為瑪麗·羅傑在六月二十二日星期天九點之後還在人世，我們有依據證明到九點為止，她是活着的。在星期三中午十二點，有人發現一具女屍漂浮在魯爾門附近的岸邊。即使我們假設瑪麗·羅傑在離開母親住所後的三個小時之內就被扔進了河的話，那麼那時距她離家只有三天——恰好三天。但是，如果兇手對她下了手，那麼，認為其動作完成能快到足以使自己在午夜之前將屍體扔進河裏的推測是愚蠢的。那些對如此恐怖罪行有罪惡感的人會選擇最漆黑的時分而非稍有亮光的時間……於是我們就明白，如果在河裏被發現的屍體是瑪麗·羅傑，那麼她在水裏的時間只能是兩天半，或者至多是三天。所有的經驗都表明，溺水的屍體，或者說在暴力致死後被立刻扔進水中的屍體，需要六到十天時間才能使其足夠腐爛到能浮出水面。即使屍體被火炮燃燒過，它也至少要五到六天的浸泡才能浮起，如果不去管它的話，它又會沉下去。那麼，我們設問，在此案中，是甚麼導致了對正常的自然過程的偏離呢？……如果屍體呈毀壞狀態在岸上被放置到星期二的晚上，那麼人們就會在岸邊發現兇手的某些痕跡。哪怕屍體是死了兩天後被扔進水中的，它是否能如此快地浮上來，這一點也很可疑。另外，最不可能的是，暴徒在犯下如此的謀殺罪行後，竟然會不附加重物就將屍體拋擲水中，而這樣的防範做起來毫不費力。"

編輯在這裏還進一步地論述，認為屍體一定在水中"不止三天了，而至少是十五天時間"，因為它腐爛得很厲害，連博韋在辨認時都頗費周折。不過，這個觀點被徹底否定了。我繼續翻譯如下：

"那麼，是甚麼事實讓博韋先生認為這屍體毫無疑問就是瑪麗‧羅傑呢？他撕開了外衣的袖子，說他發現了一些能使自己確認的標記。公眾大多猜想這些標記是由某種疤痕構成的。他擦拭着胳膊，並發現上面有汗毛——我們認為，這汗毛正如人們預先想像的那樣，是無法確定甚麼的——就像在袖子裏發現一條胳膊一樣沒甚麼結論性。當晚，博韋先生沒有返回，但是在星期三晚上的七點，他傳話給羅傑夫人，說對她女兒的調查仍在進行中。如果我們假設，在羅傑夫人的年紀和悲痛狀況下，她是不會過去的（這假設是很站得住腳的），那麼，如果他們認為那具屍體是瑪麗的話，就肯定有人會認為很有必要過去並參與調查。但是沒有人過去。在聖安德列街沒有任何人議論或聽說這件事，甚至連同一幢樓的居民都不知道。瑪麗的戀人和未來的丈夫，即住在女方母親家的聖厄斯塔什先生作證道，直到次日上午，他才聽說未婚妻的屍體被人發現之事，那時是博韋先生走進他的房間並告訴他的。對於這樣的一類消息會如此冷靜地被接受，我們覺得很是震驚。"

就這樣，這份報導竭力讓人們對瑪麗親友的冷漠留下印象，這與這些親友相信這具屍體就是瑪麗的推測不相符。這所造成的暗示是：在親友們的縱容默許之下，瑪麗從城市中消失的原因是與對她的貞潔不利的責難有關；於是，在這些親友們得知塞納河裏發現一具屍體，並與瑪麗相像時，他們就順勢讓公眾相信她死了。但是《星報》還是很草率。人們能很清楚地證實，並不存在大家所想像的冷漠；那位老夫人異常虛弱，她情緒過激，無法勝任任何事；而聖厄斯塔什遠不是冷靜地接受消息，他傷心到心緒混亂，行為幾乎瘋狂，以致博韋先生說服一個親友來照料他，阻止他參與掘墓現場的調查。另外，儘管《星報》報導說屍體由公眾出資被再次埋葬，並說瑪麗的家人堅決反對由他人慷慨饋贈的私人墓穴，而且家人沒有參加安葬儀式。我認為，雖然《星報》在有意對此印象的推波助瀾中表明了所有這一切，但所有這些都被充分地證明是不正確的。在隨後一期的報紙中，報導又盡力使人們對博韋本人產生懷疑。編輯是如下表述的：

"然後，事情發生了轉變。我們得知，有一次，當 B 夫人在羅傑夫人家中時，博韋先生正要外出，他告訴她有一位警官要來，而她，B 夫人，在他回來前一定不能告訴警官任何事，一切由他來處理……從目前的情況看，博韋先生似乎將整件事都封鎖在大腦裏，沒有他就會寸步難行，因為，不管你嘗試哪條途徑，都會撞上他……出於某種原因，他決定除了他自己，任何人都不要牽涉進此事件中，而且，根據瑪麗的男性親屬們的抗議，他還用非常奇怪的方式將他們排擠出局。他似乎非常反對讓親友們見到屍體。"

根據後來的事實，一些跡象使人們對博韋產生了懷疑。在瑪麗失蹤前幾天，有人去辦公室拜訪博韋，當時他不在，那人觀察到在門的鑰匙孔裏有一枝玫瑰花，還有一塊刻着“瑪麗”名字的板掛在附近。

　　我們從報紙上能夠搜羅的信息似乎在總體上給大家一種印象，即瑪麗是一幫暴徒手下的受害者——由於這些人的迫害，她被帶過河，遭受了暴行，並被殺害了。不過，具有廣泛影響的《商報》[25] 則強烈地反對這種被普遍接受的觀點。我從它的專欄中引用了這樣一兩段話：

　　“就老在魯爾門一帶搜尋兇手的痕跡而論，我們相信，到目前為止，案情偵察是誤入歧途了。一個像這一年輕女子一樣被公眾熟知的人，在走過了三個街區而不被人看見是不可能的；而且，任何見到她的人都應該會記住這事的，因為所有知道她的人都對她頗有興趣。她是在街道充滿了人羣時離開的……她在經過了魯爾門或是德羅梅街後，肯定會被一打以上的人認出來；可是沒有人站出來説他曾在她母親住所之外見過她，而且，除了證詞中提及她所表述過的意圖外，也沒有跡象表明她確實是出來了。她的外衣破了，包裹在她身上，而且被打結繫住了；並且，因為這樣，屍體像一捆東西似的被抬走了。如果兇手是在魯爾門附近行兇的，那麼就沒有必要對屍體做出如此的處理。屍體被發現漂浮在魯爾門附近的事實並不能證實它是在哪裏被扔進水中的……從這個不幸女子的一條襯裙上，被撕下一條長兩尺寬一尺的布，它被繫在她的下巴下面，纏繞在大腦背後，也許是為了防止她喊叫。這是一幫沒帶手帕的傢伙們幹的。"

然而，在警察局長拜訪我們的一兩天前，警察們得到了某個重要的信息，至少，這消息似乎推翻了《商報》所論述的主要觀點。兩個小男孩，他們是德呂克夫人的兒子，在魯爾門附近的樹林裏漫步時，碰巧走進了一個茂密的灌木叢，裏面有三四塊大石頭，形成了一種有靠背和腳凳的椅子。在上面的石頭上鋪着一條白色的襯裙；在第二塊石頭上的是一條絲綢圍巾。那裏還有一把女用陽傘、一副手套和一塊手帕。手帕上繡着的名字是"瑪麗·羅傑"。在四周的灌木上還有一些衣服的碎片。地面是被踩踏過的，樹叢被折斷過，到處都有搏鬥過的跡象。他們發現，在灌木叢和河流之間的柵欄被拆倒了，地面上有某種重物被拖過的痕跡。

一份名為《太陽報》[26] 的週刊對此發現作了以下的評述 —— 這些評述不過是對整個巴黎報界的觀點作出了呼應：

"所有這些物品在那裏顯然已至少有三四週時間；由於下雨，一切都嚴重發霉，並粘在一起了。有一些物品四周和上面還長了草。陽傘的綢面很堅實，但是裏面織線已經全部分解腐爛了。上面的部分是雙層和摺疊的，也都發霉破爛，並在傘被打開的情況下開裂了……那外衣的幾條碎片被灌木叢撕破，有六英吋長、三英吋寬。其中一塊是外衣的底邊，它被修補過；另一塊是裙擺上的，不是底邊。它們看上去就像被撕下來的布條，被放在荊棘叢上，離地面大概有一英尺距離……因此，毫無疑問，這令人瞠目的行兇現場已經被發現。"

緊接着這個發現，新的證據出現了。德呂克夫人作證說她在河岸不遠處，正對着魯爾門的地方開着一家路邊旅館。那附近很偏僻——異常僻靜。那裏通常是城市來的流氓們的星期日度假地，他們是坐船過河的。那個星期天下午，大約在三點鐘，一個年輕的姑娘來到了旅館，有一個臉色黝黑的年輕男子陪着她。他們兩人在那裏停留了一段時間。在他們離開時，他們走了一條通往附近某個茂密樹林的路。德呂克夫人被那姑娘的衣服吸引，因為它很像她一個已故親戚穿過的衣服。她尤其注意到了那條圍巾。在這對人離開後，一幫歹徒出現了，他們吵吵嚷嚷的，又吃又喝還不給錢，並跟着上了那對青年男女走的路。在黃昏時，他們返回了旅館，似乎非常急匆匆地過了河。

當天晚上天黑後不久，德呂克夫人和她的大兒子聽到了旅館附近有一個女人的尖叫聲。那喊聲很淒厲，不過很短暫。德呂克夫人不僅辨認出了在灌木叢中發現的圍巾，而且還認出了在屍體身上被發現的衣服。一個名叫瓦倫斯[27]的馬車夫也作證說，在那個星期天，他看見過瑪麗·羅傑和一個臉色黝黑的年輕男子一同乘渡輪到了塞納河對岸。瓦倫斯認識瑪麗，他不可能認錯的。那些在灌木叢裏被發現的東西已經全部被瑪麗的親友們辨認出來了。

在杜潘的建議下，我就這樣親自從報紙上搜集了這些證據和信息，它們還包含了一點——但是這一點似乎至關重要。就在上述這些衣物被發現後不久，好像有人看見那個喪失了生命力或幾乎像行屍走肉般的聖厄斯塔什，瑪麗的未婚夫，出現在了被大家所認為的行兇現場的附近。在他身邊有一個標有"鴉片酊"[28]的瓶子，瓶子已被倒空。他的呼吸證實了那是種毒藥。他無聲地死去了，在他身上有一封信，信中主要表明了他對瑪麗的愛，以及他要自毀的打算。

當杜潘仔細看完了我的筆記，說道："我無需告訴你，即這案件比摩格街謀殺更加錯綜複雜。它與後者有一個重要的不同。這是一個雖然殘忍，卻是普通的犯罪案例。它沒有甚麼特別超常之處。你會注意到，就因為這個原因，人們一直認為這個案子很容易解開。就因為它平常，它本該被認為難以解開。於是，最初，人們認為沒必要設酬金。G先生的眾多下屬們很快就能明白這樣的慘案很可能是怎樣、為甚麼會犯下的，他們能從很多的殺人方式中想像出其中一種，從許多的動機中找尋出一種來；因為不無可能的是，在這些無數的方式或動機中，或許就真有一種符合實情，他們想當然地認為那其中必有其一。但是，對此案的各種奇想所包含的合理性，以及這些奇想各自似乎帶有的可能性，應該被人們理解為是預示了闡明此案是困難而非容易的。我曾經說過，正是憑着那些超乎尋常的現象，理性才能謹慎地摸索到真實，假如發現真相的途徑真的存在的話，對於目前這樣的案件，應當探詢的問題不是'發生了甚麼'，而是'發生了甚麼前所未有的事'。在對萊斯巴葉[29]夫人的住所進行調查時，G先生的那些偵探們都對那些不同尋常的現象感到沮喪和迷惑，而這些現象對於一個理性而有條理的才智之人來說，卻是確定地預示了成功；可是這同一位才智之人，在面對這個香料店姑娘的案件所呈現的尋常特徵時，卻有可能陷入絕望，而且除了警察人員也能輕易取得的進展外，也說不出個所以然來。

"在萊斯巴拉葉夫人和她女兒的案子中，甚至在調查伊始，我們就確信這是一起謀殺，自殺的嫌疑是被立刻排除的。現在，我們也從一開始就排除了自殺的各種可能。在魯爾門被發現的屍體呈現的是這樣一種情形，這很難讓我們有推想出自殺的可能。但是也有人認為這具被發現的屍體並不是懸賞酬金緝拿兇手或兇手團夥案件中的、那位我們剛剛就她與警察局長達成協議的瑪麗·羅傑。我們都熟識提出此觀點的局長先生，但也不能太信任他。如果我們從被發現的這具屍體開始調查，並由此追查出兇手，發現這具屍體並不是瑪麗；或者，如果我們從活着的瑪麗着手調查，並找到了她，發現她未被殺害 —— 這兩種情況都是徒勞無益的；因為我們要承兌的人是 G 先生。因此，出於我們自身的目的，即使不是為了公道，絕對有必要的是，我們的第一步應該是確定屍體的身份就是失蹤的瑪麗·羅傑。

"《星報》的那些觀點對公眾影響很大；而且報刊自身也確信這些觀點的重要性，這從它着手寫的關於此話題的其中一篇文章的開篇態度中可以看出來 —— '在一天的幾份早報中'，它這樣寫道，'都談及了星期一《星報》上的那篇結論性的文章。'對我而言，這篇文章除了作者的熱情之外，似乎並沒有甚麼結論性。我們應該記住，總的來說，報紙的目的更多的是煽動情緒 —— 是提出論點 —— 而不是推演事實的起因。只有當前者與後者似乎是巧合時，後者的目的才被顧及。僅僅發表普通觀點的報紙（儘管這觀點或許很站得住腳），並不能從公眾中贏得聲響。民眾只有在報紙對某個普遍觀點提出尖銳的反駁時才認為它是深刻的。無論在推理中還是在文學中，最快而且最廣泛地被人賞識的就是驚世之言。但是驚世之言在兩者中卻是價值最低的。

"我的意思是説，正是瑪麗·羅傑還活着這一想法所混雜的驚人和戲劇效果，而不是這一想法的真實可信度，使《星報》對此大做文章，並確保其迎合公眾的口味。讓我們來調查一下這份報紙的主要論述；並盡力避免它闡述論點時的語無倫次。

　　"作者的首要目的是想表明，從瑪麗失蹤到發現那具浮屍之間的短暫間隔來看，這具屍體不可能是瑪麗。因此，將這段間隔縮短到最低限度就立刻成為了推理者的目標。在對這一目標的急切追求中，他最初只是草率地作出假設。他説，'如果兇手對她下了手，那麼，認為其動作完成能快到足以使自己在午夜之前將屍體扔進河裏的推測是愚蠢的'。我們就會很快，而且很自然地問為甚麼？為甚麼兇手在姑娘離開母親家之後五分鐘內就被殺的推測是愚蠢的？為甚麼認為兇手是在那天的任何時間作案的也是愚蠢的？任何時間都會有兇殺發生。但是，如果謀殺是在星期天早上九點到午夜前一刻鐘發生的，那麼兇手仍然會有足夠的時間'在午夜之前將屍體扔進河裏'。因此，這個推測恰好意味着——那個兇手根本不是在星期天作案的——而且，如果我們同意《星報》的設想，我們就容許報紙信口雌黃了。那段以'如果兇手如何如何的推測是愚蠢的'開頭的話，無論它是怎樣地被刊登在《星報》上的，也許可以被我們想像成其實是早已如此這般地存在於作者的大腦中了：'如果兇手對她下了手，那麼，認為其動作完成能快到足以使自己在午夜之前將屍體扔進河裏的推測是愚蠢的；我們認為，推測出所有這一切，並且同時推測（因為我們決定要這樣推測）屍體是直到午夜後才被扔進河裏，都是愚蠢的'——這本身就是一句非常不符合邏輯的話，但是也不像報紙上的那句話那樣完全是荒謬的。"

"如果我的目的，"杜潘接着說，"僅僅是找出破綻來反駁《星報》上這段論述的話，我就完全可以對它置之不理。不過，我們要對付的不是《星報》，而是事實真相。照現在的情形看，那句話只有一個意思；而這個意思我已經明確地説過了；但是重要的是，我們要在純粹的語言背後，尋找這些話已經明確指涉的，卻沒能傳達出來的觀點。那個記者的意圖是想説不管這場謀殺發生在星期天白天或夜晚的任何時段，兇手是不可能會冒險在午夜前將屍體抬到河邊的。事實上，這正是我要反駁的假設。那位記者推測兇手處在這樣的一種位置，在這樣的情況下，他必須得將屍體運到河邊。那麼，謀殺也可能發生在岸邊，或是就在河裏；而且，那樣的話，在白天或夜晚的任何時候，將屍體拋擲到水中就可能是最明顯和最迅速的處理方式。你會明白，我不是在暗示這是可能的，也沒有表示這與我自己的觀點是相符的。到目前為止，我的設想與案件的事實沒有甚麼關聯。我只是想提醒你注意《星報》提出觀點時的整個語氣，讓你留心文章開頭的那種片面性。

"於是，在規定了一個限度以配合自己預設的觀點之後，報紙假設道，如果這具屍體是瑪麗的話，那麼它在水裏只不過是很短的時間，報紙接着又這樣敍述：

'所有的經驗都表明，溺水的屍體，或者説在暴力致死後被立刻扔進水中的屍體，需要六到十天時間才使其足夠腐爛到能浮出水面。即使屍體被火炮燃燒過，它也至少要五到六天的浸泡才能浮起，如果不去管它的話，它又會沉下去。'

"這些論斷被巴黎的每一家報紙都默認了，除了《箴言報》[30]。這家報紙只是竭力反駁那段話中提到'溺水的屍體'的部分，它引用了五六個例子，在這些例子中，溺水的屍體短於《星報》所強調的時間，就被發現浮到水面了。但是對於《箴言報》來說，用幾個特殊的事例來反駁《星報》的重要論斷之舉，似乎有些過於缺乏哲理了。即使它有可能舉出五十個而非五個屍體在兩三天就浮上來的例子，那麼這五十個例子仍然可能被認為是《星報》所說的規律之特例，除非那規律自身被推翻。承認了這條規律，（這一點《箴言報》並不否認，它只是強調了它的特例，）那麼《星報》的論述就能發揮其充分的威力；因為這一論述並沒有自稱要牽涉到屍體在少於三天就浮到水面之可能性的問題；而且，這個可能性會對《星報》的立場有利，除非這些被幼稚地舉出的例子能在數量上足以建立起一個反對性的規律。

"你馬上就會明白，如果真有那麼一條規律，那麼所有這一切有關的論述應該被用來反對那條規律本身；為了這一目的，我們必須來檢查一下此規律的理論基礎。總的來說，人的身體既不比塞納河水輕也不比它重；這就是說，在自然情況下，人體特有的重力與它所排開的淡水重量大致相同。肥胖多肉、骨骼又小的人，以及大多數的女性都比那些消瘦而且骨骼大的人，還有男人要輕；而河水特有的比重多少是受到海潮量的影響。但是，如果不考慮潮水，或許可以這麼說，哪怕是在淡水裏，都很少有人體會真的自動沉下去。幾乎所有人在落入水中後，如果他能允許水的比重與他身體的比重恰好保持平衡——也就是說，如果他允許自己整個身體都儘可能地全部浸入水中。對於不會游泳的人來說，他正確的姿勢是與岸上的行人一樣是垂直的，頭完全後仰，並浸沒於水中；只有嘴巴和鼻孔是在水面上的。在這樣的情況下，我們應該發現人是可以毫無困難、不費力氣地浮在水中的。然而，很明顯的是，身體的重力和它排開的水的重量必須是恰好平衡的，而微不足道的力量就能打破這種平衡。例如，一條胳膊舉出水面，那麼它的支撐力就喪失了，這個重量就足以使整個頭部浸入水中，同樣，偶然借助於一塊

"哪怕是最細小的木材就能抬高頭部，使它可以四周張望。那麼，在一個不會游泳之人的掙扎中，他的雙手臂總是要向上伸，並且他會努力使頭部保持慣有的垂直位置。其結果就是嘴巴和鼻孔浸沒在水中，而他在水面下要用力呼吸的結果又使水進入了肺部。大量的水就同樣地湧入了胃部，由於充滿這些器官腔的液體與原來擴充在裏面的空氣重量是不同的，於是整個身體就變重了。根據普遍的規律，這一差別足以導致身體下沉；但是，在那些骨骼小，肌肉鬆弛肥胖的特例中，這一差別就不足以使身體下沉。這些人甚至在溺水後都不下沉。

"設想屍體是在河底，它會一直保持原狀，除非通過某種方式，它特有的重力再次變得比它排開的水量輕。這種結果是通過屍體腐爛或其他途徑達到的。腐爛產生了氣體，氣體擴充了細胞組織和所有的腔體，然後導致了令人恐懼的腫脹現象。當這種膨脹大到使屍體的體積大幅度增長，而它的品質或重量卻沒有相應增加時，它特有的比重就比排開的水量輕，於是它就立刻浮出了水面。但是腐爛受到多種因素的影響 —— 會由於各種原因而加速或延緩；例如，季節的冷暖，礦物質含量或水的純淨度，水的深淺，水的流通與停滯，身體的性質，死亡前身體的感染或無恙等。因此，很明顯，我們不能在屍體通過腐爛上浮上確定出任何精確的時間。在某個情況下，這個結果可能會在一個小時內就發生；而在其他情況下，它可能根本不發生。也有一些化學注射液能使動物的軀體在避免腐爛的情況下被永遠保存；二氯化汞就是這樣

一種製劑。但是，除了腐爛，也許，而且很普遍的是，由於蔬菜類的酸發酵使胃部產生氣體（或者在其他腔體裏由於其他原因也產生此類情形），而氣體又足以造成身體的膨脹，使身體浮上水面。放火炮的效果只是起到了震盪作用，其結果一方面能使陷入淤泥或沉積物的屍體擺脫羈絆，使它在其他條件已經成熟的情況下浮起來；另一方面，它可以震掉細胞組織中一些黏性的腐爛部分，使腔體在氣體的作用下被擴大。

　　"因此，當我們掌握了這一問題的基本理論依據後，我們就能輕鬆地檢驗一下《星報》的論斷。報紙是這樣論述的，'所有的經驗都表明，溺水的屍體，或者說在暴力致死後被立刻扔進水中的屍體，需要六到十天時間才能使其足夠腐爛到能浮出水面。即使屍體被火炮燃燒過，它也至少要五到六天的浸泡才能浮起，如果不去管它的話，它又會沉下去'。

　　"此刻，這整段話一定顯現出了一系列的矛盾和不連貫性。所有的經驗並不表明'溺水的屍體'需要六到十天時間才能使其足夠腐爛到能浮出水面。科學和經驗都證明了屍體上浮的時間是，而且必然是不確定的。此外，如果一具屍體由於被火炮燃燒過而浮出水面，並非'如果不去管它的話，它又會沉下去'，除非腐爛已經蔓延到使產生的氣體排出身體。不過我希望你注意到'溺水的屍體'和'暴力致死後被立刻扔進水中的屍體'的區別。儘管作者承認了兩者的差別，他仍然把它們歸於一類。我已經表述過溺水的屍體是如何明顯地變得比它排開的水量重，而且要不是人在掙扎中將手臂伸出水面，並在水下用力呼吸的話 —— 那喘息使水充滿了肺部原來是空氣佔據的空間，身體是根本不會下沉的。但是這些掙扎和喘息是不會發生在'暴力致死後被立刻扔進水中的屍體＇上的。因此，在後者的情況下，根據普遍的規律，屍體根本是不會下沉的——這個事實《星報》顯然是不了解的。當腐爛發展到很嚴重的程度時——當大部分的肌肉脫離骨頭時——事實上，那時候，只有到那時，我們才會看不見屍體。

「那麼，我們又如何來應對這樣一個論斷呢？即由於發現屍體漂浮時，只過去了三天，因此這具屍體不可能是瑪麗・羅傑的推論。如果溺水的是個女人，她也許根本就不會沉下去；或者，就是沉下去了，也會在二十四小時之內再次浮上來。但是沒有人推測她是淹死的；而且，如果她在被扔進水中前就死了，那麼她就會在其後的任何時間被發現浮在水面。

「《星報》還說，＇如果屍體呈毀壞狀態在岸上被放置到星期二的晚上，那麼人們就會在岸邊發現兇手的某些痕跡＇。首先，這讓人很難理解推理者的意圖。其實他的用意是表示他預見到了自己的設想有可能成為他論斷的反例——即：假如那具屍體被放在岸上兩天了，它就會發生迅速的腐爛——比它在水裏的腐爛速度更快。他認為，如果情況確實如此的話，屍體有可能在星期三浮出水面，並且他認為只有在這樣的情形下屍體才能這樣浮現。因此，他匆忙地表明，屍體並沒有放在岸上；因為，一旦如此的話，＇那麼人們就會在岸邊發現兇手的某些痕跡＇。我猜想你會對這樣的推論一笑置之的。你沒法理解就憑那具屍體在岸上的停留時間，怎麼就會使兇手的痕跡增加。我也覺得費解。

「那家報紙又繼續闡述道，＇另外，最不可能的是，暴徒在犯下如此的謀殺罪行後，竟然會不附加重物就將屍體拋擲水中，而這樣的防範做起來毫不費力＇。在這裏，請留心一下那令人發笑的思維混亂！沒有人會 —— 甚至連《星報》也不會 —— 懷疑那被發現的屍體遭受了謀殺。暴力的痕跡太明顯了。推理者的目的只是想表明這具屍體不是瑪麗，他希望證明瑪麗沒有被殺害 —— 而不是證明這具屍體沒被殺害。但是他的論述只是證實了後者。這裏是一具沒有被附加重物的屍體。兇手在把它扔進水中時，是不會不這麼做的。因此，它不是被兇手扔進河裏的。如果能證實甚麼的話，這就是能被證實的一切。這甚至連屍體的身份問題都沒涉及，《星報》費了如此周折只是否定了它前面所承認的事情，它是這樣說的，'我們完全相信那具被發現的屍體是一個被謀殺了的女性'。

"這還不是唯一的例子，在對此論點的分歧上，這位推理者甚至在無意中反駁了自己。我早已說過，他的明確目的是儘可能地縮減瑪麗失蹤和屍體被發現的時間間隔。可是我們發現他強調了一點，即從那姑娘離開母親的住所後，沒有人見過她。他是這樣說的，'我們沒有任何證據認為瑪麗·羅傑瑪麗在六月二十二日星期天九點之後還在人世'。由於他的論點明顯是片面的，他至少應該不讓它顯現出來；因為如果大家知道有人看見過瑪麗，比如在星期一，或是星期二，那麼這一時間間隔就會被大大縮短，而且，依照他自己的推論，屍體是那個女店員的可能性就會急劇下降。然而，可笑的是，《星報》卻堅持自己的觀點，完全相信由此能進一步推出總的論點。

"讓我們來重新細讀關於博韋辨認屍體的那部分論述。在有關手臂上的汗毛部分，《星報》的表述明顯不真誠。博韋先生並不是傻瓜，不可能在辨認屍體時僅僅倉促地說手臂上有汗毛。而且，任何手臂上都有汗毛。《星報》的概括性表述只不過是歪曲了證人的措辭。他一定說過這毛髮有某種特殊之處。它肯定有獨特的顏色、數量、長度或位置。

"報紙還說，'她的腳很小——腳小的人何止千萬。不管怎麼說，她的吊襪帶根本算不上是證據——她的鞋也不是——因為鞋和吊襪帶是成箱賣的。她帽子上的花也是同樣的道理。博韋先生一再堅持的是，吊襪帶的扣子被摺回過，並使帶子縮短了。這也說明不了甚麼；因為多數女人願意買一對吊襪帶回家，並把它們調節到適合它們所要纏繞的大腿尺寸，而不是在購買的商店裏就試用它們'。從這裏看，我們很難認定那個推理者是真誠的。如果博韋先生在他找尋瑪麗的屍體時，發現了一具屍體的大體尺寸與外形和失蹤的女子很相仿，他準保（這根本與衣服無關）會有一種找尋已經成功的想法。如果，除了大體尺寸和外形，他還發現屍體的手臂上有一種特殊的汗毛特徵，這與他曾在活着的瑪麗手臂上看到過的一致，他的這種想法就更堅定了；而且他信心的增長可能與那汗毛特徵的特殊性，或者說是與眾不同成正比。如果，瑪麗的腳很小，而屍體的腳也很小，那麼屍體就是瑪麗的可能性的增長比率就不會只是算術增長了，而是一種高比率的幾何增長，或是積聚性增長。再加上他所知道的姑娘失蹤那天穿的鞋子又是與屍體的相符，而且，儘管這些鞋子也許是'成箱賣的'，你至少會將可能性增加到它幾乎就是那個人的程度。那些自身對身份辨認並不算是證據的東西會通過它具有的確證位置，變成最令人確信的證據。所以，只要那頂帽子上的花也與失蹤女子所戴的相同，我們就不用繼續探究了。只要是一朵花，我們都不用繼續探究了——那麼如果是兩三朵，或是更多呢？每一接連發現的吻合就是成倍的證據——這不是證據的疊加，而是證據成千上百倍地增加。讓我們再來看一下死者身上的與那姑娘活着時使用過的相仿的吊襪帶，那麼再追究下去就有些愚蠢了。況且這些吊襪帶被發現時是縮緊的，扣子還摺回過，又恰好與瑪麗在離家不久前她自己的繫扣方式一樣。再懷疑下去就是瘋狂或虛偽了。《星報》所說的關於吊襪帶被縮短的情況其實並不多見，這正好說明了它自己在錯誤上的頑固。帶扣吊襪帶的彈性特徵就不言自明地展示了被縮短的非尋常性。它本身就具有自我調節功能，只有在很少的特殊情況下才需要再調節。從最嚴格的角度來看，瑪麗的這些吊襪帶肯定是在很少有的情況下才需要作上述的縮緊。光是這吊襪帶就足以證實她的身份了。但是被發現的屍體不僅和失蹤的姑娘有着相同的吊襪帶，還有相仿的鞋子、帽子、帽子上的花、腳、手臂上獨有的特徵，以及身體的尺寸和外形——就是說，屍體具備了瑪麗單個的和所有整體的特點。如果證明《星報》的編輯對死者的身份是真正懷有疑問，那在這樣的情形下，對他而言，也大可不必送他去接受精神病檢查。他不過是認為附和那些律師們的廢話是具有遠見的，而多數律師卻只是滿足於重複法庭的規矩條款。在此，我認為，很多被法庭所否決的證據其實在有智人士看來都是最好的證據。因為法庭是在證據認定的普遍原則的指導下行使職能的——那些都是被公認和記入法典的原則——它不願轉向特例，而這種對原則的固守，並苛刻地不理會具有衝突性的異議，無論時間的長短，也是一種能最大限度獲取事實的方式。從總體上說，這種準則按理是具有哲理性的；但可以肯定，它也會在個別事例上釀成大錯。" [31] "關於針對博韋的影射，我想你會樂意立即擯棄它們的。你早已了解到這個善良的紳士的真實品行。他是一個愛管閒事的人，情感有餘，理性不足。在真正激動的情況下，任何此類之人都願意如此表現自己，這樣就使自己容易被人懷疑為過於精明或居心不良。博韋先生（正如你的摘要所示）與《星報》的編輯有過幾次單獨的面談，並且，他因為不顧編輯的推論，斗膽提出，屍體確確實實就是瑪麗，因此而冒犯了後者。該報說，'他堅持認定屍體就是瑪麗，但是他在我們所評論的那些細節之外，卻給不出一個原委來讓大家信服'。現在無須再提及不可能舉出更強有力的證據來'讓大家信服'這一事實，我們也許注意過這樣的情況，一個人可以非常清楚地表明他相信某事，但是卻沒有能力提出一個特定的原因來讓別人相信。再沒有甚麼比個人印象更說不清楚的事了。每個人都認識他的鄰居，但是很少有人可以馬上給出他認識鄰居的原因。《星報》的編輯是無權因為博韋先生說不出確信的理由就大動肝火的。

"他的飽受懷疑更符合我關於他情感用事與好管閒事的假設，而不符合那個推理者說他有罪的暗示。一旦採取了更寬容的解釋，我們就會發現要理解鑰匙洞裏的玫瑰花、記事板上的'瑪麗'名字、'將男性親友排擠出局'、'反對讓親友們見到屍體'、告誡B夫人在他（博韋）回來前一定不能和警官交談，以及最後他'除了他自己，任何人都不要牽涉進此事件'的明顯決斷等，都並不困難。似乎毫無疑問的是，博韋是瑪麗的追求者；而她又向他賣弄過風情；於是他野心勃勃地想讓別人都認為他擁有她全部的親昵和信任。關於這個我不想再多說；而且，因為事實完全駁回了

《星報》的論斷，即認為瑪麗母親和其他親友反應冷漠 —— 這冷漠和關於他們相信屍體是那個香料店姑娘的猜測相矛盾 —— 那麼我們就得進一步探究了，就當死者的身份問題已經被我們完滿解決了。"

"那麼，"我問道，"你對《商報》的觀點如何看？"

"從實質上說，這些觀點比其他任何就此事所發表的意見都更值得注意。那些從前提得出的推論是理性而敏銳的；但是在那些前提中，至少有兩個例子的觀點是有缺陷的。《商報》意在暗示瑪麗是在離她母親家不遠處被一幫粗俗的流氓劫持的。它竭力地表述道：'一個像這一年輕女子一樣被公眾熟知的人，在走過了三個街區而不被人看見是不可能的。'這是一位在巴黎長期居住人士的觀點 —— 一位公眾人物 —— 是一位在此城市的來回活動範圍大多被限制在政府辦公室附近的人士。他知道他從自己的工作地點穿越長達十二個街區後，很少會不被人認出並向他打招呼。他明白自己有多少熟人，也知道有多少人認識他，他把自己的知名度和這個香料店姑娘的作了比較，發現兩者間沒有大的差別，於是立即就得出了結論，即這個姑娘走在路上時，會像他一樣地容易被人認出來。可是，這情況只能發生在當她的外出和他一樣是具有固定不變而按部就班的特點，而且也是在有限的同一區域時。他的往返走動在時間上是有規律性的，而且有一定界限範圍，其間有很多人會出於他的職業與自身有相似特徵的興趣而有意地觀察他。但是，總的來說，瑪麗在外走動也許會散漫些。在這個特殊的事例中，非常有可能的是，她走的路線是與平常的幾種都不同。我們所推測的存在於《商報》想法中的那種對等，只有在兩個人穿越整座城市的情況下才能被證實。在那種情形下，假設他們各自的熟人是一樣多的，那麼與相同數量的熟人相遇的機會就是相同的。就我看來，我認為，無論何時，無論瑪麗從自己的住所到姨媽家的很多路線中走的是哪一條，她在路上不碰到一個她所認識的人或認識她的人的情況，不僅是可能的，而且是完全有可能的。在對這個問題的全面而徹底的研究中，我們必須在頭腦中始終記住，哪怕是巴黎最著名人士所認識的人，在與巴黎的整個人口數量的比較中，都是非常不成比例的。

"但是不管《商報》的論述依然具有多大的影響力，當我們考慮到姑娘離開的時間時，它的力度就會大大削減。《商報》這樣說：'她是在街道充滿了人羣時離開的。'可事實並非如此。那時是早上九點。現在，除了星期天，每天早上的九點，街上確實有很多人。但是星期天的九點，人們大多是在家裏準備去做禮拜。只要你留心，你不會注意不到，每個安息日從早上八點到十點之間城市中就有一種特殊的冷清氣氛。在十點和十一點之間，街道上是有人流的，但這並不是報上所說的那麼早的時間。

"《商報》上還有另外一個觀點是缺乏觀察的。它這樣說：'從這個不幸女子的一條襯裙上，被撕下一條長兩尺寬一尺的布，它被繫在她的下巴下面，纏繞在大腦背後，也許是為了防止她喊叫。這是那些沒帶手帕的傢伙們幹的。'關於這個觀點是否站得住腳，我們會稍後再盡力研究；但是在'那些沒帶手帕的傢伙們'這句話上，編輯想指的是那羣最低俗的流氓。可是，報導所描述的是那些哪怕沒襯衫都永遠帶着手帕的人。你一定有機會觀察過，最近幾年，對那些十足的流氓來說，手帕是多麼的不可或缺。"

"那麼，"我問道，"我們如何看待《太陽報》上的文章？"

"非常可惜那個作者天生就不是一個應聲蟲 —— 本來在這件事上他可以成為這一行中最傑出的應聲蟲。他只是一一重複了那些早已刊登的評論，用值得褒揚的努力從各家報紙的論述中把它們集中了一下。他這樣寫道：'所有這些物品在那裏已至少有三四週時間，因此，毫無疑問，這令人瞠目的行兇現場已經被發現。'在這裏，被《太陽報》重申的事實實際上遠不能消除我對此事的疑慮，而且我們稍後要更細緻地將它與此事的另一個問題聯繫起來進行分析。

"目前我們必須專注於其他的調查。你不會不注意到屍體的檢查太草率了。當然，身份的問題很容易就能確定了，或者說應該早就確定了；但是還有其他問題需要明確。屍體有否被搶劫過？死者在離家時是否帶有任何珠寶首飾？如果是的話，當她被發現時還帶着它們嗎？這些重要的問題都完全沒有被證據所涉及過；還有一些同樣重要的問題也沒有被注意到。我們必須盡力通過個人的調查來確定這些問題。聖厄斯塔什的事件必須得重新調查。我對這個人沒有甚麼懷疑；但是讓我們系統地來追查一下。我們得毫無疑問地弄清楚那份關於他在星期天的活動的書面陳述是確鑿的。此類的書面陳述很容易干擾人的視線。不過，假如它內容屬實的話，我們就不必對聖厄斯塔什進行調查了。然而，如果他的書面陳述是謊言的話，那麼，他那令人懷疑的自殺事件要沒有這樣的謊言，就不會是無法解釋的事實，因此我們無需偏離常規分析的思路。

"對於此事，我認為我們應該先不考慮這場悲劇的內在因素，而是將精力集中到它的外部聯繫上。在這樣的調查中，只局限於對直接因素進行探詢，完全不考慮間接或次要的因素的做法並不是不常見的錯誤。把證據和論述限制在表面上相關的事物中也是法庭的疏於職守。但是經驗表明，而且真實的哲學也始終證明，大量的，也許是絕大部分的真理是從看似不相關的事物中得到的。即使不是恰好通過這一原則的字面意義，也是通過這一原則的實質，現代科學才決心對無法預料的事物進行推算。但是也許你不理解我。人類知識的歷史已經持續不斷地顯示出，在間接的或是偶然的、意外的事件中，我們能獲得最大量的和最有價值的發現，而且最終，在對任何發展的預期展望中，有必要不僅大量地，而且是最大限度地接受那些從偶然性中，並且從大大出乎了人們正常的期待中得到的創造。把一件事物將會是甚麼建立在現在是甚麼基礎之上的做法不再具有哲學性了。偶然性被接受成為事物基礎的一部分，我們要完全考慮或然性，並使意外和無法想像的因素歸屬進學校的數學公式中去。

"我要重申絕大部分的真理是從間接因素中獲得的這一個事實；而且，在這件事情上，只有依照這個原理的實質，我才會在目前的情況下，將調查從被無數人嘗試過的、至今沒有結果的對事件本身進行的論述轉向當前與此有關的詳細情況中。當你確定了那書面陳述的可信度後，我將比你迄今所做的要更總體一些地審查那些報紙。到目前為止，我們只是對調查情況進行了勘察；但是，事實上，如果對公眾報刊進行了一次如我所建議的那種綜合性調查後，還是獲得不了一些細節性的、對調查能起到具有指導性作用的信息的話，就很奇怪了。"

我按照杜潘的建議，對書面陳述一事作了細緻的核實。結果是，我非常肯定它們的真實性，以及聖厄斯塔什先生在此事上的清白。同時，我的朋友也以一種在我看來似乎是瑣碎而毫無目的的精密，專注並仔細地研究各類報紙檔。在一週快結束時，他將以下的摘錄放在了我的面前：

"大約三年半以前，一次與目前案件非常相似的騷亂事件發生了，即這同一個瑪麗·羅傑從王宮底層勒布朗先生的香料店失蹤了。可是，在一個星期快結束前，她又一次出現在她通常所在的櫃台，除了有點不太正常的蒼白外，她與平常沒甚麼兩樣。據勒布朗先生和她的母親說，她只是去拜訪了鄉下的某個朋友；於是該事件就很快地平息了。我們可以推測，目前的失蹤同樣也很蹊蹺，那麼，在快滿一週的時間，或者一個月的時間裏，她可能會再次回到我們當中。"——《晚報》，六月二十三日，星期一。[32] "昨天的一份晚報提到了羅傑小姐以往的一次神秘失蹤。眾所周知，在她從勒布朗的香料店失蹤的那一週裏，她是在一位年輕的海軍軍官的陪伴之下，那名男子因其行為放蕩而臭名昭著。據人們猜測，一場爭執使她受到上天的神助得以歸返。我們已得知那名浪蕩軍官的姓名，他目前駐紮在巴黎，只是由於不言自明的原因，我們不能將此公開。"——《信使報》，六月二十四日，星期二晨版。[33]

"前天，在本市近郊發生了一件最為殘忍的暴行。黃昏時分，一名紳士，偕同他的夫人和女兒僱用六個年輕男子將他們送到對岸去，當時這些男子正悠閒地划着一條船在塞納河岸邊來來回回地閒蕩着。在抵達對岸時，這三名乘客跨出了船，並向前走着，一直走到看不見船影的時候，女兒發現她把陽傘留在船上了。她返回去拿傘，於是就被這羣人抓住了，並且被拖到了水裏，她的嘴被東西塞住了，還受到了野蠻的暴行，最後被帶到岸上一個離她和父母最初下船處不遠的地方。那些歹徒目前還逍遙法外，但是警察正在追蹤他們，其中有人可望很快被緝拿。"——《晨報》，六月二十五日。[34]

"本報收到幾封來信，其目的是要證明梅奈[35]在最近那件強姦案中有罪；但是考慮此人經審訊後已被宣判無罪，另外由於來信者的論點論據似乎熱情有餘深刻不足，我們認為不宜將信的內容發表。"——《晨報》，六月二十八日。[36]

"本報收到幾封頗具説服力的來信，這些顯然來自各種管道的消息足以使我們有理由確信，不幸的瑪麗·羅傑成了星期天在城市附近侵擾民眾的無數流氓幫會中其中一幫人手下的犧牲品。此後，我們會盡力騰出版面來刊登此類評論。"——《晚報》，六月三十一日，星期二。[37]

"星期一，一名與稅務署有聯繫的駁船管理員看見一條空船漂在塞納河上。船帆被放在船艙底部。那個管理員就把船拖到了駁船管理處。次日上午，船被人取走，而沒有一個工作人員知情。現在船舵還在管理處。"——《勤奮報》，六月二十六日，星期四。[38]

讀了這些不同的摘錄，在我看來，它們不僅是不相關的，而且我沒覺出它們中有哪一條會與目前的事件相關。我等着聽杜潘的解釋。

他説道，"我目前不想詳細論述第一和第二個摘錄。我之所以摘抄它們，主要是想讓你明白警方的極端疏忽大意。就我從警察局長那裏得知的，他們並沒有從任何方面去費心地審查那個被提及的海軍軍官。但是要説在瑪麗的兩次失蹤之間沒有可推測的聯繫的話，就真的太愚蠢了。讓我們假定第一次的私奔以這對戀人間的爭吵以及那個被玩弄的姑娘回家而告終。那麼，我們現在就完全可以把第二次私奔（如果我們知道私奔再一次發生）看成是暗示了那個負心漢的重新進攻，而並不是將其視為另一個人的求愛結果 —— 我們就完全可以將其視為舊情人的'感情彌合'而不是新人的初次求愛。十有八九，那個曾經與瑪麗私奔的人會再次提議私奔，而曾被人提議私奔的她則不太可能接受另一個人提出的私奔建議。現在，請你注意一個事實，即第一次被確定的和第二次被推測的私奔的時間間隔，比我們軍艦航海的正常週期要長幾個月。難道她情人的第一次罪惡行徑由於必須得出海而被中斷，難道他趕在回來的第一時間裏繼續那還沒有被徹底完成的卑鄙企圖 —— 或者説還沒有被他徹底完成的卑鄙企圖？對所有這些事，我們都一無所知。

"不過，你會説，在第二次失蹤上，並沒有我們所想像的私奔。當然沒有 —— 但是難道我們就會説那個落空的私奔企圖也不存在？除了聖厄斯塔什，也許還有博韋，我們沒有發現瑪麗還有人們認識的、公開的、體面的追求者，也沒聽人提起過有別的甚麼人。那麼，誰是那個祕密情人呢？那人連瑪麗的親友（至少他們中的大多數）都不知道，但是星期天的早上瑪麗去見的就是他，而且瑪麗非常地信任他，以至於毫不猶豫地和他一起留在魯爾門僻靜的小樹林裏，直到夜幕降臨。設問，那個祕密情人是誰，那個至少多數親友都不知道的人是誰？而且，羅傑夫人在瑪麗離開的那個早上的奇怪預言——'我擔心我再也見不到瑪麗了'意味着甚麼？

"但是即使我們沒法想像羅傑夫人私下參與了私奔的計畫，我們總可以認為瑪麗是接受這個計畫的吧？在離開家時，她讓人們知道自己打算去拜訪住在德羅梅街的姨媽，而且讓聖厄斯塔什在天黑時去接她。那麼，乍一看，這個事實與我的推測相矛盾——但是讓我們來回憶一下。她確實是會見了某位男友，並和他一起過了河，直至下午三點才到達魯爾門，這大家是知道的。但是在這樣地答應陪伴那個人的決定中，（無論出於甚麼目的——無論她的母親知道與否，）她一定想到過她離開家時說過的打算，想過當未婚夫聖厄斯塔什在約定的時間去德羅梅街

"接她時，他會發現她並沒在那裏，就會在內心感到驚訝和懷疑。而且，當他憂心忡忡地回到住地時，會知道她還沒回家。我認為她一定想過這些事。她一定能預見到聖厄斯塔什的懊惱，以及所有人的懷疑。她不可能想到要回去承受這種懷疑；但是，如果我們假定她沒有回家的打算，那麼這種懷疑就變得無足輕重了。

"我們可以想像她是這樣想的——'我是為了私奔去見某一個人，或者我是為了其他祕密的私人目的。我很有必要不被打擾——一定得有足夠的時間讓我們遠走高飛——我會解釋說自己要去拜訪德羅梅街的姨媽，並陪她呆一天——我會告訴聖厄斯塔什到傍晚再來接我——這樣解釋的話，我就可以有儘可能長的離

家時間，而且不引起別人的懷疑和焦慮，這比其他辦法更能爭取時間。如果我讓聖厄斯塔什傍晚來接我，那之前他肯定不會來；但是如果我根本不讓他來接，我用來逃離的時間反而會縮短，因為他會指望我早點回家，而我的失蹤會更快地引起他的焦慮。那麼，如果我根本就是打算回家的——如果我只打算和那人散散步——那麼，讓聖厄斯塔什來接就不是我的做法了；因為，讓他來，他就準會確定我耍了他——這個事實是我本想永遠不讓他知道的，我可以在離開家時不告訴他我要去哪裏，可以天黑後才回家，可以告訴他我去拜訪了德羅梅街的姨媽。但既然我的計畫是永不返回了——至少要過幾個星期才回來——或者是等到隱藏了一段時間後才回來——爭取時間才是我唯一的當務之急'。

"你已經在你的記錄中注意到了，關於這個悲慘事件，最普遍的觀點是，而且從一開始就是，這個姑娘被一夥流氓殺害了。而在某種情況下，這種普遍觀點是不能被忽視的。在這個觀點自我顯現出來時——當它以非常自發的形式彰顯自己時——我們應該把它視為與直覺，即有天賦之人的個人特性相類似的一種東西。在百分之九十九的情況下，我會遵守它。但是很重要的一點是，這種輿論中不能有造勢的痕跡。這個觀點必須完全是公眾自己的；而這兩者的區別往往極難看出，極難把握。在目前的案件中，我覺得這個關於一夥流氓的'公眾觀點'，在被那個我所摘錄的第三條報導中的那個間接事件推波助瀾。整個巴黎都對發現了瑪麗，這個年輕、漂亮、聲名昭著的姑娘的屍體感到震動。這具被發現的屍體帶着遭受暴力的痕跡，並漂浮在河裏。但是現在大家都知道，在那個被推測說該姑娘被殺害的特殊時間裏，或者説在那個特殊時間前後，一夥年輕的歹徒犯下了一個與死者所遭到的性質類似，儘管程度稍輕的暴行，受害者是另一個年輕女子。一個出名的殘暴事件會影響到公眾對另一個無名事件的評判，這很令人驚奇嗎？大家等着對此做出評判，而那知名的暴行似乎恰好為此提供了方法！瑪麗也是在河裏被發現的；而這件已知的暴行也發生在這條河邊。兩場事件有很明顯的聯繫性，而真正奇妙之處卻沒有被公眾理解和把握。但是，實際上，這場如此犯下的暴行恰好證明了另一場幾乎同時發生的案件並不是這樣發生的。如果，當一夥歹徒在某個地點犯下了最前所未聞的罪行時，在相同城市的相似地點、在相同的環境下、用同樣的方式和工具、而且是在同一個時間，發生了表面看來完全相同的罪行，這簡直就是一個奇跡！可是，如果沒有如此令人驚歎的一系列巧合，那個碰巧被造勢的公眾輿論要靠甚麼來讓我們相信呢？

"在進一步探討下去之前，讓我們來考慮一下那個被人推測的謀殺現場，即在魯爾門附近的樹林裏。雖然這個樹林很茂密，但是它位於公路的附近。在樹林裏有三四塊大石頭，形成了一個有靠背和凳腳的椅子狀的東西。人們發現上面的石頭上有一條白色的襯裙；在第二塊石頭上有一條絲綢圍巾。人們還發現了一把陽傘、一雙手套，以及一塊手帕。那手帕上有'瑪麗‧羅傑'的名字。衣服的碎片散佈於四周的枝杈上。地面被人踩踏過，矮樹叢被弄斷了，這些都是劇烈掙扎的痕跡。

"雖然林中的發現博得各報刊的喝彩，而且人們一致認為它就是暴行的確切地點，但是我們得承認，有某個很好的理由可以質疑此觀點，那就是案發現場。我可以相信、或者也可以不相信它——但是有非常充分的理由讓人懷疑它。如果像《商報》所推測的，案發現場真的是在聖安德列街附近，假設兇手仍然滯留在巴黎，那麼他們自然就會對公眾的注意力被敏銳地引到了正確的方向而感到恐懼；於是，在某種心理狀況下，他們就會很快地意識到有必要盡力地分散人們的這種注意力。因此，既然魯爾門的灌木叢早已被人懷疑，那麼他們自然就有可能會有把物品放在後來它們被人發現的地方的念頭。儘管《太陽報》這樣推測了，可是沒有任何證據能證明這些被發現的物品已經放在灌木叢中有不短的時間了；然而，這裏倒還存在一個非常間接的證據來證明它們是不可能一直在那裏的，因為從那個不幸的星期天到男孩子們發現它們的那個下午的二十天當中，它們不可能沒有引起過別人的注意。《太陽報》應和了其他報紙在它之前發表的觀點，它這樣報導，'由於下雨，一切都嚴重發霉，並粘在一起了。有一些物品四周和上面還長了草。陽傘的綢面很堅實，但是裏面纖線已經全部分解腐爛了。上面的部分是雙層和摺疊的，也都發霉破爛了，並在傘被打開的情況下開裂了'。關於那些草，即所謂'有一些物品四周和上面還長了草'，很明顯，這個事實只能靠語言、即靠兩個男孩的回憶陳述來證實；因為這些男孩移動了物品，並在第三者尚未看到前把它們帶回了家。可是草是會長出來的，尤其在溫暖潮濕的天氣情況下（就像謀殺發生的那段時間），它可以僅僅在一天裏就長出兩三吋來。一把陽傘放在新覆上草皮的地上，也會在短短一週之內被新長出來的草完全遮掩的。關於發霉現象，《太陽報》編輯是如此執拗地堅持着要表述出來，他把發霉的意思在我們所摘錄的那麼簡短的段落中提及了不下三次，難道他真的沒意識到這個發霉現象的實質嗎？他有否被告知，這種霉體是種類繁多的真菌中的其中一種，它最典型的特徵是能在二十四小時內長出來並衰亡？

"因此，我們一眼就能明白，那些被用來最成功地證實這些物品已經在樹林裏'至少有三四週時間'的證據，其實是最荒謬而無效的。另一方面，人們又很難以相信這些物品在那個樹林裏的時間是長於一週的 —— 即長於兩個星期天之間的時間。那些對巴黎附近瞭如指掌的人都明白找到一個隱蔽處是極端困難的，除非那地方離郊區很遠。這樣一個在樹林裏草叢中的，未經勘探的，或者甚至說是少有人涉足的隱祕處，是一下子想不到的。就是讓那些打心底裏熱愛自然卻依然被職務牽絆於這大都市的塵土與繁忙中人 —— 讓他們中的任何一位去嘗試一下，哪怕在平日，讓他在立刻就包圍着自己的自然美景中消除對獨處的飢渴。接下來，每走一步，他都會發現，那不斷增長的魅力被一些歹徒或一羣鬧飲狂歡的流氓的聲音和人身侵擾所驅散。他就發現在茂密的樹林裏尋找清靜是徒勞的。那裏是烏合之眾出沒的特殊隱蔽地 —— 那裏有最被褻瀆的廟宇。漫遊者立刻就會從心裏感到厭惡，並逃回繁華的巴黎，巴黎不會比那裏更令人憎惡，因為它並非如此不協調地充滿了污穢。可是，如果在一週的工作日中，城市的附近都是如此被騷擾，那安息日就更厲害了！尤其是現在，當城鎮流氓被免除了工作的權利，或者説失去了慣有的犯罪機會，他就會尋找到城鎮的近郊，這不是出於對鄉村的喜愛，其實在內心他鄙視它，而是為了逃避社會的束縛和陳規。他渴望的不是新鮮的空氣和綠樹，而是鄉村的完全自由。於是，他在那個路邊旅館裏，或是在樹林中，除了他的夥伴，他不被任何目光所監視，沉溺在一切瘋狂而無度的虛假狂歡中——那是自由和酒精的聯合產物。當我重複陳述那些物品在長達超過一週的時間內，在巴黎近郊的任何一個樹林裏都一直沒被發現過的情況時，很明顯，這對於每一位冷靜的旁觀者而言，幾乎就是奇跡，對此，我就不用再贅言了。

"但是我們還有其他依據來懷疑那些物品是為了轉移人們對暴行的真正地點的注意力而被放在灌木叢裏的。首先，請你留心一下發現那些東西的日期，並將它與我從報紙上摘引的第五篇文章的日期進行比較。你會發現，在物品被找到後，幾乎在最快的時間裏，這個緊急的信息就被送到了該晚報社。儘管這些信息是各種各樣的，而且明顯來自多種管道，但是它們都指向了同一點——即，它們將大家的注意力轉移到認為這罪行是一夥人犯下的，而且案發地點在魯爾門附近。當然了，由於這些信息的緣故，或者說是公眾的注意方向被它們轉移了的原因，我們現在的懷疑並不是關於這些物品是被兩個男孩發現的一事；但是這懷疑或許，而且非常有可能是這些東西在此之前沒被孩子們發現，因為那些物品過去是不放在灌木叢裏的；它們只是後來才被放置在那裏，時間就是在消息被傳開的當天，或者是稍微提前一些，就是這些信息的罪惡創作者將它們放在那裏的。

"這個樹林很怪異——極端怪異。它異常繁茂。在它自然圍成的場地中有三塊奇怪的石頭，形成了一把有靠背和凳腳的椅子。而且，這個樹林是如此充滿藝術性，還位於離德呂克夫人的住所咫尺之遙的比鄰地區，夫人的孩子又常常仔細地觀察周圍的灌木，以尋找黃樟木的樹皮。這難道會是草率的賭注嗎？——這個賭注的贏率是一千對一——即這些男孩不用一天就能發現至少一件隱藏在綠樹成蔭的殿堂中、端放在天然御座上的物品。那些猶豫於這樣一個賭注的人，要麼自己從沒有做過孩子，要麼忘記了孩童的天性。我要重申——要理解為甚麼這些物品在被放置於這個灌木叢中長於一兩天的時間裏都沒被發現，是極其困難的；因此，不管《太陽報》是怎樣武斷和無知，我們的懷疑是很有道理的，即這些東西是相對很晚才被放在那裏的。

"但是，除了我剛才提出的，還有其他的和更有力的理由來相信它們是這樣被放置的。現在，請你費心對那些物品非常做作的擺放方式予以注意。在上面的石頭上放的是一條白色的襯裙；在第二塊石頭上的是絲綢圍巾；四周散亂分佈着的是一把傘、一雙手套、一塊帶有'瑪麗·羅傑'名字的手帕。這只是一個並不太精明的人自然會想到的儘量自然一些的擺法。但是這絕不是一種真正自然的放置方法。我倒寧願看到所有東西都在地上，而且被人踩過。在這塊有限的樹蔭中，那襯裙和圍巾幾乎不可能保持在石頭上的位置，因為它們被那麼多撕扯搏鬥的人來回拖拉過。報紙說，'地面是被踩踏過的，樹叢被折斷過，這都是搏鬥過的跡象。'——但是那條襯裙和圍巾被發現時卻好像被放在衣架上一樣。報紙還說，'那外衣的幾條碎片被灌木叢撕破，有六英吋長、三英吋寬。其中一塊是外衣的底邊，它被修補過；它們看上去就像被撕下來的布條'。在這裏，《太陽報》由於疏忽，使用了一個極其令人懷疑的片語。正如它所描述的，那些碎片確實'像被撕下來的布條'；但它們是被人有意撕下來的。布條從任何像這類面料中，由於一根荊棘的作用而被'撕下來'是最不可能發生的事之一。從這些特定的面料質地來看，刺進去的荊棘或釘子會將它們呈直角地撕開——從刺入點撕出兩條相互成直角的裂縫——但是不可能有布條被'撕下來'。我從來不知道有這樣的事，你也不會看到的。幾乎在所有的情況下，若要將一片布從這樣的面料上撕下來，就需要兩個不同方向的不同力量。如果面料有兩條邊緣線——如果，比如說，它是一塊手帕，外力要從它那裏撕出一條布，那麼，只有在這時，才可憑一股力量就可以做到。但是在目前的案子中，它是一件衣服，只有一條邊。要從它裏面撕出一塊來，而裏面又沒有邊緣線，那只能是依靠荊棘奇跡般的作用了，而且一根荊棘還無能為力。但即使靠近裙邊，也必須得兩根荊棘才行，其中一條朝兩個不同的方向，另一條朝一個方向用力。而且，這還是在邊緣沒有被捲邊的情況下。如果捲過邊的話，那就完全不可能做到了。我們由此可以明白，讓布條僅僅在'荊棘'的作用下被'撕下來'是有着無數的和巨大的障礙的；可是報紙還要讓我們相信那裏不止一條，而且很多條布都被撕下來了。甚至'其中一塊是外衣的底邊'！而且另外一塊是'裙擺上的，不是底邊'。——也就是說，它是從沒有邊緣的衣服裏面被荊棘整個地撕下來的！可以說，恐怕這事別人不信也是情有可原的。但如果從全域看，也許它們導致的懷疑還不比另一個讓人驚訝的情況強烈，即這些物品竟然就是被任何能謹慎到轉移屍體的兇手遺留在這個樹林裏的。然而，如果你認為我有意要否定這片樹林即是行兇現場的話，那你還沒有真正領會我的意圖。這裏可能發生過一件邪惡的事情，或者更可能的是，德呂克夫人那裏發生過一個意外事件。但事實上，這不是最重要的。我們並不是要努力發現現場，而是要找出作案兇手。我所引證的事情，雖然都很瑣碎，但是它們首先表明了，《太陽報》所肯定的和執意堅持的觀點是愚蠢的，第二點，同時也是最主要的是，它們讓你通過最自然的方式，對關於這個兇殺案是否是由一夥人幹的疑問進行了深入思考。

"我們只要針對外科醫生驗屍時的細節，就能重新來審視這個問題。我們只需要說，他發表的推論，在關於歹徒的數量方面，完全可以被巴黎所有著名的驗屍官嘲諷為不公正，並且是毫無根據的。我並不是說他推論的結果不可能，而是他的推論沒有根據：——難道沒有做另一種推論的充分根據？

"現在讓我們來想想'搏鬥過的跡象'；先問一下，這些跡象表示了甚麼。表示的是有一夥人。但是難道它們就沒有更像是在表示不是一夥人的意思嗎？會發生甚麼搏鬥呢——甚麼搏鬥那麼激烈而持久，居然能到處留下'跡象'呢？——竟然在一個柔弱而沒有自衛能力的姑娘和被想像出來一夥歹徒之間？不用發出聲響，只消幾條粗壯胳膊的力量之類的，一切就擺平了。受害者肯定是完全任他們擺佈的。你要記住，那些極力反對樹林就是案發現場的論述，主要說來，只是在兇手不止一個人的情況下可行。如果我們假設只有一個兇手，那我們就可以理解，而且只能理解，這場如此激烈和持久的搏鬥留下了明顯的'跡象'。

"再則，我已經提過那些物品被完全留在後來發現它們的那個樹林裏這個事實所引起的懷疑。似乎，這些犯罪證據幾乎不可能被無意中遺留在那裏。兇手有足夠的謹慎（根據推測）將屍體轉移；而兇手卻能讓比屍體本身（它的特徵很可能會很快地被腐爛所抹殺）更確鑿的證據明顯地留在行兇現場——我指的是帶有死者名字的那塊手帕。如果這是個偶然，那它就不是一夥人的偶然。我們能想像這只能是單個人的疏忽。讓我們瞧着好了，這是單個人犯下的罪行。他是和死去的鬼魂單獨相處。他被一動不動地躺在眼前的屍體嚇怕了。他的怒火衝動已經過去，那時他的心裏對自己的行為充滿了本能的恐懼。他絲毫沒有一夥人參與犯罪後必然會產生的膽量。他只是獨自面對着屍體。他顫抖着，大腦一片混亂。但是他必須得處置屍體。於是他將屍體運到河裏，遺留下了自己犯罪的其他證據；因為即使是可能的話，他也很難把所有的東西一下子都帶走，而且回來再拿也不難。但是在他到河邊的艱難跋涉中，他內心的恐懼加劇了。在路上，到處有人聲。他好多次地聽見或是想像着有看見他的人走過來的腳步聲。甚至城市的燈火都讓他心慌。在深刻的痛苦下，他長時間、頻繁地停歇，但他還是及時抵達岸邊，處置了那個可怕的重物——也許是靠了一條船。但是，這時世界還有甚麼財寶——還有甚麼樣的天網恢恢之威脅——會有力量迫使那個孤獨的兇手從那條艱辛而危險的路上返回到樹林和那血淋淋的回憶中去嗎？他不會回去，任一切結果自然發展。他就是想回去，他也沒法回去了。他唯一的想法就是立刻逃跑。他永遠地棄那些可怕的樹林而去了，就像逃避懲罰似的匿跡了。

"但是如果是一夥人幹的又會怎樣呢？他們的人數會讓他們有膽量；如果這兇惡的流氓心中竟然缺乏膽量的話；而被推測的這夥人又是純粹由兇惡的流氓組成。我認為，他們的人數會防止我所假設的會使單個罪犯感到癱軟的頭腦混亂和沒有理智的恐懼。即便我們能設想疏忽可以發生在一個人，或兩個人，或三個人的身上，那麼這個疏忽就能被四個人所補救。他們不會遺留下一切痕跡；因為他們的人數能使他們把事情一次性地完成，就沒有返回的必要了。

"再來想想我們發現屍體時，它外衣的情況，'外套上從底邊向上一直到腰部被撕開大約一尺來長，它圍着腰部繞了三圈，並被背後搭鈎狀的東西固定住'。這種做法的明顯目的就是提供一個可以拎動屍體的把手。可是如果有幾個人在，他們會想到採取這樣的權宜之計嗎？要是有三四個人，屍體的四肢不僅提供了充分的，而且是最好的把持部位。前種方法是單個人才會用的；這就使我們了解了一個事實，即'在灌木叢和河流之間的柵欄被拆倒了，地面上有某種重物被拖過的明顯痕跡'！可是，在一夥人完全可以把屍體一下子就抬過柵欄的情況下，他們會有必要為了把一具屍體拖過去而多此一舉地去把柵欄拆倒？難道這些人會這樣拖着屍體，然後留下明顯的痕跡嗎？

"說到這裏我們必須得提到《商報》的一個觀點；多多少少地，我早就評論過這個觀點。那份報紙說，'從這個不幸女子的一條襯裙上，被撕下一條長兩尺寬一尺的布，它被繫在她的下巴下面，纏繞在大腦背後，也許是為了防止她喊叫。這是那些沒帶手帕的傢伙們幹的。'

"我曾提起過，一個地道的流氓是從不會不帶手帕的。但我着重要談的不是這個事實。用到布條的原因並不是《商報》所想像的因為缺少一塊手帕，那塊被遺留在灌木叢中的手帕已經清楚地證明了這一點；其中的目的也不是'為了防止她喊叫'，這也能從布條早於那個比它的作用好很多的手帕被使用上得到證實。但是在描述布條時，報紙的措辭為'被纏繞在脖子上，纏得鬆鬆的，並被打了個結實的結'。這些詞語都非常含混，但是與《商報》對此的描述有本質上的不同。那布條有十八英吋寬，因此，儘管它是一種薄棉布，也能通過摺疊或是縱向的褶皺形成一條堅實的帶子。因此，它在被發現時就是褶皺着的。我的推理是這樣的：這個孤獨的兇手用這條繃帶拴住屍體的中部，將屍體抬出了一段距離（或是從樹林或是從其他地方）後，發現用這種方式前進，他的力氣不夠。他努力地拖着那具重物 —— 留下的跡象也證明了他確實有拖過重物的行為。既然改為拖，他就覺得很有必要在屍體頂端附加一個類似於繩子一樣的東西，它最好是被套在脖子上，這樣頭部就會防止它滑脫。於是兇手無疑就想起了屍體腰上的繃帶。要不是它纏繞在屍體上，要不是那個結一時解不開，要不是他記起來，這條布還沒有從外衣上被'撕下來'，他也許用的就是那根長帶了。從襯裙上撕一條新的會更簡單些，於是他就撕下了一條，把它繫在脖子上，就這樣拖着受害者到達了岸邊。所以，這條'布條'非得要費點周折和時間才能用，但是卻多少表明了它存在的目的 —— 即這條布條確實是被用過的，這說明使用它的需要是產生於已經拿不到手帕的時候 —— 也就是說，照我們推測的，該需要產生於兇手離開樹林（如果那裏真是作案現場）之後，而且是在從樹林通向河邊的路上。

"你會說，但是德呂克夫人的證詞（！）特地指出，在謀殺發生的重大時間前後，在樹林附近有一夥人。這一點我同意。如果在魯爾門一帶，在這場悲劇發生的前後，沒有一打像德呂克夫人所描述的團夥的話，我倒要懷疑了。雖然德呂克夫人提供的證據多少有些滯後，也確實令人懷疑，但是為自己招來責難的無賴卻只有一夥，即那個老實而謹小慎微的老婦人所說的吃了她的糕餅、喝了她的白蘭地，卻懶得付錢的那夥人。Et hinc illœ irœ[39]？

"那麼德呂克夫人的確切證詞又是甚麼樣的呢？'一幫歹徒出現了，他們吵吵嚷嚷的，又吃又喝還不給錢，並跟着上了那對青年男女走的路。在黃昏時，他們返回了旅館，似乎非常急匆匆地過了河。'

"那麼這個'非常急匆匆'很可能在德呂克夫人眼裏會顯得更嚴重些，因為她還久久地、哀怨地牽掛着她那些倒楣的糕點和酒水——對於那些糕點酒水，她還懷着一絲希望想得到補償。否則，既然天都暗下來了，她還要強調急匆匆幹嗎？這肯定是沒甚麼好奇怪的，哪怕是一夥歹徒也該急匆匆地趕回家，因為得要靠小船渡河，而且暴風雨將至，夜晚又快降臨了。

"我說的是快降臨；因為夜晚還沒有到來。當這夥'歹徒'使德呂克夫人對其急匆匆的樣子悻悻然時，只不過才黃昏時分。但是我們得知，就是當天夜裏德呂克夫人，還有她的大兒子，'聽到了旅館附近有女人的尖叫聲。'那麼，德呂克夫人又是怎麼來確定在夜裏聽到這些尖叫聲的時間段的呢？她說是'天黑後不久'。但是'天黑後不久'至少說明了是天黑了；而'在黃昏時'就肯定是白天。因此我們可以非常明確的是，那夥人是在德呂克夫人無意中聽到（？）尖叫聲之前離開魯爾門的。儘管，在所有相關的案情報導中，有關的論述正如我在與你交談中所表現出來的，都是清晰而有差別的，各家報紙或各位盲目執行命令的警察都還沒有注意到這裏面有任何總體上的矛盾。

"我只要在關於不是一夥人作案的論點上僅僅添加一點；但是這一點，至少在我看來，具有完全無法抵抗的力量。在那個大筆酬金的前提下，而且有提供重大證據就能被完全赦免的條件，在短時間裏，若在一夥粗俗的流氓中，有某一個人，或者說是任何一個人在不久前背叛了他的同謀，這並非是假想。這夥人中的任何一人，在這樣的情況下，倒並非完全是貪婪那筆酬金或是渴望赦免，而是擔心被同夥出賣。那麼，祕密至今未被解開就恰好證明了，事實上，它確實是祕密。這可怕的黑暗勾當只有一個人知道，或兩個人知道，其中一個是凡人，一個是上帝。

"讓我們來總結一下在長時間的分析後，我們所有的那點雖不充分卻是確鑿的成果。我們已經有了一個肯定的觀點，無論是德呂克夫人屋簷下發生的亡命事件，還是魯爾門附近樹林裏的謀殺案，都是由死者的一位情人，或至少是她的祕密情人所為。這個夥伴臉色黝黑。這種臉色、長帶上的'結'，還有女帽緞帶上的那個'水手結'，都說明那人很可能是一名海員。他和死者，一位風流但不卑賤的年輕女子的交情，表明了他的地位高於一般的海員。那些報紙上行文流暢而急切的報道都能很好地證明這一點。《信使報》所述的第一次私奔的情況，有助於使我們將這個海員與那個'海軍軍官'，即大家最初知道的那個將這不幸姑娘勾引的人聯繫起來。

"現在，我們最好來探討一下這個臉色黝黑之人一直不見蹤影的事。我們先得注意，他的臉色是非常黑的；肯定不是一般的黑才會讓瓦倫斯和德呂克夫人惟此特點而記憶深刻。但是為甚麼這個人會不見蹤影呢？難道他被那夥人殺了？如果是那樣的話，為甚麼那裏只有被謀殺的女子的痕跡？兩場謀殺的地點自然會被人推測是同一個地方。那麼他的屍體在哪裏呢？很有可能兇手用同樣的方式把兩具屍體都處理了。但是也有可能這個男人還活着，他是拖延着不露面，因為害怕被人指控殺了人。他的這種擔心現在可被視為理所當然——只是在事後的現在——因為已經有人證明曾看見他和瑪麗在一起——但是在兇殺剛發生後這種擔心卻不合情理。一個無罪的人的第一反應應該會去報案，並會協助辨認歹徒。這一點，也是出於策略。他已經被人看見過是和那個姑娘在一起的，他們兩人坐着一條敞篷的渡船過了河。哪怕是對一個白癡來説，公開指控兇手明顯就是最必然也是最唯一的讓自己洗脱嫌疑的辦法。我們沒法認為，在那個不幸的星期天晚上，他會既不知情也沒有察覺到發生了一件慘案。可是只有在這樣的情況下，我們才可能想像他既然活着又為何沒去報案。

"那麼我們獲得真相的方法是甚麼呢？隨着調查的深入，我們就會發現這些方法成倍地、集中地清晰起來。讓我們來仔細研究作為這個事件起因的第一次私奔，並了解一下這個'軍官'的全部歷史，包括他的近況，以及恰好在案發前後的行蹤。我們先仔細地比較寄給晚報的那些提出此案是團夥犯罪的各種不同的信件。然後，我們從這些信的風格和筆跡兩個方面來和更早寄給早報的有關信件進行比較，後者強烈地堅持認為梅奈是有罪的。完成這一切後，我們再來將這些不同的信件和已查明的軍官的手跡進行比較。通過對德呂克夫人和她的兒子，還有馬車夫瓦倫斯的反復提問，我們要盡力查明更多有關那個'臉色黝黑的男人'的相貌特徵。有技巧的詢問是不難從這些當事人中發現針對這個特定問題（或是其他問題）的相關信息的 —— 甚至這些當事人自己都沒有意識到會擁有這些信息。然後，我們來追蹤那條在六月二十三日星期一上午被一個駁船管理員撿到，而後又被人從管理處取走，而且還沒被工作人員注意到被取走的那條船。取走時，那隻船沒有舵，而且是在屍體發現之前取走的。本着謹慎而堅定的態度，我們就必然會找到這條船；因為不僅撿到它的駁船管理員能認出它，而且舵還在我們手中。帆船的舵丟了，一般人是絕不會若無其事，連問也不問的。讓我再插一個問題。當時並沒有登出過船被撿到的啟事，船是被悄悄地拿到管理處，又被人悄悄地弄走的。但是船主或是僱主 —— 在沒有啟事的情況下，他們怎麼可能會快到星期二一早就會得知船在星期一才停好的地點呢？除非我們設想那個駁船管理處和海軍方面有某種聯繫 —— 是某個個人的長期聯繫才導致了有人能察覺出它細微的利害關係 —— 它瑣碎的小事。

"談到那個孤獨的兇手拖着屍體來到岸邊時，我早就提到過他利用一條船的可能性。現在我們就明白了，瑪麗·羅傑是從船上被丟入水中的。這是自然而然會發生的。把屍體扔在岸邊的淺水區裏是無法匿屍的。受害者背上和肩膀上的特殊印記説明是船底的肋材摩擦造成的。那具屍體被發現時並沒附加重物也證實了這個觀點。如果它是從岸邊被扔進水中的，就會加上重物。我們只能把沒有重物解釋為可能兇手在離開前忘了這個防範措施。他在要把屍體弄到水中時，無疑就注意到了自己的疏忽；但是那時附近已經沒有補救的東西了。他寧願冒其他的險也不會返回那可惡的岸上去。在把那可怕的負擔卸載後，兇手就會立刻返回城裏。然後，他會在某個僻靜的碼頭跳上岸。但是那船——他會將它繫上嗎？他太倉促了，無暇顧及繫船之類的事。而且，等船靠碼頭了，他就會覺得這樣是留下了不利於自己的證據。他自然是想丟開所有與他的罪責相關的東西，越遠越好。他不僅要從碼頭逃跑，而且他不會讓船停在那裏。於是他肯定會任它漂走。讓我們繼續假設下去——第二天早晨，這個兇手驚恐萬分地發現那船被人撿起並留在他每天都會去光顧的地方——也許那個地方是由於他的工作緣故才頻頻涉足的。第二天晚上，他不敢拿舵，就把船轉移了。那麼現在那個無舵的船在哪裏呢？這是我們首先要發現的事物之一。我們一發現它，那成功的曙光就會顯現。這條船會指引我們，以連我們自己都會驚訝的飛快速度，找到那個在亡命的安息日的午夜就使用過該船的人。鐵證會相繼疊現，而兇手也會就此被緝拿。

（由於一些我們不該詳述的原因，而它們對許多讀者來說是不言自明的，在此，我們就冒昧地將那些從杜潘所獲得的清晰而細微的線索中追溯出來的細節部分從我們手邊的稿子上省去了。我們認為只須簡要地交代一下，我們所推測的結果都發生了；而且警察局長也按期地履行了與杜潘爵士的協議條款，儘管有些勉強。坡先生的文章是以下面的話為結語的。——編者按[40]）

"你們會認為我說的無非是巧合罷了。關於這個話題，我上述所講的已經足夠。我自己從內心裏不相信超自然。自然和上帝是兩回事，這沒有人會否定。後者創造了前者，他能隨意地控制或改造它，這也是毋庸質疑的。我説的是'隨意'；因為這是依照意願，而不是如愚頑的邏輯之所謂的依照權力。並不是神不能調整他的準則，而是我們為調整想像出了一個可能的必要性，這一舉動會傷害神。這些準則原本就包含了在將來會發生的一切偶然。在上帝眼中，一切都是現在。

"我要重申一下，我所説的這些事只是巧合。而且，在我所涉及到的事物中，人們會發現，就已知的命運而言，在不幸的瑪麗‧塞西莉亞‧羅傑斯的命運和瑪麗‧羅傑在人生的某個時期的命運之間，存在着一條平行線，當人們考慮到這相似性有着驚人的準確度，其理性便會困惑無措。我認為人們將會看到所有這一切。但是，當看到上述時期中的那個瑪麗的悲慘遭遇，當看到圍繞着她的迷霧被撥開時，讀者可別猜測我是想暗示這條平行線在延伸，或者甚至是想暗示在巴黎發現這個殺害了巴黎女店員的兇手所使用的方法，或者在類似推理上所運用的方法，都會引出類似的結果。

"因為就這種猜測的後半部分而言，大家應該考慮到，在兩個案件的事實中，哪怕最瑣碎的變化都可以通過徹底混淆兩件事實的過程而引出最嚴重的錯誤估計；這就很像在算術上，一個錯誤，其自身也許是微不足道的，但可以在運算過程中的每一步中以其不斷倍增的作用力最終導致與正確結果大相徑庭的答案。而就這種猜測的前半部分而言，我們一定要記住，我所提到的概率演算拒絕所有關於平行線延伸的觀點 —— 它以強有力而明確的態度拒絕這些想法，即不容許以此早已被延長並被弄得精確無誤的平行線來作為其計算比例。這是這些反常推測中的其中一種，雖然運用的是完全不符合數學規律的思維，卻是惟有數學家才能真正接受的。例如說，很難讓普通讀者相信，一個擲骰子的人連續兩次擲出 6 來，足可以賭他第三次不會再擲出 6 來。如果有人這麼提議，通常會立刻遭到才智之人的否定。前兩擲結束後，這兩次就是過去的事實了，它們應該不會對將來的投擲有甚麼影響。擲 6 的幾率似乎正好應該與骰子在任何平常時間被擲時一樣——也就是說，它只受其他各次甩擲的影響，而這些甩擲結果或許是骰子造成的。這一觀點非常明確，要想反駁這個觀點，只會更多地遭到嘲笑，而不是表示尊重的

"關注。這裏產生的錯誤——一個讓人覺得有點惡作劇似的重大錯誤——我無法自稱在我目前有限的篇幅中將它揭示出來，而且如果從哲學的角度看，它也無需被揭示。或許我至少可以這麼說，它形成了一連串無窮錯誤中的一個，這些錯誤發生在推理過程中，是推理力求詳細探詢真相而造成的。"

（張瓊譯）

5

被竊的信

Nil sapientiæ odiosius acumine nimio.[41]

—— 塞內加

巴黎，18××年的某個傍晚，秋風陣陣，我和朋友 C·奧古斯特·杜潘一起，在他位於聖日爾曼區杜諾街 33 號四樓住宅後廂的小書房，或稱藏書室裏，悠閒地享受着沉思和用海泡石煙斗抽煙的雙重樂趣。我們兩人至少有一個鐘頭深深沉浸在無語之中，隨便哪個人都能看出，我們都專注地看着那使屋裏氣氛顯得凝重的一圈圈青煙而出神。至於我，我正琢磨着黃昏初上之時兩人所交談的幾個話題，我指的是摩格街的事件，以及關於瑪麗·羅傑被謀殺的謎案。因此，當公寓門一開，走進了我們的老朋友巴黎警察局的 G 先生時，我覺得那完全是一種巧合。

我們對他表示了由衷的歡迎，這個人，雖然讓人有點瞧不起，倒也能讓人樂一陣，而我們也有幾年沒見他了。我們一直在暗處坐着。此時杜潘站起身來想點上燈，但一聽 G 先生說是來向我們請教，或者說是來向我的朋友請教，想聽聽他關於某件十分麻煩的公務的意見，便沒點燈又坐了回去。

"如果這是一件需要動腦筋的事情，"杜潘說着並沒有去點上燭芯，"我們還是在暗處談論的比較好。"

"這是你的又一個怪異念頭，"警察局長説道。這位局長習慣於把自己無法理解的事情都説成"怪異"，因此便身處於"怪異"軍團之中。

"千真萬確，"杜潘説着給這位來訪者遞上了一支煙斗，又往他跟前推了把靠椅。

"這回是甚麼難事啊？"我問道，"但願別又是甚麼謀殺之類的。"

"呵，不是，根本不是那件子事。其實，這件事情真的非常簡單，我絲毫不懷疑我們自己就能很好地解決它，可是我轉念一想，也許杜潘先生願意聽聽其中的細節，因為這件事的確太怪異了。"

"既簡單又怪異，"杜潘説道。

"沒錯，也不完全那樣。實際情況是，這件事一方面十分簡單，可又讓我們怎麼也摸不着頭腦，這讓我們都覺得疑惑不解。"

"也許正因為事情簡單才讓你們做不好，"我朋友説道。

"你這是在胡説八道些甚麼呀！"警察局長開心地大笑着説道。

"也許其中的神祕太明顯了，"杜潘説。

"天吶！誰曾會動過這樣的念頭？"

"有點太不言自明了。"

"哈！哈！哈！——哈！哈！哈！——呵！呵！呵！"來訪者給逗樂了，大笑起來，"咳，杜潘，你這是要讓我笑死啊！"

"到底是件甚麼樣的事情？"我問道。

"好，聽我告訴你，"警察局長説着長長地、緩緩地、深沉地吐了口煙，在椅子上端坐好身子。"我用不了幾句話就全告訴你們了。但在我細説之前得先警告你們，這件事可是絕密的，要是讓人知道了我把它泄漏給了別人，我這位子很可能就得丟。"

"説吧，"我説道。

"要麼別講，"杜潘説道。

"那好吧。我從上層得到一個私人信息，王室又一份極其重要的文件被竊。竊走這封信的人查到了，這一點毫無疑問，有人看見他拿的。而且文件還在他手裏，這一點也清楚了。"

"是怎麼知道的？"杜潘問道。

這位局長説道，"文件一旦從偷竊者那裏出手 —— 就是説，根據他肯定設計好的目的來處理這份文件 —— 就會發生某些結果，可實際上這樣的結果卻並沒有發生。因此，根據文件的性質，根據這樣的事實，這一點就很明顯了。"

"請説得再明確一些，"我説道。

"好吧，我可以説到這麼個地步，即掌握這份文件的人擁有了一種權力，而這種權力在某一階層中具有很高的價值。"局長挺喜歡這樣的外交辭令。

"我還是不甚明白，"杜潘説道。

"還不明白？咳，如果把文件透露給第三方 —— 我們就不説他的姓名了 —— 就會使一位地位極其尊貴的人士的名譽受到損害。這就使掌握這份文件的人佔了上風，捏住了那位尊貴人士的把柄，並使其聲譽掃地，不得安寧。"

"可是，"我插了進去，"這樣的上風，必須是偷文件的人確信丟文件者知道他就是竊賊。誰竟敢 —— "

"這位偷文件的人，"G先生說道，"就是D大臣，世界上沒有他不敢做的事情，管他是丈夫之為還是小人之舉。偷的手法真是又聰明又大膽。這份文件——坦白地說，是一封信——是該文件的主人單獨在王宮裏時收到的。她正看着信，這時另一位貴族突然闖了進來，她尤其不願意讓他看到這封信。匆忙中她試圖把信塞進抽屜，卻塞不進，只好把信攤開着擺在了桌子上。不過，信紙最上方寫的是地址姓名，下面的內容沒有展現出來，信便不太引人注意。就在這時候，D大臣進來了。他那山貓般狡詐銳利的目光立刻就注意到了那份文件，認出了地址姓名的筆跡，看出了收信人的慌張，揣摩出了她的祕密。他用慣常的方式匆匆地來了一遍公事公辦，便掏出了一封和桌上那封有點相像的信，展開來，裝出要看信的樣子，然後把它緊緊疊放在那封信邊上。他接着又聊了約十五分鐘時間，談的都是公事。最後，他告辭的時候，順手拿走了那封他沒有權利拿的信。而信的主人雖然看見了，卻因為還有第三方就站在她身邊而不敢喊出來。大臣溜了，把自己那封無關緊要的信留在了桌上。"

"瞧，"杜潘對我說道，"你想了解的佔上風的原因都在了——偷信人完全清楚丟信人對他的了解。"

"沒錯，"局長回答道，"過了幾個月之後，這樣的權力在政治場合上變得非常危險起來。信的主人日復一日地更加堅信必須把信要回來。可是這件事又無法公開進行。最後她萬般無奈，讓我來負責處理。"

"我相信，"杜潘說着吐出了一串優美的煙圈，"這是她能希望甚至是能想像到的最英明的辦事人了。"

"你過獎了，"局長說道，"不過，可能有人是這麼想的。"

"很明顯，"我說道，"正如你所說的，信還在這位大臣的手裏，而使他佔上風的是擁有這封信而不是拿它派具體的用場。一派用場，他就不再有這樣的權力了。"

"對，"G說道，"我正是按這樣的想法進行的。我首先考慮的是要對大臣下榻之處來一番徹底的搜查，可讓我為難的是，搜查一定不能讓他本人知道。特別是我被告誡說，一旦讓他有理由懷疑我們的計劃，情況將變得十分危險。"

"可是，"我說，"對這樣的調查你可是相當專業的。巴黎警察局從前常做這樣的事。"

"沒錯，正因為如此，我才沒有絕望。這位大臣的日常起居也讓我有機可乘。他經常徹夜不回，他的僕人不多。他們都睡在離主人套房很遠的房間裏，另外，這些人都是那不勒斯人，很容易就喝得酩酊大醉。你知道，我手裏的鑰匙，可以打開全巴黎任何一扇房門或櫥櫃的門。三個月來，沒有一個晚上我不在D的住處呆上大半夜，親自搜查那地方。這件事關係到我的名譽，告訴你們一個天大的祕密，那筆酬金數目很大。等我完全相信這偷信人比我還機敏得多時，便不再去搜查了。我覺得已經把所有可能藏着這封信的角落都查遍了。"

"但是有沒有這樣的可能，"我提出了自己的看法，"儘管信也許是在大臣手裏，這應該是毫無疑問的，但他是否可能把信藏在了別處而不是自己的住處呢？"

"這不大可能，"杜潘說道。"照宮廷上目前的特殊情況看，特別是據說D某人也捲入其中的那些陰謀，說不定甚麼時候就會立刻需要這份文件——隨時都會有人命令立刻拿出這份文件。這一點和掌握這份文件幾乎具有同樣的重要性。"

"能隨時拿出這份文件？"我問道。

"就是説，能隨時銷毀這份文件，"杜潘答道。

"對，"我説，"很明顯，文件就在他住處。至於説他是否會把文件帶在身上，我們可以認為這樣的可能性根本不存在。"

"完全正確，"局長説道。"他有兩次受到突然檢查，就像遭到攔路搶劫一樣，他在我親自監視下被仔細搜過身。"

"你還不如省了這些麻煩，"杜潘説道。"我看，這 D 某人並非愚鈍之輩，既然如此，他肯定預料到會有突然搜查，這是當然之事。"

"的確不是徹頭徹尾的笨蛋，"G 説道，"不過他是個寫詩的，而我認為寫詩的人離笨蛋不過一步之差了。"

"對，"杜潘若有所思地長長地吸了口海泡石煙斗，説道，"儘管我本人也一直蠢笨地在寫一些打油詩甚麼的。"

我説："你能不能仔細説説你搜查的情況？"

"好，事實上，我們搜得從容不迫，甚麼地方都搜遍了。幹這樣的事情我早已經驗豐富了。我在整棟樓裏一個房間一個房間地查，每個房間要查上整整七夜。我們首先檢查套房裏的家具。能開的抽屜都開一遍，我想你是知道的，對受過正規訓練的警察來説，再'祕密的'抽屜也能找得到。在這樣的搜查中誰要是被'祕密'抽屜蒙過去了，那就是個大傻瓜。事情明擺着的。每一個櫥裏都會有某些體積——就是空間——需要弄清楚。我們有詳細的規則。一段線條五十分之一的差別都會引起我們的注意。查完櫥我們查椅子，還用你見過我們使用的那種細長的針刺探枕頭。我們還卸下桌面。"

"幹嘛這麼做？"

"有時候想藏東西的人會搬開桌面或其他家具的類似板面，在家具的腿上挖洞，把東西藏在洞裏，再把板面放回去。牀架支柱的頂端和底部也能這樣用。"

"但敲一敲聽聲音不就會發現是否有空洞了嗎？"我問道。

"根本不會的，只要在東西放進空洞時裏上足夠厚的棉花。另外，在這個案子中，我們必須不弄出任何聲響。"

"但你也不可能把所有能這樣挖個洞藏東西的家具都翻個遍呀。信紙可以被捲縮成很細很細的形狀，體積和大號的毛線針相差無幾，這樣，它就能插進椅子橫檔這樣的東西裏去。你沒把所有的椅子都拆散了吧？"

"當然沒有，但是我們幹得更漂亮 —— 我們用一架高倍放大鏡，檢查了他住處的每一把椅子上的每一根橫檔，檢查了每一件家具上的每一處榫頭。上面要是有一絲最近被人撥弄過的痕跡，我們立刻就能注意到。比如說，鑽洞時留下的一星木屑，看起來會像一隻蘋果那樣明顯。膠水痕跡有沒有異常，榫頭有沒有空隙，等等，都保證會被我們查出來。"

"我看你連鏡子都查了，細看了鏡面玻璃和襯板之間的縫隙，還刺過了牀褥和牀單，窗簾地毯都在你搜查之列。"

"那是當然，這樣把家具的每一個部分都徹徹底底地搜了個遍之後，我們就搜查這屋子本身。我們把整個屋子的地面分解成小塊，每一塊都標上數字，一塊都不會漏掉，然後我們對整個屋子每一平方英吋的地面都細細搜查，還包括兩間緊鄰的房子，和前面一樣，用了放大鏡。」

「緊鄰的兩處房子！」我叫了起來，「你一定費了不少的事吧。」

「是的，不過那筆酬金也是十分可觀的。」

「你把屋子周圍的地面都包括進去了？」

「周圍的地面都鋪着磚。在那裏倒沒遇上太多的麻煩。我們檢查了磚石之間的青苔，發現沒有被人動過的痕跡。」

「你肯定還檢查了 D 某人的文件，還翻查了他書齋裏的書？」

「當然啦，每一疊文件每一個包裹我們都翻看過，我們不僅翻遍了每一本書，還翻遍了每本書裏的每一頁，而不是像有些警察那樣拿着書晃幾下就算完成任務了。我們還測量了每本書封面的厚度，測得極為精確，因為每一張封面都用放大鏡細細查過。要是哪本書的裝幀最近被人做過手腳，這樣的事實絕不可能逃脫我們的注意。有五六卷書是新近從裝幀店裏送來的，我們還仔細地用針直着插進封套裏探過。」

「你們還查過地毯下面的地板嗎？」

「那還用問。我們把每塊地毯都掀起來看過，還用放大鏡檢查了下面的地板。」

「還有牆紙？」

「查了。」

「地窖呢？」

「查了。」

「那麼，」我說道，「你做的推測就全錯了，那封信並不像你猜想的那樣藏在那個地方。」

“恐怕你這是說對了，”局長說。“瞧，杜潘先生，你說我該怎麼做？”

“徹底搜查那地方。”

“這絕對沒有必要了，”G回答道。“我千真萬確地相信，那封信不在那座官邸裏。”

“那我也給不了你甚麼更好的建議了，”杜潘說道。“不過，你能準確描述一下那封信的樣子嗎？”

“當然能！”局長說着掏出一個記事本，大聲地讀着那份丟失的文件的內外部特徵，特別是外部特徵。讀完信件特徵後不久，他便告辭了，一臉的沮喪神情，我從未見這位好好先生如此沮喪過。

又過了個把月時間，他再次來訪，發現我們和上一次的情況差不多。他還是拿了支煙斗，拉過把椅子，聊起了一些尋常的話題。終於我問道：

“呃，G先生，那封丟失的信如何了？我想你最後一定下了決心，沒在大臣身上弄巧成拙吧？”

“去他媽的大臣。沒錯，我是按杜潘說的又搜查了一遍，可我早知道那準又是白忙一場。”

“你說過的，他們提出的獎賞數額有多大？”杜潘問道。

“怎麼，數字不小 —— 的確是一筆相當可觀的酬金，我不想說出準確的數字，但是我要這麼說，誰能幫我獲得那封信，要我給他開一張五萬法郎的個人支票我真不會介意。事實上，事件的重要性在與日俱增，獎金最近又翻了一番。不過，即使漲上三倍，我也無法再進一步了。”

"是啊是啊，"杜潘咬着海泡石煙斗吸一口吐一句地説道。"G先生 —— 我真 —— 覺得 —— 你在 —— 此事上 —— 並沒有 —— 竭盡 —— 全部的力氣。我覺得 —— 你還能 —— 再做一點點 —— 努力。呃？"

"怎麼做 —— 該怎麼辦？"

"咳 —— 這件事情 —— 呼呼 —— 你可以 —— 呼呼 —— 找人請教請教嘛，呃？ —— 呼，呼，呼。你還記得那個阿伯內西的故事嗎？"

"不，該死的阿伯內西！"

"當然！你盡可以説他該死。可是從前有個有錢的吝嗇鬼，想揩他的油，想法子讓阿伯內西白開張處方。為此，他安排與對方私下會面聊天，繞着彎子把自己的情況告訴醫生，聽起來就像是想像中的一個病人的病情。"

"'就讓我們假設，'那吝嗇鬼説道，'他有如此這般的症狀，醫生，您會讓他服用甚麼藥呢？'"

"'服用甚麼藥！'阿伯內西説道，'當然是讓他服從勸告啦。'"

"可是，"警察局長説着有點沉不住氣了，"我可是完全願意服從勸告的，還準備支付酬金呢。誰要是能在這件事情上出手相幫，我真的願意出五萬法郎。"

"既然如此，"杜潘邊説邊拉開抽屜拿出一本支票本，"你還不如按剛才説的數目給我開一張支票。等你簽上名，我就把那封信交到你手上。"

我驚呆了。局長也顯得萬分震驚。有好幾分鐘，他在那裏一動不動，一言不發，張着嘴巴，怔怔地直盯着我的朋友，眼珠似乎都要從眼眶裏突出來了。過了一會，他似乎稍微鎮定了些，抓過一支筆，幾度停頓幾眼茫然之後，終於寫好了這張五萬法郎的支票，簽上名，把它遞給了坐在桌子對面的杜潘。後者仔細看了看支票，把它夾進了自己的小記事本裏，然後用鑰匙打開了書桌的一隻分格抽屜，取出一封信，遞給了局長。這位官員喜出望外，緊緊捏住，雙手顫抖着展開信紙，迅速掃視了一眼其中的內容，然後跌跌撞撞衝向房門，也顧不上甚麼禮節，頭也不回地出了房間，出了屋子，而且自從杜潘讓他開具支票以來，他連一句話都沒説過。

等他走了之後，我的朋友開始細細解釋起來。

"巴黎的警察的確自有一套，十分能幹，"他説道，"他們有毅力，很聰明，也很老練，對自己職責所需的知識掌握得十分精通。因此，當 G 先生向我詳細描述他在 D 宅裏搜查的情況時，我完全相信他已經做了令人滿意的調查 —— 在他努力的範圍之內。"

"在他努力的範圍之內？"我問道。

"是的，"杜潘説。"他們採取的措施不僅是最好的，而且執行得也絕對完美。那封信要真是放在他們的搜索範圍內，這些傢伙一定會找到，毫無疑問。"

我只是微微一笑 —— 但是他在講這番話時的神情卻十分認真。

"他們的措施就其本身來説是很好的，"他繼續説道，"而且執行得也很好，而主要的缺陷就在於，這些措施並不適用於這樣的案子和這樣的人。對局長而言，某些極為聰明的想法反倒成了普羅克拉斯提斯之牀 [42]，迫使他按此制定自己的計畫。可在處理手中的案子時，他始終在犯錯誤，不是想得太深就是想得太淺，而許多小學生都會比他思考得更合理。我就知道有個八歲的孩子，他在猜單雙的遊戲中成功率之高，讓所有的人都讚歎佩服。遊戲很簡單，是用彈子玩的。一個人手心裏捏上幾顆這樣的玩意，然後問對方彈子是雙數還是單數。如果猜對了，猜數的人就贏一顆彈子，猜錯了就輸一顆。我說的那孩子把全校孩子的彈子全贏去了。當然啦，他猜單雙是有一點方法的，主要就是觀察和估計對手的機智程度。比如，對手是一個大傻瓜，緊攥着拳頭問他，'單還是雙？'這位小學生回答，'單'，輸了，可第二次再猜他就贏了，因為他暗想，'這傻帽第一猜時捏的是雙數，而他那點腦子也只夠他在第二猜時捏單數了。因此我就猜單。'——結果他猜單而且贏了。如果遇上比那傻帽稍多一點頭腦的，他就這樣想，'這傢伙發現第一次我猜了單數，第二次時他的第一衝動就是像前一個傻帽那樣簡單地把數字從單改成雙，但是他轉念一想，這樣改太簡單了，最後他決定仍然捏雙數。因此我要猜雙'。他猜了雙，贏了。同學們都說這孩子'好運氣'，可他的這套推理從根本上說到底是怎麼回事？"

"只是把推理人的智力與其對手的智力做比照，"我說道。

"對了，"杜潘說道，"我問那孩子是用甚麼樣的方法來進行如此徹底的比照並最終取得成功的，他這樣回答我：'我想發現對方有多聰明、多笨、多善、多惡的時候，或者想發現對方此刻在想些甚麼的時候，我就在自己的臉上做出儘可能和對方一樣的神情，然後就看看這時候自己心裏會產生甚麼樣的念頭或情感，能配得上這樣的神情。'這小學生的回答，觸及了使拉羅什富科、拉布吉夫、馬基亞維里和卡巴內拉等人看似高深莫測的前提。"

"如果我沒弄錯你的意思，"我說道，"推理人的智力與對手的重合程度，取決於他能在多大程度上精確地計算對手的智能。"

"從實用目的來說，的確如此，"杜潘回答道，"而這位局長和他的那羣部下卻屢屢失敗，首先是因為他沒有進行這樣的比照，其次是因為他錯算或者說根本就沒有計算他們與之打交道的對手的智力。他們只考慮自己的想法有多麼聰明，在搜查東西時只想到他們自己會藏的那些地方。他們在一定程度上是對的——即他們自己的智力忠實地代表了常人的妙計，但是，當具體某個罪犯的狡詐與他們的思維特徵不一致時，那罪犯當然就把他們騙過了。當罪犯的智力超過他們時，這樣的結果準會發生，當罪犯的智力不及他們時，這樣的結果也常會發生。他們的調查原則從不隨機應變。即使受異常的緊急情況之迫使——被某筆酬金驅使——他們最多也只是將辦事的老方法擴展一點，極端一點，但從不觸及其根本。比如說，在 D 某人的案子中，他們對基本原則做過甚麼改動沒有？鑽孔、打眼、探測，敲敲打打，用放大鏡觀察，把建築面積分解成平方英吋再編號登記，這一切不就是在把那個或那套搜查原則應用到極端嗎？而這套原則不就是建立於局長在自己長期工作中已經熟悉了的對於人類智力的認識之上的嗎？難道你沒注意到嗎，他認定，凡是要把一封信藏起來的人，雖然不一定都會把信藏進椅子腿上鑽出來的洞裏，卻至少會聽從那個建議把信藏在椅子腿上鑽出的洞裏的類似念頭，把信藏在某個隱蔽的暗洞或角落裏。難道你也沒注意到，這樣藏東西的祕密角落，只適用於普通情況，而且也只有普通智力水準的人才會想到。因為在所有藏匿行為中，把藏匿物置於何處——以這種祕密方式來藏匿——總是最先被假定並被推測出來的。由此，發現被藏匿物根本就不取決於搜尋者多麼敏銳，而完全取決於其是否細心，是否有耐性和決心。當案子十分重要——或者對警方來說十分重要，懸賞也相當可觀時，上面所說的那些素質一向都是制勝的因素。我說過，如果這封丟失的信就藏在局長的搜查範圍之內，換句話說，如果此信是以局長所能想像的方式藏匿起來的，那要找到這封信根本就不成問題。你現在該明白我這麼說的意思了吧。然而，這位局長卻完全被弄得暈頭轉向了，他之所以失敗，其間接原因就在於他認定，由於這位大臣有詩人的名聲，他便一定是傻瓜。局長認為，傻瓜都是詩人，並因此得出結論，即詩人皆傻瓜，從而徹底地犯了一個周延全稱肯定判斷之謂項的邏輯錯誤。”

“不過此人真是詩人嗎？”我問道。“我知道他們是兩兄弟，兩人都有點文學才氣。不過我知道那個當大臣的曾寫過很深奧的微積分學方面的東西。他是個數學家，不是詩人啊。”

“你錯了，我對他很了解，他是個數學家兼詩人。正因為他既是詩人又是數學家時，他推理能力很強，而如果他僅僅是個數學家，他就根本無法推理，這樣就會在局長面前束手就擒了。”

“你太讓我吃驚了，”我說道，“你說的這些和所有人的觀點完全矛盾。你不是想徹底否定人們經過幾個世紀的研究探索才建立起來的觀點吧。長久以來，人們都認為數學推理就是推理之極致。”

"'Il y a à parier，'"杜潘引用尚福爾的一句原話回答道，"'que toute idée publique，toute convention reçue，est une sottise，car elle a convenue au plus grand nombre.'[43]我告訴你，數學家們竭盡全力地散佈你剛才提到的那個傳播廣泛的謬誤，即使把這一謬誤宣傳為真理，它還是個謬誤。例如，他們利用本來可以用於更好目的的方法，把'解析'這個術語偷偷加在了代數學上。法國人是這一欺瞞的始作俑者。但是，如果說一個術語有甚麼重要性的話，如果說詞語是從其應用中獲得價值的話，那麼，'解析'一詞所表示的'代數'含義，和拉丁語中'ambitus'表示'野心'、'religio'表示'宗教'、'homines honesti'表示'一羣品格高尚的人'等沒甚麼兩樣。"

"我看，你得和巴黎的一些代數學家好好爭論一番了，"我說道，"不過你接着說吧。"

"我不同意這樣的觀點，認為在抽象邏輯之外還能有以任何特定形式出現的推理，也不認為這樣的推理會有任何價值。我特別不同意經數學方式演繹出的推理。數學是形式和數量的科學，數學推理只是將邏輯應用於觀察形式和數量。把所謂純粹代數的真理說成是抽象或普遍真理，就是犯了大錯。如此大的錯誤，居然還被人普遍接受，真讓我大為不解。數學公理並非公理——即普遍真理。比如，數學關係——如形與數——所適用的，用在倫理學上經常就大錯特錯。在研究後者的學問中，集合體等同於整體的說法就經常是不正確的。在化學中那些公理也不適用。對動機研究它們也不適用，因為當兩個各有其特定價值的動機聯合到一起時，其價值並不一定等同於各自價值之和。數學上還有很多其他的真理，其真理性也僅限於數學關係之中。但是數學家們卻習慣上從其有限真理出發，以為它們具有絕對的普適性——而世人也的確以為它們具有普適性。布萊恩特在其高深的《神話》一書中就提到了人們犯錯誤的一項類似的緣由，他說，'儘管我們並不相信異教傳說，但卻不斷忘卻這一點，經常把傳說當作存在着的現實加以援引。'對於代數學家來說，他們本身就是異教，他們就相信這樣的異教傳說，他們之援引傳說，與其說是由於記憶差錯，不如說是出於頭腦中無法解釋的糊塗。簡而言之，我從未碰到過一個純粹數學家，除了求等根之外還能讓人對其表示信任，或不在暗中把 $x^2 + px$ 絕對且無條件地等於 q 當作自己信奉的準則的。你要是願意，不妨試試對這些先生中的某一位說，你相信在有些場合下，$x^2 + px$ 並不完全等於 q，一讓他明白你的意思，就得趕緊逃開去，不然，他一定會給你一頓狠揍。"

當我對他上述之辭只是付之一笑時，杜潘繼續說道："我的意思是，如果大臣只是一個數學家，局長就決沒有必要給我寫這張支票了。然而，我認識的他卻既是數學家又是詩人，因而我使用的方法便是根據他的能力來制定的，還參考了他所處的境況。我還知道他是宮廷中人，而且是個膽子很大詭計多端的傢伙。我想，這樣的人絕不會意識不到警方行動的常規模式。他不會沒料想到——事實也證明他的確料到了——他會遭遇突擊檢查。我想，他一定預見到自己的住處會遭到祕密搜查。他經常夜不歸宿，警察局長很高興地認為這對他的成功搜查有所幫助，我卻認為都是詭計，為的是給警方提供徹底搜查的機會，好讓他們得出 G 先生後來的確得出的結論——即信不在那地方。我還感覺到，剛才我不厭其煩地向你仔細講述的那一整套思路，講到警方搜查被藏匿物的行動牽涉到那條不變的原則——我覺得這一整套思路肯定會在大臣的腦子裏閃過，這肯定會使他放棄任何通常的藏匿地點。我想，他的腦子肯定不至於笨得想不到這一點，即他在旅館的住所中最祕密最隱蔽的暗處，在警察局長的目光、探針、小鑽和放大鏡之下，都會如最平常的衣櫥那樣毫無祕密可言。最後，我發現他會被迫轉向簡單化，哪怕不是有意做出的處心積慮的選擇。你也許還記得，第一次和警察局長見面時我就說，這件讓他如此費心的案子之所以顯得神祕，完全有可能是因為它其實十分的簡單明瞭，而局長聽了卻大笑起來。"

"沒錯，"我說道，"我清楚地記得他那副開心的樣子。當時我還真以為他要笑得抽風了呢。"

"物質世界與非物質世界之間有着許多十分接近的類似，"杜潘繼續說道，"所以許多真理可以用修辭方式表示，比如可以用暗喻或明喻來加重論點的力度，或使描述更為豐滿。例如，慣性原理在物理學和玄學中似乎是相同的。在前者，體積較大的物體比體積較小的更難推動，而其後的動量則與這樣的難度成正比；在後者，儘管能力更大者的智力運動起來比能力較差者更有力，更經久，更富有變化，在開始動作之時，他們卻總是不太情願，遲疑猶豫。再有，你是否注意過，甚麼樣的商店門上的路牌最引人注意？"

"這我倒從來沒想到過，"我說。

"有一個找字遊戲，"他接着說道，"是在一張地圖上玩的。遊戲的一方要求另一方找出一個特定的詞——城市、河流、國家或帝國的名稱——簡而言之，就是那五顏六色令人目眩的圖面上的詞。遊戲的新手一般都讓對手去尋找字體印得最細小的名稱，想以此為難對方，而老手則專挑那些字體很大，橫過整幅地圖的那些名稱。這就像那些字體過大的街牌，因過分醒目反而不容易讓人注意到。這種視覺疏漏正好與思維疏忽相類似，由於這樣的思維疏忽，使聰明人對那些明顯是不言自明的事實視而不見。但是這一點似乎正好在警察局長的智力能力之上或之下，使他從來沒想過，這大臣也許或可能就把這封信放在所有人的眼皮底下，誰都沒能夠發現它。

"這位 D 大臣的確膽子大、腦子活、善辨析、很聰明。我覺得如果他想好好利用這封信，那信一定就在伸手可及之處，又考慮到警察局長所獲得的十分肯定的證據，證明那封信不在這位大人物進行的普通搜索的範圍之內。我越思考這些問題，就越堅信，這大臣為了把信藏起來，採用的權宜之計既精明又周全，那就是根本不把信藏起來。

"我前後考慮周到，便備上一副綠色鏡片的眼鏡，挑了個晴朗的上午，不請自去了大臣官邸。D 先生在家，呵欠連天，一副懶洋洋的神情，裝出極為倦怠的樣子。他也許是世上最最精力充沛的人——但這只是他在人背後的樣子。

"我對他有來有往，發着牢騷說眼睛不管用，非戴眼鏡不可了，而在鏡片的掩護之下，我小心地徹底地掃視了整個房間，但表面上裝出在專心和主人交談。

"我特別注意了他座位邊上的那張大書桌，桌面上亂七八糟地攤着幾封信和其他的文件，還放着一兩件樂器，幾本書。

然而，我細細搜索良久，並未發現甚麼能讓人感到特別懷疑的東西。

"最後，我環顧室內，視線落在一隻華而不實的用裝飾着金銀絲線的硬卡紙做成的卡片盒架上，盒子拴着一根骯髒的藍色緞帶，掛在壁爐架正中稍低一些的一個小銅球上。盒架有三四層，裏面放着五六張訪客名片和一封信。後者表面髒兮兮的，皺皺的，被人從中間幾乎一撕為二——一眼看去，主人似乎因為它毫無用處而本想把它全撕掉的，可一轉念又改變了主意，將它留了下來。信封上蓋着一個很大的黑色印戳，能十分清晰地看見那個 D 字押碼，收信人地址姓名是纖細的女性筆跡，收信人正是 D 大臣本人。信被不經意地、甚至似乎有些不屑一顧地扔在了卡片盒架最上層的格子裏。

"我一瞥見這封信，便斷定它就是我要找的那封。沒錯，從表面上看，它和警察局長向我們詳細描繪的那封完全不同。這封信的印章大而黑，上面有 D 字押碼，而那封信上的又小又紅，上面是 S 家族的公爵紋章。這封信上大臣親收的地址，字跡小而帶有女性特徵，而那封信上寫的是致某位元王室成員，字體明顯粗大剛勁。只有兩封信的大小相同。但是，這些差別太厲害，太過分了。骯髒的、被撕壞的信封和 D 某人實際上有條不紊的習慣根本不相符合，完全說明是一個有意為之以騙人相信那不過是一份毫無價值的文件的詭計。考慮到這一切，再加上那信又擺放在那麼特別顯眼的地方，讓來人一眼便可看見，這就完全符合我先前所做的結論了。我說，這些事實對一個心存疑慮的訪客來說，就最有力地證明了他內心的懷疑。

"我儘量拖延拜訪時間，一邊興致勃勃地和大臣就某個話題談論着，我清楚知道，這個話題永遠會讓他很感興趣並十分激動，而我真正的注意力則一直放在那封信上。我在心裏仔細記下了信封的外觀和放在盒架上的樣子，還獲得了一個發現，徹底消除了我所有可能的細小懷疑。在仔細觀察信封邊緣時，我注意到那裏有點不正常的毛糙。那邊緣的磨損，就像是有人把一張硬紙摺過來後，用摺疊機壓平，然後再反方向按原來的摺痕摺回去。這一發現足以讓我清楚地看出，這封信被他像手套似地內外翻了過來，重新寫上地址姓名，蓋上封簽。於是我向大臣道過日安，匆匆告辭，走的時候在桌上留下一隻金質的鼻煙盒。

"第二天上午，我去拿回那隻鼻煙盒，兩人又接着前一天的話題熱切地談開了。正談得起勁，就在官邸窗外傳來一聲很響的好像是手槍射擊的聲音，緊接着就是幾聲充滿恐懼的尖叫，亂哄哄的人羣大呼小叫起來。D 某人衝到窗前，推開窗子，朝外看去。我便趁機走到盒架前，拿起那封信塞進衣袋，把一封一模一樣的（從外表看）信放在原處。這封信是我在自己的住處準備好的，那個 D 某人的封簽是用麵包塊做的印章按上去的。

"街上的混亂是一個拿着火槍的冒失傢伙引起的。他在一羣女人和孩子中間開了槍。事後查明，槍裏並沒有裝子彈，那傢伙就被當成瘋子或酒鬼放了。我一拿到看見的那封信便跟着 D 某人走到窗邊去了，那傢伙一走，D 就從窗邊走了回來。沒等多久，我就向他告辭了。那假裝瘋子的人是我花錢僱來的。"

"可是你幹嘛還要用一封一模一樣的信把原信換回來呢？"我問道。"你第一次去的時候就拿過來一走了之豈不更好嗎？"

"這位 D 某人可是個不要命的，"杜潘回答道，"而且膽大包天。再者，他住的官邸裏有不少對他十分忠心的僕從。我要是按你說的胡亂行事，我可能就無法活着從大臣的住處出來了。善良的巴黎人恐怕就再也見不到我了。不過，除了這些考慮之外我還有一個目的。你知道我的政治傾向的。在這件事情上，我充當了那位夫人的支持者。那大臣十八個月以來一直牢牢把她控制在自己的權力之下。這一下可倒過來了 —— 因為他並不知道信已經不在他手裏，所以仍然會按信在他手裏的情況對她進行訛詐。這樣，他立刻會在政治上遭遇滅頂之災。他的失敗將既突然又令他難堪。facilis descensus Averni[44]，這話說得真不錯，可正如卡塔拉尼在談論歌唱時所說，在各種各樣的爬升中，升高總比降低容易得多。在目前這一事例中，我對那跌下去的人沒有同情 —— 至少沒有憐憫。他是個可怕的惡魔，一個無法無天的天才。然而，當他受到那位被警察局長稱之為‘某位人士’的她的反擊時，走投無路，一定會去打開我留在他盒架裏的那封信。我承認我很想看看他那時候腦子裏會有怎樣的念頭。"

"怎麼？你在信封裏塞了甚麼特別的東西了？"

"咳 —— 讓信封空着總不太好吧，那可是在羞辱人了。在維也納的時候，這位 D 某人做過一次對不起我的事情，我那時平心靜氣地告訴過他我會記着的。我知道他發現有人竟然把他給耍了，肯定想弄清楚對手的身份，因此，不給他點提示就有點可惜

了。他十分熟悉我的筆跡，我就在空白紙片的中央直接抄下了這
樣的話——

    '—   —Un dessein si funeste,
    S'il n'est digne d'Atrée, est digne de Thyeste.' [45]

    "這句話摘自克雷比雍之《阿特柔斯》。" [46]

（張沖譯）

6

厄舍屋的倒塌

Son cœur est un luth suspendu; Sitôt qu'on le touche il résonne.[47]

—— 貝朗瑞

那年秋季的某一天，整天乏味、幽暗、寂靜，雲層抑抑，低浮在天空，我騎馬獨自穿越了一片落寞陰森的曠野，夜幕降臨時，發現不遠處就是那憂鬱感傷的厄舍屋。不知為何，初初的一瞥，一種無法排解的陰鬱就在我心底彌漫開來。我說無法排解，是因為要在往常，哪怕是大自然中最荒涼恐怖的景象，也能挑起人的詩意和情感，讓人感覺到一點欣喜，可這次面對的景象，卻怎麼也無法使我的情緒得到緩解。我看着面前的景致 —— 那座孤宅，那周圍質樸簡潔的風景 —— 那荒涼的壁牆 —— 空洞的窗眼 —— 幾簇繁茂的莎草 —— 幾棵朽木的蒼白樹幹，內心縈繞着一種極度的消沉。這消沉幾乎無法用任何塵世感情來比擬，只能說像鴉片吸食者幻夢初醒時的狀態：那種重新墜落凡生的苦澀，那種面紗脫落的驚懼。我心裏一片冰冷，感到消沉難受，感到一種無藥可救的思想枯竭，任憑怎樣想像都無法激發半點莊嚴感。我收輯沉思：這是甚麼？這令我想起厄舍屋就如此心力交瘁的是甚麼？這是一個完全無法破解的謎，而我也無力與凝神思索時那向我襲來的飄渺幻想展開搏鬥。我只好接受這個不盡如人意的論斷，即，毋庸置疑的是，那是非常單純的自然物質的結合，它形成了一種感染人的力量，而要對這一力量進行分析卻超越了人之所能。我認為，只要把景致中的各個細節、畫面中的各個筆觸的組合變動一下，就足以緩解或消除那令人悲傷的氣氛。於是我一邊這麼想着，一邊策馬走向宅邊那個寧靜的、波光粼粼的水潭，潭邊石頭陡峭，水色幽黑可怖。我俯身看看潭水，渾身一陣戰慄，比方才更為驚慌：因為我看見灰色莎草變形的倒影，樹幹猙獰，窗眼洞然。

可是，此時我卻打算在這棟陰鬱的大屋裏駐留幾週。屋子的主人羅德里克·厄舍曾是我孩提時的好夥伴；但我們已多年未見。然而，最近我在國內偏遠的地方收到了一封信──是他寫的──信中文字十分急迫，使我不得不親自前往給予答覆。信上的手書顯出他焦慮不安的跡象，寫信人提到自己身罹重病──一種使他的思緒壓抑思維混亂的病，還提到他非常渴望見到我，說我是他最好的、事實上也是他唯一的私交，說他抱着嘗試的念頭，希望我能去陪伴他，使他舒心，使病痛得以緩解。信中還諸如此類寫了其他一些內容。他的邀請顯然情真意切，讓我來不得絲毫猶豫。於是，儘管這樣的召喚聽來奇怪，我對此卻只能從命。

雖然我們在孩提時代一直是親密的夥伴，但我對這位仁兄真的知之寥寥。他一直異常緘默，積習頗深。然而，我很清楚，他那古老的家族從不為人知的年代起，就以脾性裏獨特的敏感而著稱，歷經悠長的歲月，這種敏感在許多高雅藝術著作中展現出來，近年來，又反覆在慷慨而謙虛的慈善活動中，在對於錯綜複雜之事的熱情投入中顯現出來，他對後者的投入甚至比對傳統的、更易被接受與認可的音樂之美更為專注。我還了解到一個顯著的事實，即歷史悠久的厄舍家族的血脈，無論在哪一代，香火都不旺盛；換言之，整個家族一直一脈單傳，只在很短的時期裏有過微小的例外。我想到，這屋子的特點和主人的氣質竟然如此相像，又想到這一家族的個性竟然如此完善地被保留下來，經過幾個世紀仍可能代代影響，這使我感到，正是這一不足，或許由於間接的因素，最終，子嗣繼承的遺產和姓氏竟會如此同一，使府邸原來的名字變成了這個古雅、雙關的"厄舍屋"稱號，在農夫們稱呼它時，似乎即有家族又有家族宅邸之意。

我曾說過，我那多少有些孩子氣的實驗——即俯視水潭——的唯一效果，是為了加深初次的怪異印象。毫無疑問的是，我對自己迷信思想正迅速增強的意識——我為何不如此界定呢？——反而使這種迷信更為加劇。我早就知道，這是一切以恐懼為基調的情感自相矛盾的法則。而且，可能就是因為這個原因，當我再次從宅屋在潭中的倒影抬高視線，看着物體本身時，我腦海裏出現了一個奇怪的幻象——那幻象如此荒謬，事實上，我提到它，不過是想顯示壓迫我的這種感覺有着生動的力量。我如此想像着，真的相信整個宅邸和這一區域，以及與之密切相關的事物，都充滿了一種奇特的氛圍——這種氛圍和天空中的大氣無甚關係，卻散發着朽木、灰色牆垣以及寂靜的水潭的氣息——那是一種瘟疫般的神祕氣息，陰鬱、呆滯，辨別不清，並帶有沉悶的色彩。

我擺脫了這無疑是夢幻般的精神狀態，更細緻地觀察着這幢宅邸的真面目。它的主要特徵似乎有些過分古老的味道。悠長歲月使房屋的褪色非常厲害。建築表面遍佈着細小的菌類植物，它們從屋簷垂下來，形成了一張細密交織的網。然而所有這一切都沒有顯示出異常的頹廢跡象。其間的工匠技藝絲毫未損，而且宅屋在依然完美協調的各部位和每一塊石頭的風化狀態之間呈現出一種狂亂的衝突。這種不協調在很大程度上使我想到了某個不常使用的地下室裏的木制結構，那裏毫不通風，那些木製結構已經腐朽多年，然而，除了這大片的腐朽跡象，其構造沒有絲毫不穩定的徵兆。也許細心的觀察者可以發現一個幾乎不被注意到的裂痕，這裂痕從正前方的屋頂開始，蜿蜒曲折地經過牆垣，直到消逝在黯淡的水潭中。

看到此番光景，我騎馬經過一條通向宅屋的短道。等候着的僕人幫我牽走了馬，我走進了大廳那哥特式的拱門。一個男僕躡手躡腳一言不發地領我穿過許多幽暗錯綜的過道，進入主人的書房。一路上，我看到很多事物，不知道怎麼的，都使我早先說過的那種朦朧情緒越發強烈起來。雖然我周圍的事物——天花板上的雕刻、牆壁沉鬱的帷幔、烏木地板的漆黑，以及我邁步經過時就發出咿咿聲的有着鬼魅般紋章的戰利品，都不過是或類似我幼年時就已熟悉的東西，雖然我會毫不猶豫地承認自己對那一切是多麼熟悉，我仍然很驚訝地發現，這些平常的景象所激發起來的幻象竟是如此的陌生。在樓梯上，我遇到了家庭醫生。我覺得他的表情混雜着些許陰險和窘困。他慌張地和我打了個招呼就走了下去。男僕猛地推開一扇門，引我走到他主人面前。

我所在的房間非常寬敞，天花很高，窗戶狹長、帶着尖頂，離漆黑的橡木地板相當的高，從室內很難伸手企及。微弱的紅色光線從格窗玻璃射入，剛好照清楚屋裏那些較為顯眼的物品；然而，我再用力都無法看到房間的最深處，或是拱形和格紋天花的深處。黑色的帷幔垂在牆壁上。家具總體顯得擁擠、阻塞、古舊，而且破敗。四處散放着許多書籍和樂器，但絲毫未給房間增加任何活力。我感到正呼吸着令人憂傷的空氣。四處彌漫着凝滯、強烈，並且無法驅散的陰鬱氣氛。

　　厄舍一見我走進去，便從他方才一直平躺着的沙發上站起身，生氣勃勃地熱情招呼我，起初我認為，這熱情有點真誠過度——帶着厭世者勉強的笑容。可我看了看他的臉，確信他是完全真誠的。我們坐了下來，他沉默着，我半是同情半是畏懼地凝視着他。可以肯定，在這樣短的時間中，沒有一個人的變化會像羅德里克·厄舍那樣令人如此害怕！我很難讓自己承認眼前這蒼白的男人就是我的童年夥伴。不過他的面部特徵一直都這麼特別：臉色慘白，眼睛又大又亮，無比清澈，嘴唇有些削薄，沒甚麼血色，曲線卻異常美麗，他的鼻子有着精致的希伯來風格，可是鼻孔卻比通常的要寬大得多；他的下巴造型優美，但不夠凸顯，缺乏精神活力；遊絲般的頭髮異常柔軟纖細——這些特徵，加上太陽穴上方部位的過分開闊，使他的整體面容顯得令人難忘。此時，這些主要特點以及它們的慣有表情雖然只是更顯著了些，可是它們帶來的變化卻如此巨大，讓我有點認不清眼前這人到底是誰了。尤其是他皮膚的那種可怕的慘白，以及眼睛中奇特的光澤讓我驚訝，甚至產生了畏懼心理。那綢緞般的頭髮也被毫不在意地蓄長了，而且，當這些輕柔纖細的頭髮飄拂着而不是垂在臉龐時，我怎麼也無法將他奇異的表情與任何常人聯繫在一起。

朋友舉動的不連貫性立刻令我感到吃驚 —— 那是一種不協調；我很快就發現，這種不協調是因為他竭力而徒勞地掙扎着要克服習慣性的痙攣 —— 那是過度的精神緊張。事實上，我對這特點還是有些準備的，不僅是因為他的信，還由於我對他少年時期的某些特性的回憶，以及從他獨特的身體形態和脾氣中得出的推論。他的舉止時而活潑時而沉鬱，他的聲音時而緊張和優柔寡斷 (這時他的元氣似乎暫時凝止了)，時而簡潔有力 —— 那種乾脆、有分量、從容而低沉的發音 —— 那種沉重、自控，完美協調的喉音，這狀態也許在神迷的醉漢或不可治癒的鴉片吸食者最強烈的興奮中才能聽到。

就這樣，他談及了邀我造訪的目的，他想見到我的熱切渴望，以及他期待我能給予的撫慰。他非常詳盡地闡述他所感受到的自己疾病的特點。據他說，這是一種與生俱來的、家族遺傳的不幸，他對治療已經感到絕望，但他很快又補充說，這只不過是一種肯定會很快停止的神經疾病。它體現在諸多異樣的感覺中。他的詳細描述中，有一些令我產生興趣，也使我困惑；儘管，這也許是他敍述所用的術語和總體講述風格在起作用。他深受一種病態的感官敏銳的折磨；他只能吃最淡而無味的食品；只能穿某種質地的服裝；花卉的香味令他壓抑；他的眼睛甚至在很微弱的光線下都感到難受；而且，只有某些特殊的聲音以及弦樂器的樂音才不讓他產生恐懼。

我發現他深陷在一種莫名的恐懼中。"我會衰竭下去的，"他說，"我准會在這樣可悲的愚蠢中衰竭下去。就這樣，就這樣死去，不會有別的死法。我害怕將來的事，不是怕事件本身，而是怕它們的結局。一想到所有這些會波及我不勝負荷的靈魂的事，哪怕是最微不足道的，我就渾身發抖。實際上，我不厭惡危險，除了危險帶來的絕對效果——驚慌。在身心疲憊的可憐狀態下，我感到這種時刻遲早會來臨，到那時，在與那殘酷的幽靈——恐懼的搏鬥中，我一定會同時失去生命和理智。"

另外，我還不時地從他支離破碎、模棱兩可的暗示中，發現他精神狀態上另一個怪異的特點。他被某種迷信的感覺束縛着，這感覺與他的住所有關，而在此居住了那麼多年，他卻從未設法去深入了解。由於他談及迷信的影響力時表達得晦澀朦朧，我無法重述；那純粹是他祖屋的形式與內涵中的奇異性所造成的一種影響。他說，由於長期受此折磨，他的精神承受着一種負擔——那是灰暗的牆垣和塔樓，以及映照着它們的幽晦水潭，最終給他的精神生活帶來的影響。

然而，儘管不無猶豫，他還是承認，在這種奇特的、折磨着他的陰鬱中，大部分可以被追溯到一個更自然和明顯得多的本源，那就是他妹妹嚴重而持久的頑疾。事實上，這根子就在於，他心愛的妹妹顯然已瀕臨死亡。妹妹是他多年來唯一的生活伴侶，也是他在世上的唯一親人。"她一死，"他帶着令人難忘的苦澀說道，"我（我，這個絕望而脆弱之人）就成為古老的厄舍家族遺留在人世的最後子嗣。"他說這話時，瑪德琳小姐（因為人們都這麼稱呼她）正從屋子那一頭走過，即刻消失了，而且她沒有注意到我的存在。我對她懷有一種驚懼交加的情緒。我的目光追隨着她隱退的腳步，一種恍惚的感覺壓抑着我。最終，一扇門在她身後關閉，我的視線本能而熱切地在她兄長的臉上探詢着。

可是他把頭埋在手裏，我只能感到，有一種異乎尋常的蒼白在他瘦削的手指上蔓延，指縫間滴着感傷的眼淚。

瑪德琳小姐的病長期以來一直令醫生們困頓無措。一種久積的冷漠，身體的日益衰竭以及雖短暫卻頻繁的強直性昏厥，都是她這疾病的特殊症狀。迄今為止，她一直頑強地支撐着與疾病抗爭，不使自己最終纏綿病榻，但是，在我抵達厄舍屋當天傍晚，她終於屈從了死神的淫威（那晚她兄長用難以言表的痛苦聲音告訴了我）。於是我意識到，我對她的那一瞥或許就成了最後一瞥——就是說，我將再也見不到活着的這位小姐了。

隨後幾天，無論是厄舍先生還是我，都沒再提及她的名字。在這期間，我忙於努力緩解朋友的憂鬱。我們一同作畫、閱讀，或者我恍如幻夢般地傾聽他激動而即興地彈撥着如泣如訴的六弦琴。就這樣，因為彼此間越來越親密，我便得以全面洞悉他的心靈深處，我也越痛苦地感覺，自己試圖鼓舞他精神的所有努力是徒勞的。他的沉鬱好比一種與生俱來的本性，像一道恒久的憂鬱之光，籠罩在精神和物質宇宙中所有的物體上。

在我朋友那變幻不定的構思中，有一個不那麼抽象的或許可以勉強用語言表示出來。那是一幅小小的圖畫，畫面上是一條無限悠長的長方形地窖或隧道，裏面的牆壁低矮、光滑、潔白，並且沒有中斷或其他裝飾物。畫面的某些補充部分表明，這洞穴在地表底下很深的地方。在它巨大的範圍中，任何部位都看不到出口，也看不到火炬或其他人為的光源；可是大量強烈的光束在其中到處晃動着，使整個空間沉浸在一片可怕而不適當的輝煌中。

我剛才提到過厄舍那病態的聽覺神經，它使患者無法忍受一切音樂，除了弦樂器的某些聲音之外。也許，因為他僅局限於彈奏六弦琴，便很大程度上使他的演奏帶有奇異古怪的特點，不過他即興曲中充滿激情卻不能歸結於這個原因。他那些幻想曲的曲調和歌詞裏（因為他常常邊彈邊即興演唱）的激情肯定是、也一定是情感高度匯聚和集中的效果，我在前面暗示過，這只有在他不自然的興奮到達頂峯的特殊時刻才看得到。我很容易地記住了其中一首狂想曲的歌詞。在他演唱它時，我對這歌詞印象極為深刻，或許是因為在歌詞意義的深處，或在它神祕的意蘊中，我覺得自己第一次察覺到，厄舍已經完全意識到他那玄虛的理性正搖搖欲墜。這首詩題名為《幽靈出沒的宮殿》，文字大致如下，儘管或許不太準確：

在山谷幽壑的最綠處，

善良天使曾住在

一座美好而高貴的宮殿 ——

輝煌燦爛的宮殿 —— 巍然屹立。

在思想君王的領地中 ——

它巍然佇立！

看見過如此精美的建築。

金光燦燦的旗幟

在宮殿頂上飄拂；

（這 —— 這一切 —— 都已是悠遠的往昔歲月）

每一絲溫柔的空氣都徜徉在

那甜美的日子裏，

沿着宮殿的粉牆白壁，

一抹芬芳插翅而飛。

這快樂山谷的漫遊者

透過兩扇明亮的窗戶，

望見精靈們翩然起舞

隨着古琴悦揚的旋律；

御座上端坐着

（王族貴冑！）

王國的國君，周身的榮耀與堂皇，

與他的身份完全相當。

珠光寶氣的璀璨

裝飾着美麗宮殿大門，

穿門而入的是翩然，翩然

且恒久閃爍的

一隊回音仙女，她們的神聖職責

只是歌唱，

用無與倫比的優美嗓音，

頌揚國王的聰明智慧。

可是邪惡穿着憂傷的衣袍，

侵襲了王座至高的尊貴；

（啊，讓我們悲慟，因為明天不再

讓他恩蒙黎明，一片荒涼！）

他的宮邸，那輝煌的

燦爛和昌盛

僅成了一則依稀的故事

被亙古的歲月埋葬。

山谷中的遊歷者，

透過通紅的窗戶望見

許多鬼魅般遊移的影子

伴隨着不和諧的樂曲；

這時，彷彿洶湧可怖的河流

穿透了黯然的門扉，

那駭人的一羣不斷地沖過，

大笑着——但笑容不再。

那天夜晚，他突然告訴我瑪德琳小姐過世了，並說他打算將她的屍體存放兩週（在屍體最終下葬前），安置於宅邸主牆內眾多地窖中的一間，這時，我禁不住想起那本書中所述的瘋狂儀式，以及它對這位疑病患者可能產生的影響。然而，這古怪程序中的世俗因素是我感到不能隨意質疑的原因之一。兄長執意要執行他的決定（他就是這麼對我說的），是考慮到死者疾病的怪異特徵，考慮到她的醫生會有急切而冒昧的探訪，還考慮到家族墓地在荒郊野外、無遮無蔽之處。我不否認，我想起剛到厄舍屋時在樓梯上看到的那人不祥的臉色，便根本不想反對他採取那個我認為至多不過是一種既無害也不違常理的預防措施了。

在厄舍的請求下，我親自幫他安排臨時的停屍場地。屍體已經被置於棺材內，我們兩人單獨把棺材抬到了暫時歇息地。停放屍體的地窖（它很久沒開啟過，空氣令人窒息，我們的一個火把差一點熄滅了，這使我們幾乎沒法觀察環境）狹小、潮濕，並且根本無法讓光線透進來。它位於我臥房正下方地下深處。很顯然，它只在很久遠的封建時代才被使用過，最糟糕的是用作城堡主樓的監獄，後來被用作儲藏火藥或是其他一些易燃易爆物質。它的部分地板，以及我們抵達那裏要走過的長拱道的整個內部都被細緻地包上了銅。門是塊厚重的鐵板，也採取了類似的保護措施。當它依着門鉸鏈而移動時，因巨大的重量而發出異常尖銳刺耳的聲音。

我們在恐懼之地把棺材放到支架上時，稍稍移動了一下這哀傷的重負上尚未釘住的蓋子，看了看棺材中人的遺容。我第一次注意到兄妹之間相像得驚人。厄舍也許察覺了我的想法，咕噥着解釋了幾句，從中我了解到，死者和他是孿生兄妹，而且他們之間一直存在着交感，那共同的感受有着一種幾乎無法被人理解的本質。不過，我們的目光在死者身上沒有停留太久——因為我們心懷畏懼。使這個姑娘正當青春就香消玉殞的疾病，就像所有強直性昏厥症一樣，在她胸口和臉部徒然地留下一片微弱的紅暈，嘴角上那絲令人懷疑、揮之不去的微笑，在死亡中顯得尤為可怕。我們扣上棺蓋，釘上釘子，然後關閉鐵門，步履蹣跚地走了出來，走回大屋樓上同樣陰鬱的房間。

那之後，又過去了幾個痛苦悲哀的日子，我朋友的精神錯亂情況發生了明顯變化。他正常的舉動已經消失。他忽視或是忘卻了日常生活中的消遣，從一個房間徘徊到另一個房間，腳步急促、淩亂、迷惘。如果可以這麼說的話，他慘白的臉色呈現出更令人恐怖的色調——但是他眼中的亮澤消退了。曾經時而沙啞

462

的聲音也匿跡了；取而代之的是發抖的顫音，彷彿透着極端的恐懼。有時候，我真覺得他那不肯停歇的痛苦內心裏藏着某種沉重的祕密，為了要透露這祕密，他竭力想鼓起必需的勇氣。有時，我又被迫把所有一切歸結為純粹的、令人費解的狂顛的反覆無常，因為我看到他長久地盯着虛空，極度地專注，似乎在傾聽某個想像中的聲音。無怪乎他的狀態是那麼駭人——也那麼感染着我。我覺得，他那古怪卻令人難忘的迷信念頭正緩慢地、難以預料地向我襲來。

尤其是在把瑪德琳小姐放入地窖後的第七或第八天的深夜，我上牀就寢，便充分體會到他這種感情的強烈性。時間一點一點流逝——我絲毫沒有睡意。我竭力想用理智驅逐一直籠罩着自己的緊張情緒，並努力相信，所有的緊張感受，大多數是受了房間裏陰暗家具的影響——是因為黑色襤褸的帷幕，它們被正在迫近的暴風雨擾動着，一陣陣地在牆上來回搖擺，晃晃悠悠地把牀上的東西吹得沙沙作響，可任憑我怎麼努力都制止不了。一陣不可抑制的顫抖逐漸蔓延我的全身；最後，我的心頭盤旋着一種完全沒來由的驚慌。我喘息着，掙扎着，想擺脫這感覺，我從枕頭上欠起身子，急切地凝視着房間的黑暗深處，傾聽着——我不知自己為何這麼做，只知道這是一種身體被激發起的本能反應——我聽到某種低沉、模糊的聲音，它們在暴風雨的間歇中傳來，聲音間隔很長，而且我不知它們來自何方。我被一種強烈的恐懼震懾着，這恐懼莫名其妙，又難以忍受。我匆匆穿上衣服（因為我感覺自己整夜都睡不着了），在房間裏來來回回地疾走着，努力使自己從這糟糕的情形中振作起來。

如此這番地，我還沒走上幾個回合，就注意到隔壁樓梯上有輕輕的腳步聲。我馬上就辨別出這是厄舍的腳步。即刻，他就輕輕地叩響了我的門，然後提着一盞燈走了進來。他的面色像平常一樣慘白——但是他眼裏還帶着一種瘋狂的熱切——舉動中有一種明顯被克制着的歇斯底里。他的樣子令我吃驚——但當時我最不堪忍受的是獨守長夜的寂寞，我甚至樂意接受他這樣子，把這當成一種解救。

　　"難道你還沒看見嗎？"在他沉默地向四周凝望了片刻後，他突然説話了，"你還沒看見嗎？——可是，等一等！你會看見的。"他邊説邊小心地掩住那盞燈，快步走到其中一扇窗子邊，猛地推開窗，窗外正起着暴風雨。

　　奪窗而入的那陣猛烈的狂風幾乎將我們連根拔起。這確實是一個狂風與凄美交加、恐懼與美麗並存的夜晚。旋風顯然是在我們附近聚集着能量，因為風向出現了頻繁而強烈的偏移；極度凝聚的雲朵（它們壓得非常低，幾乎要碰到房屋的塔樓）並沒有阻止我們感受這栩栩如生的速度，從各個方向飛速而來的風，並沒有消失在遠方，而是相互撞擊在一起。我是説，即使雲層極度密集，也不妨礙我們感受到這一切——只是我們沒瞧見月亮星星，也沒有閃電劃過。但是，那巨大而騷動的氣團下方的表面，就像所有在我們身邊的地面物體一樣，正閃爍着一種異常的光，它是光線微弱而清晰可見的氣態發散物，它蔓延着，籠罩了整座宅邸。

　　"你不能——不該看這個！"我邊戰慄着對厄舍説，邊推搡着將他從窗口拉回一張椅子上。"這些讓你迷惑的東西不過是普通的閃電——或者是水潭的沼氣才造成那麼可怕的景象。我們把窗

關了吧 —— 這空氣會凍着你，對你身體有害。這裏有一本你喜歡的傳奇故事，我來讀，你來聽 —— 這樣我們就能一起熬過這個可怕的夜晚了。"

我拿起來的那本古書是蘭斯洛特・坎甯爵士的《瘋狂的約會》，我稱它為厄舍的所愛是出於無奈的揶揄，並非認真；因為事實上，此書粗俗乏味，十分冗長，很少有東西能激發起我那具有高雅而神聖念頭的朋友之興趣。然而，它是當時唯一能伸手可及的書；於是我懷着朦朧的希望，希望朋友那被煽起來的興奮，恰好可以在我朗讀的那些極端愚蠢的東西 (因為精神錯亂過程中充滿了與此類似的異態) 中得以緩解。如果我真的可以憑着他在傾聽 —— 或表面在聽 —— 這故事時那種狂野而過度的快活情緒來下判斷的話，我也許真能慶幸自己這主意奏效了。

我讀到了故事中最為人熟知的那部分，講到主人公埃塞爾雷德尋求和平地進入隱士的住地，但沒有成功，便要強闖進去。我記得那敍述的文字是這樣寫的：

"於是，生性勇猛的埃塞爾雷德憑着自己的強力，並且在酒力的作用下，再也無法等待和那一貫固執陰險的隱士談判。可是，埃塞爾雷德感覺雨水滴落在肩膀上，擔心暴風雨將至，便掄起釘頭錘一陣重擊，很快就在門上砸出一個窟窿，他伸進佩戴着臂鎧的手使勁地拉着，頓時將那門撕裂、扯斷了，幹木板空洞的響聲令人心驚膽戰，久久地回蕩在森林裏。"

剛念完最後一句話，我感到一陣驚慌，停頓了一會；因為我感覺到 (儘管我隨即推斷這是我興奮的幻想在欺騙自己) —— 我感覺到，從房屋遠處傳來了清晰的回聲，這也許與蘭斯洛特・坎甯爵士所詳細描述的破碎和撕裂的聲音幾乎完全相似（只是它顯然更沉悶而單調些）。毋庸置疑，是聲音的巧合引起了我的注意，因為窗戶框架的唭嗒聲，以及狂風不斷增強的混雜聲，本身並不能引起我的興趣，也不至於驚擾我。我繼續讀下去：

"勇士埃塞爾雷德走進大門，但並沒有發現那個陰險隱士的蹤影，他感到又氣又驚，只見一條遍體鱗片、吐着火舌的巨龍在白銀鋪地的黃金大殿前守衛着，牆上掛着一個閃閃發光的黃銅盾，上面鑴着如下銘文——

進入此殿，便為主人；

殺了火龍，即贏此盾。

埃塞爾雷德舉起釘頭錘，向龍頭擊去，巨龍墜落在他面前，停止了毒烈的呼吸，它發出一聲尖利的慘叫，極其可怕刺耳，令人戰慄，埃塞爾雷德不得不用手捂住了耳朵，想回避這可惡的、前所未聞的叫聲。"

我又一次驟然停住了，感到極度的驚訝——因為，在那一瞬間，我毫無疑問地確實聽到了（儘管我說不出它是從哪個方向來的）一個低沉而且顯然是遙遠的、淒厲的、拖長的並且最為異常的尖叫或刺耳的聲音——恰好與我根據書中描寫所想像出來的那條龍的異樣的慘叫相吻合。

我被那不尋常的巧合壓抑着，被無數矛盾衝突的感受壓抑着，滿心的驚訝和極度恐慌，可我依然保持足夠的鎮定，以免被朋友看出來，刺激他那過敏的神經。我沒法確定他是否注意到了那令人困惑的聲音；雖然能肯定的是，在剛才幾分鐘裏，他的舉止發生了奇怪的變化。他本來位於我正前方，可現在已慢慢地轉開椅子，把臉正對着房間的大門。在這樣的情況下，我雖然能看見他嘴唇在顫抖，彷彿正在無聲地呢喃，可是卻看不見他的整個面部。他的頭垂在胸前——但是我知道他沒有睡着，我從他圓睜着的呆滯雙眼的側面輪廓中得以如此判斷。他身體的動作也證實了這一點——因為他輕輕地、迅速地、不停地左右搖擺着。我很快地注意到了這一切，並繼續朗讀蘭斯洛特爵士的作品，故事是這樣繼續的：

"此刻，勇士從那條龍可怕的慘叫中回過神來，想到了那面黃銅製的盾，想到要驅散那上面的妖術，他把那畜生的屍體移開，無畏地踏過白銀地板，走向懸掛盾牌的那面牆壁。但是沒等他走到那裏，那面盾牌就跌落到他腳邊的白銀地板上，發出一聲可怕而清脆的巨聲。"

這幾個字剛從我嘴裏讀出來，我便感到一陣清晰、空洞、金屬的、響亮的然而又顯然是沉悶的迴響——彷彿一面黃銅盾真的重重地落到了銀地板上。我驚慌失措地跳起來；但是厄舍那有節奏的搖擺絲毫沒受干擾。我沖到他坐着的椅子旁。他眼睛緊盯着前方，整個臉部變得像石頭般僵硬。可是，當我把手放在他肩膀上時，他渾身猛烈地戰慄着，雙唇顫抖着一絲慘淡的微笑。我發現他在低聲地、急促地、喋喋不休地咕噥着，好像沒有意識到我的存在。我彎下身子靠近他，終於聽到了他那可怕的話語。

他的聲音彷彿有着一種超人的力量，帶來了符咒的效力，他指向的那道又大又沉的黑檀木房門，兩扇古老的門扉竟慢慢開啟。這是風造成的——但是，門外確實站着高挑而覆蓋着裹屍布的厄舍家的瑪德琳小姐。她白色的袍子上面血跡斑斑，憔悴的身軀明顯地帶着痛苦掙扎的痕跡。有那麼一會，她一直顫抖着，在門檻上來回搖晃着——然後，她發出低沉的呻吟，沉重地跌在她哥哥身上，在臨死前強烈的、最後的痛苦中，將哥哥壓倒在地板上，哥哥立刻也變成了一具死屍，成了自己預言過的恐怖的犧牲品。

我驚慌地逃出了這間屋子，逃離了這座宅子。穿過那古老的石道時，外面依然狂風不已。突然，一道強光射在道路上，我回頭想看一下這怪異的光束從何而來；因為我身後只有那座巨大的房子和它的陰影。光亮來自那輪圓圓的、正在落下的、血紅的月亮，它那時正明豔地透射過那曾經幾乎是無法辨清的裂縫，我在前面提到過的那條從房頂蜿蜒曲折地延伸到屋腳的裂縫。我凝望着，裂縫迅速地擴展開來——一陣強烈的旋風吹過——月亮的整個球體立刻湧現在我眼前——那堵高牆轟然倒塌，我眼前一片暈眩——一陣長長的喧囂聲傳來，就像萬頃波濤洶湧而來——我腳下那深邃而陰潮的水潭黯然地匯攏，無聲無息，淹沒了"厄舍屋"的殘垣碎瓦。

（張瓊譯）

7
紅死病假面

"**红**死病"摧殘這個國家已經很長時間了，人們從來沒遇見過如此致命而可怕的瘟疫。它的主要體現和標誌就是鮮血——那殷紅、恐怖的鮮血。患者會有尖銳的疼痛和驟然的暈眩，然後毛孔大量出血，並逐漸糜爛。患者身體上，尤其是臉部的那些猩紅血跡，就是讓病人隔離於親友的幫助和安慰的瘟疫符咒。疾病的整個發作、惡化以及死亡過程，只要半小時。

但是普洛斯彼羅親王卻是快樂、無畏和睿智的。當領地人口減至一半時，他從宮廷的騎士淑女中召集了一千名健壯而無憂無慮的朋友到自己身邊，和他們一同隱居到他的一個城堡形宅院中。那是一個寬敞雄偉的建築，很符合親王個人那古怪而威嚴的品位。一道堅實巍峨的牆壁將宅院包圍，牆上有幾扇鐵門。朝臣們進入時，帶了熔爐和沉重的鐵錘，進宅院後就焊上了門閂。他們決定，萬一內部有人發生突然的絕望或是瘋狂衝動，也不讓他們有任何途徑出入此地。宅院裏供給充足。在這樣的防範措施中，朝臣們應該能抵抗疾病的傳染。這種時刻，外面的世界就只能聽之任之，再去為之憂傷或深思是愚蠢的。親王提供了所有的享樂設施，有小丑、即興表演者、芭蕾舞蹈演員、樂師、美女以及葡萄酒。宅院裏擁有所有這一切，包括安全，而宅院外面則是"紅死病"。

在隱居的第五或第六個月快結束時，外面的瘟疫發展到了最倡狂的時候，普洛斯彼羅親王舉辦了一個盛況空前的假面舞會，以款待隨他而去的那一千位朋友。

假面舞會的場面很是奢華。但是先讓我描述一下其中的各個房間。那裏有七個房間——是堂皇的套間。在許多宮殿中，這樣的套房呈現出修長筆直的景象，摺疊門可以兩面滑動，一直貼到牆面，因此整體看來幾乎一覽無餘。然而，這裏的套間就特色迥異了；其間可以看出公爵對奇異古怪的鍾情。房間的排列非常不規則，因此一眼只能看到一個房間。房間每二十或三十碼就有一個急轉彎，而每一轉都給人一種新的印象。在左右兩邊牆壁的中央，是一個高而狹窄的哥特式窗戶，望出去是封閉的走廊，走廊在套房中蜿蜒延伸着。這些窗戶上安裝着彩色玻璃，玻璃的顏色隨着它開啟的那個房間中裝飾的主色調而發生相應的變化。例如，在東端的房間裏懸掛飾物都是藍色的——它的窗玻璃也是鮮明的藍色調。第二個房間的裝飾和掛毯是紫色的，那裏的窗格玻璃也是紫色的。第三個房間通體為綠，窗戶亦如此。第四個房間的裝飾和光線設計則是橘紅色的——第五間是白色調——第六間呈紫羅蘭色。第七間屋子被緊緊地包裹在黑天鵝絨帷幔中，帷幔自天花板和牆面垂下，層層疊疊地打着褶皺，垂落在同一質地和色調的地毯上。但是，惟有此間屋子，窗戶的顏色沒有與裝飾一致。窗玻璃是深紅色的——是殷紅的鮮血顏色。在七個房間裏，四處散佈或從屋頂垂吊着大量金色裝飾，但都沒有燈或枝狀燭台，在這組房間中也沒有發出任何的燈光或燭光。但是在連接這組房間的走廊上，在每扇窗的對面，立着一個沉重的三腳架，上面擺放着火盆，火光透射進彩色玻璃，把房間照得耀眼閃亮，就這樣，一種豔麗、奇異、多姿多彩的景象產生了。但是在西面，或者説是那間黑色的房間裏，那流瀉在帷幕上的火光穿過了血紅的窗玻璃，顯得極其恐怖。人們進入房間時，他們的面容在光的映照下顯得十分狂野。因此，很少有人能有足夠的勇氣涉足其間。

也就是在這間屋子裏，正對着西面牆壁，立着一口巨大的黑檀木製成的鐘。鐘擺來回擺動着，發出乏味、沉重、單調的叮噹聲；當分針在鐘面上走過一圈時，鐘就敲響了整點的報時，於是從黃銅製成的鐘腔裏發出了一種清晰、響亮、深沉和極富音樂性的聲音，但是這音調及重音是如此特殊，在每一個整點，樂隊的樂師就會禁不住將他們的表演停止片刻，傾聽着鐘聲；就這樣，跳華爾茲的人也必然會停止舞蹈，整個歡快的羣體會出現短暫的驚惶；而且，當鐘聲仍在繼續時，最輕佻的人會變得臉色蒼白，較為年長和穩重的人會將他們的手撫過前額，彷彿處於困惑的幻想或沉思中。但是鐘聲徹底停止後，輕快的笑聲立刻就蔓延了整個人羣；樂師們相互望瞭望，微笑着，似乎在笑自己的緊張和愚蠢，並且低聲地互相發誓説下一次鐘響不會再有類似的情緒了；然後，過了六十分鐘後（期間有三千六百秒鐘飛逝而過），又一次敲鐘開始，又會發生與前面同樣的驚惶、顫抖和沉思。

可是，儘管有這樣一些事發生，這還是一次歡快而盛大的狂歡。公爵的品位獨特，他對色彩和視聽效果頗具慧眼。他輕視純粹時髦的裝飾風格，在設計上非常大膽和熱烈，而且在構思上富有奔放華麗的光彩。有一些人可能會覺得他很瘋狂，他的追隨者並不這麼認為。因此，很有必要去聽、去看、去接觸他，然後大家才會確信他並不瘋狂。

在這次盛大的慶典中，他指導設計了七個房間中大部分的可移動裝飾；正是他個人的設計風格才使戴假面的人獨具特色。他們肯定很怪異。舞會上到處是眩目、閃爍的光芒，充滿了刺激和幻影——很多都曾在《愛爾那尼》一劇中見到過。那裏還有配着不相稱的肢體和道具的古怪人物。

那裏還有一些諸如瘋子般穿戴風格的瘋狂裝飾，有許多美麗、嬉鬧、怪異的服飾，有些衣服很可怕，很能激發起人的厭惡感。事實上，在七個房間裏往來穿行的是各種各樣的夢。而且，這些夢四處糾結扭動着，承載着房間裏的色調，使樂隊瘋狂的音樂彷彿隨着他們的腳步聲做出了回應。可是不久，站在天鵝絨廳房中的黑檀木鐘敲響了。於是，有那麼片刻，除了那鐘聲，一切都沉靜下來，一片寂靜無聲。那些夢在佇立中是僵直冰冷的。但是，鐘聲消逝了——它們只僵持了一瞬間——接着，在它們離去時，身後飄蕩着一聲輕快、柔和的笑。於是，音樂再次奏響，夢又活了，更加快樂地來回扭曲着，三腳架處的光焰流溢過窗玻璃，產生出絢爛多彩的色調，如影隨形般被這些夢牽引着。但是，七個房間中最西面的那間屋子裏，沒有戴假面者敢於逗留；因為正夜色闌珊，透過血紅的窗玻璃，流淌着更顯殷紅的光；而且，那黝黑的帷幕也令人驚駭；人一踏上那裏的黑色地毯，臨近的那口黑檀木鐘那裏就傳來一聲壓抑的隆隆聲，相比那些在更遠處的其他房間裏沉湎於尋樂的人來說，進入此房間的人會感到那聲音聽來更為莊嚴肅穆。

但是其他房間裏已經人滿為患了，人們的心在狂烈而富有活力地搏動着。狂歡的熱潮逐浪推升，直到最後午夜的鐘聲敲響。然後，正如我所說的，音樂停歇了；華爾茲舞蹈者的旋轉緩和下來；一切都像前次一樣進入了令人不安的平息中。不過這一次鐘聲敲了十二下。於是，或許這次有更多的思想潛入進來，那些狂歡的人們陷入的沉思也更長久。也許正因為如此，直到最後一聲鐘響的回聲完全寂靜下來，很多人才有空注意到一個先前未被任何人注意的戴假面具的人。於是，關於這個新來的戴假面的人的傳聞在低聲耳語中散佈開了，最後整個人羣發出了一陣嗡嗡聲，或者說是咕噥聲，它充滿了不快和驚訝 —— 接着，最終這聲音透出了恐慌、驚懼以及憎惡。

從我前面描述的那羣幻象中，也許大家能推想出，那些尋常的外形激發不出如此的騷動。事實上，那晚的假面舞會對參加者幾乎沒作任何限制，但那個假面人做得有些過頭了 [48]，他逾越了親王哪怕是相當寬泛的禮儀規範。就是那些最不拘小節的鹵莽人士，在強烈的情緒波動下，心靈都會感到震動。

甚至對那些徹底迷失自我，認為生與死不過是一樣的玩笑之人，都有一些玩笑是開不得的。實際上，當時整個人羣都似乎強烈地感受到，在那個陌生人的裝扮和舉止中，沒有絲毫的才智和禮節。那人的體形高大、消瘦，從頭到腳籠罩在裹屍布中。他那遮掩面容的假面做得和僵屍的臉部惟妙惟肖，就是最細緻的觀察都肯定很難找出破綻。可是，即使周圍那些瘋狂的尋歡作樂之人對此並不贊同，他們或許還能忍受一下。不過，那人竟過分到扮演紅死病。他的罩袍上浸染着鮮血 —— 還有他寬闊的額頭，以及臉部的所有器官，都佈滿了可怕的殷紅色。

普洛斯彼羅親王的目光落到這個幽靈般的形象上（那人緩慢而莊嚴地移動着，彷彿要全身心地投入這個角色，並在跳舞的人羣中昂首闊步地來回走着），他渾身震顫，出於驚恐或是厭惡，他最初的表現是強烈的痙攣；但是接下來，他的額頭就憤怒得發紅了。

"誰膽敢，" —— 他向站在身旁的朝臣們嘶啞地質問着 —— "誰膽敢開這樣褻瀆神明的玩笑？把他抓起來，剝了他的面具 —— 那樣我們就知道誰該在日出時在城牆上被絞死！"

普洛斯彼羅親王是在東邊或者説是藍色的房間裏説這番話的，他的聲音在七個房間裏響亮而清晰地迴盪着，因為親王是豪放而粗獷之人，在他揮手之際，音樂聲戛然而止。

那時，親王站在藍屋裏，身旁有一羣臉色蒼白的朝臣。他剛開口講話時，人羣向那入侵之徒簇擁過來，發出一陣輕微的騷動聲，那人剛才還近在咫尺，即刻，他就從容而堂皇地靠近了正在説話之人。但是，人羣中對那人的瘋狂猜測中帶有某種莫名的敬畏，使全場頗受觸動，誰都沒有伸手去抓他。因此，他不受阻撓地走到親王身旁一碼距離的範圍，然後，彷彿一陣衝動，壯觀的人羣都從各個房間的中央縮回到牆壁旁，那人繼續走着，邁着那種從一開始就使他顯得與眾不同的莊嚴而慎重的步伐，從那藍色屋子走到紫色屋子 —— 從紫色到綠色 —— 從綠色到橘色 —— 又到了白色屋子 —— 甚至快要到達紫羅蘭色的房間。然而這時候，普洛斯彼羅親王為自己片刻的懦弱而感到發瘋般的憤怒和恥辱，他急忙地衝過六個房間，由於異常的懼怕鎮住了全場，沒有人跟隨親王。他抽出了匕首，將它高舉着，猛烈而急速地向那正在離去的人衝了上去，和他只有三四尺的距離，而後者已經到達了最頂端的天鵝絨房間，他猛一回頭，迎着那個追逐而來的人。然後，那裏傳出了一聲淒厲的喊叫 —— 那把匕首墜落在黑色地毯上，發出了若隱若現的幽光。即刻，死去的普洛斯彼羅親王俯臥在地毯上。接着，尋歡者們瘋狂而絕望的勇氣被煽動起來，狂歡的人流猛地湧進了那間黑色房間，他們抓住了那個假面人，他高大的身體屹立在黑檀木鐘的陰影中，一動不動。可是人們瞠目結舌地發現，他們粗暴而蠻橫地觸摸着的那裏屍布和僵屍般的面具中，沒有任何有形的實體。

這時，大家才確認了紅死病的到場。他在夜晚像竊賊般地潛入，使那些狂歡者在他們尋歡作樂之際，在鮮血浸染的廳堂中，一一墜地，並在倒下時頹然死去。而且，隨着最後那個放浪者生命的終結，那口黑檀木鐘也壽終正寢，那個三腳架的火焰亦隨之熄滅。黑暗，腐朽和紅死病以其無邊無涯的浩大聲勢統佔了一切。

（張瓊譯）

8

過早埋葬

有些題材絕對吸引人，但又太過恐怖，無法寫成正規的小說。純粹的浪漫主義作家必須回避這樣的題材，否則就會冒犯眾人，令人厭惡。只有當嚴格和莊重的真實允許我們這麼做時，使用這些題材才是妥當的。例如，我們因為強渡別列茨那河 [49]、里斯本大地震、倫敦瘟疫、聖巴托洛繆大屠殺，或是加爾各答土牢裏一百二十三名犯人的窒息死亡的敍述中那極其強烈的"令人愉悦的痛苦"而戰慄。但這些敍述中，正是事實 —— 是現實 —— 是歷史使人觸目驚心。如果它們是杜撰的事件，那我們只會深惡痛絕。

我剛才提到了歷史記載的幾件非常著名而令人畏懼的災難，但是在這些事件中，災難的規模給人留下的強烈印象並不亞於災難的性質。我無須提醒讀者，在漫長而枯燥的人類災難記錄中，我可以挑選許多比這些大規模災難更加具有本質痛苦的個人事例。那真實的悲慘，事實上 —— 那極度的悲哀 —— 是獨特的，而不是廣泛的，那可怕而極端的痛苦是由個體的而非羣體的人來承受 —— 為此，讓我們感謝上帝的仁慈。

毫無疑問，對於許多單純的凡人而言，生生活埋是那些極端中最恐怖的。凡是愛思考的人幾乎都不會否認，活埋是經常、而且很頻繁發生的事。那分隔了生與死的界線最多是幽暗而模糊的，誰能說從哪裏完結，又從哪裏開始呢？我們知道，在一些疾病中，表面的生命力會完全停止，然而，更確切地說，那些停止只是暫停。它們只是在那令人無法理解的身體機構中短暫停滯。過了某一個階段，某種無形的神祕元素又開始運轉起神奇的小齒輪和具有魔力的輪子。那根銀線並未永遠鬆弛，那隻金碗也沒有徹底破碎。可同時，靈魂去哪裏了呢？

　　然而，除了這些必然的結論外，從先驗的角度看，某種原因一定會導致某種結果 —— 即眾所周知的這類機能暫停的病例，自然一定會時常導致過早埋葬現象 —— 除了這一點，我們有直接的醫療證據和普通實例來證實，許多這樣的埋葬的確發生過。有必要的話，我馬上就能找出一百個真實例子。其中有一例非常值得注意，這件事或許對我的一些讀者來說歷歷在目，它發生在不久以前，事發地點在附近的巴爾的摩市，該事件引起了令人痛苦的、強烈的、而且是廣泛的震驚。一位非常令人尊重的市民 —— 他是著名的律師，也是國會議員 —— 他的妻子突然患上一種急性的怪病，這病症使醫生們徹底地束手無策。她經歷了巨大的痛苦後死了，或者被認為是死了。事實上，沒有人對此表示懷疑，也沒有任何理由懷疑她實際上並沒有死亡。她表現出死亡的一切正常跡象。臉部呈現出通常的萎縮而凹陷的輪廓，嘴唇也是常有的大理石般的蒼白，眼睛毫無光澤，身體冰涼，脈搏也停止了跳動。過了三天，屍體還沒有被埋葬。在這三天裏，屍體變得石頭般僵硬。總之，人們催促要馬上辦葬禮，因為大家認為屍體很快就要腐爛了。

　　這位女士就停放在她家族的墓穴，此後三年裏沒人打開過。後來，要開啟墓穴放一個石棺進去。但是，哎呀！這位丈夫將面臨着怎樣的恐怖啊！他要親自打開那扇門！當大門向外轉開時，一樣白色而可怕的東西嗒嗒響着掉在他懷裏。那是他妻子的殘骸，包在尚未發霉的裹屍布裏。

經過縝密的調查，大家認為，很明顯，她在被埋葬後的兩天內又復活了；然後她在棺材裏掙扎着，使棺材從支架、或者是從擱板上掉落下來，棺材因此而破裂，使得她掙脫出來。有人無意中留了盞灌滿了煤油的燈在墓穴中，燈被發現時煤油已耗盡；不過，它也許是由於蒸發而耗完的。在走下那可怕的墓窟的階梯的最上頭，有一塊很大的棺材碎片，從這一點看，她似乎曾竭力用它來敲鐵門，以引起別人的注意。這樣過後，由於極度的恐懼，她也許暈厥了，或者可能就死了；而且在跌倒的過程中，她的裹屍布纏在了某個向內突起的鐵製物體上。就這樣，她保持着直立狀態，然後腐爛掉。

1810 年，法國發生了一起活埋事件，此事的諸多情形有助於證實一個觀點，即事實確實比小說更離奇。故事的女主人公是維克托里娜·拉福加德小姐，一位出自名門的年輕姑娘。她富有，而且非常漂亮。在她眾多的追求者中，有一位名叫朱利安·博敍埃的巴黎窮文人，或者說是窮記者。他的才華與親切和善的個性引起了這位女繼承人的關注，他似乎真的被她深愛着。但姑娘與生俱來的驕傲使她最終決定拒絕記者的求婚，和一位名叫雷奈勒先生結了婚。雷奈勒先生是一位銀行家，也是一名頗有名聲的外交能手。然而，婚後，這位紳士忽視她，或許更確切地說甚至還虐待她。和他一起過了幾年悲慘的生活後，她死了，——至少她的狀態是那麼接近死亡，騙過了任何見到她的人。她被埋葬了

──不是在墓穴，而是在她出生的鄉村，在一個普通的墳墓裏。她的戀人滿心絕望，但依然沉浸在深切的愛的回憶中，他從首都來到這鄉村所處的偏僻之地，懷着浪漫的企圖，想挖出那具屍體，拿走她一縷秀髮。他到了墓地，午夜時分他挖出了棺材，打開它，並開始取頭髮。這時，他被那雙睜開的迷人雙眸吸引住。事實上，那位女士是被活埋的。她的生命力還沒有完全消逝，在戀人的撫摸下，她從被人誤解為是死亡的昏睡中蘇醒。他瘋狂地背着她來到了自己在鄉村的住所，並憑着豐富的醫學知識給她服用了一些很有效的補藥。最後，她復活了，並認出了救她的人。她依然和他住在一起，直到逐漸地徹底恢復元氣。女人少有鐵石心腸的，這愛的最後一課足以打動她的心。於是，她將心交給了博敍埃，再也沒有回到丈夫身邊，而是對丈夫隱瞞了自己復活的消息，和戀人一起私奔到美國。二十年後，兩人返回法國，以為時間已經大大改變了女人的容顏，朋友們不會認出她。但是他們錯了。因為，實際上，雷奈勒先生一眼就認出了她，並要認領妻子。她拒絕了，於是法庭判決支持她的拒絕，認為由於這一奇特情形已持續了很久，他作為丈夫的權利已不僅合理而且合法地終止了。

萊比錫的《外科醫學雜誌》是一份很有權威和質量的期刊，一些美國書商總是很願意翻譯並重印它，該刊在最近一期中就登載了一件具有上述特點的非常令人憂傷的事件。

一位身材高大、健康強壯的炮兵軍官從一匹失控的馬上摔下來，頭部嚴重撞傷，他當場失去了知覺，顱骨輕微骨折，但醫生發現它沒有導致生命危險。開顱手術很成功。他被放了血，而且還採用了很多其他的常規救治措施。然而，他卻慢慢陷入了一種越來越令人絕望的昏迷狀態中，最後被確認為已經死亡。

當時天氣很暖和，他就被倉促地埋在了一個公墓裏。他是在星期四下葬的。隨後的那個星期天，公墓像往常一樣遊人擁擠。中午時分，一個農夫說了一段話，激起了強烈的騷動。農夫說當他坐在那位軍官的墳頭時，他清楚地感到地面在震動，好像下面有人在掙扎似的。起初沒有人把那農夫的話當真；但是他表露出明顯的恐懼，而且固執地一再堅持自己的說法，這最終對人羣發生了作用。人們很快拿來鐵鍬，不到幾分鐘時間就挖開了墳墓，原來那墓穴本來就挖得很淺，很讓人覺得寒磣。這時，軍官的頭露了出來，當時，他看上去是死了的樣子，但是他在棺材裏幾乎坐直了身體，在猛烈的掙扎中，棺材的蓋子都被他頂起了一部分。

於是他立刻被送往最近的醫院，院方認為他依然活着，儘管正處於昏厥狀態。幾個小時後，他蘇醒了，還認得出他的熟人，而且還斷斷續續地訴說自己在墳墓裏所遭的罪。

從他所講述的來看，情況顯然是這樣的，他被埋葬後，肯定有一個小時以上的時間是清醒的，然後就陷入了麻木。墳墓挖得很草率，而且很疏鬆，蓋上的土又極其具有滲透性。這樣，就透進了必要的空氣。他聽到頭上有人羣的腳步聲，就拼命地讓別人聽到他的動靜。他說，可能就是墓地的喧鬧，才將他從沉睡中喚醒的，但是他一醒，就完全意識到自己正處於恐怖的境地。

根據記錄，這位病人狀態不錯，從一定程度來看，似乎能完全康復，但是他卻成了騙人的醫學實驗的受害者。醫生對他採取了電擊療法，一次猛烈的電擊後他突然昏迷 —— 電擊療法有時候是會導致這樣的情況發生，然後就再沒有醒來。

不過，提到電擊療法，我想起了相關的一件著名的、非常離奇的活埋事件。當時，該療法使倫敦的一位被埋了兩天的年輕律師恢復了元氣。此事發生在 1831 年，當時，無論在甚麼情形下談起它，都能引起非常強烈的反響。

那位名叫愛德華·斯特普爾頓的病人明顯死於由斑疹傷寒而起的高燒，還有併發的一種不知名的病症。後者引起了治療大夫的好奇心。對於他表面的死亡，醫生請求他的親朋同意進行驗屍檢查，但是遭到了拒絕。像往常一樣，既然請求被拒絕，醫生們就決定挖出屍體，再悄悄地、從容不迫地解剖它。在和倫敦眾多掘墓團夥中的一家談妥後，很快就將一切安排就緒。於是，葬禮後的第三個夜晚，那具屍體被人從八英尺深的墓穴中掘出，置放在一家私人醫院的手術室裏。

屍體腹部上被長長地切了一刀，看到屍體依然新鮮，外表沒有腐爛，解剖者便想到了使用電擊療法。試驗一個接着一個，除了通常的結果外，解剖者沒有發現任何特異之處，除了有一兩次，屍體的抽搐比一般的抽搐更顯得有生命跡象。

夜已很深，都快到黎明了，最後，眾人認為最好立刻就進行解剖。但是一位醫學學生特別希望能驗證一下自己的理論，堅持要在胸部肌肉上進行一次電擊。於是他們在胸腔上草草地切了個口子，匆匆接上電線，這時，病人突然以急促但並不是抽搐的動作從手術台上站起來，走到地板中央，緊張地環顧了幾秒鐘，然後——他說話了。他說的話人們很難聽明白，但卻是一字一詞的，音節也十分清晰。說完後，他重重地倒在地板上。

一時間，大家都嚇呆了——但情況緊急，使他們很快恢復了理智。看來，斯特普爾頓先生還活着，儘管他處於昏迷狀態。眾人趕緊給他用藥，使他蘇醒過來，並很快恢復了健康，回到了朋友們身邊——不過一開始並沒有讓他的朋友們知道他復活的事，直到不再擔心他舊病復發為止。朋友們的震驚——他們的狂喜和驚訝——是可以想像的。

　　然而，這事最令人驚訝的奇特之處，是斯特普爾頓先生自己講述的那段話。他聲稱自己在整個過程中並不是完全麻木的——在遲鈍而模糊的感覺中，他知道在自己身上發生的所有事，從他被醫生宣判死亡起，一直到他暈厥後倒在醫院的地板上。他認出解剖室時曾經竭盡全力說出話來，可卻無人能聽懂，那句話就是"我還活着"。

　　這類事例可以很輕鬆地就找到許多，但是我不打算再講了。因為事實上，我們沒必要用這些來確證過早埋葬的事實的確存在。我們從這類事例中想到，其實我們很少有能力察覺這樣的情況，因此我們必須承認，這樣的事情在我們並不知曉的情況下也許在頻繁發生。實際上，墓地被挖掘——無論是出於甚麼目的或以何等規模——時，人們總會發現那些殘骸擺着令人生疑和恐懼的姿態。

　　這種懷疑真的很可怕——但是更可怕的是厄運！也許我們不用猶豫就可以這樣斷言，沒有任何事比過早埋葬能對肉體和精神產生更可怕的極度痛苦：人的肺部要經受無法承擔的壓力，潮濕的土壤令人窒息，身體緊貼裹屍布，被狹窄堅硬的空間包裹，純粹黑夜般的漆黑，寂靜就像海一般地席捲而來，那看不見卻感受得到的終極征服者蠕蟲——這一切，再加想到上面的空氣和青草，想到親愛的朋友們如果知道這情況就會飛身來解救自己，同時又意識到他們永遠沒法得知，知道我們無望的命運就是真正的死亡，我認為，所有這些想法，給依然跳動的心靈帶來了可怕而無法忍受的恐懼，為此，就是最勇敢無畏的想像都一定會畏縮。我們不知道世上有這樣的痛苦折磨，這種地獄最深處的恐懼，我們做夢都想不到它的一半。因此，所有關於這話題的敍述都令人產生深刻的興趣。然而，在話題本身令人蕭穆敬畏的氣氛中，這興趣完全並尤其依賴於我們對相關事件真實性的深信不疑。我現在要講述的就是我親身了解的——是我自己真實的個人經歷。

有好幾年，我一直遭受一種奇怪病症的折磨，在沒有其他更確切名稱的情況下，醫生稱其為強直性昏厥。儘管此病的直接和誘發因素、甚至實際的診斷仍然很令人費解，但是它明顯的和表面的特徵人們卻相當了解。它的變異似乎主要體現在程度的輕重上。有時候，病人在過度的嗜睡狀態下，只躺了一天或者更短的時間，在此期間，他失去知覺，看上去一動不動，但還能依稀察覺其心臟的跳動，身體的溫熱尚存，面頰中央有輕微的血色，而且如果用鏡子貼近嘴唇的話，我們可以發現肺部有遲鈍的、不均勻的、而且是緩慢不定的運動。然而有時候，這種迷睡狀態會持續幾週——甚至幾個月。這時，最細緻的觀察和最嚴密的醫學測試都無法分辨出在患者病發狀態和我們所認為的完全死亡之間的實際差異。很多情況下，他被朋友們從過早埋葬的厄運中拯救出來，不過這只是因為朋友們了解他以往曾經有過強直性昏厥的情況，從而會進一步產生懷疑，最重要的是，這懷疑是因為他身上沒有出現腐爛跡象所引發的。幸好，這種病情的發展很緩慢。雖然它最初的發作引人注目，但症狀並不明顯。緊接着，病情發作變得越來越明顯，持續時間一次比一次長。在這種情況下，就存在着不能被埋葬的主要理由。那些第一次發作就意外地顯示出極端症狀的不幸者，幾乎都不可避免地會被活生生地送進墳墓。

我自己的病情和那些醫學書上所提到的沒有太大的不同。有時候，沒有任何明顯原因我就會倒下去，然後一點一點地陷入一種半是昏厥半是沉睡的狀態，在這種狀態中，我沒有痛覺，沒法動彈，或確切地說，是沒法思考，只有一種的生命意識，能模模糊糊地感到那些圍在我牀邊的人的存在。這情況一直持續着，直到我突然又從這種病發狀態中完全恢復知覺。有的時候，我會迅速而劇烈地被病情擊倒。我感覺噁心、麻木、冰涼而且暈眩，接着立刻就倒在地上。然後，好幾個星期裏，一切都是空虛、黑暗、沉寂，四周空無一物，只有完全的毀滅。然而，我從這樣的發作中醒過來，其復蘇之緩慢與發作之驟然成正比，就好像孤獨失所的乞丐在寂靜而漫長的冬夜遊蕩在街巷，最後迎來了黎明一樣——之前的一切是那麼緩慢，那麼令人疲倦，而突然間，靈魂的曙光重又歸來，這時候又那麼令人愉悅。

然而，除了迷睡的傾向，我的健康狀況總的看來還不錯；我也沒意識到自己是在遭受着一種普遍疾病的打擊——除非我通常的睡眠中的特殊表現會真地被人看作是病發所致。當我從沉睡中醒過來時，我沒法一下子完全恢復知覺，而且在好幾分鐘時間裏，我依然很恍惚和迷惑，總體的智力，尤其是記憶力，還處於一種徹底的中止狀態。

我的整個感受中並沒有肉體上的疼痛，但精神上的困擾卻是無窮的。我的想像力變得很恐怖，還說着"關於蠕蟲、墳墓和墓誌銘"的話。我迷失在死亡的幻想裏，過早埋葬的念頭一直在我腦海裏盤旋。我為之戰慄的可怕危險日夜折磨着我。對於死亡，思緒的折磨令我難以忍受，而對於過早埋葬，這痛苦就達到了極點。當冷酷的黑暗覆蓋世界時，我在自己恐怖的念頭中戰慄，就像靈車上顫動的羽毛。當我的本性再也忍受不了這種失眠時，我得掙扎着入睡，因為一想起醒來時可能會發現自己躺在墳墓中，我就不寒而慄。而且當我最終沉入睡眠時，這也只是一下子衝進了一個幻象的世界，在那裏，那個被埋葬的念頭張着巨大的、黑色的、幽暗的翅膀，盤旋着，凌駕在上空。

　　從那些在夢中壓抑着我的無數陰鬱意象中，我只挑選了獨一無二的一個記錄於此。我想我是陷入了一種全身僵硬的昏厥，它滯留的時間和發病的程度超乎尋常。突然，有一隻冰冷的手放在我的前額，然後一個不耐煩的、急促不清的聲音在我耳畔說着"起來！"

　　我坐了起來，四周一片漆黑。我看不到讓我起來的那個人，想不起自己是甚麼時候昏厥的，也不知道自己剛剛躺在哪裏。我一動不動，努力地回憶着，那涼涼的手猛地抓住了我的手腕，急躁地搖着，然後那急促的聲音又響起來了：

　　"起來！我不是讓你起來嗎？"

　　"那你，"我問，"是誰？"

　　"我在自己生活的地方無名無姓，"那聲音很悲哀地回答我，"我過去是人，但現在是鬼。我過去很無情，但現在很慈悲。你

一定感到我在發抖 —— 我說話時牙齒打顫，但這不是因為冰冷的夜晚 —— 這無盡的黑夜，而是這恐懼令我無法忍受。你怎麼還能這樣平靜地睡？這些劇烈疼痛的呻吟使我無法安睡。這些景象我承受不了。起來！和我一起去外面的黑夜，讓我為你打開墳墓。這難道不是痛苦的景象嗎？ —— 看呀！」

我看了；那個無形的人依然抓着我的手腕，他已經打開了全人類的墳墓；每個墳墓散發出腐屍微弱的磷光，於是我能看到最深處，看到那裏裹着屍布的屍體，它們和蠕蟲一起沉浸在憂傷而蕭穆的深睡中。可是，唉！真正沉睡的卻比那些根本沒有入睡的少千百萬；那裏有微弱的掙扎，那裏彌漫着憂傷的不安，從那無數深深的坑洞裏，從被埋葬人的裹屍布上，傳來了憂鬱的沙沙聲。在那些似乎在寧靜長眠的人當中，我看到很多人都改變了最初下葬時那僵直不安的樣子，程度或輕或重。在我盯着看時，那聲音又對我說：

「難道這不是 —— 哦！難道這不是一個令人憐憫的景象嗎？」可是沒等我找到回答的話語，那個身影已鬆開我的手腕，磷光熄滅了，所有的墳墓都猛地合上了，從墳墓裏傳來一陣絕望的喧囂，不斷重複着：「難道這不是 —— 哦，上帝，難道這不是令人憐憫的景象嗎？」

類似這樣的幻象在夜晚呈現出來，日益將它們可怕的影響滲入我清醒的時日中。我的神經變得極為衰弱，於是我屈服於無盡的恐慌。我不敢駕車，不敢走路，不敢沉溺於任何要讓我離開家的活動。事實上，當那些知道我有強直性昏厥傾向的人不在身邊時，我就不敢再信任自己，害怕一旦陷入了一次尋常的發作中，就會在真實情況被確診前遭埋葬。我懷疑最親近的朋友的關心和忠誠。我害怕，一旦我陷入了比往常時間更長的昏厥中，他們或許會被人說服，認為我不會恢復了。我甚至擔心，在我給大家帶來了這麼多的麻煩後，他們說不定會樂於將任何延長了的發作作為徹底擺脫我的充足理由。無論他們怎麼努力用最嚴肅的諾言向我保證都沒用。我強迫他們發出最莊重的誓言，保證無論怎樣他們都不會埋了我，除非腐爛已經蔓延到不能再保留屍體。但即使如此，我極度的恐懼還是聽不進任何勸說 —— 不接受任何安慰。我開始實施一系列精心的防範措施。此外，我讓人把家族的墓穴造得可以從裏面輕易地打開。只要在那根長長的，伸入墓穴的槓桿上輕輕一摁，它就會讓鐵門很快向後轉開。我還在那裏做了安排，讓空氣和光自由進入，並放置了盛有食物和水的容器，我從棺材裏就能伸手拿到。棺材裏面墊得溫暖而柔軟，上面的蓋子和地下室鐵門遵循一樣的開啟原則，還添加了彈簧，確保連身體最微弱的運動都足以自由操縱它。除了這些，墳墓的頂上還吊着一個很大的鈴，那條繩子被設計成能伸進棺材的一個洞口，就這樣，繩子可以被繫在屍體的一隻手上。但是，唉！與人類的命運抗衡有甚麼用呢？甚至連這些設計精良的安全設施，都不足以把經受這些宿命折磨的不幸之人從最深的活埋痛苦中解救出來！

這一天終於來了 —— 就像以往經常發生的那樣，它來了 —— 我發現自己從徹底的無意識中進入了第一次微弱而模糊的生存感覺。慢慢地 —— 像龜行那麼緩慢地 —— 精神黎明那微微的曙光來臨了。我感到一陣遲鈍的不安，漠然忍受着麻木的疼痛。沒有焦慮 —— 沒有希望 —— 沒有努力。然後，過了一個漫長的間歇，耳邊響起一陣鈴響；又過了更長的一段時間，肢端有了一陣刺痛和麻癢感；然後是一陣彷彿遙遙無期的舒適的靜止，在此期間清醒感正掙扎着進入思想；接着，又是短暫地陷入了麻木狀態；然後就猛地醒來了。最後，一個眼皮上有輕輕的顫動，很快地，又是一陣電擊的恐懼，它強烈而模糊，把血液洶湧地從太陽穴輸送到心臟。這時，我才第一次積極地努力思考，然後首次試圖回想起甚麼。然後，出現了局部而短暫的記憶。這時，記憶掌握了控制權，從一定程度上，我意識到了自己所處的狀態。我感到自己不是從普通的睡眠中醒來，回想起我遭遇了強直性昏厥。最後，一陣衝動巨浪般襲來，我震顫的靈魂被那可怕的危險壓垮了 —— 被那個幽靈般盤桓不去的念頭壓垮了。

被這種幻覺籠罩後的幾分鐘時間裏，我靜止不動。這是為甚麼呢？因為我無法鼓起勇氣移動自己。我不敢努力去確信自己的命運，但是我心中有聲音在向我低語這是真的。一陣絕望 —— 不像其他的痛苦所喚起的那種絕望 —— 在長久的猶豫不定之後，只有絕望在激勵着我開啟那沉重的眼皮。我睜開眼睛。一片漆黑 —— 完全的漆黑。我知道發作過去了，知道自己的病症危機早已離去。我知道自己已徹底恢復了視覺功能。可是周圍很黑，全黑的，黑夜般強烈而徹底的昏暗始終持續着。

我竭力想叫喊；嘴唇和乾澀的舌頭痙攣着一起用勁，但空洞的肺部發不出聲音來，它似乎被覆在上面大山一般的重量所壓，我喘着粗氣，每一次掙扎着大口吸氣時，心都怦怦直跳。

在企圖大聲喊叫的努力中，下巴動了動，讓我感覺到它們被綁了起來，就像平常對死者所做的一樣。我也覺得自己躺在某個堅硬的東西上；而且，我的兩側也有一種類似的被緊緊包裹的感覺。到那時，我還沒有試着動一動我的四肢，此刻我猛地舉起一直是手腕交叉地擺在那裏的雙臂。我的雙手碰到了堅硬的木質材料，它在我臉部上面不超過六英吋的地方。最後，我不再懷疑自己是躺在一個棺材裏。

這時，在我經歷的這所有無盡的痛苦中，一個甜美的天使般的希望出現了 —— 因為我想到了自己的防範措施。我扭動身體，間歇地用力想頂開棺材蓋：它沒動。我動了動手腕想拉繫鈴的繩子：沒有找到它。這時，這安慰永遠地飛走了，而更嚴酷的絕望籠罩着我；因為我禁不住想到我自己精心準備的軟墊子也沒了。接着，我的鼻子也突然聞到了一種強烈而特殊的潮濕泥土的氣息。我的結論是不可反駁的，我沒有在家族墓穴裏，我陷入昏厥時並沒在家 —— 周圍是陌生人 —— 甚麼時候，或是怎麼昏厥的，我都記不得了 —— 是那些陌生人把我像狗一樣埋了起來 —— 然後把我釘在普通的棺材裏 —— 並將它扔進了 —— 深深地、深深地，而且是永遠地扔進了某個普通而不知名的墓地。

這可怕的結論進入了我心靈的最深處，我又一次地掙扎着想大聲喊叫。這次我成功了。一聲悠長、狂野、持續而痛苦的尖厲叫喊或是嚎叫在黑夜的地底迴盪。

"喂！喂，這裏！"一個粗啞的聲音回答道。

"見鬼！這是怎麼回事！"第二個聲音説。

"別吵了！"第三個聲音響起來。

"你這樣狂叫是甚麼意思，像隻野貓似的？"第四個聲音説道。於是，我被一夥長相粗野的人抓着，並被胡亂地搖晃了好幾分鐘。他們沒有把我從沉睡中喚醒——因為我喊叫時已經徹底醒了——但是他們讓我完全恢復了記憶。

這事發生在弗吉尼亞的里士滿附近。我在一位朋友的陪伴下，沿詹姆斯河岸下游走了幾英里去打獵。夜晚來臨時，我們遇到了一場暴雨。河邊停着一隻小型的單桅帆船，船艙裏裝載着花園用的肥土，這為我們提供了唯一可躲雨的地方。我們就充分地利用了它，並在那裏過了夜。我在船僅有的兩個鋪位中的一個上睡下了——重量六七十噸的單桅帆船上的鋪位是怎麼樣的就可想而知了。我躺的那個位置還沒有牀墊。它的最大寬度是十八英吋，從底部到頭上的甲板處的距離也一模一樣。我發現要把自己塞進去異常困難。但是，我還是睡得很熟。因為沒有做夢，沒有做噩夢，我醒來時的所有幻覺自然都因我周圍的環境而起，來自我慣有的思維傾向，來自——這我也暗示過了——感官恢復時的困難，尤其是要在沉睡醒來後很長的時間裏重新恢復記憶。那些搖醒我的人是船上的工作人員以及卸貨工人。泥土的氣味就是裝載物自身發出來的。我下巴上的繃帶是一塊絲綢手帕，我用它來代替常用的睡帽包頭的。

然而，我當時承受的折磨無疑和真的墳墓沒甚麼兩樣。它們很可怕——實在太可怕了；但事情總是否極泰來。因為這過度的驚嚇使我精神必然產生劇烈反應，我的心靈得到了調整——獲得了平衡。於是我出國旅行，我做大量的鍛煉，呼吸着天空自由的空氣。我思考着其他的問題，而不是死亡。我扔掉了醫學書，焚燒了"巴肯"[50]，不再閱讀《夜思》[51]，不讀關於墓地的浮誇詩文，不看鬼怪故事——例如本篇。總之，我變了個人，過着正常人的

生活。從那個難忘的夜晚以後，我徹底拋開了自己那令人恐怖的
擔憂，我的強直性昏厥病症也隨之消失了，也許，對於這一病症，
前者與其説是結果，倒毋寧説是起因。

　　有時候，即使在冷靜的理智看來，我們悲哀的人性世界或許
也會和地獄很相像，但人類的想像並不是能泰然探索每一個洞穴
的卡拉蒂絲。唉！大量關於埋葬的恐怖事件並不能完全被當作奇
思怪想，但是，就像陪着阿弗拉斯布沿着奧克蘇斯河 [52] 航行的那
些魔鬼，他們肯定得睡覺，要不他們就吞噬了我們 —— 必須讓他
們沉睡，否則我們就完蛋。[53]

（張瓊譯）

9

陷坑與鐘擺

Impia tortorum longos hic turba furores
Sanguinis innocui, non satiata, aluit.
Sospite nunc patria, fracto nunc funeris antro,
Mors ubi dira fuit vita salusque patent.

（此四行詩是在巴黎雅各賓俱樂部
原址所建市場的幾個入口處寫的。）

此時，我依然繼續小心翼翼地向前走着，記憶中湧上了成千的關於恐怖的托萊多的傳言。關於那裏的地牢，流傳着一些關於怪異事物的故事 —— 我把它們稱為傳說，但是它們很怪異，可怕得令人不敢重述，除非是通過耳語。難道我要留在這個黑暗的地下世界裏被餓死嗎；或者甚至會有更可怕的命運在等着我？那些結局是死亡，而且是比平常的死亡更痛苦，我太了解法官的品性，這是毋庸置疑的。這種折磨的方式和時間是佔據或擾亂我心靈的一切。

我伸出的雙手終於碰到了甚麼堅實的障礙物。那是一面牆，好像是磚石牆壁 —— 滑滑的、黏黏的，冰冷冰冷。我順着它走，由於受到某些古代的小說敍述的影響，我的步子謹慎而充滿狐疑。然而，這麼做並不能使我確定地牢的大小，因為我可能會轉一圈再回到原地，而且自己對此又毫無知覺，因為各處的牆面沒有一點差別。因此我要找到那把在我被帶入法庭時放進口袋的刀，但是它不在了，我的衣服被換成了粗糙的嗶嘰面料的麻袋布。我是想把刀鋒插進磚石牆壁上的某條細細的裂縫裏，這樣就能辨認出我的出發位置。儘管在我錯亂的幻覺中，這件事情最初似乎不可完成，但難度畢竟並不太大。我從袍子的邊緣撕下一塊布，把它完全展開，垂直於牆壁鋪在地上。當我圍着牢房摸索時，准會在轉過一圈時踩到這塊布。我想，至少是這樣的；但是我沒考慮地牢的大小，也沒想過自己的虛弱。地面又潮又滑，我蹣跚着向前走了一會，就絆倒了。極度的乏力使我俯臥在地上；當我躺下時，睡意頓時向我襲來。

我醒來時，伸出一條胳膊，發現在我旁邊有一條麵包和一大罐水。我累得不想思考，只管貪婪地吃喝起來。不久，我又重新不辭辛勞地圍着牢房走，並終於碰到了那塊嗶嘰布。到從我摔倒的地方，我已經數過有五十二步，加上我接着又走了四十八步，直到那塊布的位置。這樣就總共移動了一百步。如果兩步為一碼，我推算出這個地牢周長五十碼。不過我在牆上碰到了很多角，因此我猜不出這地窖——我不得不認為這是個地窖——的形狀。

我這樣探究並沒有目的，當然也不抱任何希望。但是一個隱約的好奇促使我繼續探究下去。我放棄了牆壁，決定橫穿過這個地牢。最初，我走得格外小心，因為儘管地面是堅硬的材料，卻因為黏滑而危險。不過，最後我鼓起勇氣，毫不猶豫地跨出了堅定的步子——儘量努力走直線。我這樣前進了大約十到十二步，被撕過的袍子邊緣纏住了我的雙腿，我一腳踩上去，重重地一頭栽倒了。

這一跤跌得我暈頭轉向，一下子沒能明白這多少有些令人吃驚的情況，但是幾秒鐘後，雖然我還趴在地上，卻馬上注意到是甚麼原因了。是這樣的——我的下巴支在牢房的地面上，但我的嘴唇和頭頂的位置雖然似乎比下巴還低，但是沒有撞到甚麼。同時，我的前額好像浸在濕冷的水汽中，而且一股特殊的腐爛黴菌的氣味鑽入了鼻孔。我伸手一摸，渾身戰慄地發現我跌倒在一個圓坑的邊緣，坑的大小我一下子沒法確定。我摸索着坑沿下面的磚石，摳出一小塊碎片，把它扔進深洞裏。過了好幾秒鐘，我傾聽着它在下滑時碰在坑壁上的迴響，最後，它發出一聲沉悶的掉進水裏的聲音，緊接着是很響的回音。同時，頭頂上傳來了一個很像是門扇迅速開合的聲音，一道微弱的亮光突然穿透了陰暗，又頓時消失了。

我清楚地明白了自己前面是即將到來的末日，並暗自慶幸那使我免於墜落陷坑的及時的一跤，再走一步，我就從這世界隱身了。而這剛被躲避了的死亡，有着某種我認為是與宗教法庭審訊有關的故事中言過其實而荒誕的特徵。對於在死亡暴政下的受害者，他們可以選擇直接的肉體痛苦的死，或是最可怕的精神恐懼的死。他們留給我的是後一種死法。在長期的折磨中，我變得神經衰弱，連聽到自己的聲音都要發抖，無論怎麼看，我都是眼前各種折磨方式最合適不過的對象。

精神上的興奮使我許久都睡不着，但是最終我又沉入夢鄉。醒來時，發現自己的身邊像以前一樣又有了一條麵包和一大罐水。灼熱的焦渴消耗着我的體力，於是我把罐子裏的水一飲而盡。水裏一定下了藥，因為我還沒喝完，就有種無法抵抗的昏昏欲睡感。我又陷入沉睡中——像死一樣地沉睡着。我當然不知道它持續了多久，但是當我又一次睜開眼睛時，周圍的事物都看得見了。在一陣強烈的、地獄般的亮光下——那光線來自何處我一開始還沒法確定——我看見了牢房的大小和形狀。

我對大小的推測完全錯了。那整個一圈牆壁不超過二十五碼。有那麼幾分鐘，這個事實讓我有一種枉然的感覺，真的很枉然！因為，在我所處的這個可怕的境遇中，還有甚麼會比這地牢的大小更微不足道呢？但是我的靈魂卻對這些瑣碎之事充滿了瘋狂的興趣，而我則盡力地想找出自己測量上發生錯誤的原因。真相終於在我腦海裏閃現。在我第一次企圖探察時，我數到了五十二步，然後就跌倒了。那時我肯定離那塊嗶嘰布只有一兩步路，實際上，我幾乎已經圍着地窖走了一圈。然後我就睡着了，醒來後，我一定是往回走了——就這樣，我推測出的那一圈幾乎是實際的兩倍。我混亂的大腦沒能使我注意到我是從左邊開始走的，而結束時的牆卻在右邊了。

關於牢房的形狀，我的感覺也欺騙了我。在我摸索着走時，我發現了很多彎角，於是就推斷出它的形狀很不規則。徹底的黑暗對一個從昏迷或睡夢中醒來的人效果太強了！這些彎角無非就是一些彼此距離不等的淺凹陷，或者是裂縫。牢房的大體形狀是正方形的。我先前以為的磚石牆好像應該是鐵，或是其他金屬，連成了巨大的板塊，彼此的縫合或連接處便形成凹陷。整個牢房的金屬表面被粗糙地塗滿了各種可怕而令人厭惡的圖案，即起源於宗教迷信的陰森恐怖的圖案。魔鬼們帶着威脅人的氣勢，骷髏一般瘦骨嶙峋，還有其他更為可怕的圖案彌漫並污損着牆面。我發現這些怪物們都非常清晰，但是色彩顯得暗淡而模糊，似乎是潮濕的空氣所致。我還注意到了地板，它是石頭的，中間裂開了一個圓形的陷坑，我曾僥倖沒有墜落於此；但是那是地牢裏唯一的陷坑。

我費力地看，還是不甚清晰：因為我個人的身體狀況通過睡眠已經發生了很大的改變。這時，我直挺挺地仰臥在一個低矮的木框架上。在那上面我被腰帶狀的一條長帶子牢牢地固定住了，帶子在我的四肢和身體上繞了好幾圈，只有頭部是自由的，我的左胳膊費大力氣還可以動彈，能從我身邊放在地上的一個陶製的盤子裏拿食物。讓我感到恐懼的是，我看到的那個大水罐被人拿走了。我感到恐懼是因為我被無法忍受的焦渴折磨着。那焦渴似乎是迫害我的人設計好要刺激我的 —— 因為盤中的食物是調味辛辣的肉。

我仰望着牢房的天花板，它離我大約有三十或四十英尺，結構和牆壁相仿。其中的一塊上有一個非常古怪的形狀吸引了我全部的注意。畫的是時間老人像，就像人們通常所接受的那個樣子，只是他手握的長柄鐮刀被換掉了。開始不經意地一看，我推測那個畫出來的替代物是一個巨大的鐘擺，就像我們在古董鐘上看到的那樣。然而，在這個裝置的形狀中，有某種東西使我更加關注。當我直直地抬頭凝視着它（因為它的位置恰好在我正上方），幻覺中它好像在動着。這個幻想立刻就得到了證實。它的擺動幅度很小，當然也很慢。我有些害怕地看了它幾分鐘，但更多的是驚訝。最後，看着它單調的運動，我感到疲倦了，就把視線轉向了牢房的其他物品。

　　一陣輕微的聲音引起了我的注意，我朝地板看，發現有幾隻巨大的老鼠在穿過地板。老鼠是從我右面視線領域中的井裏爬出來的。在我盯着看時，它們正成羣結隊地爬出來，很匆忙的樣子，目光貪婪，被那塊肉的氣味誘惑着。為此，我得要費力費神地把它們嚇跑。

　　要講述我當時數着鋼刀擺動次數時那長久的、比死還可怕的恐懼又有何益！一寸一寸地 —— 一縷一縷地 —— 那下降像是只有過幾個世紀才會讓人覺出來 —— 它下降着，依舊在下降着！一天天過去了 —— 可能是有好多天過去了 —— 它在我上方近在咫尺地擺着，彷彿用它辛辣的呼吸拂着我。那強烈的鋼鐵氣味沖進我的鼻孔。我祈禱着 —— 我用祈禱勞煩上蒼讓它下降得更快些。我變得狂暴瘋癲，掙扎着要迫使自己抬起來迎接那搖擺着的可怕彎刀。後來，我忽然平靜下來，躺下來對着閃爍的死亡微笑，像一個孩子對着稀罕的小玩意一般。

　　我又陷入了一陣完全的知覺麻木，時間很短暫。因為當我又蘇醒時，並沒覺得鐘擺有任何可以察覺的下降。但是這時間可能很長 —— 因為我知道有惡魔在記錄我的昏厥，而且他可以隨意地制止擺動。這次醒來後，我還是覺得非常 —— 哦！無法形容的 —— 噁心和虛弱，好像經歷了長時間的虛脫狀態。即使在那段時間的痛苦中，人的本能使我渴望食品。我費力掙扎着儘量將左手伸到綁繩所允許的地方，拿到了很小的一塊老鼠吃剩的殘留物。當我把一部分塞進嘴裏時，腦海裏閃過一種隱約的想法 —— 一種帶有希望的高興。可是希望與我何干?它是 —— 正如我説的 —— 一種隱約的想法,人總是會有很多這樣的念頭,但從來實現不了。我覺得那是一種帶有希望的高興,但我也感到那想法在成形過程中就夭折了。我徒勞地想努力實現這個念頭 —— 重新獲得它。長期的折磨幾乎已經耗盡了我正常的思維能力。我成了個愚笨的人 —— 一個白癡。

鐘擺的擺動方向與我豎躺的身體成直角。我感到那個月牙是預備穿透我的心臟的。它會磨損我外袍的嗶嘰布料 —— 會返回並再次進攻 —— 一次 —— 又一次。儘管它那可怕的寬邊(大約有三十英尺或更長)以及它下墜時嘶嘶作響的氣勢,都足以使鐵牆分裂,但是要損毀我的外袍依然需要幾分鐘時間。想到這裏,我停住了,我不敢想下去。我凝神於此念頭 —— 似乎只要抓住它不放,我就能阻止那鋼鐵的墜落。我強迫自己想像那月牙鋼刀擦過外衣時發出的聲響,想像衣服被撕開時給自己的神經帶來的那種特有的驚栗。我想像着所有這些無聊的細節,直到牙關顫抖。

它墜落着 —— 穩穩地潛進。面對着它下降和橫向速率的對比,我懷有一種瘋狂的快感。向右 —— 向左 —— 橫掃一切 —— 帶着那該死的靈魂尖叫!向着我的心臟,帶着老虎般鬼鬼祟祟的迫近步伐!我又笑又嚎,內心滿是各種各樣的念頭。

它墜落着 —— 勢在必行而無情地下降着!它就在離我胸口三寸處搖擺着!我拼命掙扎 —— 想猛力地掙脱出我的左手臂,它只有肘關節以下的部位可以活動,我能費力地將手從身旁的盤子處移到我的嘴巴,但僅此而已。如果我能把肘部以上的繫結掙斷,我就能抓住並竭力制止這個鐘擺,而且還能盡力阻止這場崩落!

沒等我把頭放回原位，腦海中突然閃過一個念頭，準確地說，那隱約的逃脫念頭我曾經暗示過，當時在我把食品送到焦灼的雙唇處時，它曾或明或暗、不太明確地漂浮在我的思緒中。此刻整個想法出現了——雖然、不很明晰——卻是完整的。懷着緊張而絕望的神情，我立刻着手去實現這個想法。

在很多小時裏，我所緊貼着並躺着的那個木架子一直被大羣老鼠簇擁着。它們瘋狂、無畏、貪婪，用紅色的眼睛盯着我，彷彿在等待着，直到我僵硬靜止後成為它們掠奪的食品。我思忖着，"它們在陷坑裏習慣吃些甚麼東西呢？"

儘管我費力地阻止它們，它們還是吞噬了盤子裏幾乎所有的食品，只剩下了一小塊。我習慣用左手在盤子上前後搖動揮舞，可最終那無意識而單調的動作失去了效力。這羣老鼠歹徒在貪婪的進食過程中，頻頻地用尖銳的牙齒咬我的手指，我的手指上還殘留着一些油膩而辛辣的食物碎末，於是我拼命地把手在我可以夠到的繃帶上擦拭，然後，把手從地板上舉起，屏住呼吸靜靜地躺着。

起初，那羣貪食的動物很吃驚，對這一變動——這種靜止感到恐懼。它們警惕地向後緊縮，很多老鼠逃回了那個陷坑。但是這只持續了一會。我並沒有看錯它們的貪婪。它們看到我依然沒有動靜，一兩隻最勇敢的老鼠就跳上木架，嗅着繃帶。這似乎是讓全體沖上來的信號，於是它們從陷坑裏重新匆忙地湧上來。它們貼近木頭——攀了上來，有幾百隻老鼠跳上我的身體。那鐘擺有節奏的運動對它們根本不起作用。它們避開鐘擺的衝擊，忙着對付那被塗抹過的繃帶，它們壓着我——一堆堆重疊地擠在我身上。它們在我脖子上翻騰，那冰涼的舌頭探詢着我的嘴唇；在它們蜂擁而至的壓力下，我的半個身體幾乎都僵直了，無法言說的噁心堵滿了我的胸口，沉重的濕冷感在我內心激發起陣陣寒意。但是我覺得只要一分鐘，那場鬥爭就將停止。我明確地感到那繃帶鬆解了，知道不止一處已經肯定被咬斷。我以驚人的毅力靜靜地躺着。

當我放棄那企圖，掙扎着站起身時，我突然看出了牢房裏的神祕變化。我曾注意到，雖然牆上的圖形輪廓是足夠清晰的，但是那顏色顯得模糊而不確定。這些顏色此刻，而且在瞬間顯現出一種驚人而極其強烈的光澤，使那些鬼魅而兇惡的圖畫更加恐怖，甚至能使比我神經健全的人都不寒而慄。那惡魔的雙眼帶着狂野而可怕的生動性，從每一個方向瞪着我，那些目光我從未領教過，而且它們閃動着恐怖的火焰一般的光澤，令我沒法想像它們竟是幻覺。

傳來一陣嘈雜的嗡嗡人聲！一陣好像許多小號同時吹起的響亮聲音！一陣刺耳的聲響，彷彿上千雷鳴在翻騰！那可怕的牆壁迅速後退了！我正向着深淵墜落、暈厥時，一條手臂伸過來抓住了我。那是拉薩爾將軍的手。法國軍隊已經進駐了托萊多，宗教法庭已經落到了它對手的掌控之中。

（張瓊譯）

10

泄密之心

真的！—— 緊張 —— 我一直到現在都非常、非常地緊張！可是你為何要說我瘋了呢？那病痛使我的感覺更加敏銳 —— 而不是毀壞 —— 不是麻木了它們。尤其是我的聽覺，它極其靈敏。我聽到了在天堂和人間的一切聲音，聽到地獄中有許多事物。我怎麼會瘋了呢？聽着！並且請注意我能多麼神志健全 —— 多麼平靜地對你講述這整個故事。

我沒法説出這念頭最初是怎樣進入我大腦的；但是一旦我想到了它，它就日夜縈繞在心頭。沒有任何目標，也不懷甚麼慾望。我愛這老頭，他從沒虧欠或傷害過我。我對他的錢財毫不眼熱。我想那是因為他的那隻眼睛！沒錯，就是它！他有一隻禿鷹的眼睛 —— 灰藍色的，薄霧輕蒙。每當它注視着我，我就血液僵冷；於是，逐漸地 —— 非常緩慢地 —— 我下定決心要了結這老頭的性命，這樣我就能一勞永逸地逃離那隻眼睛。

這就是關鍵所在。你覺得我瘋了，覺得瘋子是沒有理智的。可是你真該親眼目睹，你該看看我對這事處理得有多聰明 —— 多謹慎 —— 多有遠見 —— 多隱蔽！

在我除掉這老頭之前的整個一週裏，我從沒對他如此友好過。每天晚上，大約午夜時分，我轉動他門上的插銷，並開了門 —— 哦，幹得如此輕柔！然後，當門開到足夠探進頭去時，我將一個黑色燈籠放進去，它整個地被遮蔽着，密封着，透不出一點光線。然後，我將頭猛地探進去。哦，看到我如此巧妙地探進頭去，你沒準會笑的！我慢慢地移動腦袋——非常、非常地緩慢，這樣我就不會吵醒老頭了。我花了一個鐘頭才把整個腦袋塞進門縫中，這樣我就能看到他正躺在牀上。哈！——瘋子會如此聰明嗎？然後，當頭完全探入房間後，我就小心翼翼地解開燈籠——哦，我是多麼小心——謹慎（以防摺合處發出吱吱的響聲）——我把燈籠解到只能透出一道細細的光線，光落在了那隻禿鷹般的眼睛上。在七個漫漫長夜中，我都如此這般地行事——每晚都是在午夜時分——可是我發現那隻眼睛總是緊閉着，因此，我就無法動手了；因為惹惱我的並不是那個老頭，而是他那隻邪惡的眼睛。每天早晨，破曉時分，我就勇敢地走進房間，大膽地對他說話，親切地喊他的名字，並詢問他那晚過得如何。所以，你明白，他要是能懷疑每天晚上恰好零點的時候，我都盯着他睡覺的話，他可真得是個非常深謀遠慮的老人才行。

到第八個晚上，我比平常更加謹慎地打開了門。鐘錶的分針比我開門的速度更快，我從沒像那天晚上一樣地感受到自己所擁有的力量——還有我的智慧。我幾乎控制不住那種勝利感。設想一下，我站在那裏，一點一點地打開了門，而他連做夢都想不到我那些祕密的行為和思想。想到這些，我暗暗地笑了。也許他聽到了聲音，因為他在牀上突然地動了起來，好像受了驚嚇似的。此刻你也許認為我退縮了——但是我沒有。他的房間如同黏稠漆黑的瀝青一般幽暗（因為出於防止竊賊之故，百葉窗緊閉着），因此我明白他是看不到房門被打開的，於是我繼續一點點地向前推着門。

我把腦袋探了進去，並且準備解開燈籠，當我的大拇指觸摸到那個錫製的扣件時，老頭從牀上彈身而起，叫了起來——"誰？"

我靜止不動，默不出聲。整整一個小時我都沒有動過一塊肌肉，同時我也沒聽到他躺下的聲音。他依然直坐在牀上傾聽着——恰好與我每晚傾聽牆壁裏報死蟲的聲音一樣。

這時，我聽到一聲輕微的呻吟，並知道那是極度恐懼的聲音。它不是因為疼痛或憂傷才發出的呻吟——哦，不是！——它是人在不堪承受驚懼時，從靈魂深處發出的低沉而壓抑的呻吟。我對這種聲音很了解。許多夜晚，在午夜時分，當整個世界都沉睡時，它就從我自己的內心湧上來，並隨着它可怕的回聲而漸漸深沉，於是那些恐懼就困擾着我。我説我很了解它。我了解這個老人的感受，並且同情他，儘管在內心我暗自發笑。我知道，從第一個輕微的響聲驚得他在牀上翻了個身之後，他就一直清醒地躺着，他的驚慌一直在增長。他不斷努力想像着這些都是空穴來風，卻又做不到。他一直對自己説——"這只不過是煙囪裏的風——只是一隻老鼠在爬過地板"，或者"這僅僅是一隻蟋蟀發出的一聲鳴叫"。是的，他一直在努力用這些假設來安慰自己；但是他發現這些都是徒勞的。完全是徒勞的；因為當死亡正迫近他時，死神已經將自己黑色的陰影投射在他身前，並包圍了這個受害者。正是這種不被察覺的陰影那令人憂傷的感染力才使他感到——儘管他並未耳聞目睹——使他感到房間裏有我腦袋的存在。

我等了很久，等得非常耐心，沒等聽到他躺下，我決心打開一點點——打開燈籠裏那極其微小的縫隙。於是我這樣做了——你沒法想像我做得有多躡手躡腳，有多靜悄悄——直到，最終，一條微暗的光線，就像蜘蛛結出的絲那麼細的，從縫隙中透射出來，落在那隻禿鷹眼睛上。

它睜着——大大地睜着——我盯着它，變得憤怒起來。我看得清清楚楚——它渾然一片呆滯的藍色，蒙着一層可怕的紗，這使我脊髓不寒而慄；但是我根本看不到老人的臉或身體：因為，彷彿出於本能，我已經徑直將光線準確地投了那該死的地方。

此刻，難道我沒有告訴過你，你所誤解為瘋狂的只不過是感官上的過於敏銳嗎？——此刻，告訴你，我的耳邊傳來了一聲低沉、單調、迅速的聲音，就像包在棉花裏的表發出的響聲。我也很了解這樣的聲音。那是老人心臟在搏動。它更激發了我的憤怒，就像鼓聲鼓舞了戰士的勇氣。

可是即使如此，我依然克制自己，並保持靜止，幾乎不發出呼吸聲。我一動不動地把持着燈籠，想試試自己能讓光線在那隻眼睛上保持怎樣的穩定。這時，那可惡而連續的咚咚的心跳聲加強了，它變得越來越快，逐漸響起來。那老頭的恐懼一定達到了極端！它變得越發強烈，告訴你，越來越強烈！——你懂我的意思嗎？我對你說了我很緊張：我真是這樣。此刻，在夜深人靜的時刻裏，在那老房子可怕的沉寂中，這聲音如此奇怪，它令我產生無法自控的恐懼。然而，我還是多抑制並佇立了幾分鐘。可是那搏動聲變得愈發強烈！我想那顆心一定要爆炸了。於是，一種新的焦慮佔據了我——那聲音可能會被鄰居聽到！那老頭命該此時了！我大叫一聲，猛地打開燈籠，跳進了房間。他尖叫了一下——只叫了一次。剎那間，我把他拖到了地上，並將那張沉重的牀推到他身上。然後我亢奮地笑起來，發現事情就此了結了。但是，好幾分鐘裏，心臟帶着壓抑的聲音跳動着。然而我並不感到惱火；這聲音隔牆聽不到。最終，它停歇了。老頭死了。我移開牀，檢查了屍體。是的，他徹底斷氣了。我把自己的一隻手放在那心臟上，如此維持了好幾分鐘。那裏沒有心跳了，他完全死了，那眼睛再也不會令我煩惱了。

倘若你依然認為我瘋了，只要我描述自己在藏匿屍體時的謹慎和明智，你就不會再這樣認為了。夜晚行將結束，我幹得很匆忙，但是卻做得悄無聲息。首先，我肢解了屍體，砍下了腦袋、胳膊和大腿。

然後我從房間的地板上掀起三條厚木板，將屍體的所有部分分別放置其中，然後非常巧妙地、敏捷地把木板放回原位，如此，肉眼 —— 甚至老天 —— 都察覺不出任何異樣處。沒有甚麼要洗拭的 —— 沒有任何的污跡 —— 沒有血跡甚麼的痕跡。對此我極其謹慎，一個浴缸就盛下了這一切 —— 哈！哈！

當我幹完了這所有的事，已經四點了 —— 天黑得像午夜一般。當時鐘報時之際，街邊的大門被敲響了。我輕快地下樓去開門，—— 我現在還有甚麼可害怕的？三個男人走了進來，他們非常謙和地自我介紹，説自己是警官。一位鄰居在夜裏聽到了一聲尖叫：他疑心發生了謀殺案，就向警署報了案，於是他們（這些警官）就被派來對附近地帶進行查看。

我笑了 —— 我有甚麼好害怕呢？我對這幾位先生表示歡迎，並告訴他們，那聲尖叫是我自己在夢中發出的。我又説，那個老人去鄉下了，目前不在家。我領着他們在房子裏到處轉了轉，讓他們搜查 —— 好好地搜查。最後，我帶他們去了老頭的房間。我讓他們看了他的財物，它們都完好無損。我信心十足，滿懷熱情地把椅子移進房間，希望他們坐下來解解乏。我自己則因為勝券在握而毫無畏懼，恰好將自己那張椅子放在了藏匿被害者屍體的地方。

警官們很是滿意，我的舉止令他們信服。我感到徹底的輕鬆。他們坐着，而我則愉快地回答他們的問題，和他們聊着家常。可是，不久，我覺得自己變得越來越蒼白，並盼着他們離開。我覺得頭疼，並且在幻覺中感到耳鳴：可是他們依然坐着，仍舊在閒聊。耳鳴聲越來越清晰——它持續着，並且更加清楚起來。為了擺脫這種感覺，我就更肆意地説話，但是它連綿不斷而且越發明顯——直到最後，我發現那聲音並不是從我耳朵裏發出的。

毫無疑問，此刻我顯得非常蒼白——但我越發放肆地説着話，並且提高了聲調。可是那聲音仍然越來越響——我該怎麼辦？那是一種低沉、單調、迅速的聲音——和包裹在棉花裏的鐘錶所發出的聲響非常相像。我大口呼吸——然而警官們並沒聽到。我説得更快了——情緒更加激越；可是那聲音還在漸漸增強。我站起身來爭論着一些瑣事，聲調很高，做着猛烈的手勢，可是那聲音還在漸漸增強。他們幹嗎還不走？我在地板上來回重重地踏步，仿佛被這些人的見解弄得很惱火——可是那聲音還在漸漸增強。哦，老天！我能怎麼樣？我唾沫四濺——説着胡話——詛咒着。我轉動着自己坐過的那張椅子，在地板上摩擦着，但是那聲音強烈得到處都是，並且持續加強。它變得越來越響——越來越響——越來越響！那些人還在樂滋滋地閒聊着，笑着。難道他們沒聽到嗎？萬能的上帝啊！——不，不！他們聽到

了！——他們起了疑心！——他們知道了！——他們正在嘲笑
我的恐慌！——我當時這樣想着，現在也這樣認為。這種痛苦才
是最要命的！這種嘲弄是最不可忍受的！我再也忍受不了這種偽
善的笑容了！我覺得自己非得大聲喊出來，否則就要死了！——
而此刻那聲音——又來了！——聽！更響了！更響了！更響了！
——

"壞蛋！"我尖聲叫着，"別再裝了！我坦白！——打開木板！
——這裏，在這裏！——那是他可惡的心臟在跳！"

（張瓊譯）

完

註解

1　斯瓦姆默丹（Swammerdamm，1637—1680），荷蘭博物學家。

2　小山羊在英文中是 kid，和後面所提及的船長基德（Kidd）類似。

3　"a" 在英文裏是 "一個" 的意思，"I" 則是 "我" 的意思，兩者都很多見。

4　該名號與主教一詞在英文中讀音相近。

5　惠斯特，四人玩的一種牌戲，橋牌的前身。

6　薛西斯，波斯國王。

7　拉丁文，指 "和諸如此類的（角色）"。

8　伊壁鳩魯（西元前 341—270），古希臘唯物主義和無神論者。

9　意為："第一個字母已失去了原來的發音。"

10　舊法國金幣，一個金幣值 20 法郎。

11　莫里哀《貴人迷》第一幕第二場。

12　弗朗索瓦·歐仁·維多克（1775—1857），曾為拿破崙組建國家警員總隊，後建立了一個由他管理的私人偵探所。

13　法文，意思是：我應付得圓通得體。

14　引自盧梭的小說《新愛洛伊斯》，法文意為 "否認事實，無中生有"。

15　最初發表《瑪麗·羅傑疑案》時，作者認為不需要現在所增補的這些注腳；但本故事所依據的這場悲劇已過去多年，作者認為還是應該加上這些注腳，並對故事的總體構思進行了一些說明。一個名叫瑪麗·塞西莉亞·羅傑斯的年輕姑娘在紐約附近被殺害。儘管她的死引起了強烈而持久的轟動，但是直到這篇小說寫成並出版之時（1842 年 11 月），疑案一直未被破解。在本故事中，作者假托敘述一個巴黎女店員的死亡，雖然只參照了瑪麗·羅傑斯的謀殺案實際情況中的一些非關鍵部分，但作者在每個細節中都追隨這個疑案的實質。因此，小說中的所有論據都適用於真實事件：而對真相的調查則是本文的目的。《瑪麗·羅傑疑案》是在遠離慘案現場的情況下寫成的，除了可提供信息的報紙之外，沒有其他的調查途徑。因此，作者並不掌握許多如果親臨現場並進行勘察所能得到的信息。然而，記錄在下面的這件事實或許並不算不妥：兩名證人（其中一人是小說的敍述者德呂克太太）在小說發表之後很久，在不同的時間裏提供的證詞不僅充分證實了此文總的推論，而且還完全證明了這一推論所依據的全部是假設的主要細節。——原注（本篇小說的注腳除特別注明外均為作者原注。）

16 諾瓦利斯是馮·哈登貝格（Von Hardenburg）的筆名。——譯者注

17 即拿索街。（坡在注腳中對應於正文裏的地名、人名分別為紐約及紐約附近的地名和瑪麗·羅傑斯案件有關人士的姓名。——譯者注）

18 即安德森。

19 即哈德遜河。

20 韋赫肯區。

21 即佩恩先生。

22 克羅姆林。

23 《紐約信使》週刊。

24 即《紐約喬納森兄弟報》，主編為H·赫斯廷斯·魏爾德先生。

25 《紐約商報》。

26 《星期六費城郵報夜刊》，編輯為C·I·彼德森先生。

27 即亞當。

28 鴉片酊，一種作止痛劑或毒藥的藥劑。——譯者注

29 參見《摩格街謀殺案》。

30 即《紐約商業廣告報》，編輯為斯通上校。

31 "一條基於客體性質之上的理論會由於客體的不同而難以自圓其説；而依據事物起因設置論題的人則會因為其結果不同而停止評判。因此，任何國家的法理學都表明了，當法律成為了一門學科和一種體系，它就失去了公正性。盲目專注於分類原則已導致法律出錯，這錯誤只要觀察立法機關是如何頻繁地被迫站出來修復自身系統所喪失的公正便可得知。"——蘭多。（蘭多是賀瑞斯·賓尼·華萊士所用的筆名，他曾於1838年匿名出版小說《斯坦利》，本段文字引自該小說。——譯者）

32 《紐約快報》。

33 《紐約先驅報》。

34 《紐約信使問詢報》。

35 梅奈是最初涉嫌並被捕的當事人之一，但因缺乏證據而獲釋。

36 《紐約信使問詢報》。

37 《紐約晚郵報》。

38 《紐約旗幟報》。

39 怒由此生？—— 譯者注

40 此按語是坡本人自行插入，由最初發表本小説的雜誌加上去的。

41 拉丁文，即：智者所惡莫過於機靈。

42 Procrustes，古希臘傳説中人物，他將被他抓到的人放在一張鐵牀上，比牀長的人，被其砍去長出的部分；比牀短的人，被其強行拉長。

43 法語：你可以相信這個事實：所有流行的見解和公認的慣例都是愚蠢的，因為大多數人覺得它們可以接受。

44 拉丁文：下地獄容易。

45 法語：如此歹毒之計，若比不過阿特柔斯，也配得上堤厄斯忒斯。

46 即法國劇作家克雷比雍（1674—1762）根據希臘神話寫成的悲劇《阿特柔斯與堤厄斯忒斯》（1707）。劇中堤厄斯忒斯誘姦了其兄邁錫尼國王阿特柔斯之妻；作為報復，阿特柔斯殺了堤厄斯忒斯的三個兒子並烹熟讓其食之。

47 法語：他的心是繃緊的魯特琴；只要觸碰它，就會產生迴響。

48 原文為 out-Heroded Herod，是比希律王更希律王的意思，希律王（Herod）是以殘暴著稱的猶太國王。這裏表述的是行為過分、過頭了。

49 指拿破崙軍隊於 1812 年遠征俄國，撤退時強渡別列茨那河。

50 威廉·巴肯的《家庭醫學》是當時最流行的醫學參考書，在 1769 至 1854 年間共印 29 版。

51 即英國詩人愛德華‧揚格（1683—1765）所著長詩《哀怨，或關於生命、死亡和永生的夜思》。

52 今稱阿姆河。

53 坡在這裏暗指威廉‧貝克福德的《瓦特克》（1798），書中的主人公國王瓦特克在其女巫母親的影響下成了魔王地獄迷宮裏的迷途之魂。坡在這裏間接提到這個故事，是他從華萊士的小説《斯坦利》（1838）中讀到的，書中還有阿弗拉斯布沿着奧克蘇斯河航行的故事。